AMERICAN BORN CHINESE

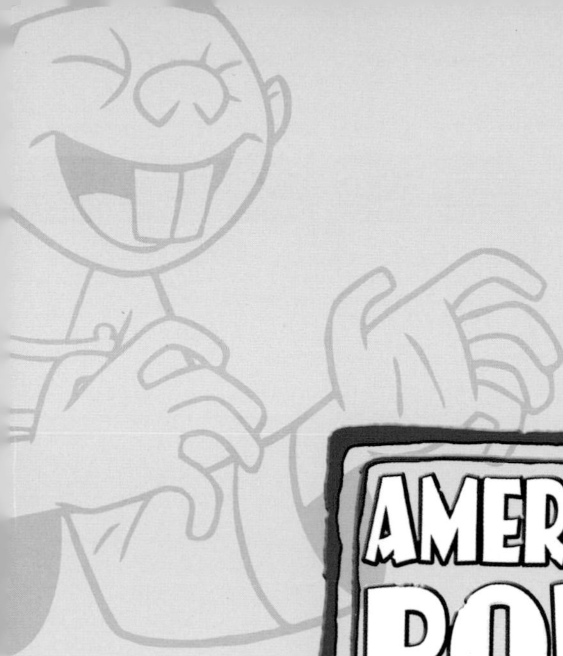

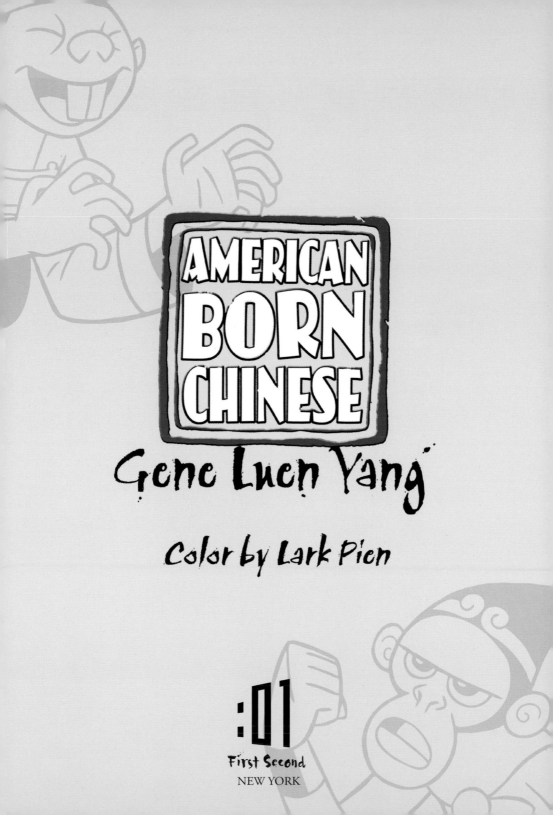

AMERICAN BORN CHINESE

Gene Luen Yang

Color by Lark Pien

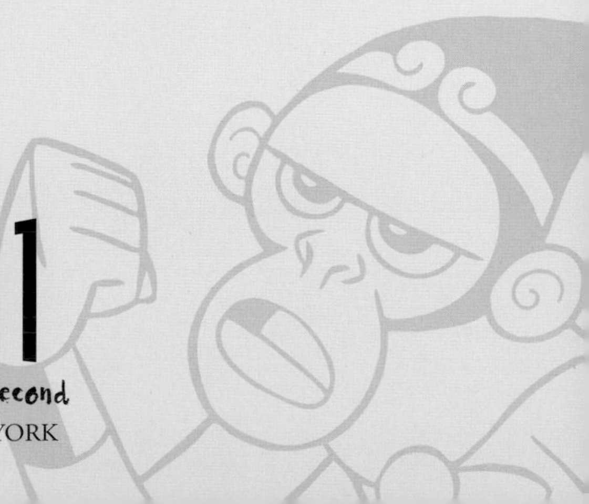

:01 First Second

NEW YORK

To Ma,
for her stories of the Monkey King

And Ba,
for his stories of Ah-Tong, the Taiwanese village boy

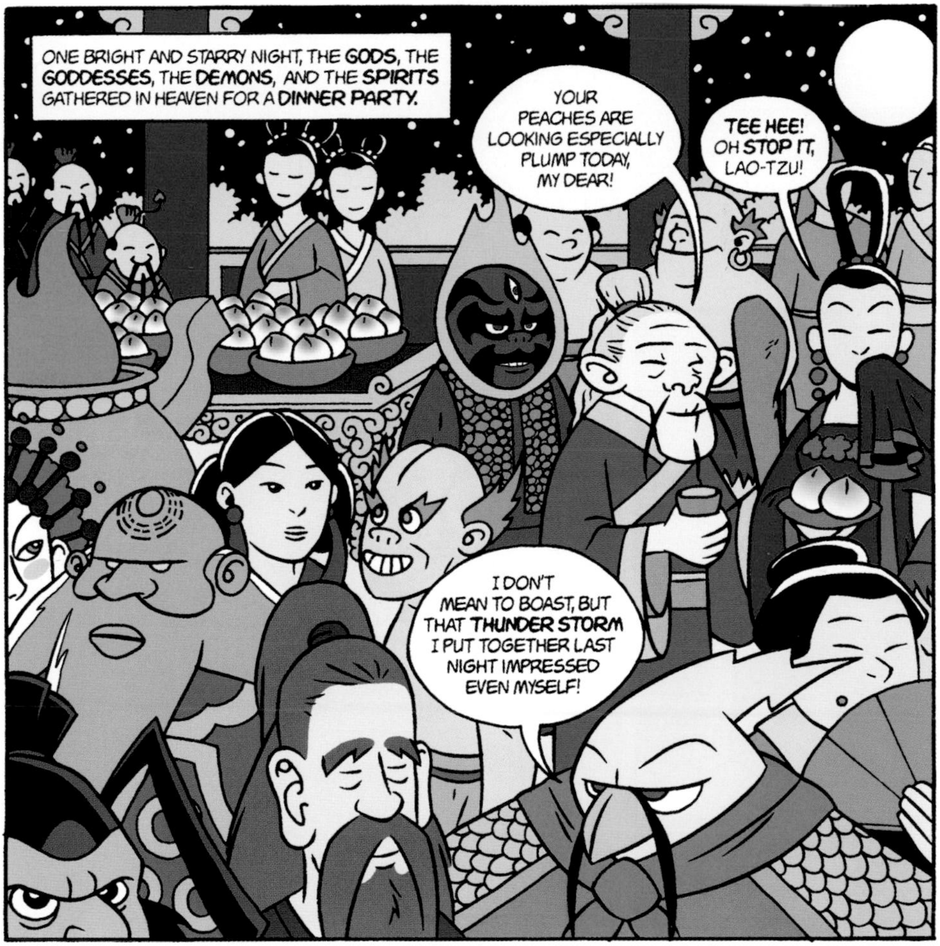
ONE BRIGHT AND STARRY NIGHT, THE GODS, THE GODDESSES, THE DEMONS, AND THE SPIRITS GATHERED IN HEAVEN FOR A DINNER PARTY.
YOUR PEACHES ARE LOOKING ESPECIALLY PLUMP TODAY, MY DEAR!
TEE HEE! OH STOP IT, LAO-TZU!
I DON'T MEAN TO BOAST, BUT THAT THUNDER STORM I PUT TOGETHER LAST NIGHT IMPRESSED EVEN MYSELF!

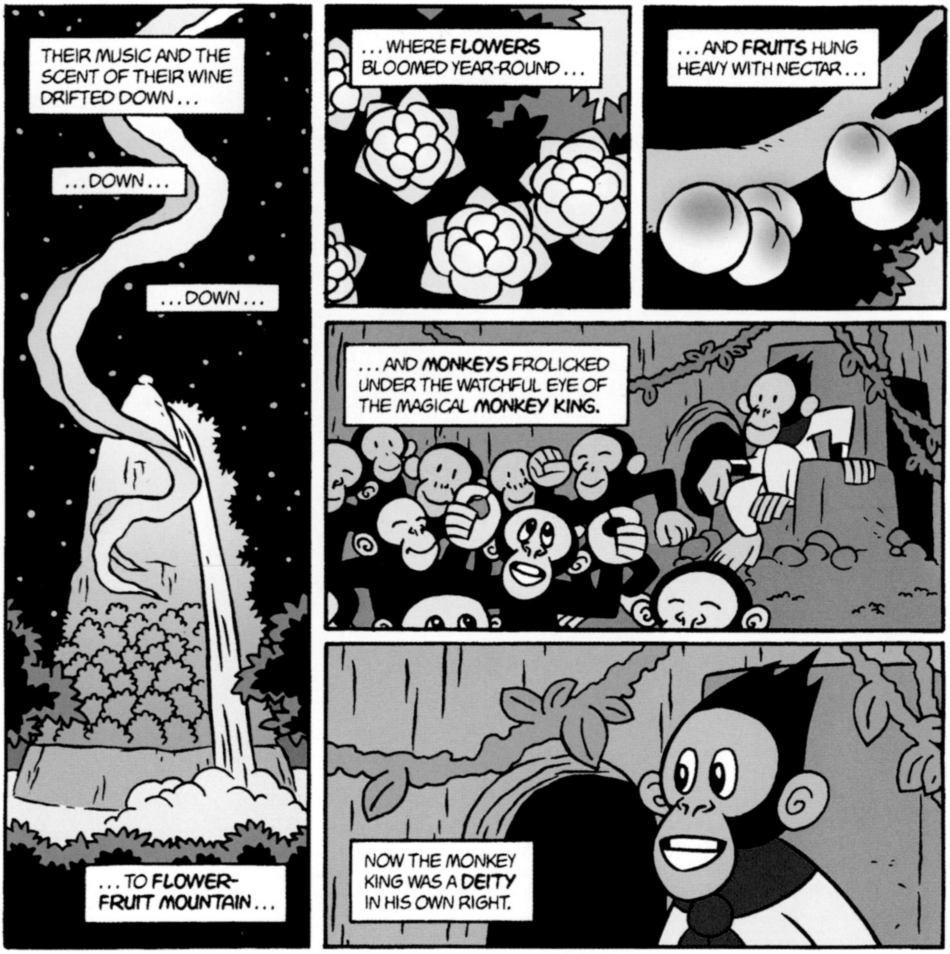
THEIR MUSIC AND THE SCENT OF THEIR WINE DRIFTED DOWN . . .
. . . DOWN . . .
. . . DOWN . . .
. . . TO FLOWER-FRUIT MOUNTAIN . . .
. . . WHERE FLOWERS BLOOMED YEAR-ROUND . . .
. . . AND FRUITS HUNG HEAVY WITH NECTAR . . .
. . . AND MONKEYS FROLICKED UNDER THE WATCHFUL EYE OF THE MAGICAL MONKEY KING.
NOW THE MONKEY KING WAS A DEITY IN HIS OWN RIGHT.

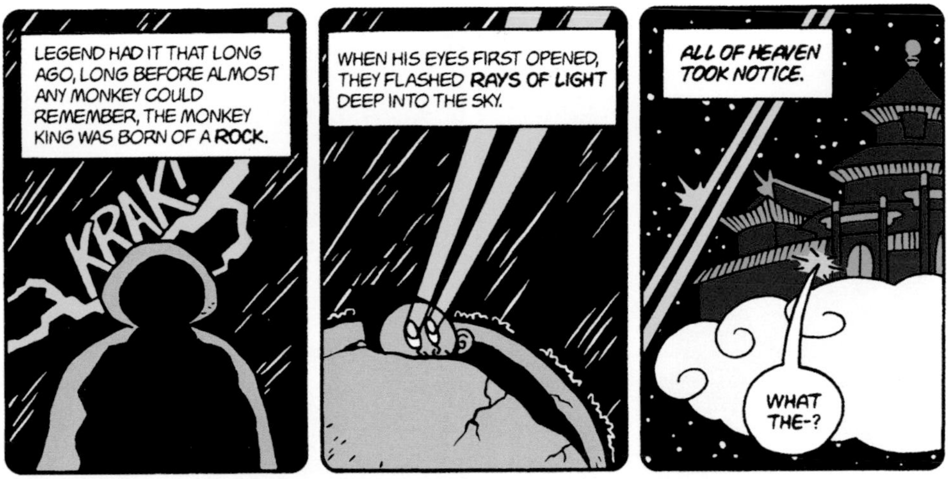
LEGEND HAD IT THAT LONG AGO, LONG BEFORE ALMOST ANY MONKEY COULD REMEMBER, THE MONKEY KING WAS BORN OF A **ROCK**.
KRAK!
WHEN HIS EYES FIRST OPENED, THEY FLASHED **RAYS OF LIGHT** DEEP INTO THE SKY.
ALL OF HEAVEN TOOK NOTICE.
WHAT THE-?
SOON AFTER, HE PURGED **FLOWER-FRUIT MOUNTAIN** OF THE **TIGER- SPIRIT** THAT HAD HAUNTED IT FOR CENTURIES.
HE ESTABLISHED HIS **KINGDOM** AND MONKEYS FROM THE FOUR CORNERS OF THE WORLD **FLOCKED** TO HIM.

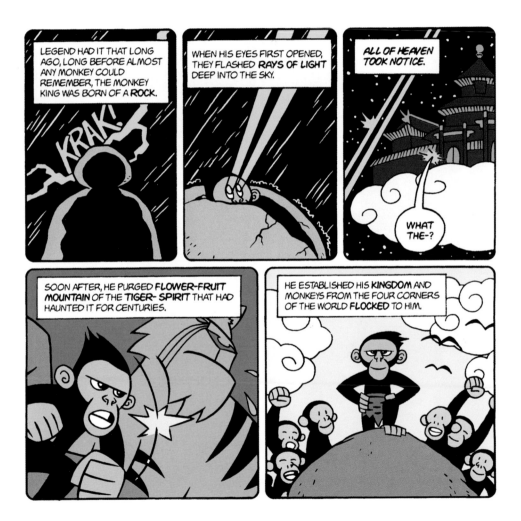

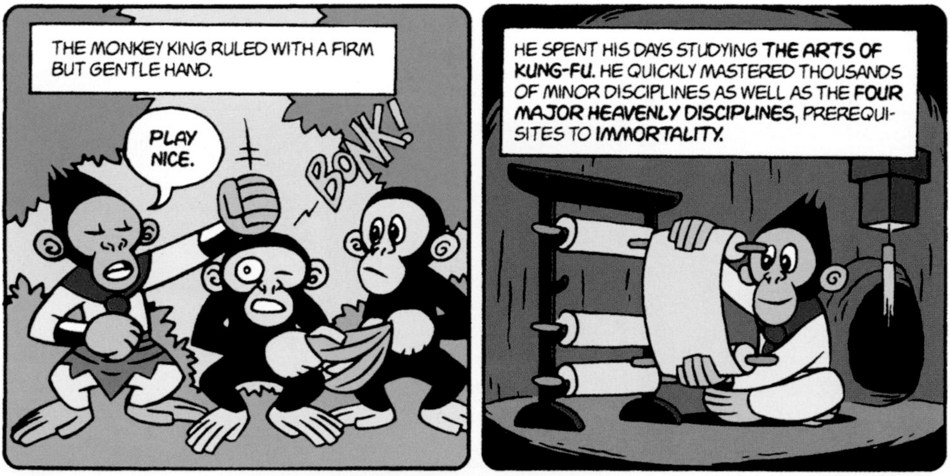
THE MONKEY KING RULED WITH A FIRM BUT GENTLE HAND.
PLAY NICE.
BONK!
HE SPENT HIS DAYS STUDYING **THE ARTS OF KUNG-FU.** HE QUICKLY MASTERED THOUSANDS OF MINOR DISCIPLINES AS WELL AS THE **FOUR MAJOR HEAVENLY DISCIPLINES**, PREREQUISITES TO **IMMORTALITY.**
DISCIPLINE ONE: FIST-LIKE-LIGHTNING
電
KRAK!
DISCIPLINE TWO: THUNDEROUS FOOT
BOOM!
雷

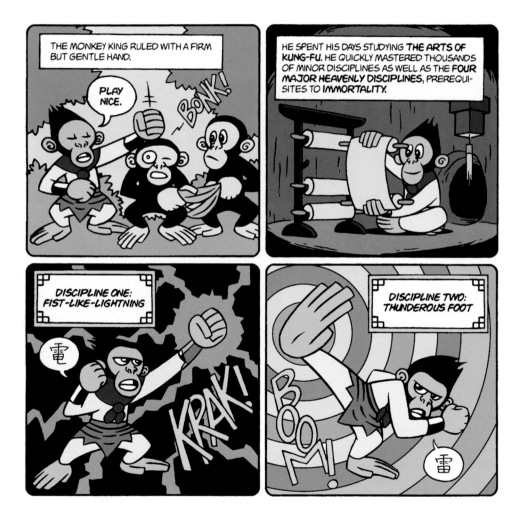

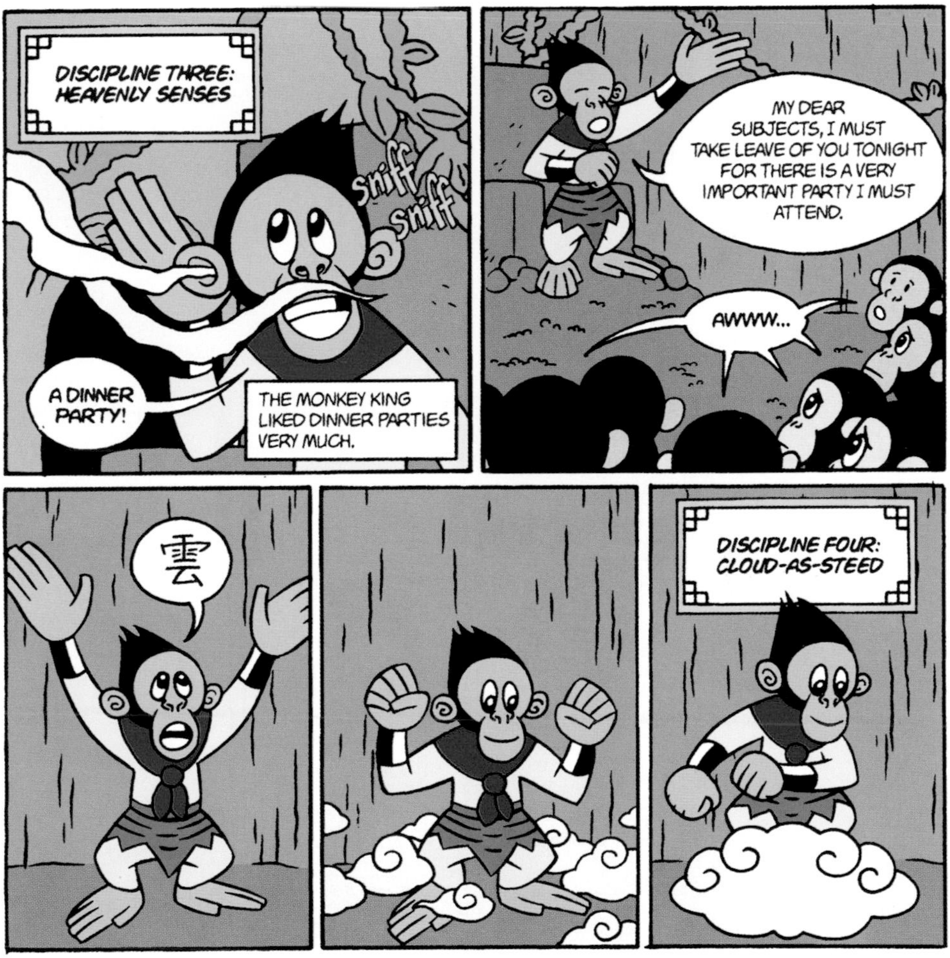
DISCIPLINE THREE: HEAVENLY SENSES
SNIFF SNIFF
A DINNER PARTY!
THE MONKEY KING LIKED DINNER PARTIES VERY MUCH.
MY DEAR SUBJECTS, I MUST TAKE LEAVE OF YOU TONIGHT FOR THERE IS A VERY IMPORTANT PARTY I MUST ATTEND.
AWWW...
雲
DISCIPLINE FOUR: CLOUD-AS-STEED

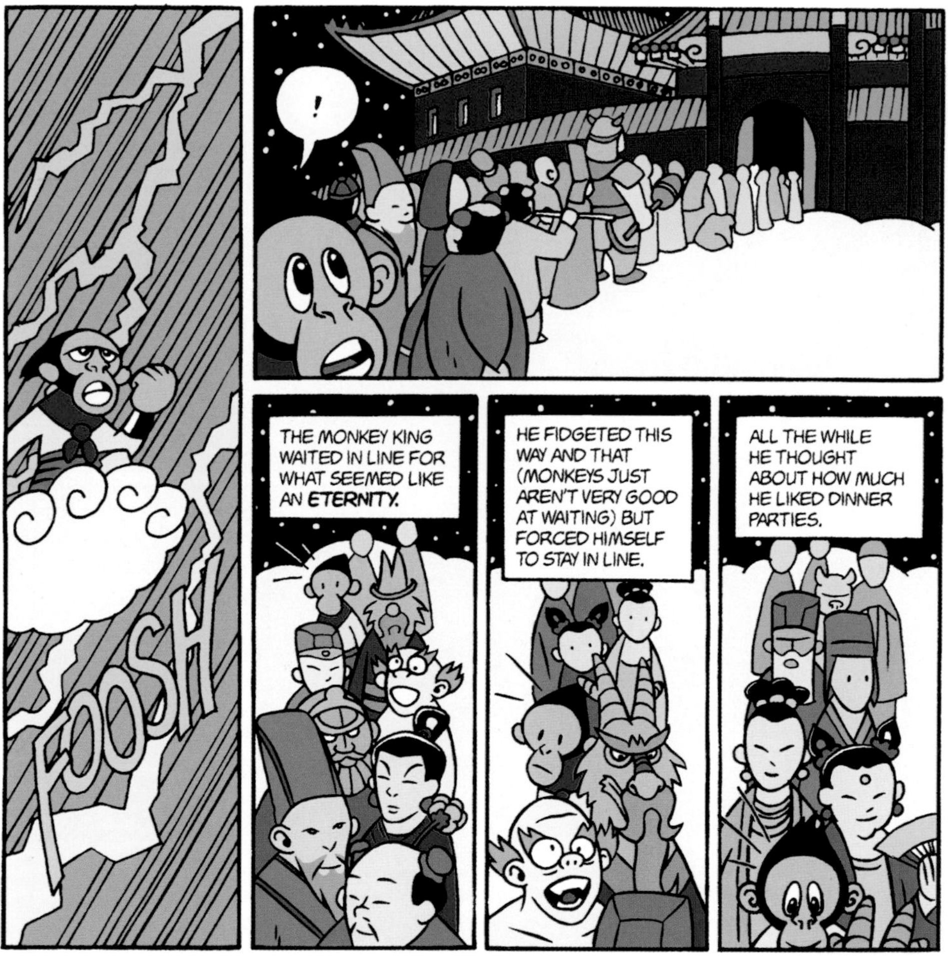
FOOSH
!
THE MONKEY KING WAITED IN LINE FOR WHAT SEEMED LIKE AN **ETERNITY.**
HE FIDGETED THIS WAY AND THAT (MONKEYS JUST AREN'T VERY GOOD AT WAITING) BUT FORCED HIMSELF TO STAY IN LINE.
ALL THE WHILE HE THOUGHT ABOUT HOW MUCH HE LIKED DINNER PARTIES.

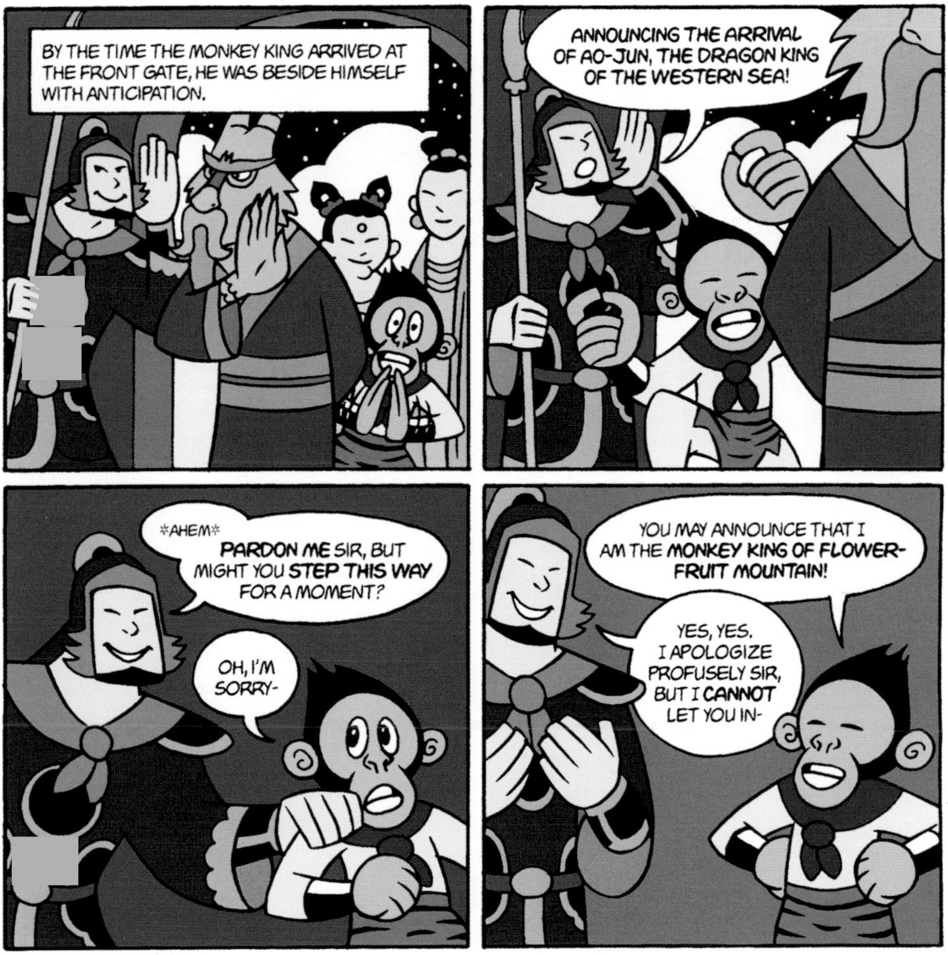
BY THE TIME THE MONKEY KING ARRIVED AT THE FRONT GATE, HE WAS BESIDE HIMSELF WITH ANTICIPATION.
ANNOUNCING THE ARRIVAL OF AO-JUN, THE DRAGON KING OF THE WESTERN SEA!
AHEM PARDON ME SIR, BUT MIGHT YOU STEP THIS WAY FOR A MOMENT?
OH, I'M SORRY-
YOU MAY ANNOUNCE THAT I AM THE MONKEY KING OF FLOWER-FRUIT MOUNTAIN!
YES, YES. I APOLOGIZE PROFUSELY SIR, BUT I CANNOT LET YOU IN-

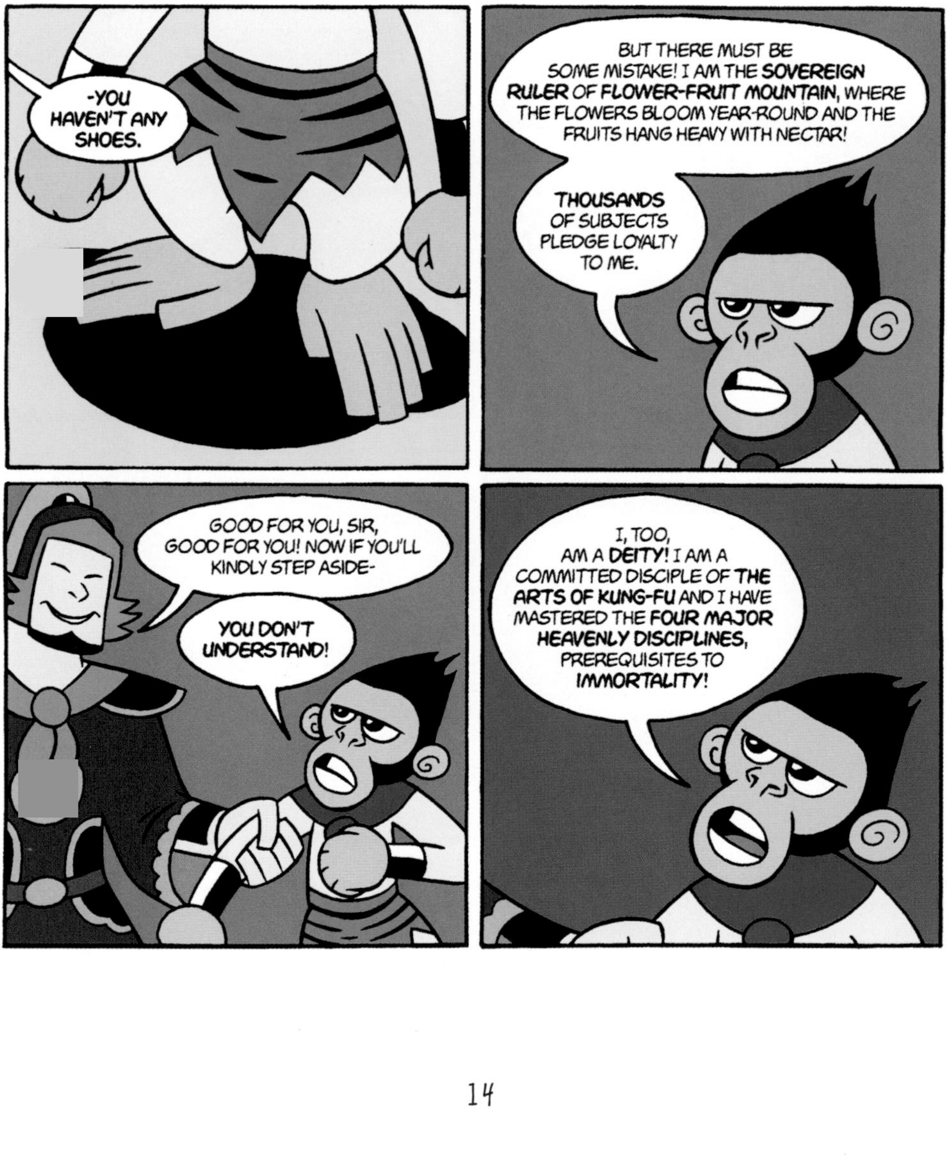
-YOU HAVEN'T ANY SHOES.
BUT THERE MUST BE SOME MISTAKE! I AM THE SOVEREIGN RULER OF FLOWER-FRUIT MOUNTAIN, WHERE THE FLOWERS BLOOM YEAR-ROUND AND THE FRUITS HANG HEAVY WITH NECTAR!
THOUSANDS OF SUBJECTS PLEDGE LOYALTY TO ME.
GOOD FOR YOU, SIR, GOOD FOR YOU! NOW IF YOU'LL KINDLY STEP ASIDE-
YOU DON'T UNDERSTAND!
I, TOO, AM A DEITY! I AM A COMMITTED DISCIPLE OF THE ARTS OF KUNG-FU AND I HAVE MASTERED THE FOUR MAJOR HEAVENLY DISCIPLINES, PREREQUISITES TO IMMORTALITY!

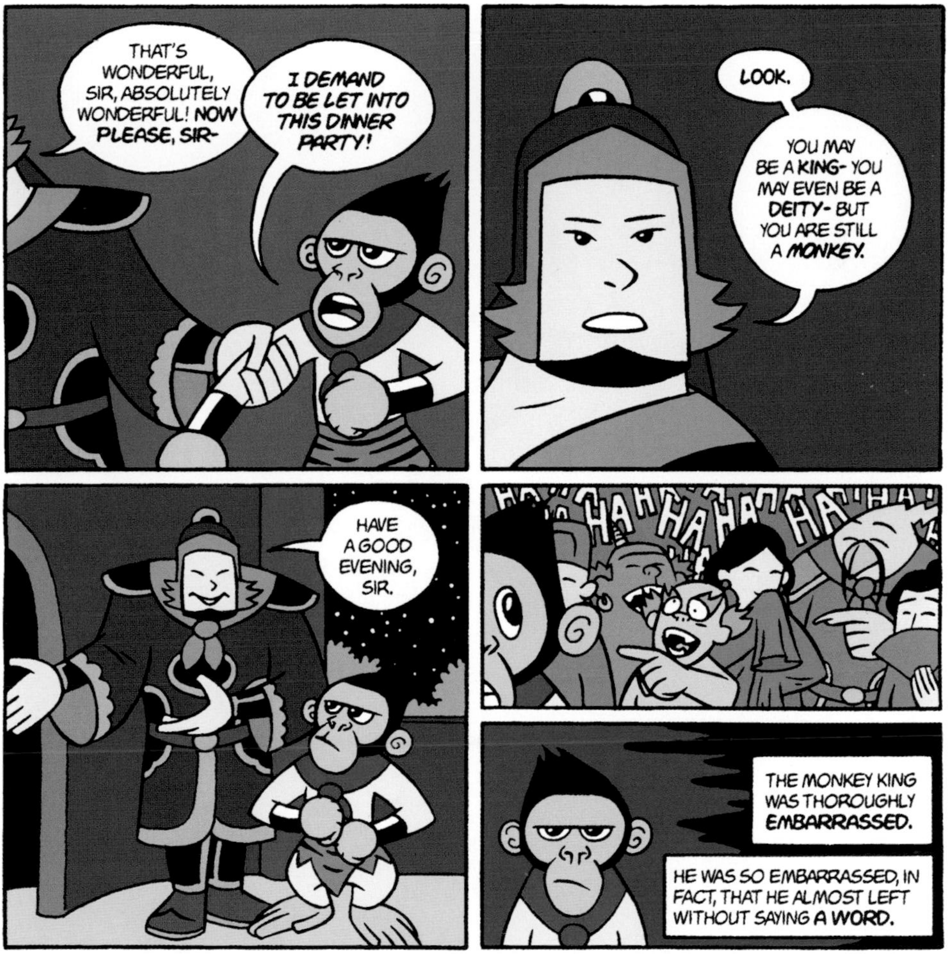
THAT'S WONDERFUL, SIR, ABSOLUTELY WONDERFUL! NOW PLEASE, SIR-
I DEMAND TO BE LET INTO THIS DINNER PARTY!
LOOK.
YOU MAY BE A KING- YOU MAY EVEN BE A DEITY- BUT YOU ARE STILL A MONKEY.
HAVE A GOOD EVENING, SIR.
THE MONKEY KING WAS THOROUGHLY EMBARRASSED.
HE WAS SO EMBARRASSED, IN FACT, THAT HE ALMOST LEFT WITHOUT SAYING A WORD.

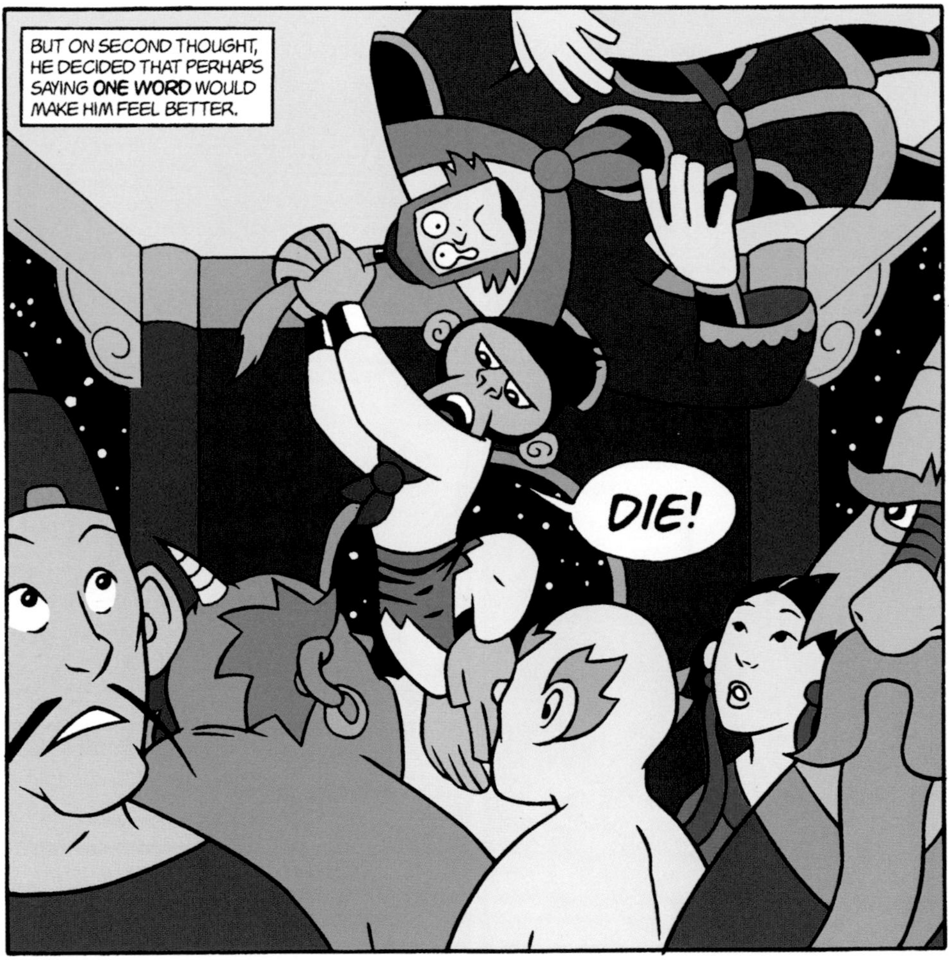
BUT ON SECOND THOUGHT, HE DECIDED THAT PERHAPS SAYING **ONE WORD** WOULD MAKE HIM FEEL BETTER.
DIE!

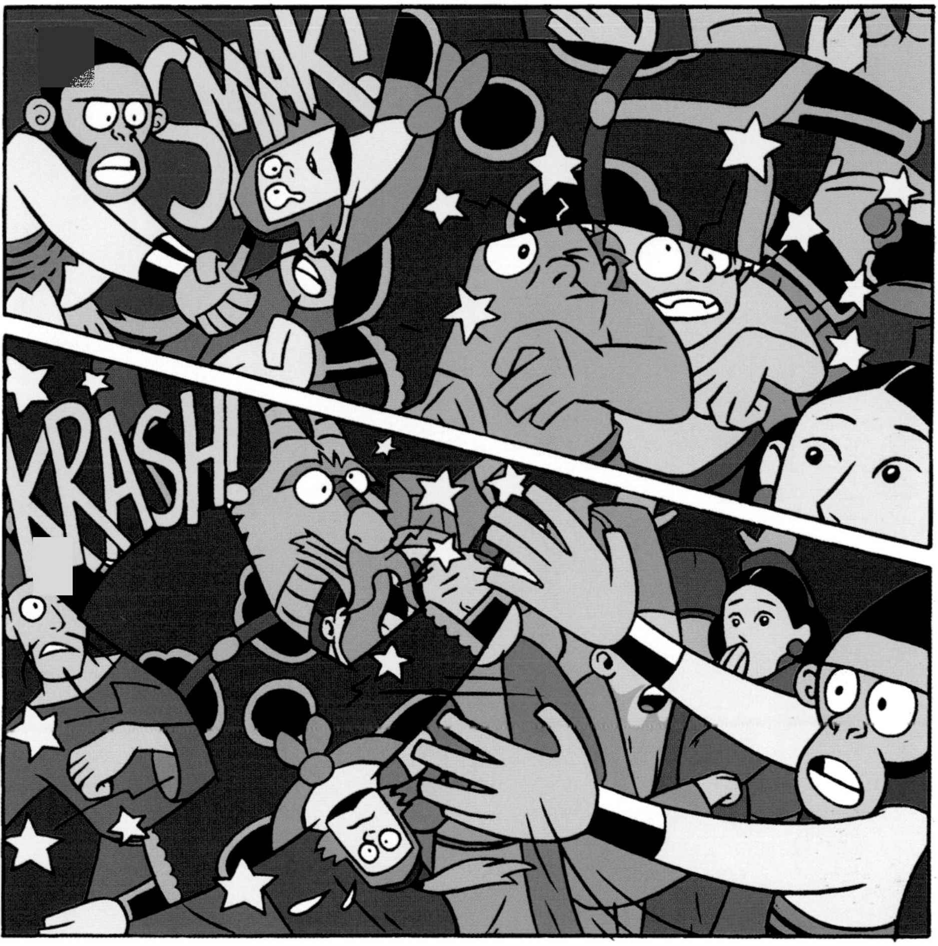
SMAK!
KRASH!

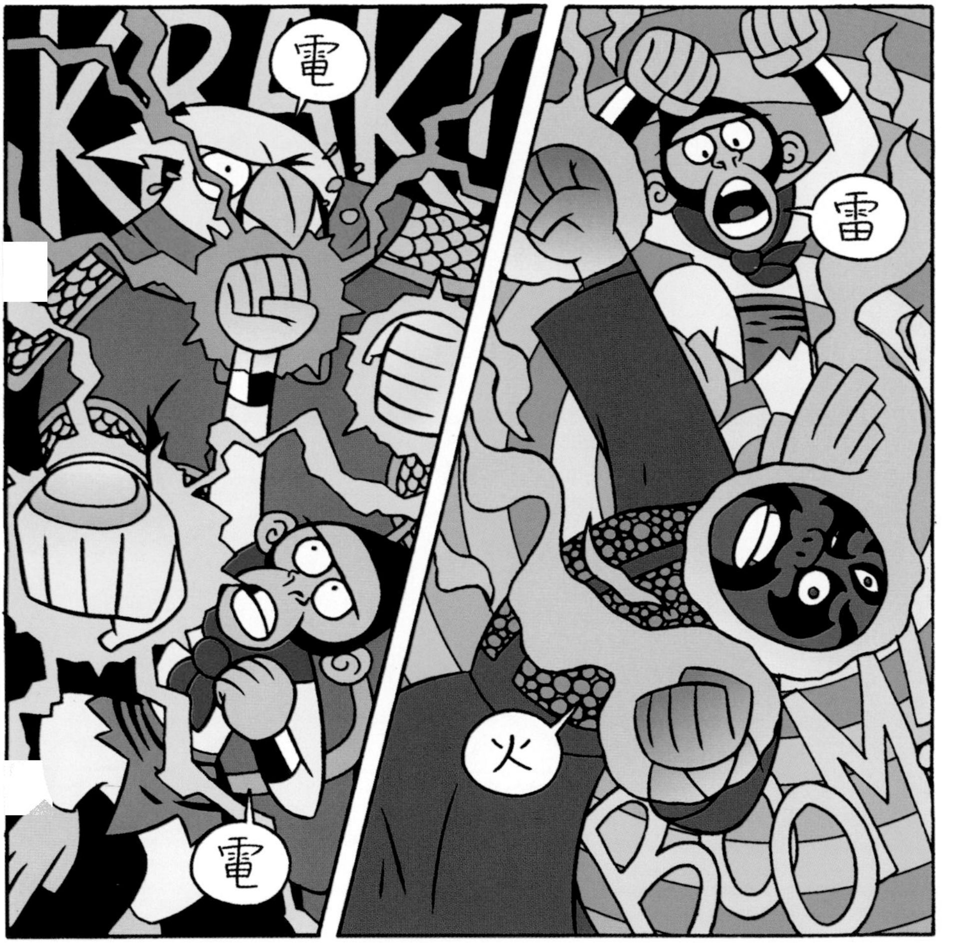
電
電
雷
火
BOOM!

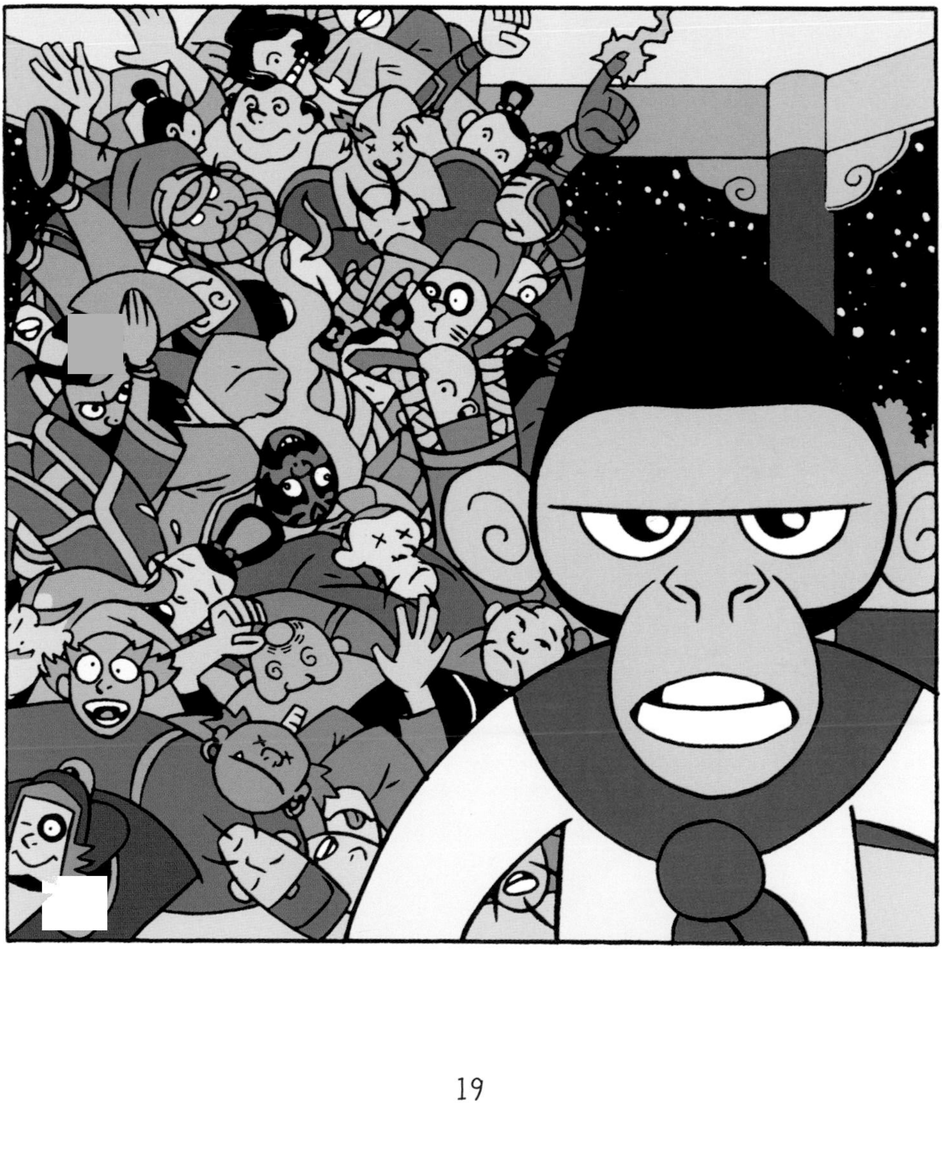

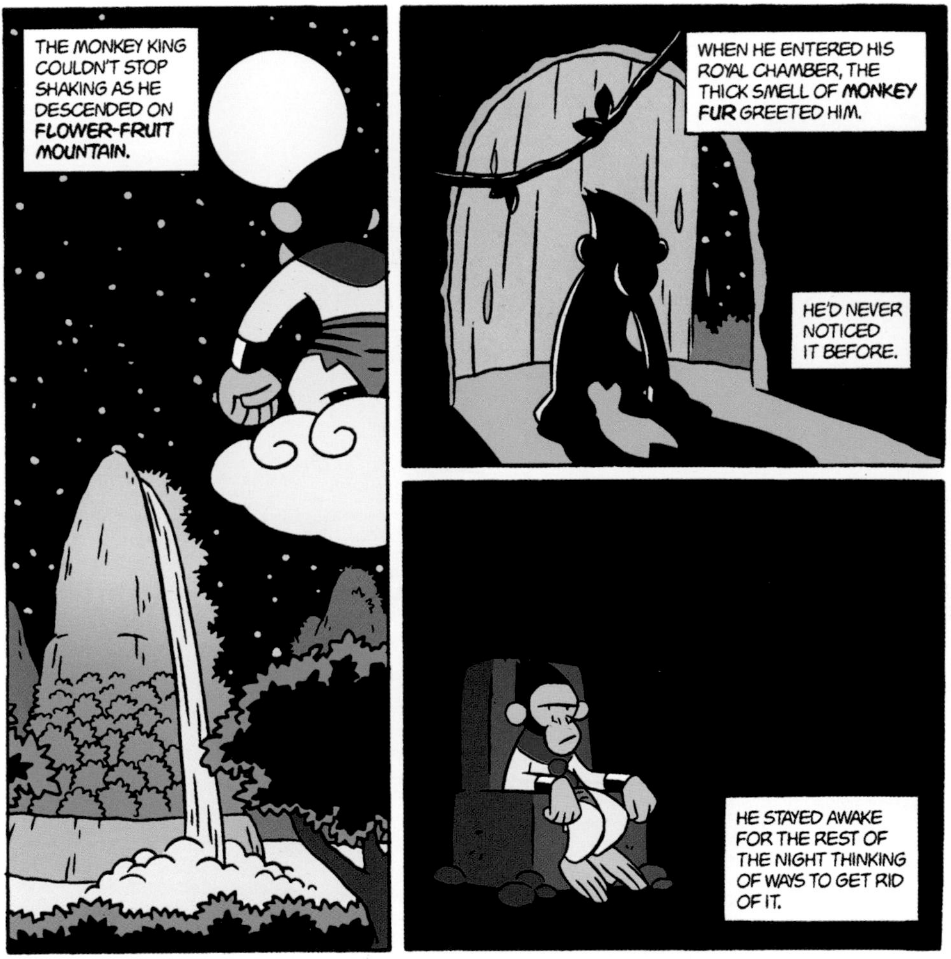
THE MONKEY KING COULDN'T STOP SHAKING AS HE DESCENDED ON **FLOWER-FRUIT MOUNTAIN.**
WHEN HE ENTERED HIS ROYAL CHAMBER, THE THICK SMELL OF **MONKEY FUR** GREETED HIM.
HE'D NEVER NOTICED IT BEFORE.
HE STAYED AWAKE FOR THE REST OF THE NIGHT THINKING OF WAYS TO GET RID OF IT.

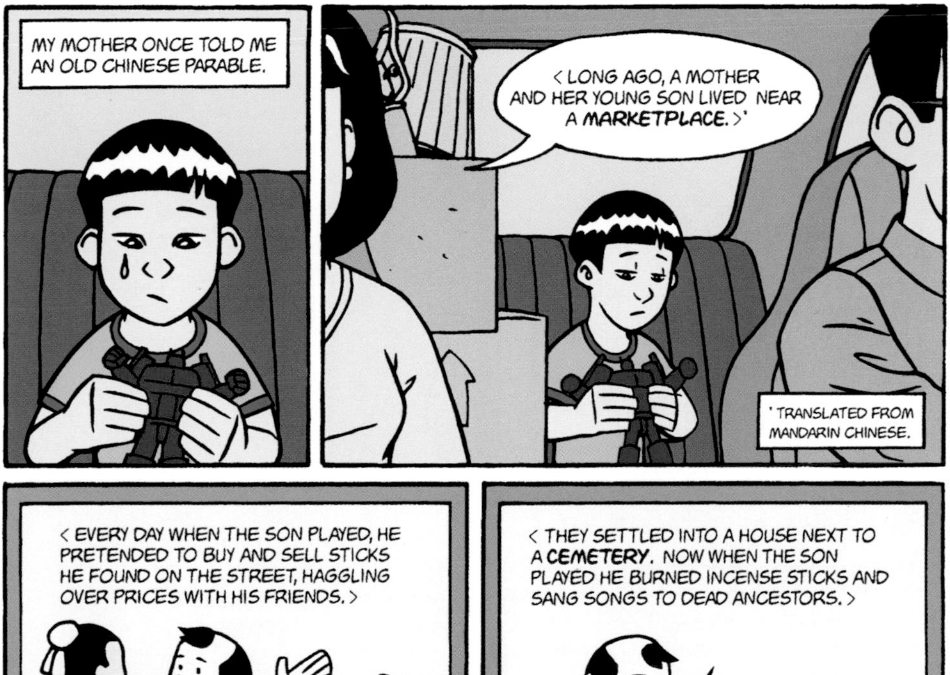
MY MOTHER ONCE TOLD ME AN OLD CHINESE PARABLE.
< LONG AGO, A MOTHER AND HER YOUNG SON LIVED NEAR A **MARKETPLACE.** >*
* TRANSLATED FROM MANDARIN CHINESE.
< EVERY DAY WHEN THE SON PLAYED, HE PRETENDED TO BUY AND SELL STICKS HE FOUND ON THE STREET, HAGGLING OVER PRICES WITH HIS FRIENDS. >
< THE MOTHER DECIDED TO MOVE. >
< THEY SETTLED INTO A HOUSE NEXT TO A **CEMETERY.** NOW WHEN THE SON PLAYED HE BURNED INCENSE STICKS AND SANG SONGS TO DEAD ANCESTORS. >
< THE MOTHER DECIDED TO MOVE AGAIN. >

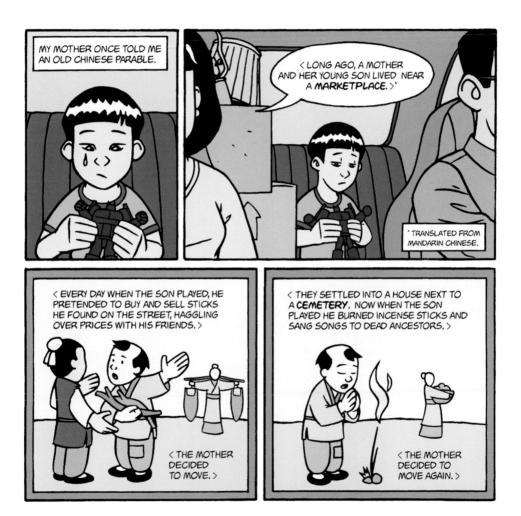

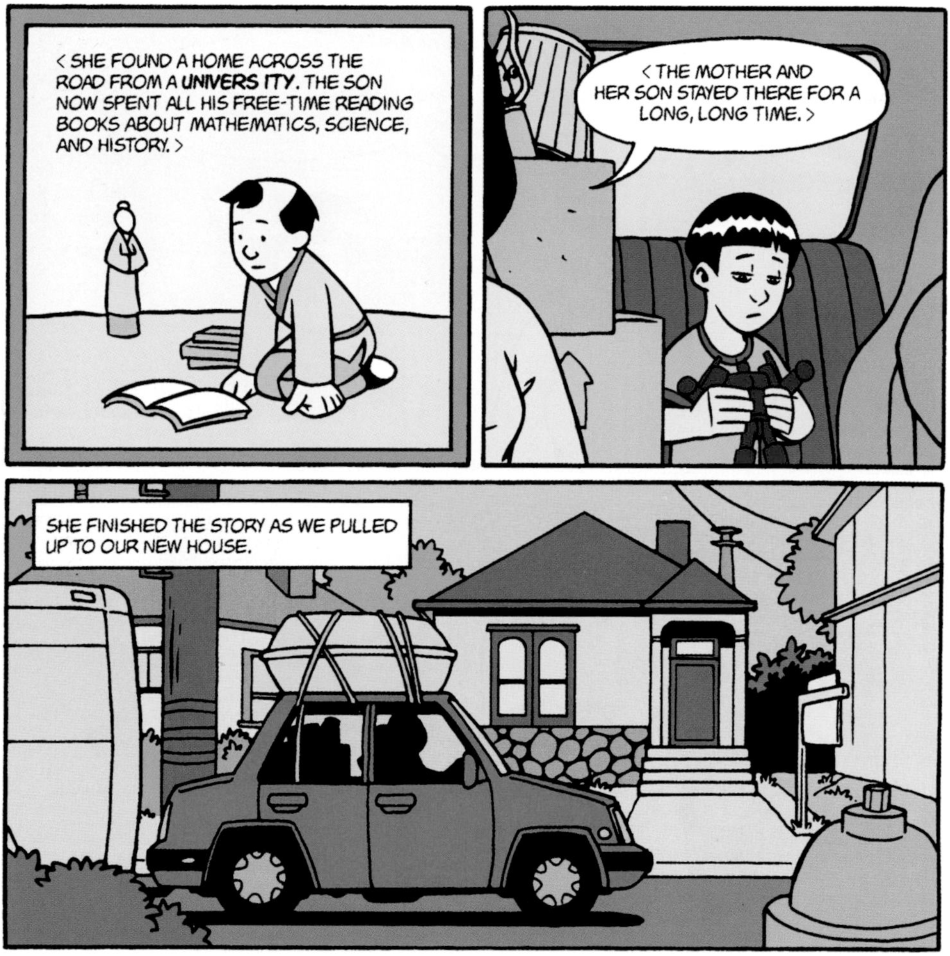
< SHE FOUND A HOME ACROSS THE ROAD FROM A **UNIVERS ITY**. THE SON NOW SPENT ALL HIS FREE-TIME READING BOOKS ABOUT MATHEMATICS, SCIENCE, AND HISTORY. >
< THE MOTHER AND HER SON STAYED THERE FOR A LONG, LONG TIME. >
SHE FINISHED THE STORY AS WE PULLED UP TO OUR NEW HOUSE.

MY PARENTS ARRIVED IN **AMERICA** AT THE SAME AIRPORT WITHIN A WEEK OF EACH OTHER.

IRONICALLY, THEY DIDN'T MEET UNTIL A YEAR AND A HALF LATER, IN THE LIBRARY OF SAN FRANCISCO STATE UNIVERSITY. THEY WERE BOTH GRADUATE STUDENTS.

FOR TUITION MONEY, MY MOTHER WORKED AT A CANNERY.

MY FATHER SOLD WIGS DOOR-TO-DOOR.

SUAVE!

EVENTUALLY, MY FATHER BECAME AN ENGINEER AND MY MOTHER A LIBRARIAN. JUST BEFORE I WAS BORN, THEY MOVED INTO AN APARTMENT NEAR SAN FRANCISCO **CHINATOWN**. WE STAYED THERE FOR NINE YEARS.

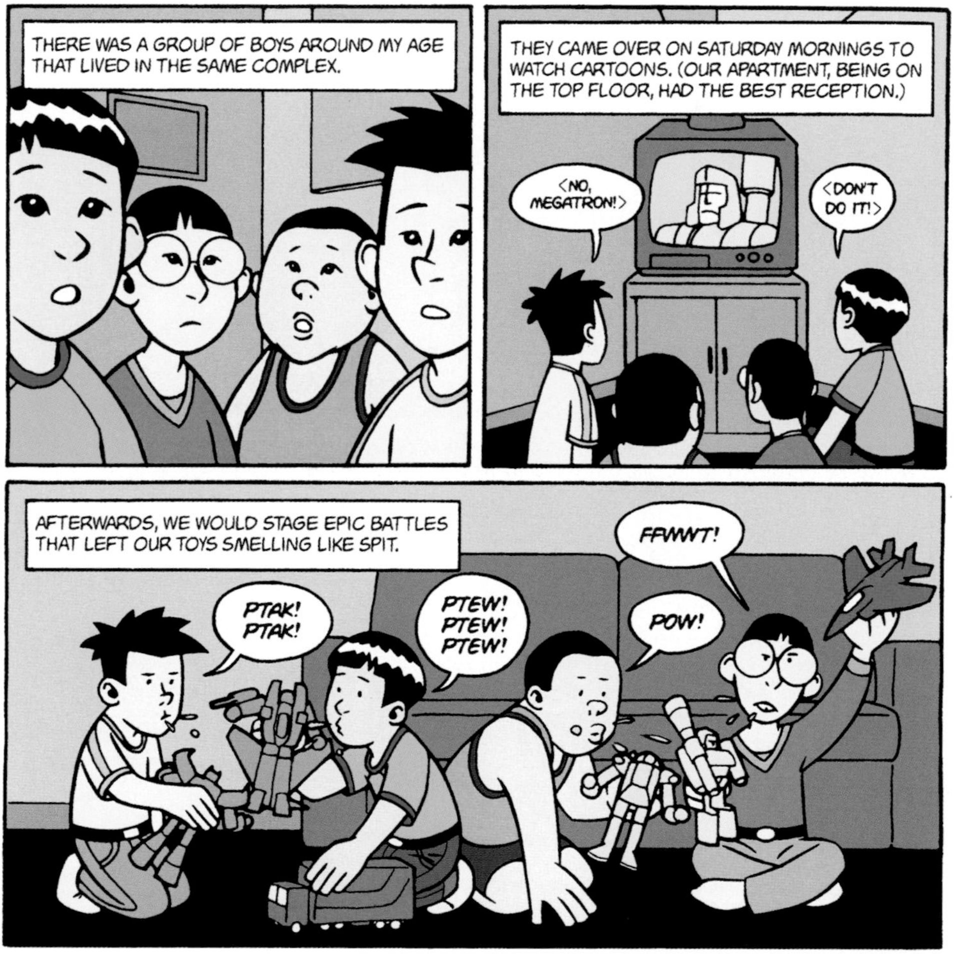
THERE WAS A GROUP OF BOYS AROUND MY AGE THAT LIVED IN THE SAME COMPLEX.
THEY CAME OVER ON SATURDAY MORNINGS TO WATCH CARTOONS. (OUR APARTMENT, BEING ON THE TOP FLOOR, HAD THE BEST RECEPTION.)
<NO, MEGATRON!>
<DON'T DO IT!>
AFTERWARDS, WE WOULD STAGE EPIC BATTLES THAT LEFT OUR TOYS SMELLING LIKE SPIT.
PTAK! PTAK!
PTEW! PTEW! PTEW!
POW!
FFWWT!

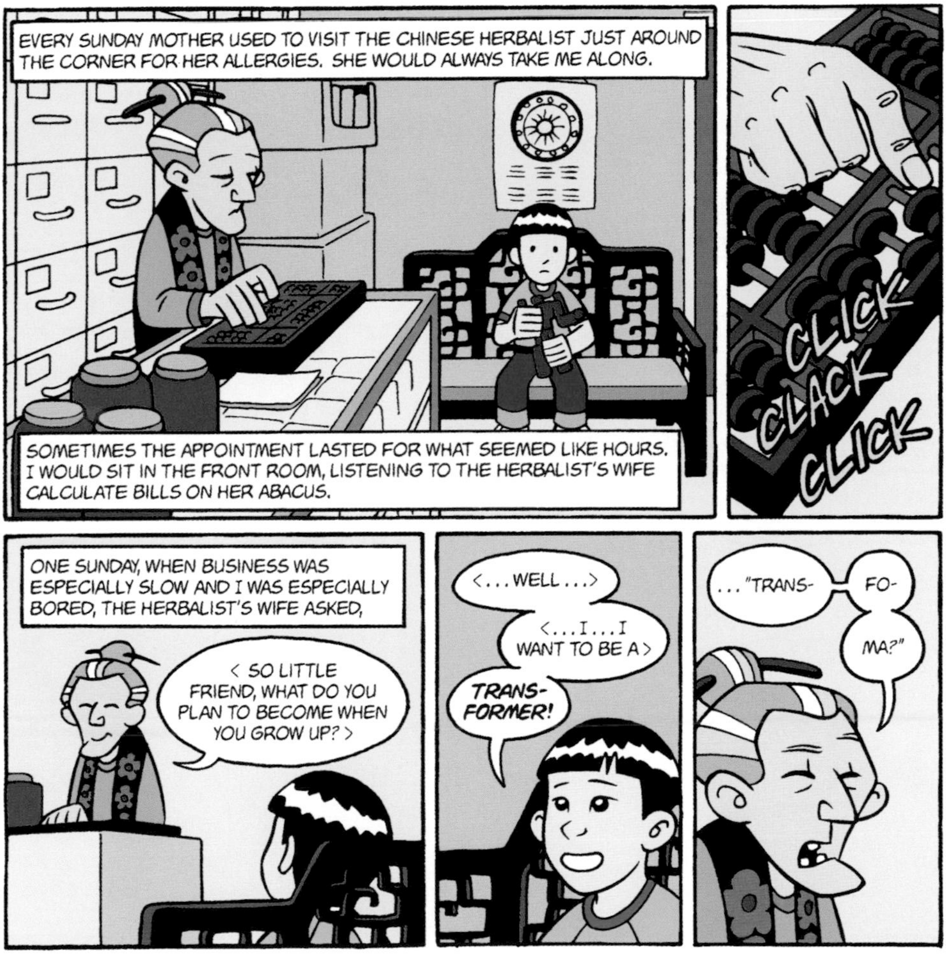
EVERY SUNDAY MOTHER USED TO VISIT THE CHINESE HERBALIST JUST AROUND THE CORNER FOR HER ALLERGIES. SHE WOULD ALWAYS TAKE ME ALONG.
SOMETIMES THE APPOINTMENT LASTED FOR WHAT SEEMED LIKE HOURS. I WOULD SIT IN THE FRONT ROOM, LISTENING TO THE HERBALIST'S WIFE CALCULATE BILLS ON HER ABACUS.
CLICK
CLACK
CLICK
ONE SUNDAY, WHEN BUSINESS WAS ESPECIALLY SLOW AND I WAS ESPECIALLY BORED, THE HERBALIST'S WIFE ASKED,
< SO LITTLE FRIEND, WHAT DO YOU PLAN TO BECOME WHEN YOU GROW UP? >
< . . . WELL . . . >
< . . . I . . . I WANT TO BE A >
TRANS-FORMER!
. . . "TRANS-
FO-
MA?"

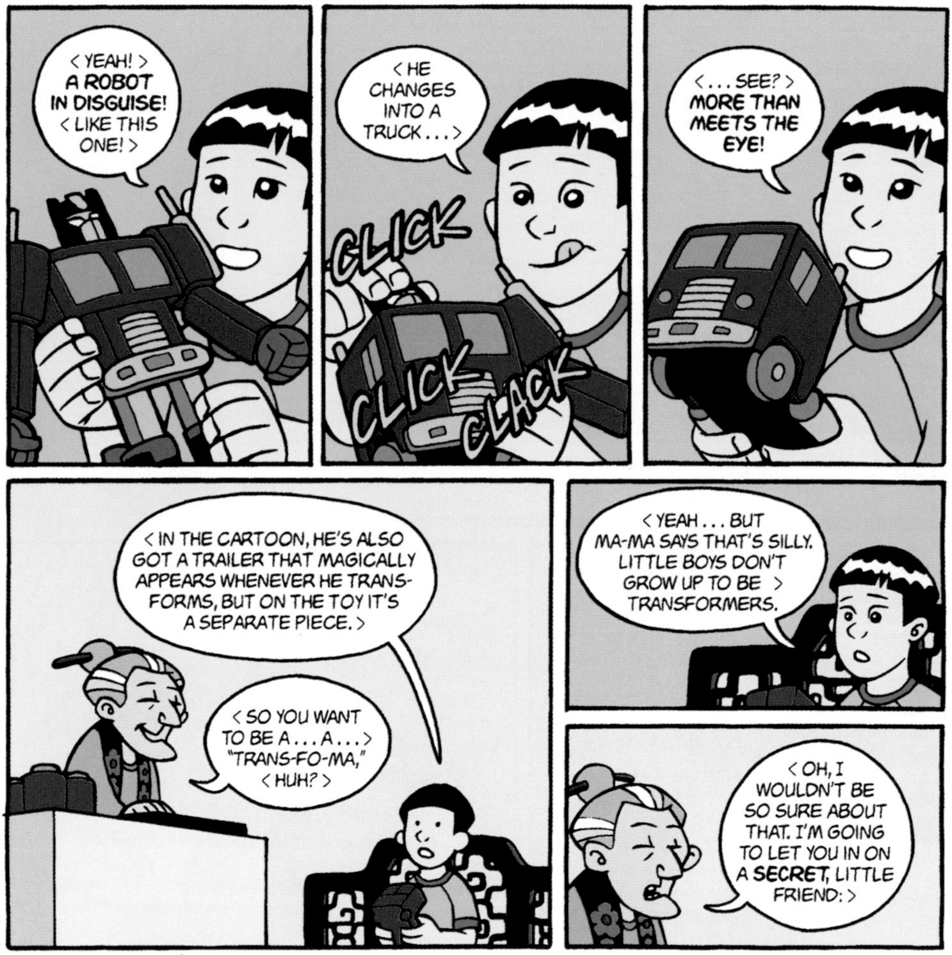
< YEAH! > **A ROBOT IN DISGUISE!** < LIKE THIS ONE! >
< HE CHANGES INTO A TRUCK . . . >
CLICK
CLICK
CLACK
< . . . SEE? > **MORE THAN MEETS THE EYE!**
< IN THE CARTOON, HE'S ALSO GOT A TRAILER THAT MAGICALLY APPEARS WHENEVER HE TRANS-FORMS, BUT ON THE TOY IT'S A SEPARATE PIECE. >
< SO YOU WANT TO BE A . . . A . . . > "TRANS-FO-MA," < HUH? >
< YEAH . . . BUT MA-MA SAYS THAT'S SILLY. LITTLE BOYS DON'T GROW UP TO BE > TRANSFORMERS.
< OH, I WOULDN'T BE SO SURE ABOUT THAT. I'M GOING TO LET YOU IN ON A **SECRET**, LITTLE FRIEND: >

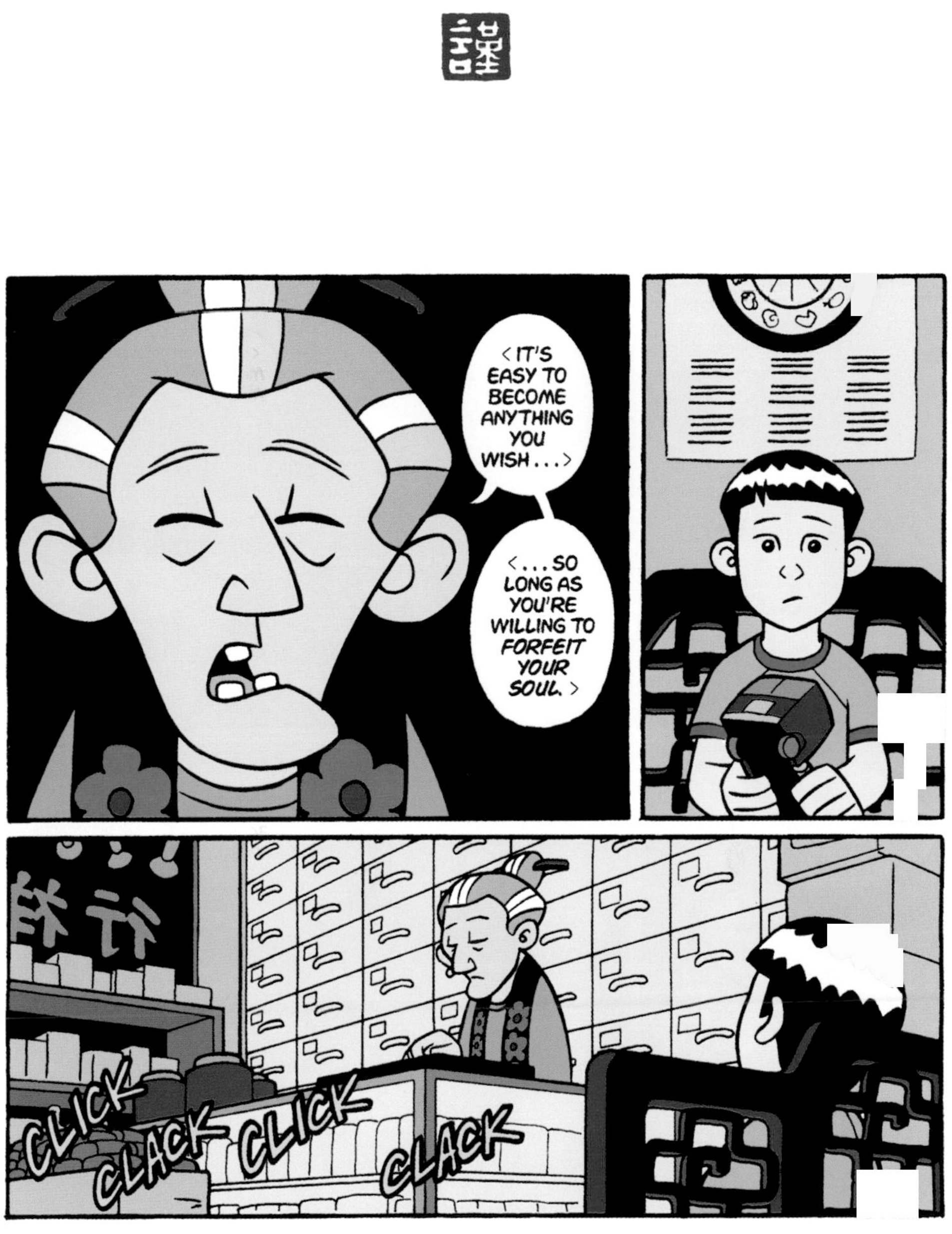
<IT'S EASY TO BECOME ANYTHING YOU WISH...>
<...SO LONG AS YOU'RE WILLING TO FORFEIT YOUR SOUL.>
CLICK
CLACK
CLICK
CLACK

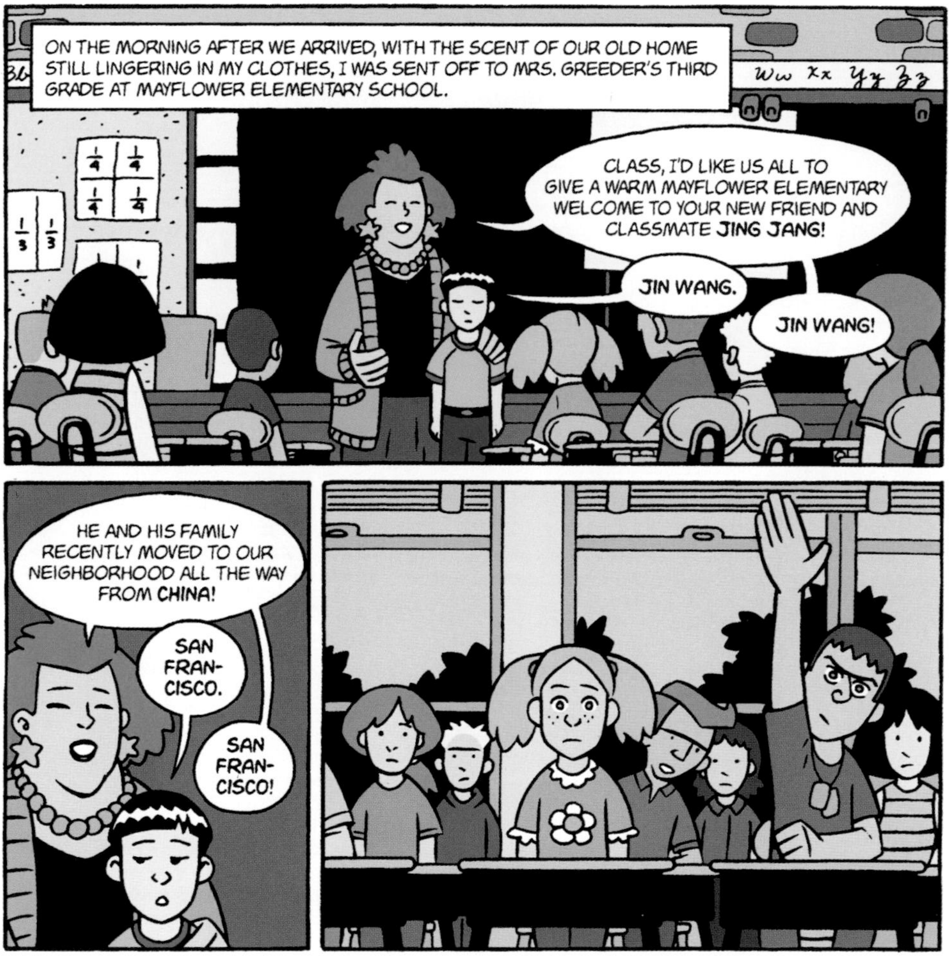
ON THE MORNING AFTER WE ARRIVED, WITH THE SCENT OF OUR OLD HOME STILL LINGERING IN MY CLOTHES, I WAS SENT OFF TO MRS. GREEDER'S THIRD GRADE AT MAYFLOWER ELEMENTARY SCHOOL.
Ww Xx Yy Zz
CLASS, I'D LIKE US ALL TO GIVE A WARM MAYFLOWER ELEMENTARY WELCOME TO YOUR NEW FRIEND AND CLASSMATE **JING JANG**!
JIN WANG.
JIN WANG!
HE AND HIS FAMILY RECENTLY MOVED TO OUR NEIGHBORHOOD ALL THE WAY FROM **CHINA**!
SAN FRANCISCO.
SAN FRANCISCO!

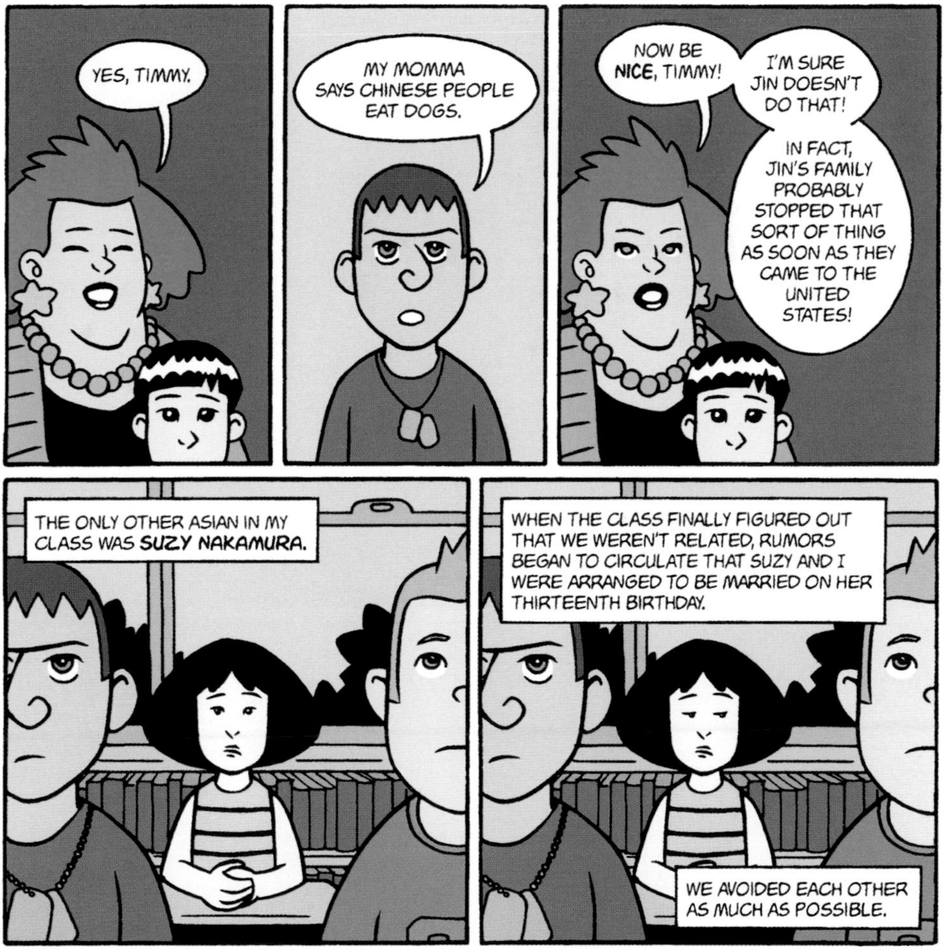
YES, TIMMY.
MY MOMMA SAYS CHINESE PEOPLE EAT DOGS.
NOW BE **NICE**, TIMMY!
I'M SURE JIN DOESN'T DO THAT!
IN FACT, JIN'S FAMILY PROBABLY STOPPED THAT SORT OF THING AS SOON AS THEY CAME TO THE UNITED STATES!
THE ONLY OTHER ASIAN IN MY CLASS WAS **SUZY NAKAMURA**.
WHEN THE CLASS FINALLY FIGURED OUT THAT WE WEREN'T RELATED, RUMORS BEGAN TO CIRCULATE THAT SUZY AND I WERE ARRANGED TO BE MARRIED ON HER THIRTEENTH BIRTHDAY.
WE AVOIDED EACH OTHER AS MUCH AS POSSIBLE.

謹

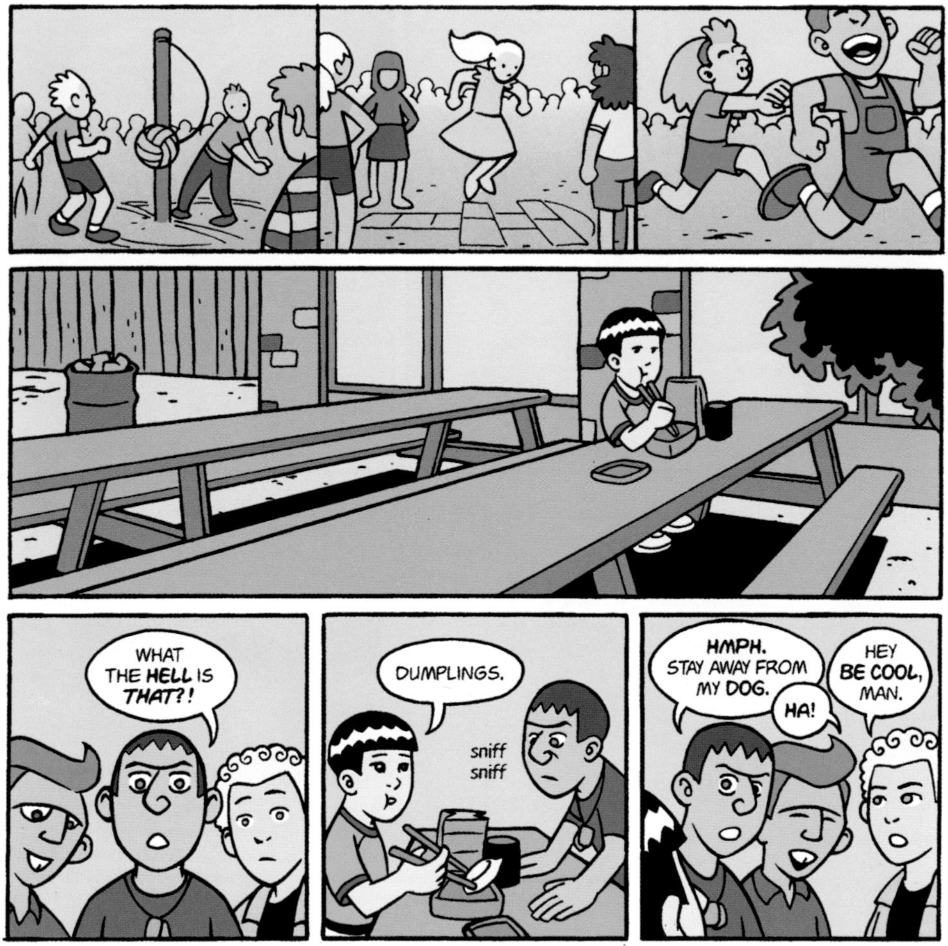
WHAT THE HELL IS THAT?!
DUMPLINGS.
sniff sniff
HMPH. STAY AWAY FROM MY DOG.
HA!
HEY BE COOL, MAN.

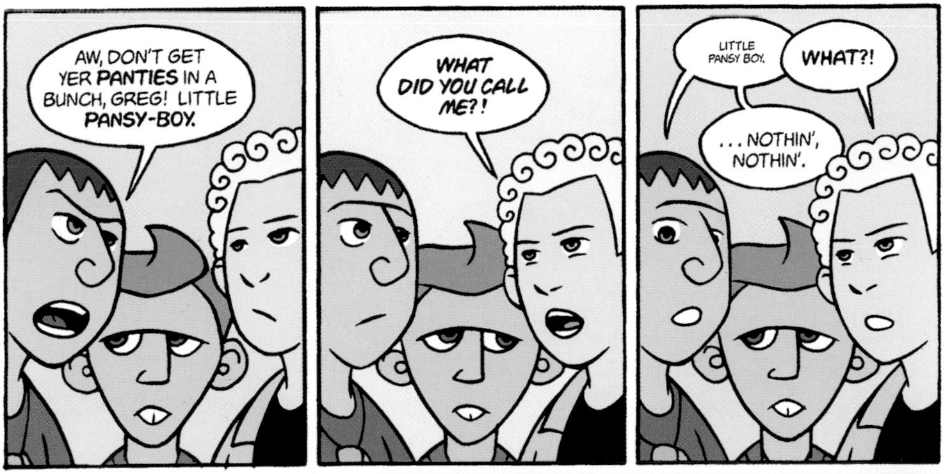
AW, DON'T GET YER PANTIES IN A BUNCH, GREG! LITTLE PANSY-BOY.
WHAT DID YOU CALL ME?!
LITTLE PANSY BOY.
WHAT?!
...NOTHIN', NOTHIN'.
COME ON. LET'S LEAVE BUCKTOOTH ALONE SO HE CAN ENJOY LASSIE.
HA HA! "BUCK-TOOTH!"

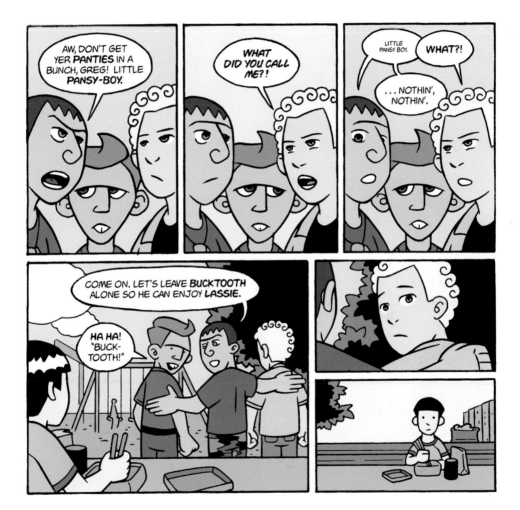

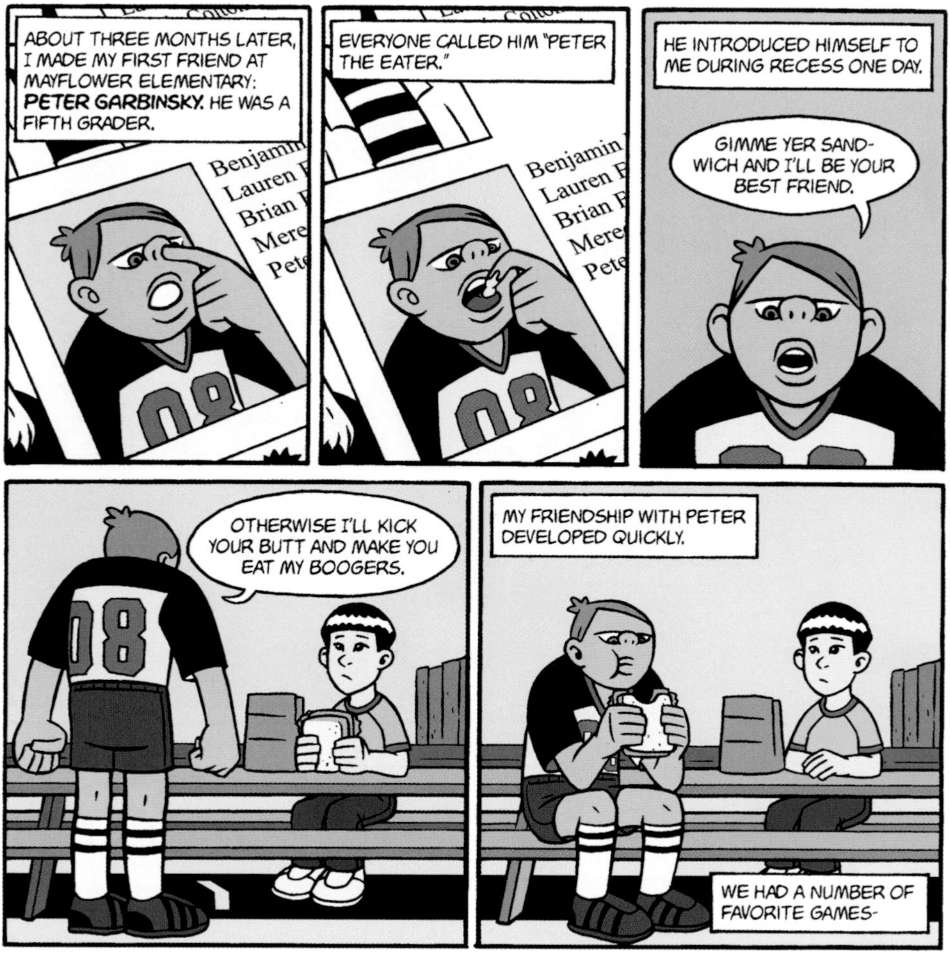

ABOUT THREE MONTHS LATER, I MADE MY FIRST FRIEND AT MAYFLOWER ELEMENTARY: **PETER GARBINSKY.** HE WAS A FIFTH GRADER.
Benjamin
Lauren
Brian
EVERYONE CALLED HIM "PETER THE EATER."
HE INTRODUCED HIMSELF TO ME DURING RECESS ONE DAY.
GIMME YER SANDWICH AND I'LL BE YOUR BEST FRIEND.
OTHERWISE I'LL KICK YOUR BUTT AND MAKE YOU EAT MY BOOGERS.
MY FRIENDSHIP WITH PETER DEVELOPED QUICKLY.
WE HAD A NUMBER OF FAVORITE GAMES-

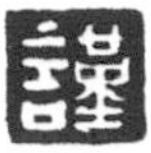

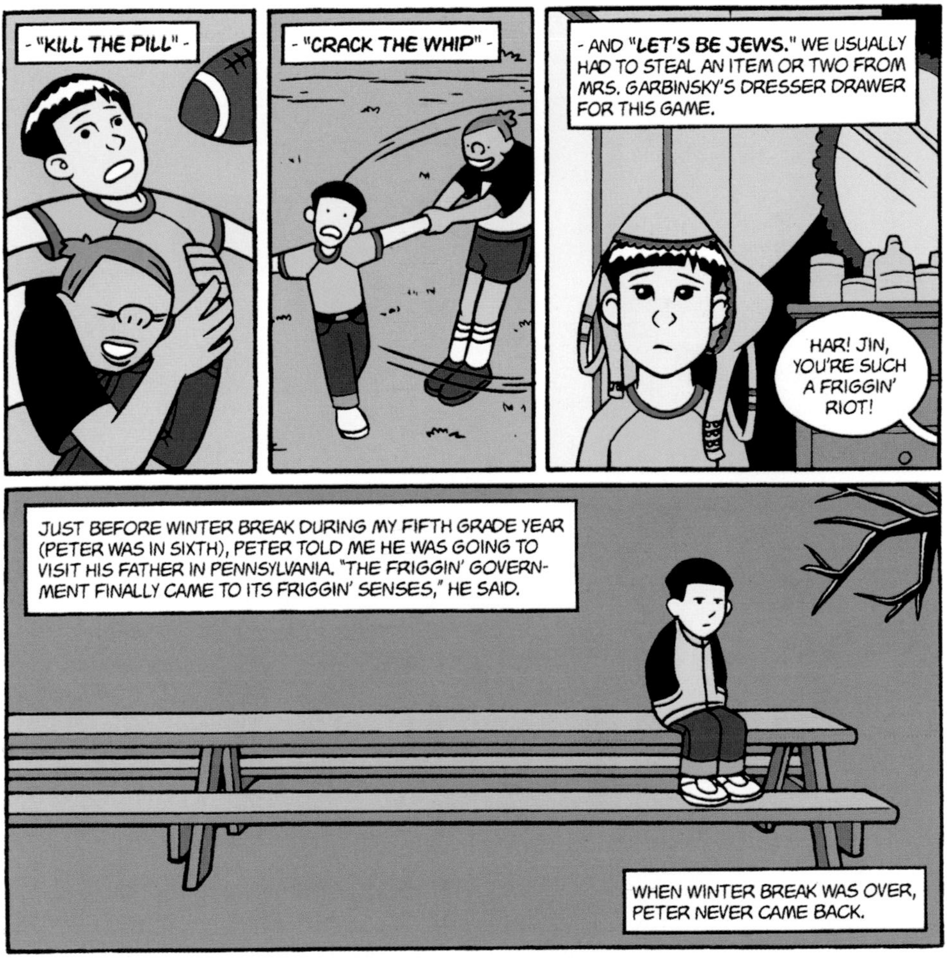
- "KILL THE PILL" -
- "CRACK THE WHIP" -
- AND "**LET'S BE JEWS.**" WE USUALLY HAD TO STEAL AN ITEM OR TWO FROM MRS. GARBINSKY'S DRESSER DRAWER FOR THIS GAME.
HAR! JIN, YOU'RE SUCH A FRIGGIN' RIOT!
JUST BEFORE WINTER BREAK DURING MY FIFTH GRADE YEAR (PETER WAS IN SIXTH), PETER TOLD ME HE WAS GOING TO VISIT HIS FATHER IN PENNSYLVANIA. "THE FRIGGIN' GOVERNMENT FINALLY CAME TO ITS FRIGGIN' SENSES," HE SAID.
WHEN WINTER BREAK WAS OVER, PETER NEVER CAME BACK.

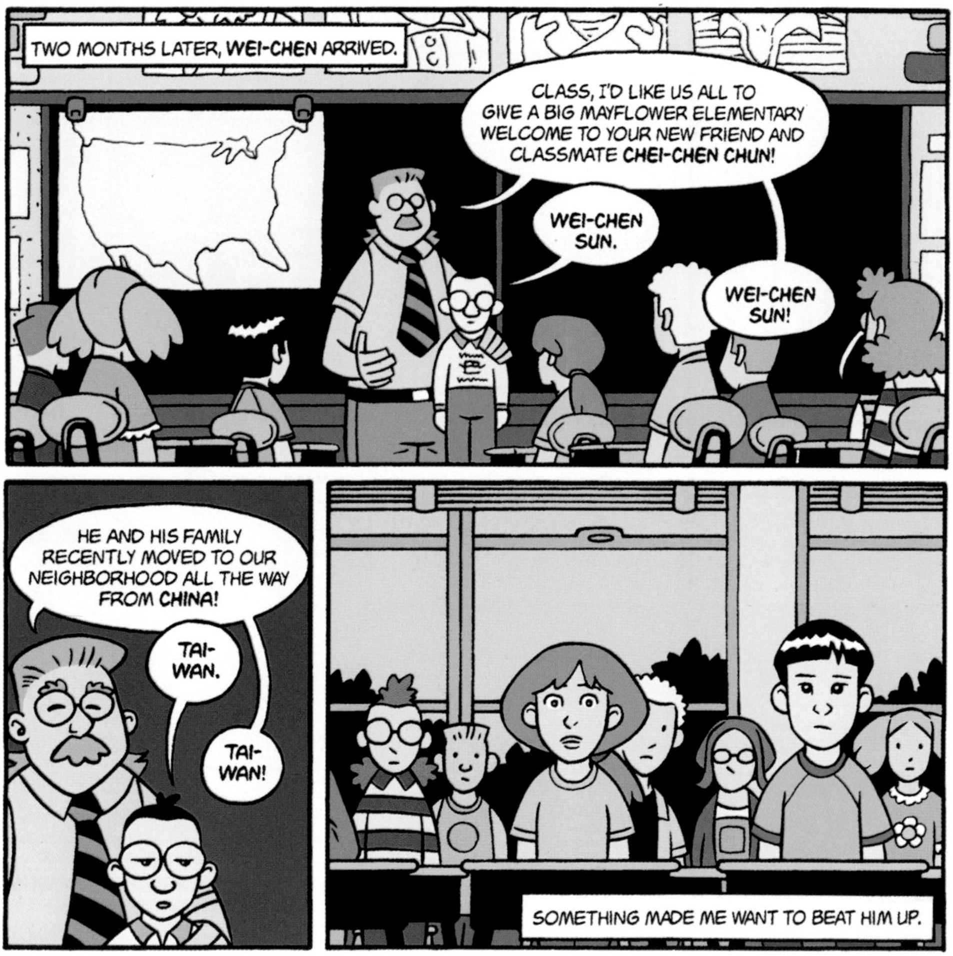
TWO MONTHS LATER, WEI-CHEN ARRIVED.
CLASS, I'D LIKE US ALL TO GIVE A BIG MAYFLOWER ELEMENTARY WELCOME TO YOUR NEW FRIEND AND CLASSMATE CHEI-CHEN CHUN!
WEI-CHEN SUN.
WEI-CHEN SUN!
HE AND HIS FAMILY RECENTLY MOVED TO OUR NEIGHBORHOOD ALL THE WAY FROM CHINA!
TAI-WAN.
TAI-WAN!
SOMETHING MADE ME WANT TO BEAT HIM UP.

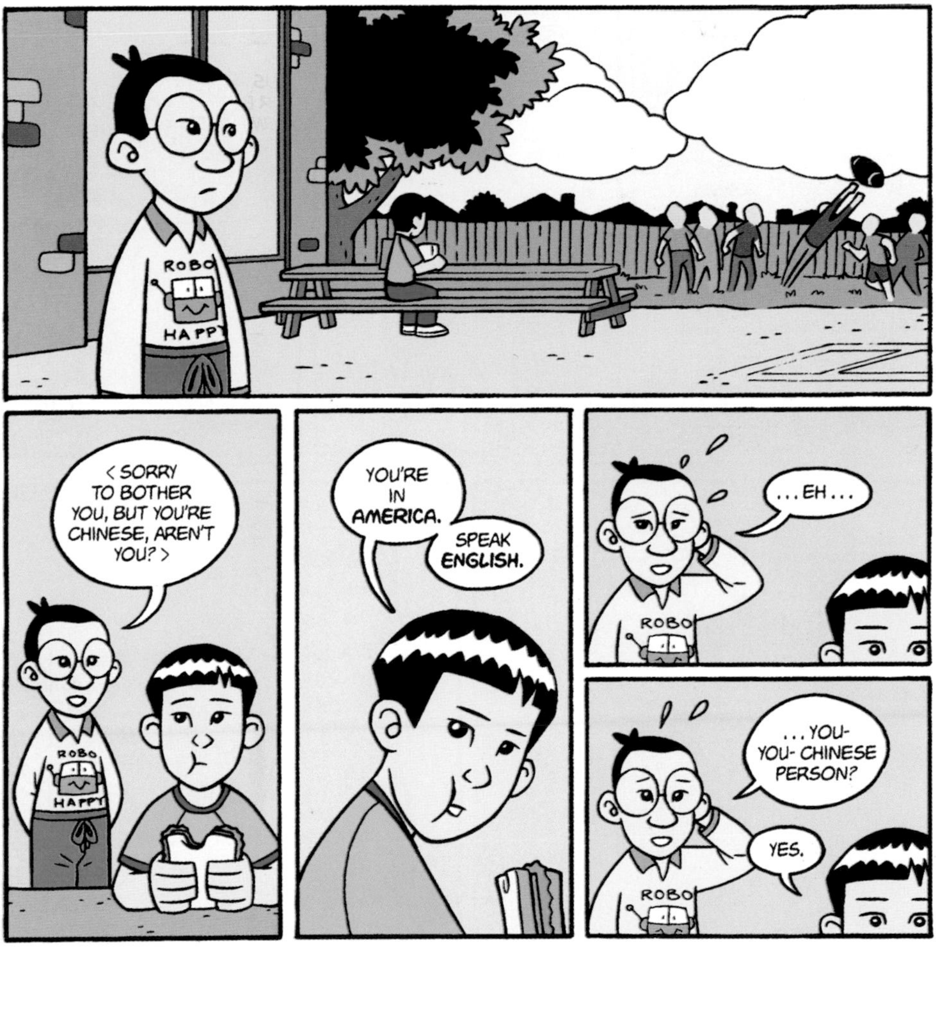
ROBO HAPPY
< SORRY TO BOTHER YOU, BUT YOU'RE CHINESE, AREN'T YOU? >
YOU'RE IN AMERICA.
SPEAK ENGLISH.
...EH...
...YOU- YOU- CHINESE PERSON?
YES.

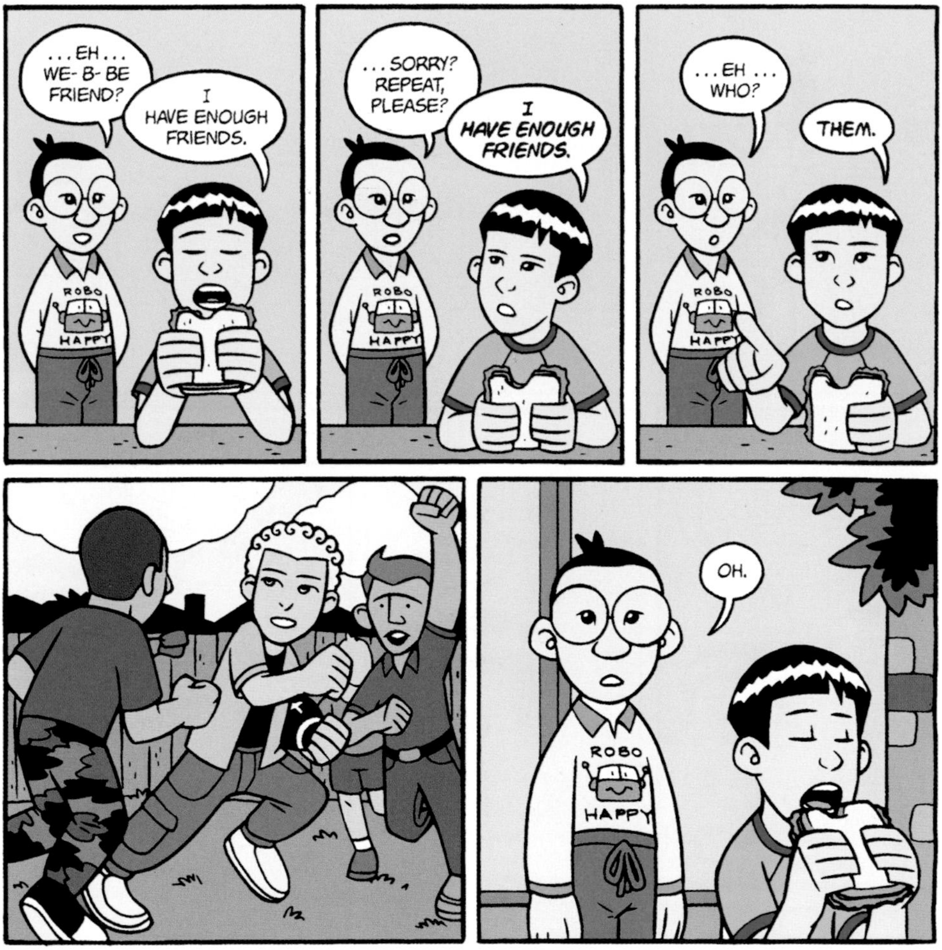
...EH... WE- B- BE FRIEND?
I HAVE ENOUGH FRIENDS.
...SORRY? REPEAT, PLEASE?
I **HAVE ENOUGH FRIENDS.**
...EH... WHO?
THEM.
OH.

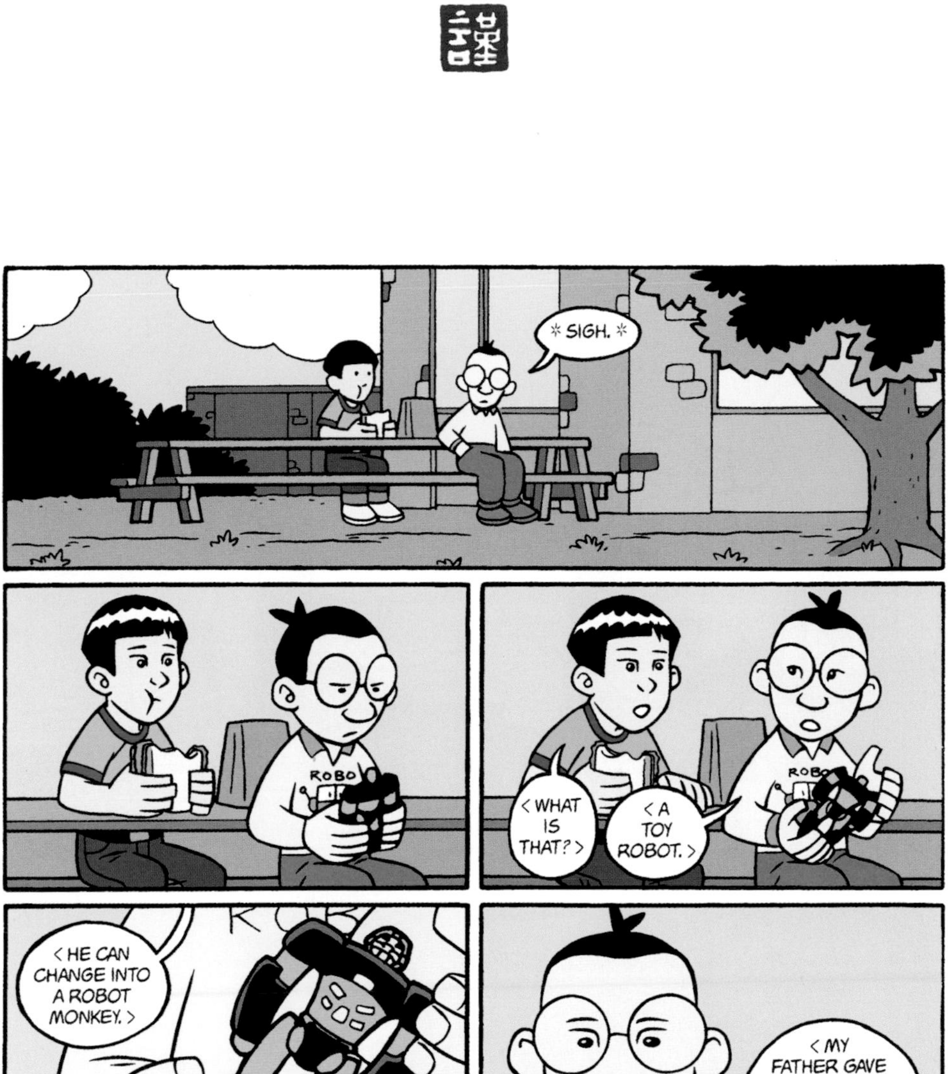

* SIGH. *
ROBO
< WHAT IS THAT? >
< A TOY ROBOT. >
< HE CAN CHANGE INTO A ROBOT MONKEY. >
< MY FATHER GAVE IT TO ME JUST BEFORE I LEFT. AS A GOOD-BYE PRESENT. >

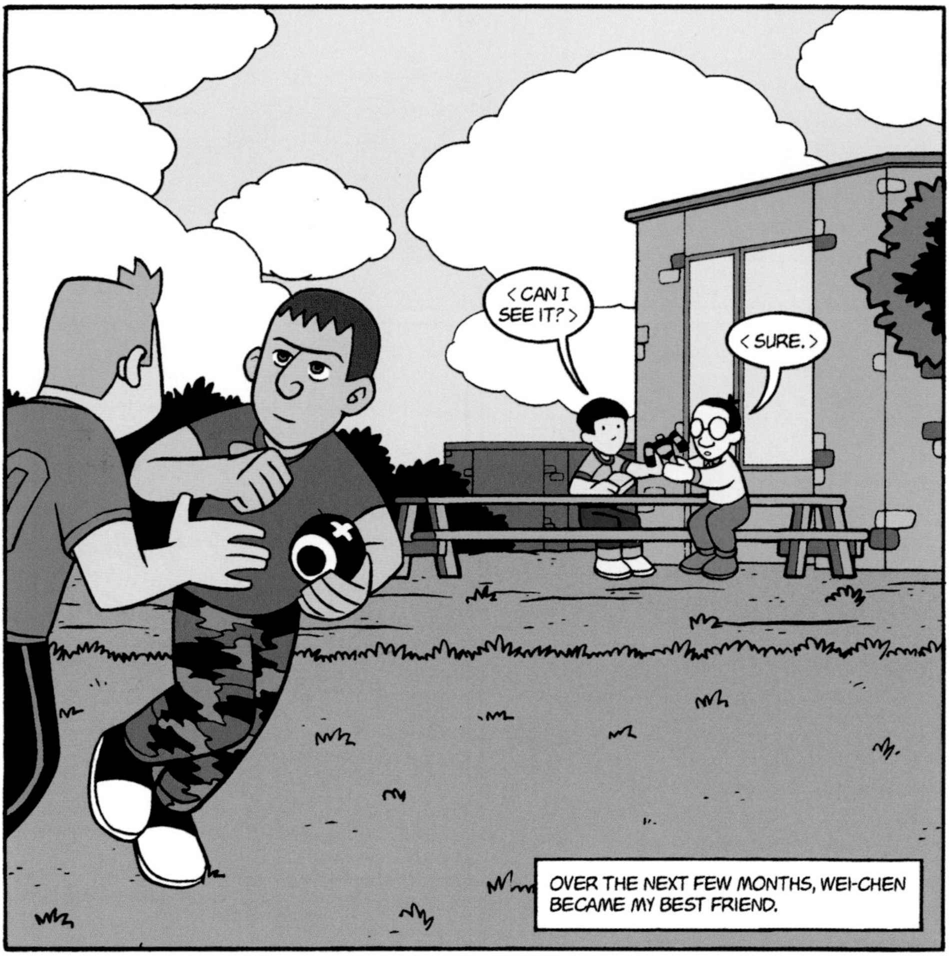
< CAN I SEE IT? >
< SURE. >
OVER THE NEXT FEW MONTHS, WEI-CHEN BECAME MY BEST FRIEND.

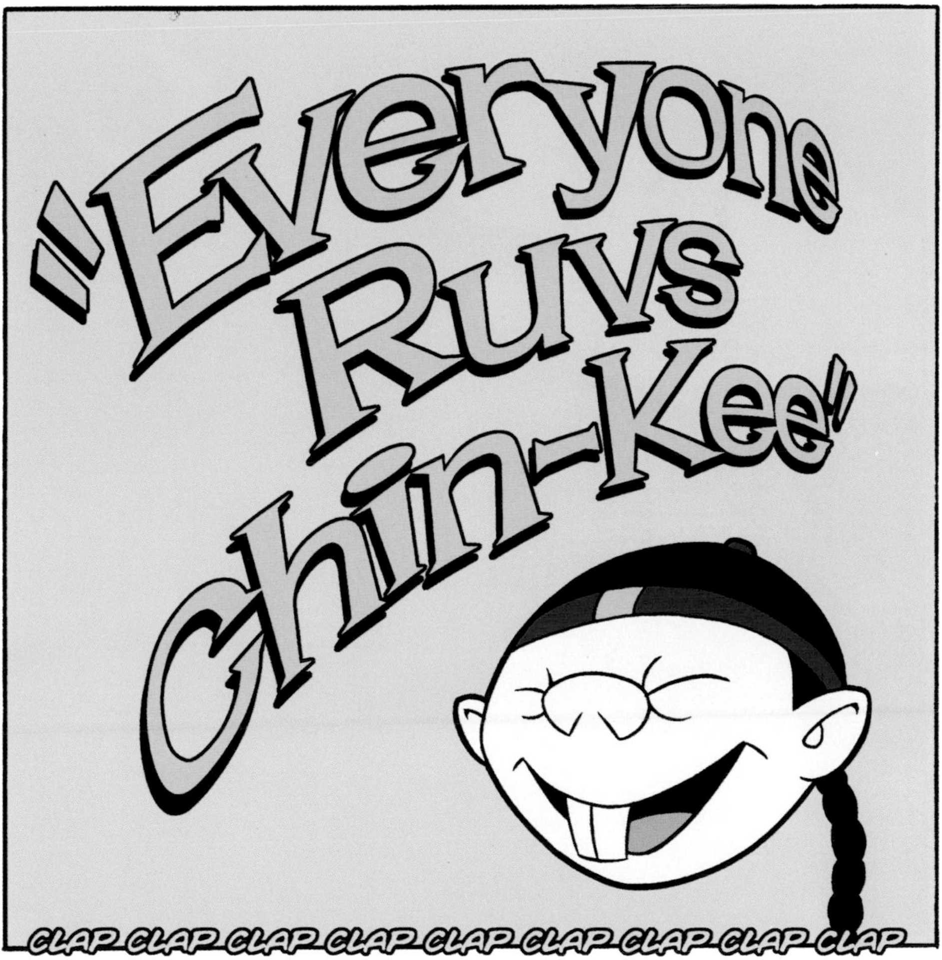
"Everyone Ruvs Chin-Kee!"
CLAP CLAP CLAP CLAP CLAP CLAP CLAP CLAP CLAP

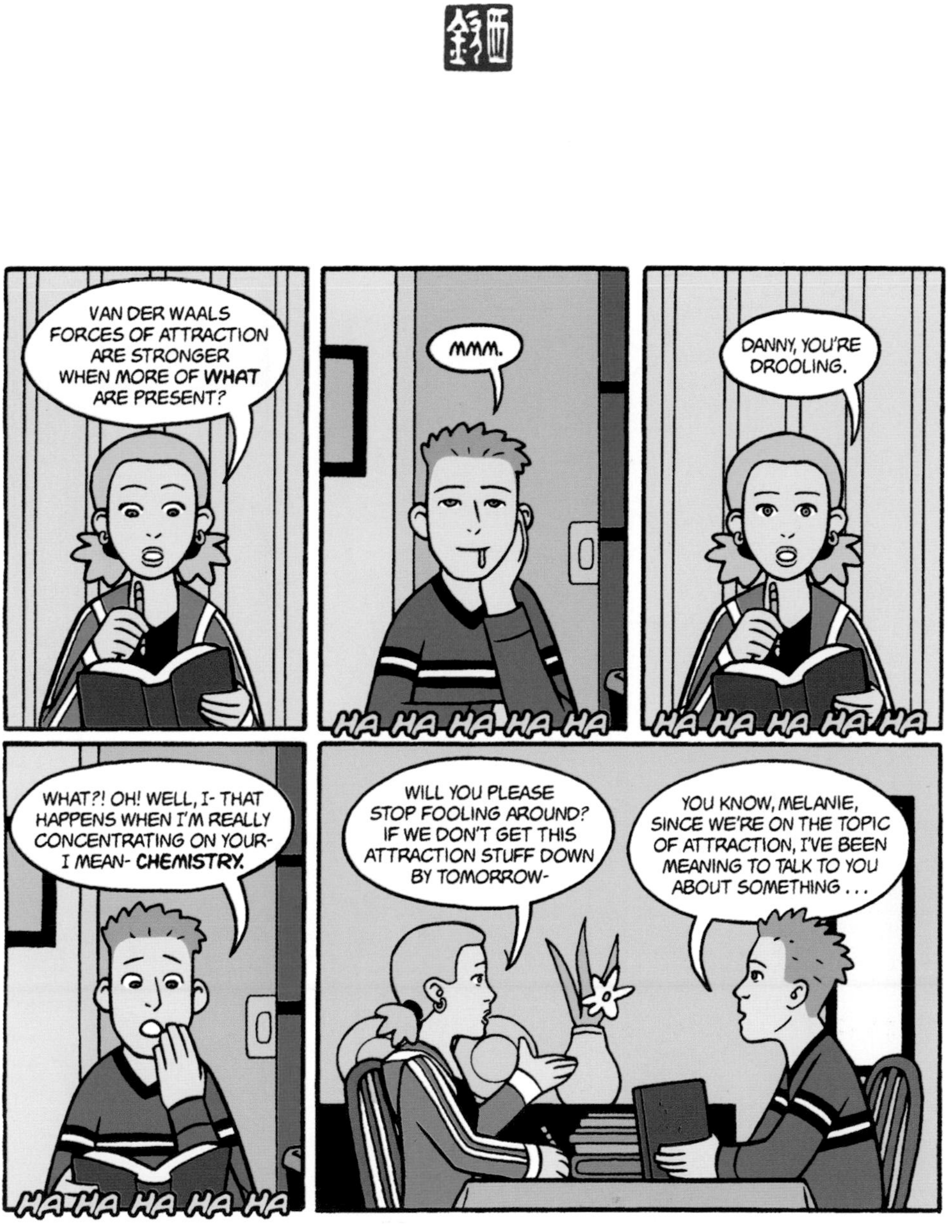
VAN DER WAALS FORCES OF ATTRACTION ARE STRONGER WHEN MORE OF WHAT ARE PRESENT?
MMM.
HA HA HA HA HA
DANNY, YOU'RE DROOLING.
HA HA HA HA HA
WHAT?! OH! WELL, I- THAT HAPPENS WHEN I'M REALLY CONCENTRATING ON YOUR- I MEAN- CHEMISTRY.
HA HA HA HA HA
WILL YOU PLEASE STOP FOOLING AROUND? IF WE DON'T GET THIS ATTRACTION STUFF DOWN BY TOMORROW-
YOU KNOW, MELANIE, SINCE WE'RE ON THE TOPIC OF ATTRACTION, I'VE BEEN MEANING TO TALK TO YOU ABOUT SOMETHING . . .

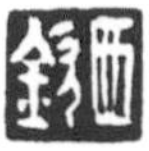

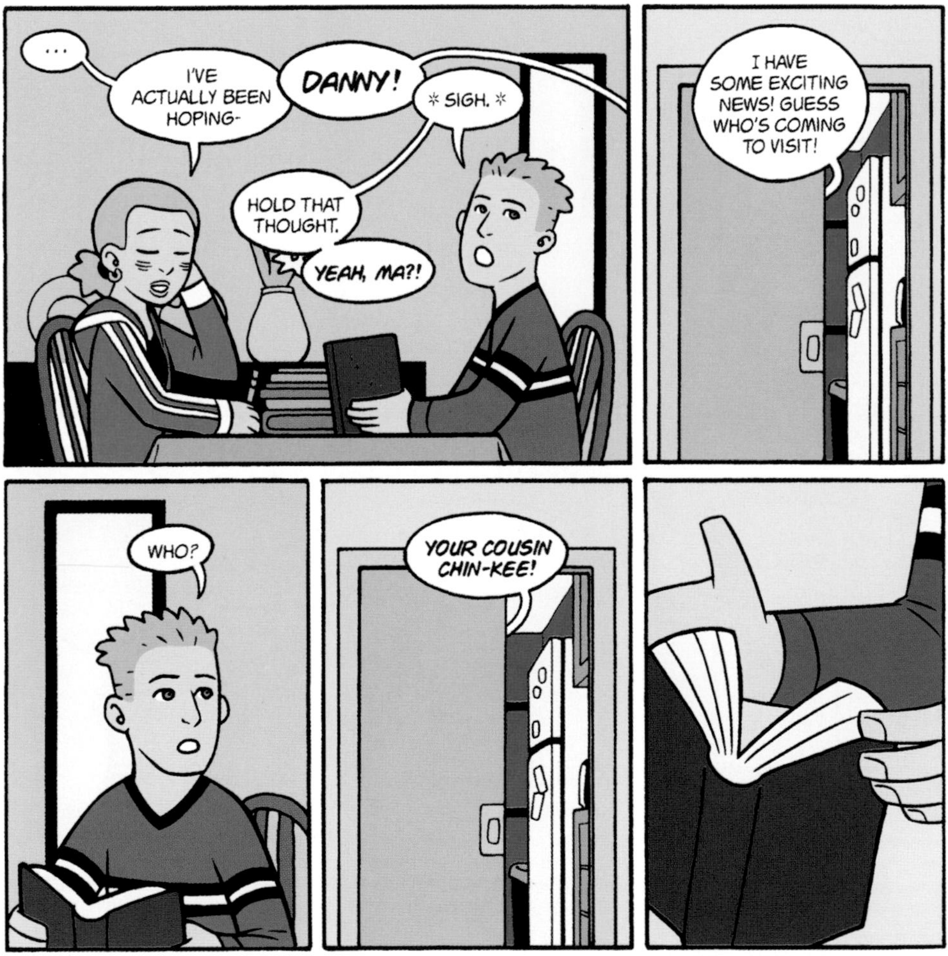
...
I'VE ACTUALLY BEEN HOPING-
DANNY!
✲ SIGH. ✲
HOLD THAT THOUGHT.
YEAH, MA?!
I HAVE SOME EXCITING NEWS! GUESS WHO'S COMING TO VISIT!
WHO?
YOUR COUSIN CHIN-KEE!

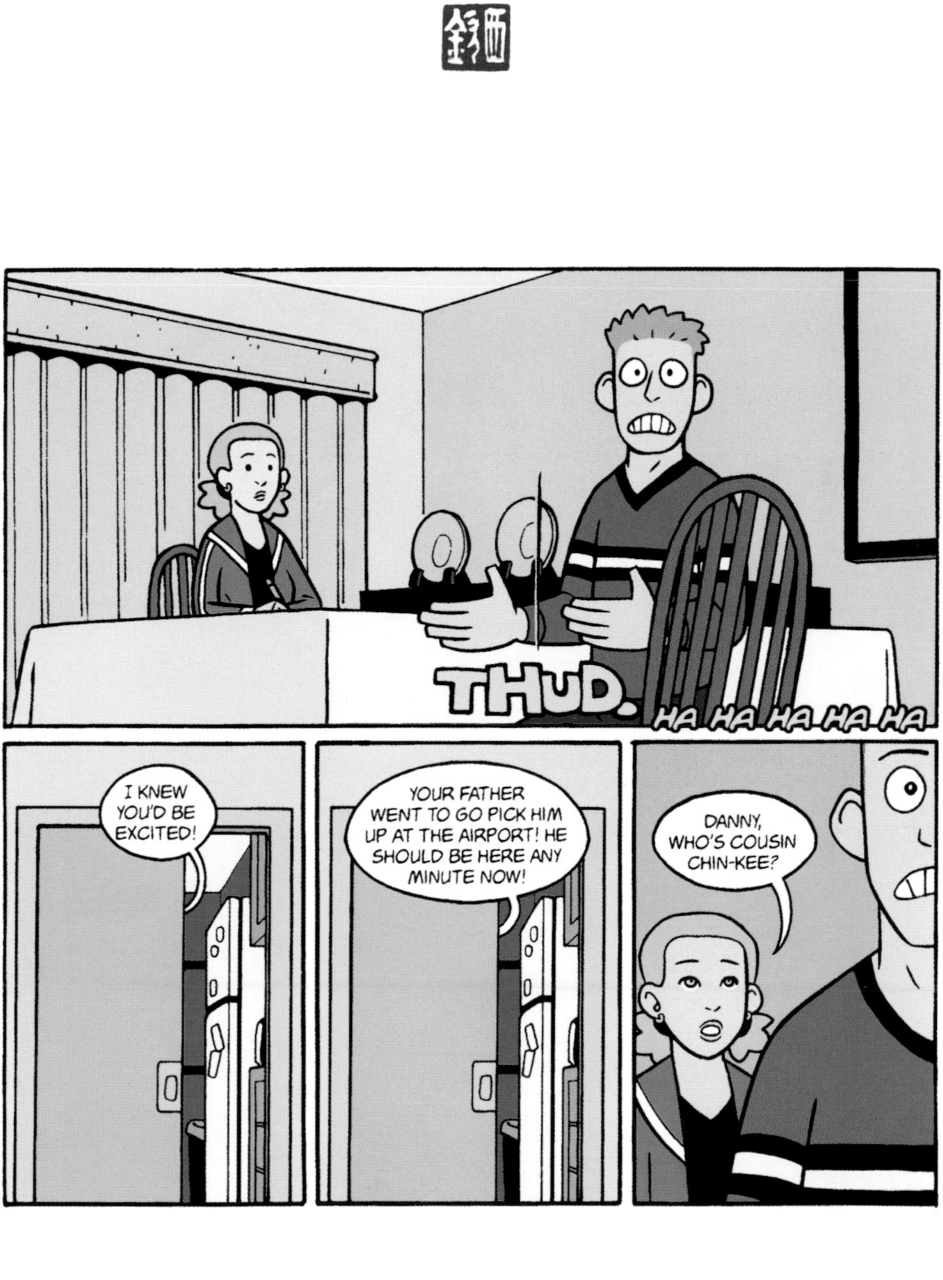
THUD.
HA HA HA HA HA
I KNEW YOU'D BE EXCITED!
YOUR FATHER WENT TO GO PICK HIM UP AT THE AIRPORT! HE SHOULD BE HERE ANY MINUTE NOW!
DANNY, WHO'S COUSIN CHIN-KEE?

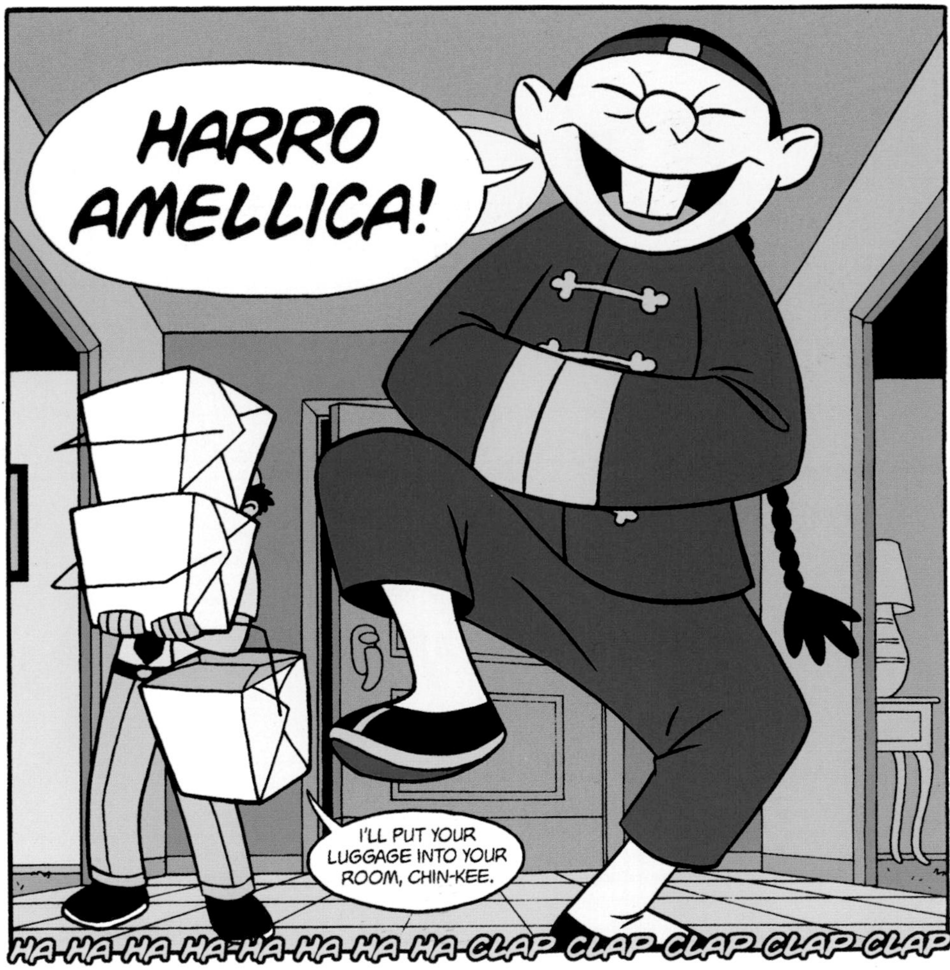
HARRO AMELLICA!
I'LL PUT YOUR LUGGAGE INTO YOUR ROOM, CHIN-KEE.
HA HA HA HA HA HA HA HA CLAP CLAP CLAP CLAP CLAP

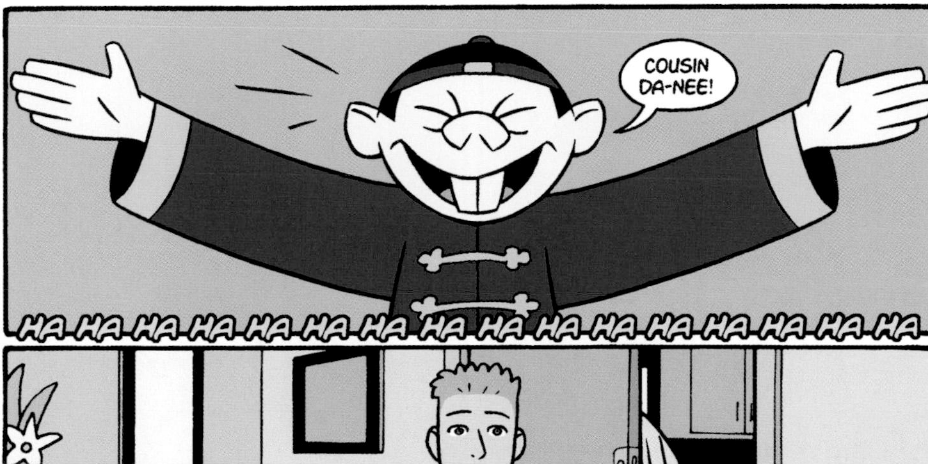
COUSIN DA-NEE!
HA HA HA HA HA HA HA HA HA HA HA HA HA HA HA HA
RONG TIME NO SEE! CHIN-KEE HAPPY AS **GINGER ROOT** PRANTED IN NUTRITIOUS MANURE OF **WELL-BRED OX!**
...
HI CHIN-KEE.
HA HA HA HA HA HA HA HA HA HA HA HA HA HA HA HA

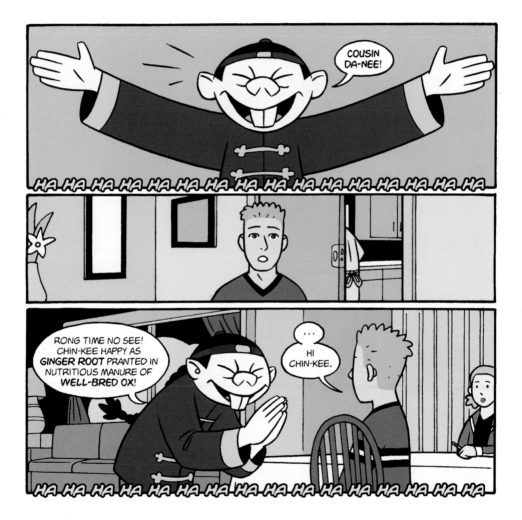

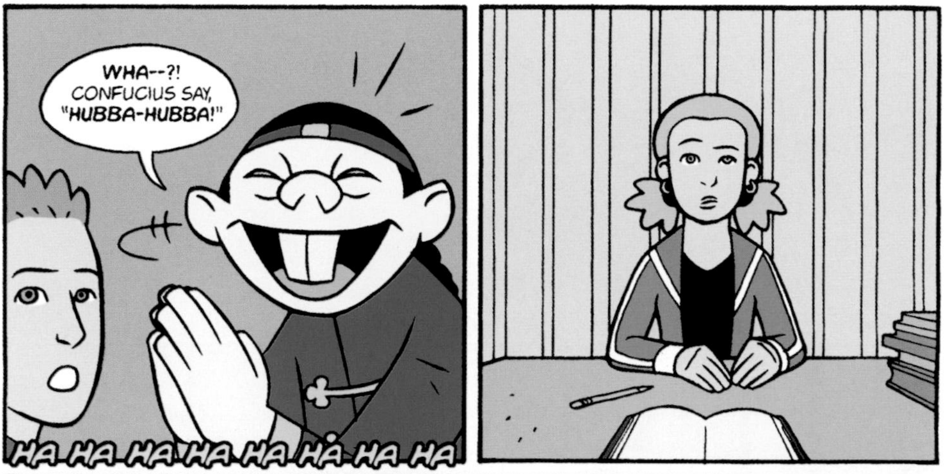
WHA--?! CONFUCIUS SAY, "HUBBA-HUBBA!"
HA HA HA HA HA HA HA HA HA
SUCH PLETTY AMELLICAN GIRL WIFF BOUNTIFUL AMELLICAN BOSOM! MUST BIND FEET AND BEAR CHIN-KEE'S CHILDREN!
HA HA HA HA HA HA HA HA HA HA HA HA HA HA HA HA

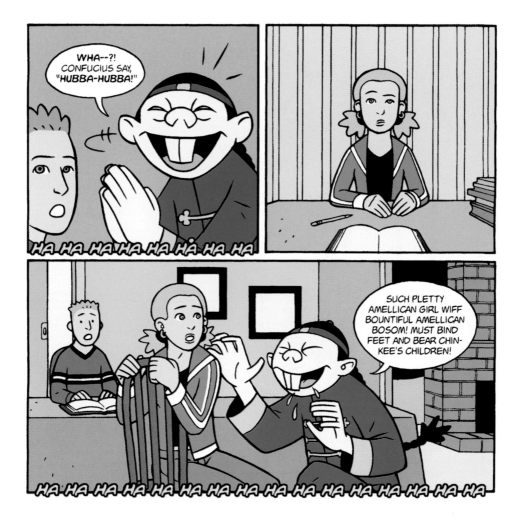

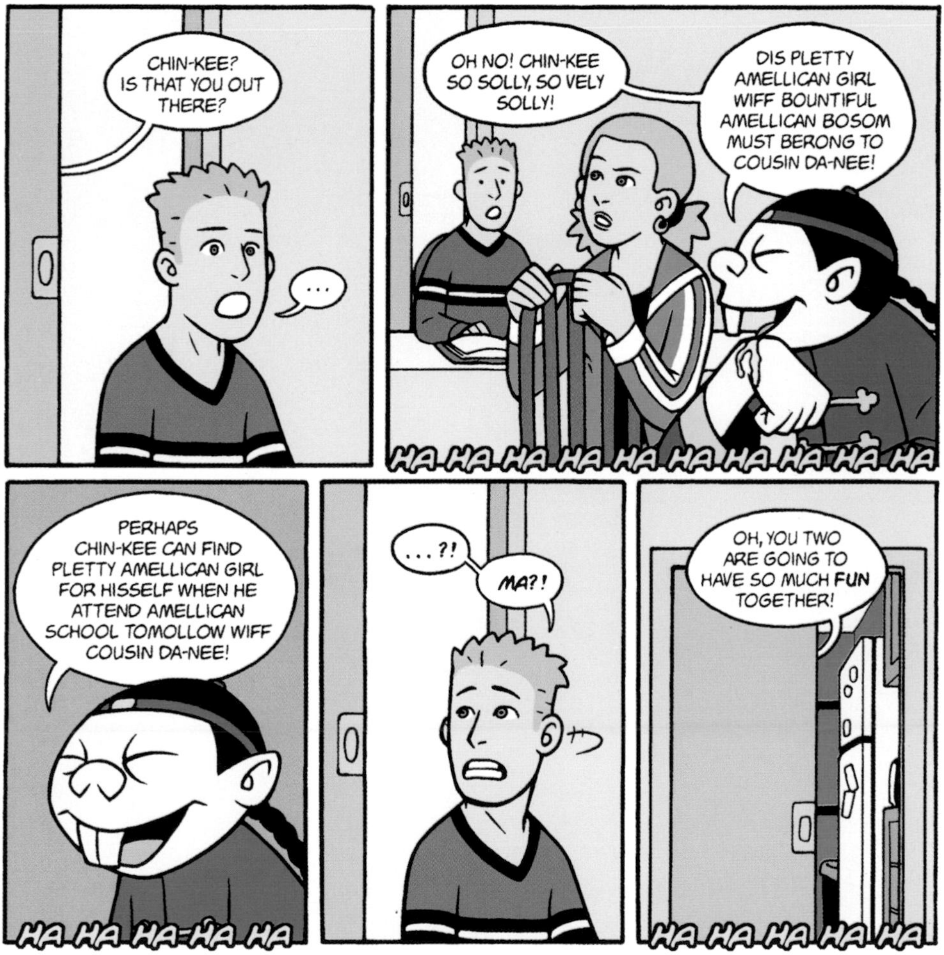
CHIN-KEE? IS THAT YOU OUT THERE?
. . .
OH NO! CHIN-KEE SO SOLLY, SO VELY SOLLY!
DIS PLETTY AMELLICAN GIRL WIFF BOUNTIFUL AMELLICAN BOSOM MUST BERONG TO COUSIN DA-NEE!
HA HA HA HA HA HA HA HA HA HA
PERHAPS CHIN-KEE CAN FIND PLETTY AMELLICAN GIRL FOR HISSELF WHEN HE ATTEND AMELLICAN SCHOOL TOMOLLOW WIFF COUSIN DA-NEE!
HA HA HA HA HA
. . . ?!
MA?!
OH, YOU TWO ARE GOING TO HAVE SO MUCH FUN TOGETHER!
HA HA HA HA HA HA

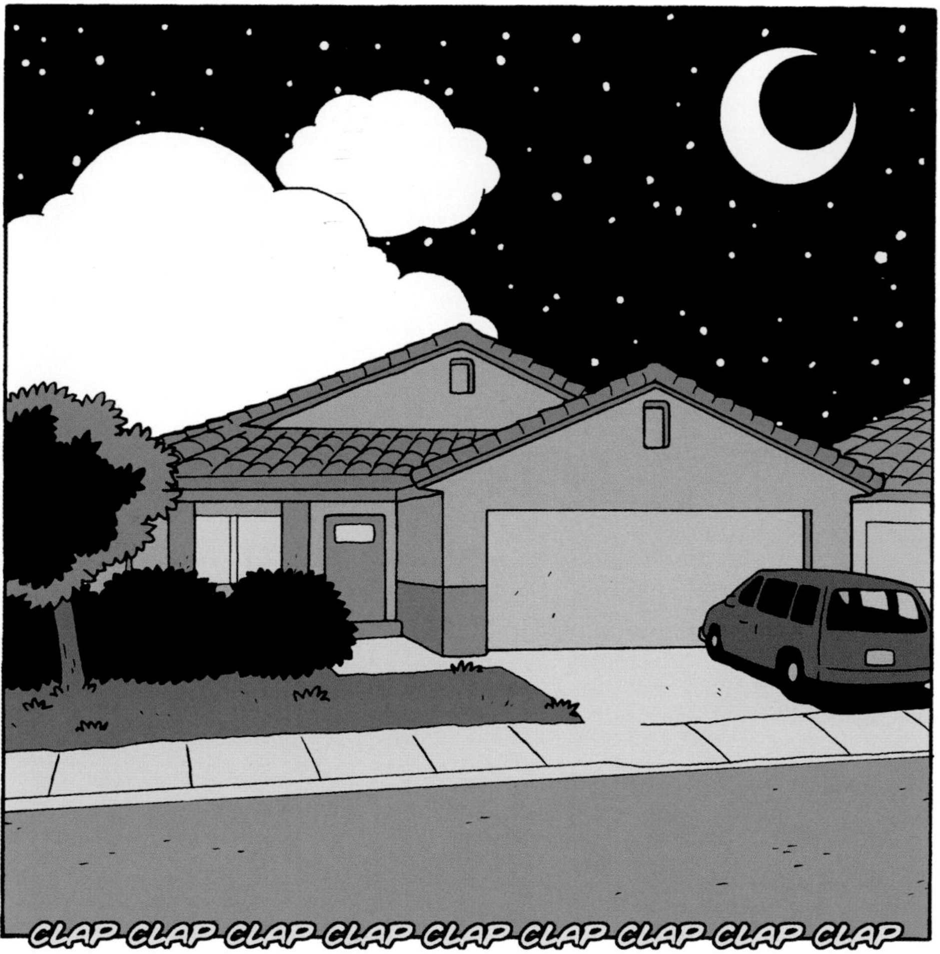
CLAP CLAP CLAP CLAP CLAP CLAP CLAP CLAP CLAP

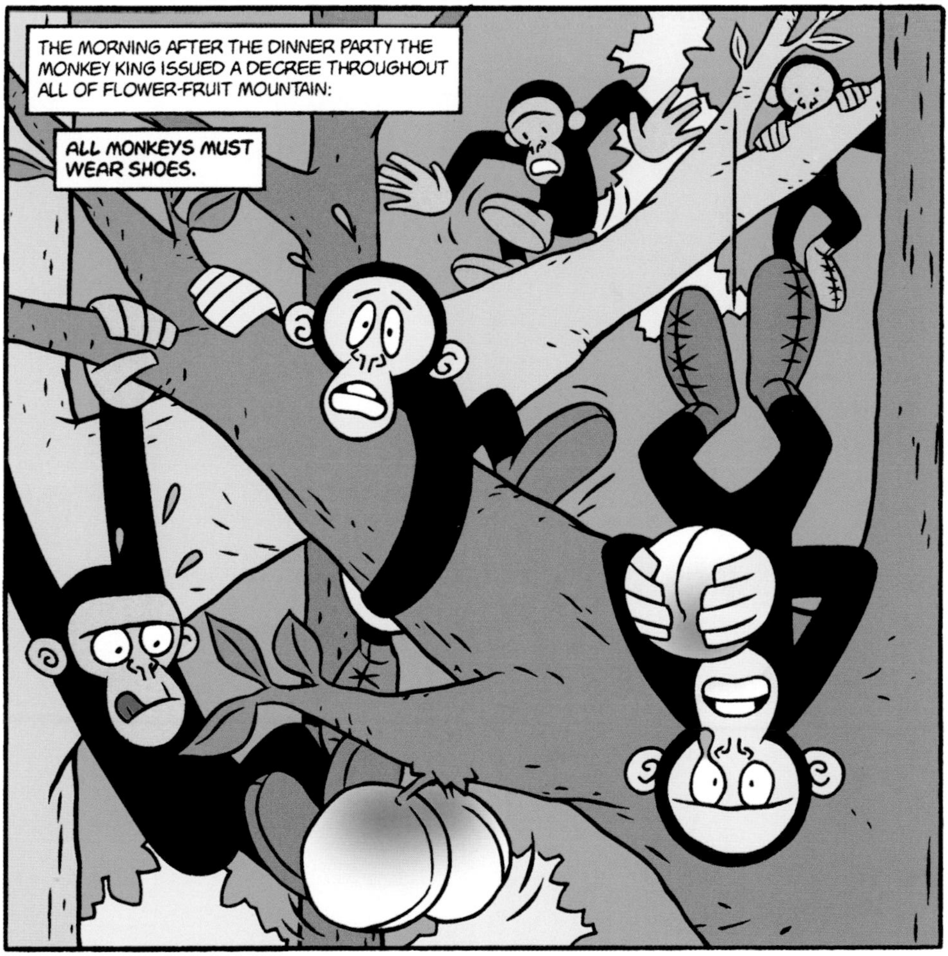
THE MORNING AFTER THE DINNER PARTY THE MONKEY KING ISSUED A DECREE THROUGHOUT ALL OF FLOWER-FRUIT MOUNTAIN:
ALL MONKEYS MUST WEAR SHOES.

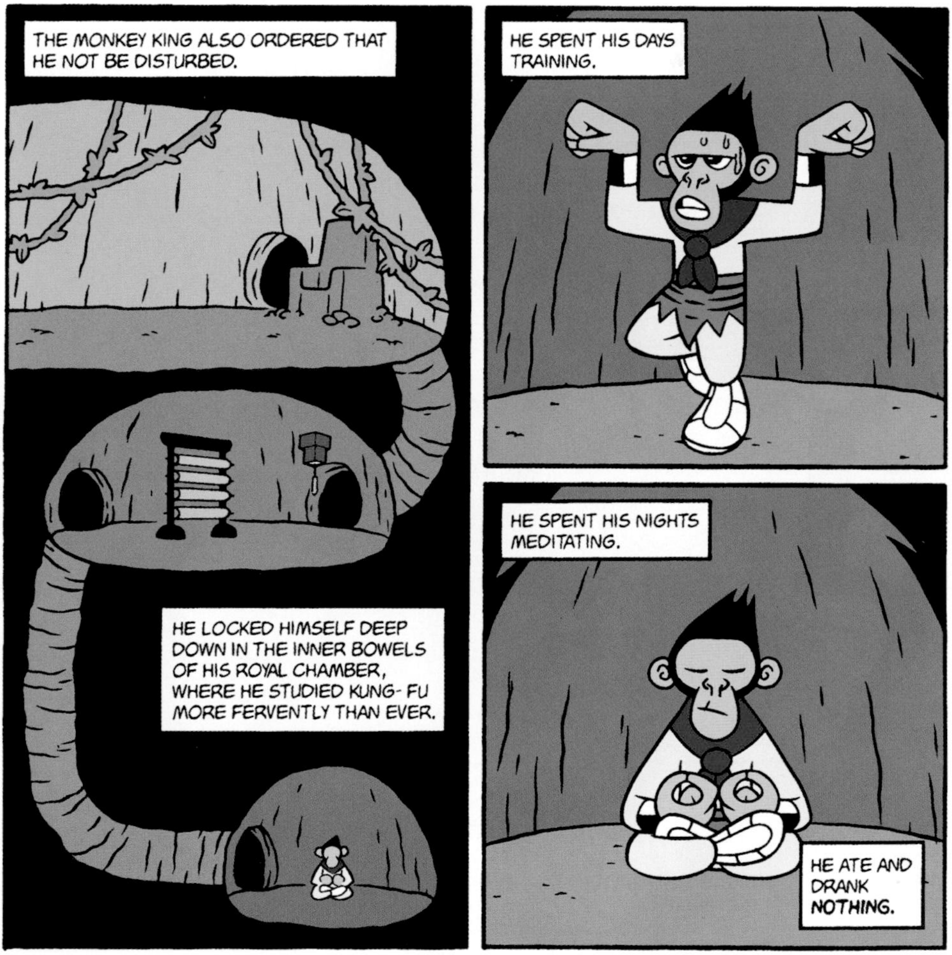
THE MONKEY KING ALSO ORDERED THAT HE NOT BE DISTURBED.
HE LOCKED HIMSELF DEEP DOWN IN THE INNER BOWELS OF HIS ROYAL CHAMBER, WHERE HE STUDIED KUNG-FU MORE FERVENTLY THAN EVER.
HE SPENT HIS DAYS TRAINING.
HE SPENT HIS NIGHTS MEDITATING.
HE ATE AND DRANK **NOTHING.**

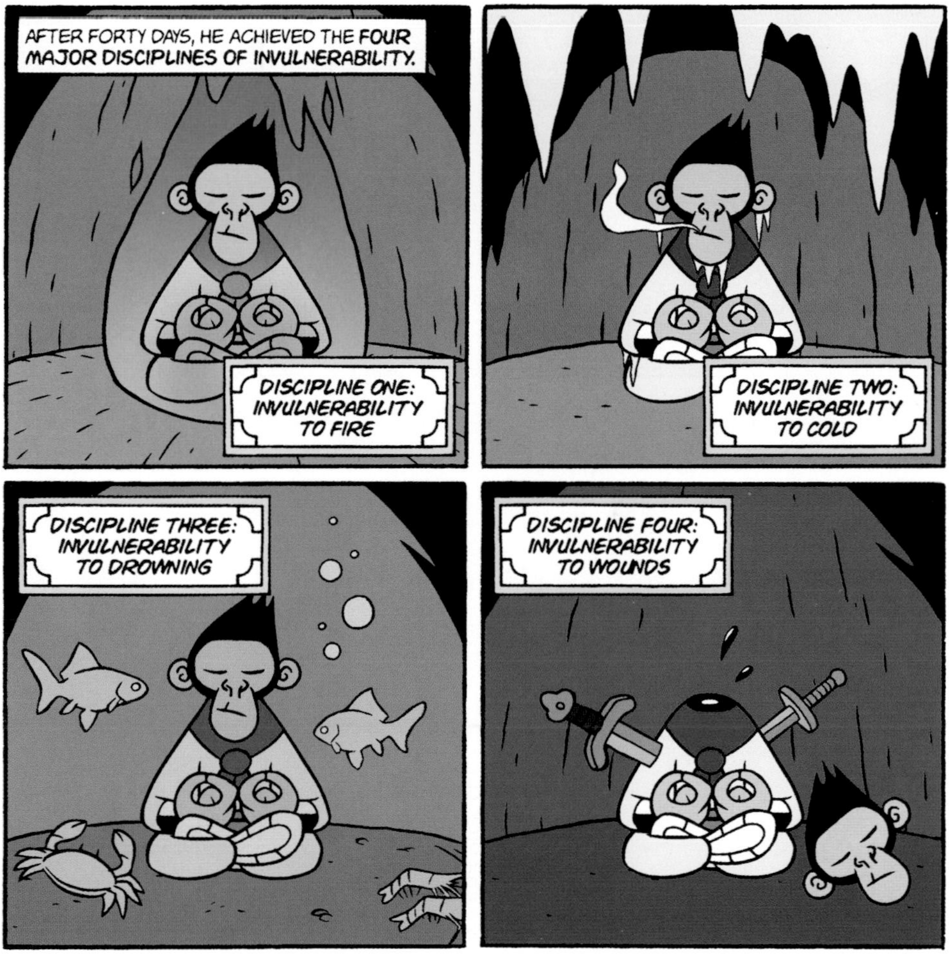
AFTER FORTY DAYS, HE ACHIEVED THE FOUR MAJOR DISCIPLINES OF INVULNERABILITY.
DISCIPLINE ONE: INVULNERABILITY TO FIRE
DISCIPLINE TWO: INVULNERABILITY TO COLD
DISCIPLINE THREE: INVULNERABILITY TO DROWNING
DISCIPLINE FOUR: INVULNERABILITY TO WOUNDS

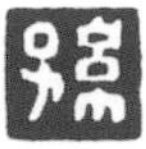

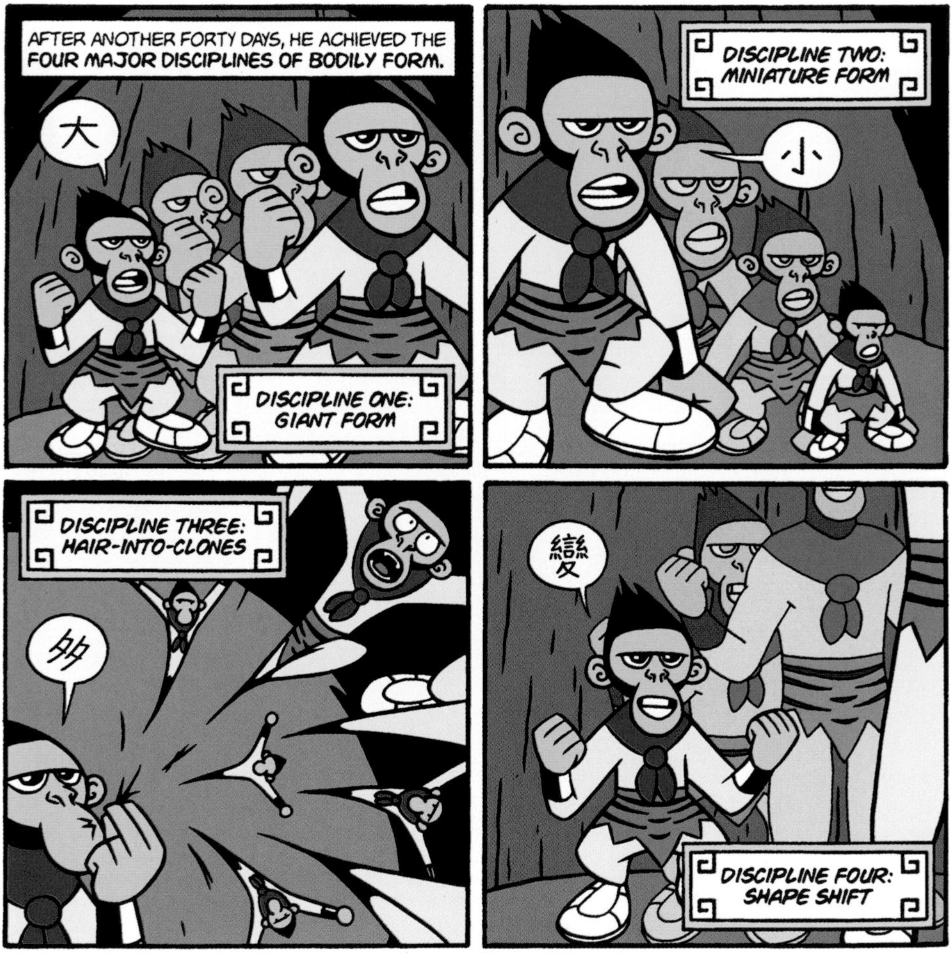

AFTER ANOTHER FORTY DAYS, HE ACHIEVED THE FOUR MAJOR DISCIPLINES OF BODILY FORM.
大
DISCIPLINE ONE: GIANT FORM
DISCIPLINE TWO: MINIATURE FORM
小
DISCIPLINE THREE: HAIR-INTO-CLONES
夠
DISCIPLINE FOUR: SHAPE SHIFT

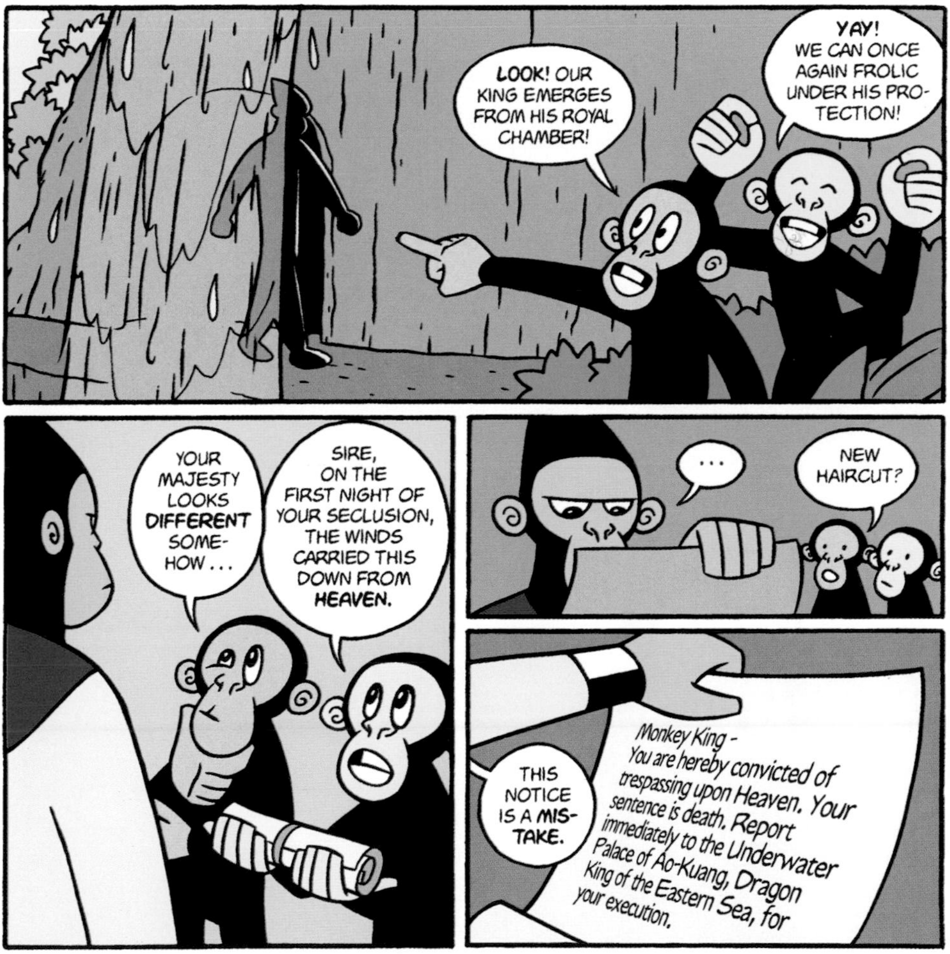
LOOK! OUR KING EMERGES FROM HIS ROYAL CHAMBER!
YAY! WE CAN ONCE AGAIN FROLIC UNDER HIS PROTECTION!
YOUR MAJESTY LOOKS DIFFERENT SOMEHOW . . .
SIRE, ON THE FIRST NIGHT OF YOUR SECLUSION, THE WINDS CARRIED THIS DOWN FROM HEAVEN.
. . .
NEW HAIRCUT?
Monkey King - You are hereby convicted of trespassing upon Heaven. Your sentence is death. Report immediately to the Underwater Palace of Ao-Kuang, Dragon King of the Eastern Sea, for your execution.
THIS NOTICE IS A MISTAKE.

THIS "MONKEY KING" IT SPEAKS OF NO LONGER EXISTS, FOR I HAVE MASTERED TWELVE MAJOR DISCIPLINES OF KUNG-FU AND TRANSCENDED MY FORMER TITLE!
I SHALL NOW BE CALLED-
-THE GREAT SAGE, EQUAL OF HEAVEN!
WOULD YOUR MAJESTY LIKE A BANANA?
YUMMY BANANA!
...

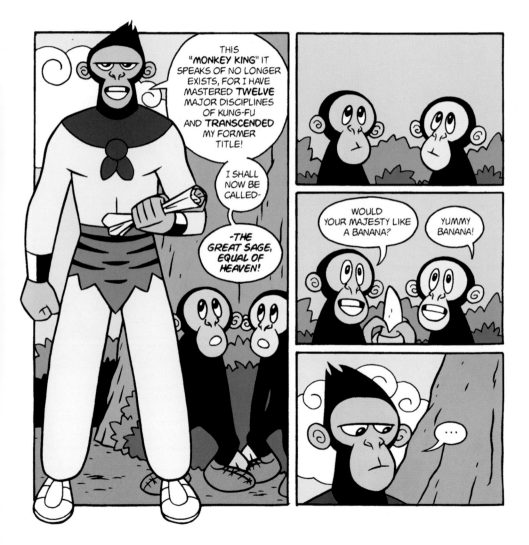

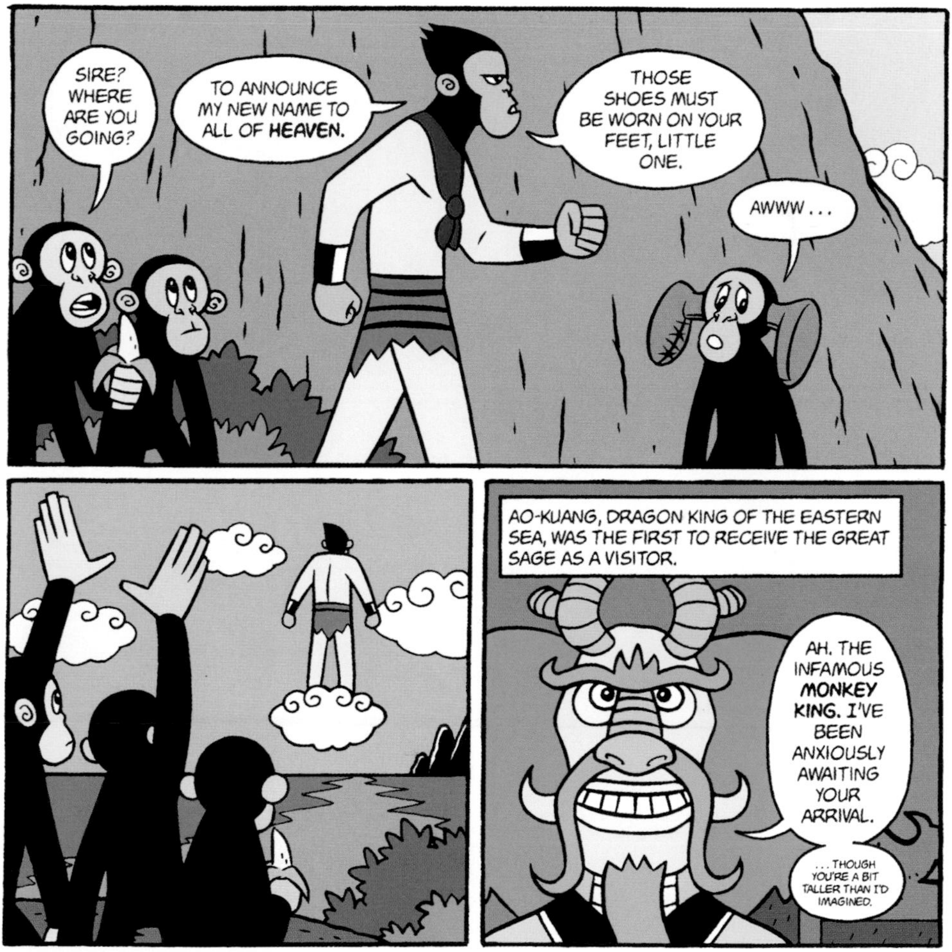
SIRE? WHERE ARE YOU GOING?
TO ANNOUNCE MY NEW NAME TO ALL OF HEAVEN.
THOSE SHOES MUST BE WORN ON YOUR FEET, LITTLE ONE.
AWWW . . .
AO-KUANG, DRAGON KING OF THE EASTERN SEA, WAS THE FIRST TO RECEIVE THE GREAT SAGE AS A VISITOR.
AH. THE INFAMOUS MONKEY KING. I'VE BEEN ANXIOUSLY AWAITING YOUR ARRIVAL.
. . . THOUGH YOU'RE A BIT TALLER THAN I'D IMAGINED.

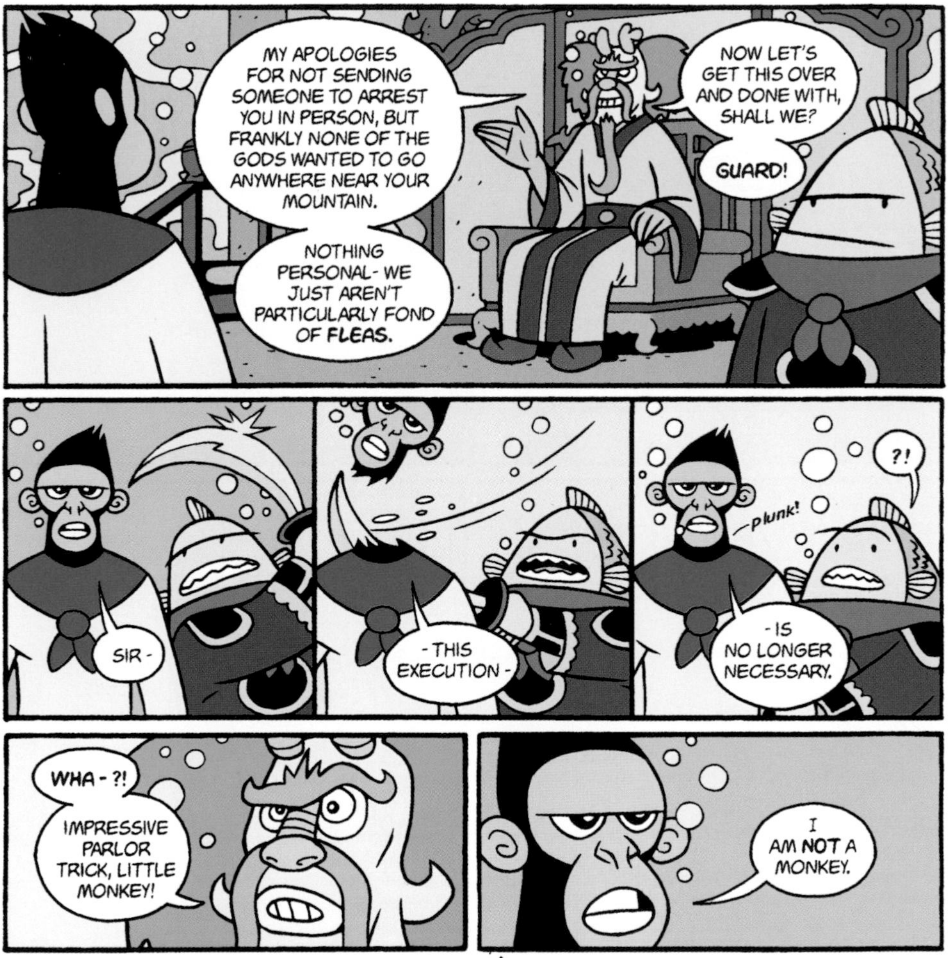
MY APOLOGIES FOR NOT SENDING SOMEONE TO ARREST YOU IN PERSON, BUT FRANKLY NONE OF THE GODS WANTED TO GO ANYWHERE NEAR YOUR MOUNTAIN.
NOTHING PERSONAL- WE JUST AREN'T PARTICULARLY FOND OF **FLEAS.**
NOW LET'S GET THIS OVER AND DONE WITH, SHALL WE?
GUARD!
SIR -
- THIS EXECUTION -
-plunk!
?!
- IS NO LONGER NECESSARY.
WHA - ?!
IMPRESSIVE PARLOR TRICK, LITTLE MONKEY!
I AM **NOT** A MONKEY.

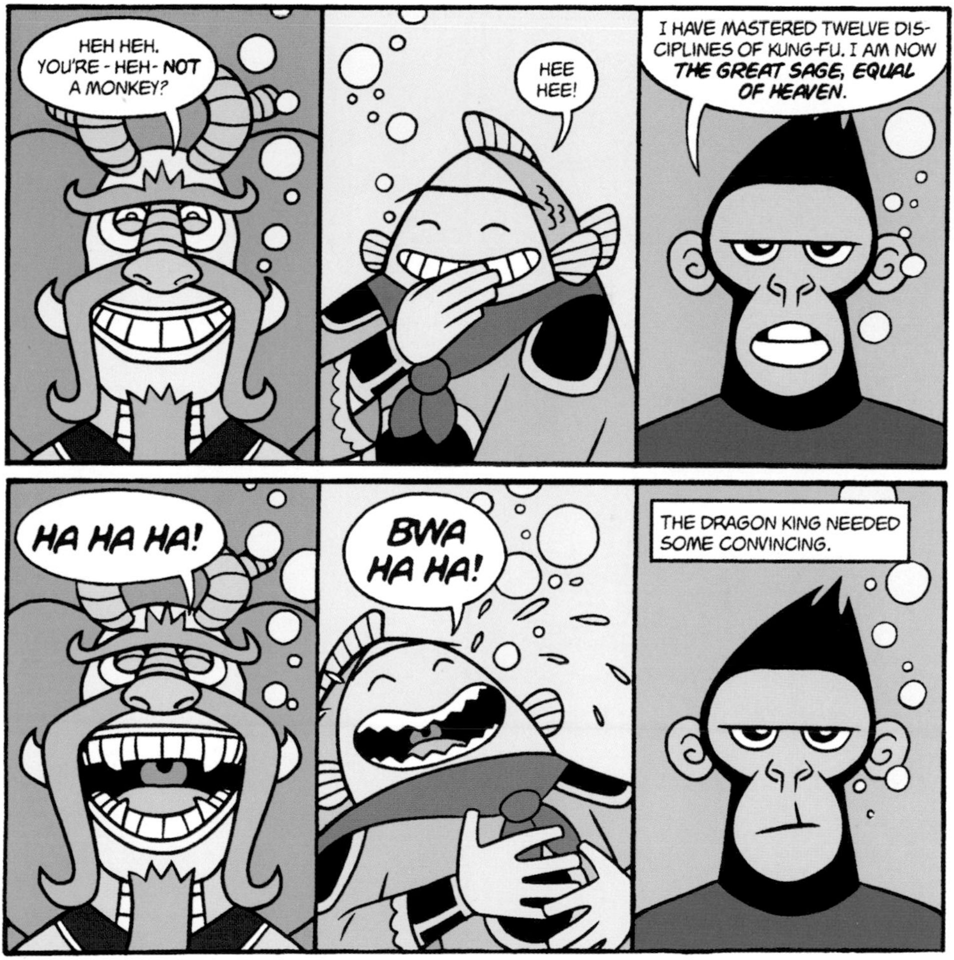
HEH HEH. YOU'RE - HEH - NOT A MONKEY?
HEE HEE!
I HAVE MASTERED TWELVE DISCIPLINES OF KUNG-FU. I AM NOW THE GREAT SAGE, EQUAL OF HEAVEN.
HA HA HA!
BWA HA HA!
THE DRAGON KING NEEDED SOME CONVINCING.

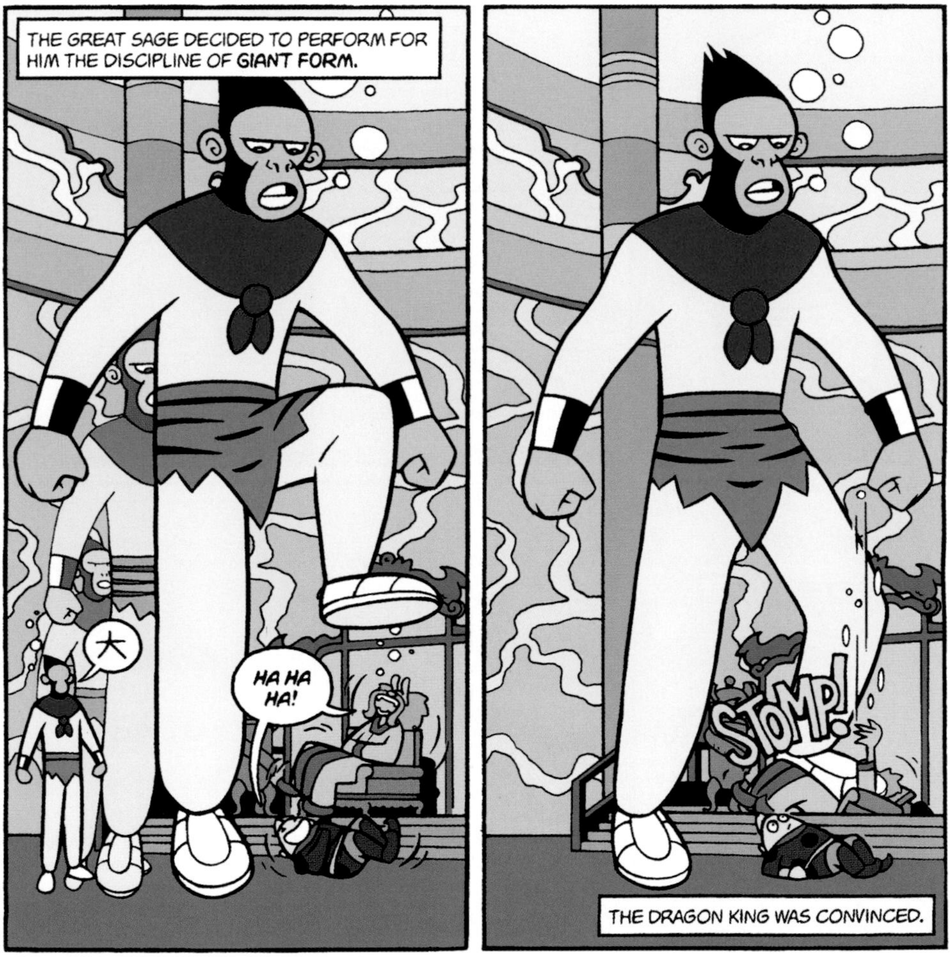
THE GREAT SAGE DECIDED TO PERFORM FOR HIM THE DISCIPLINE OF GIANT FORM.
大
HA HA HA!
STOMP!
THE DRAGON KING WAS CONVINCED.

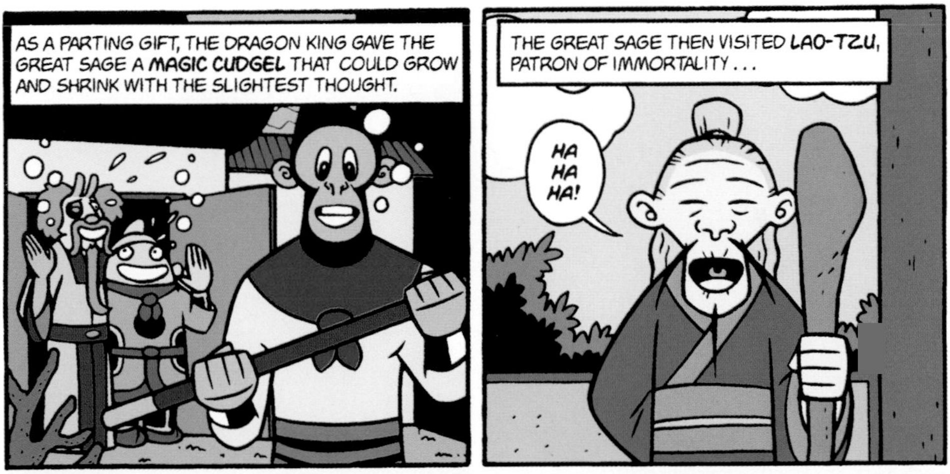
AS A PARTING GIFT, THE DRAGON KING GAVE THE GREAT SAGE A MAGIC CUDGEL THAT COULD GROW AND SHRINK WITH THE SLIGHTEST THOUGHT.
THE GREAT SAGE THEN VISITED LAO-TZU, PATRON OF IMMORTALITY . . .
HA HA HA!
. . . YAMA, CARE-TAKER OF THE UNDERWORLD . . .
TEE HEE!
. . . AND THE JADE EMPEROR, RULER OF THE CELESTIALS.
HAW HAW HAW!

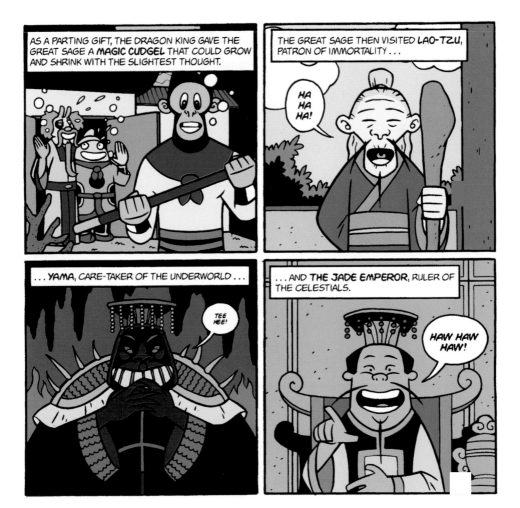

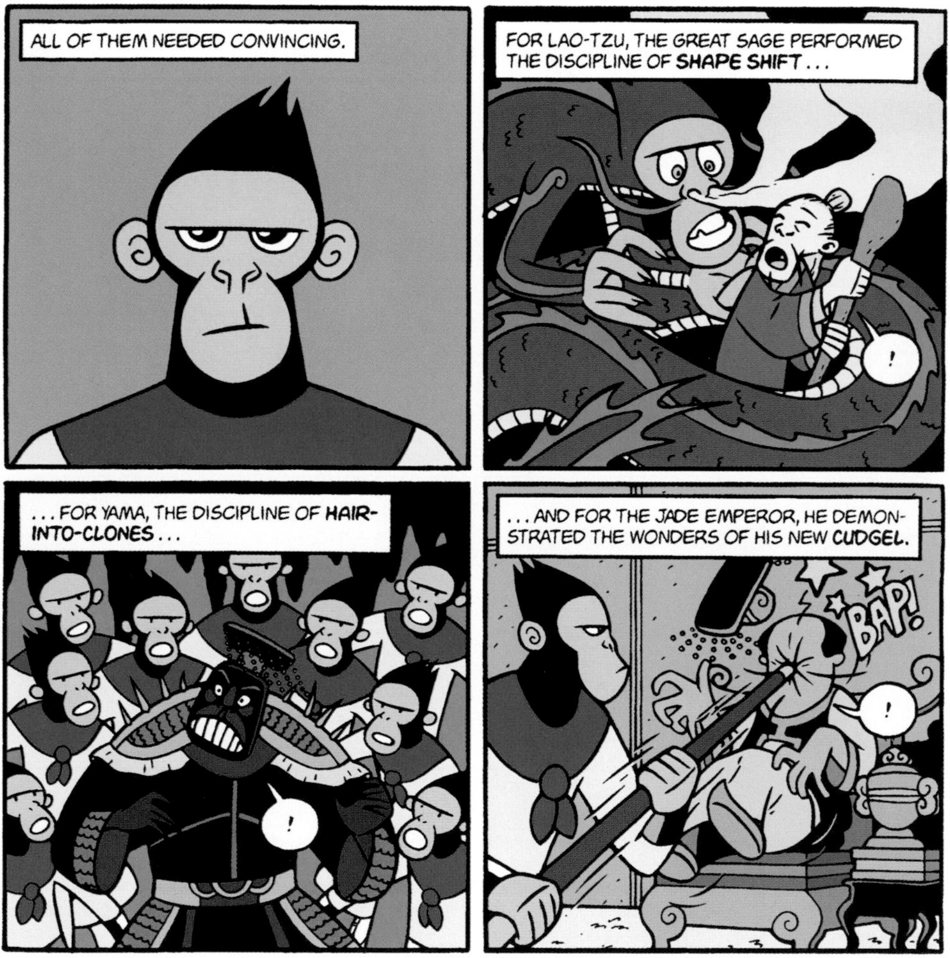
ALL OF THEM NEEDED CONVINCING.
FOR LAO-TZU, THE GREAT SAGE PERFORMED THE DISCIPLINE OF SHAPE SHIFT . . .
!
. . . FOR YAMA, THE DISCIPLINE OF HAIR-INTO-CLONES . . .
!
. . . AND FOR THE JADE EMPEROR, HE DEMONSTRATED THE WONDERS OF HIS NEW CUDGEL.
BAP!
!

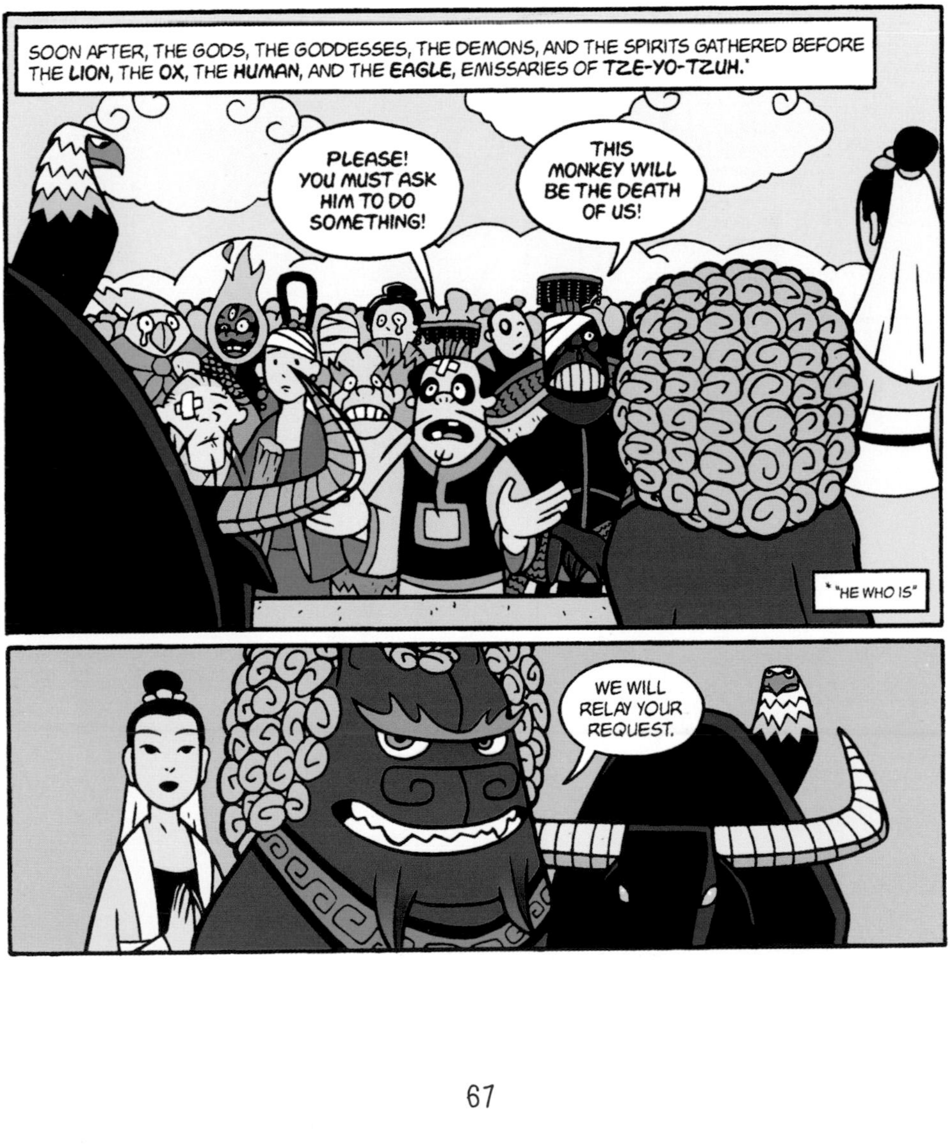
SOON AFTER, THE GODS, THE GODDESSES, THE DEMONS, AND THE SPIRITS GATHERED BEFORE THE **LION**, THE **OX**, THE **HUMAN**, AND THE **EAGLE**, EMISSARIES OF **TZE-YO-TZUH.***
PLEASE! YOU MUST ASK HIM TO DO SOMETHING!
THIS MONKEY WILL BE THE DEATH OF US!
* "HE WHO IS"
WE WILL RELAY YOUR REQUEST.

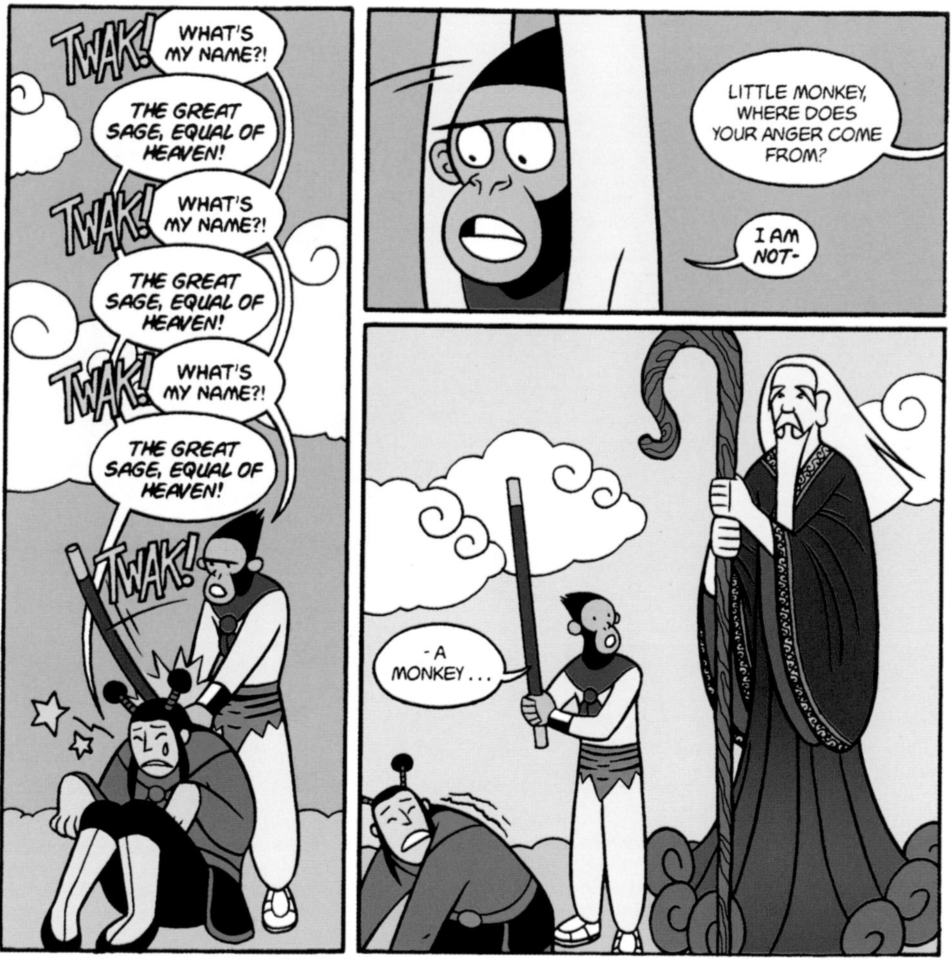
TWAK!
WHAT'S MY NAME?!
THE GREAT SAGE, EQUAL OF HEAVEN!
TWAK!
WHAT'S MY NAME?!
THE GREAT SAGE, EQUAL OF HEAVEN!
TWAK!
WHAT'S MY NAME?!
THE GREAT SAGE, EQUAL OF HEAVEN!
TWAK!
LITTLE MONKEY, WHERE DOES YOUR ANGER COME FROM?
I AM NOT-
-A MONKEY...

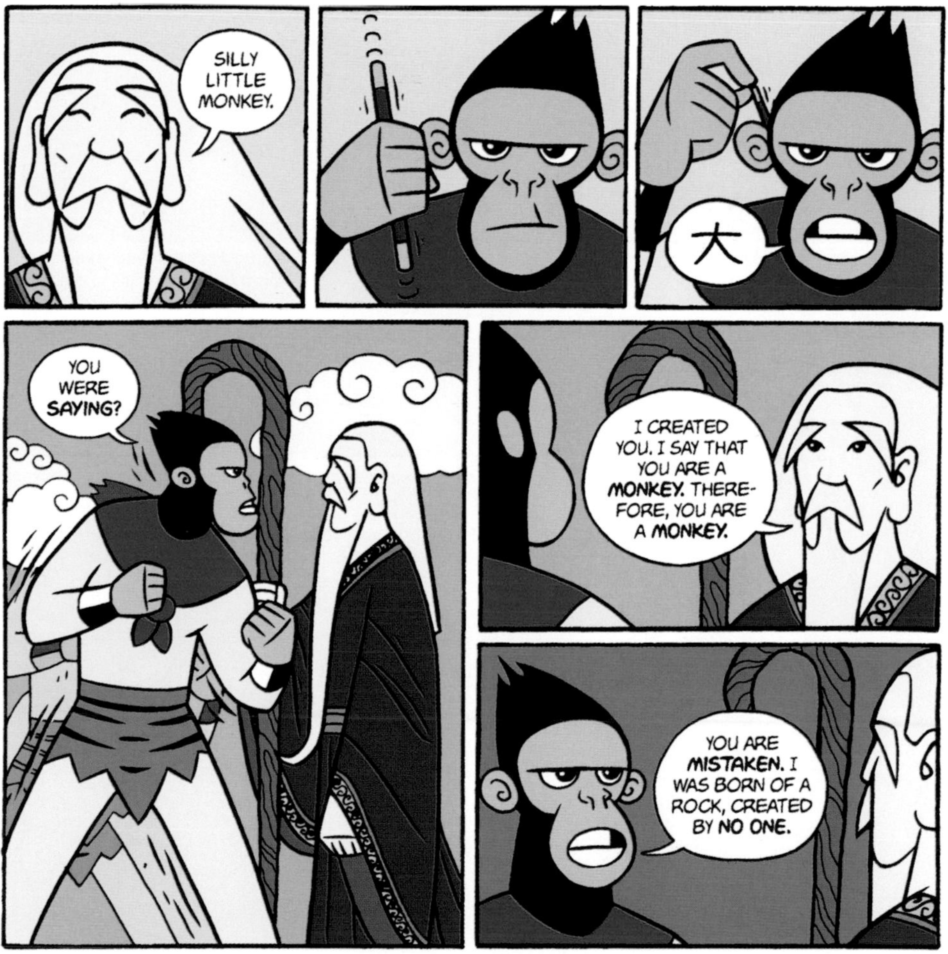
SILLY LITTLE MONKEY.
大
YOU WERE SAYING?
I CREATED YOU. I SAY THAT YOU ARE A MONKEY. THERE-FORE, YOU ARE A MONKEY.
YOU ARE MISTAKEN. I WAS BORN OF A ROCK, CREATED BY NO ONE.

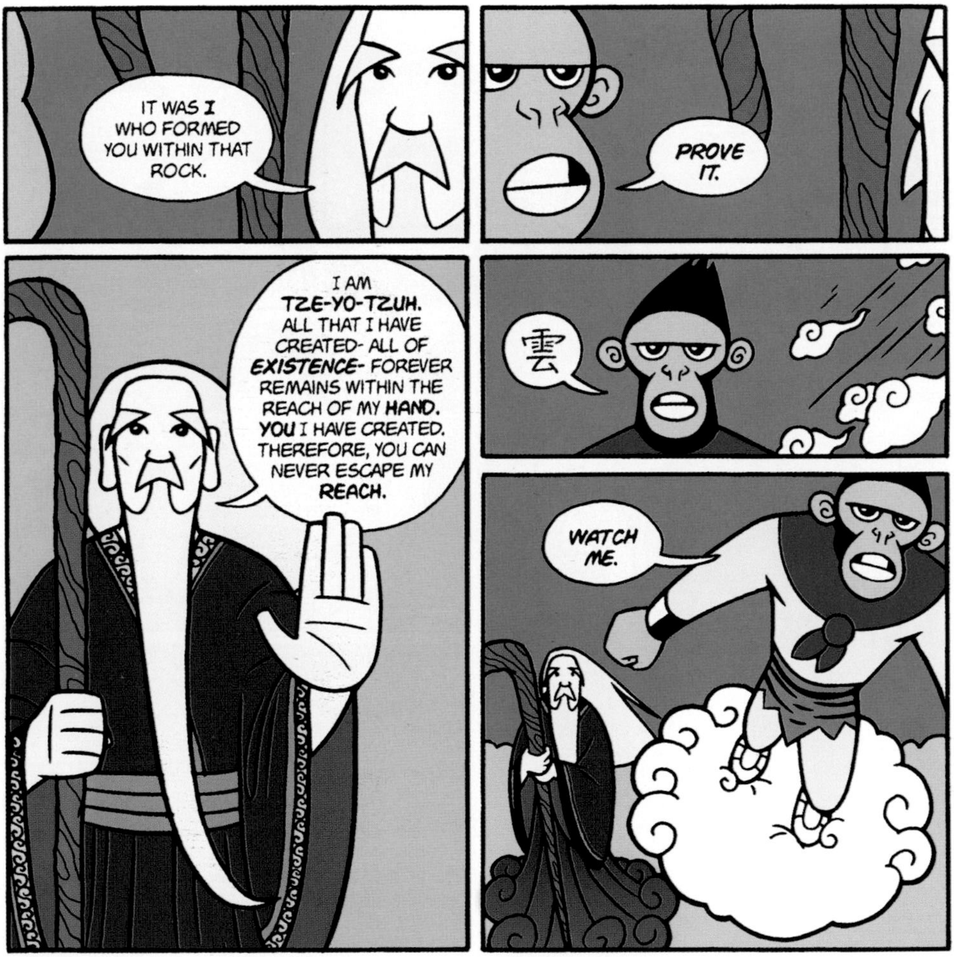

IT WAS I WHO FORMED YOU WITHIN THAT ROCK.
PROVE IT.
I AM TZE-YO-TZUH. ALL THAT I HAVE CREATED- ALL OF EXISTENCE- FOREVER REMAINS WITHIN THE REACH OF MY HAND. YOU I HAVE CREATED. THEREFORE, YOU CAN NEVER ESCAPE MY REACH.
雲
WATCH ME.

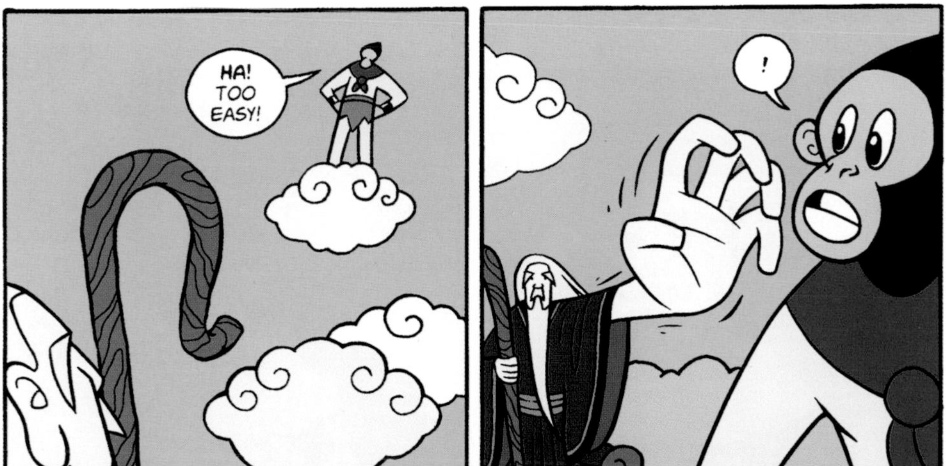
HA! TOO EASY!
!
THE GREAT SAGE FLEW WITH AS MUCH FURY AS HE COULD MUSTER.

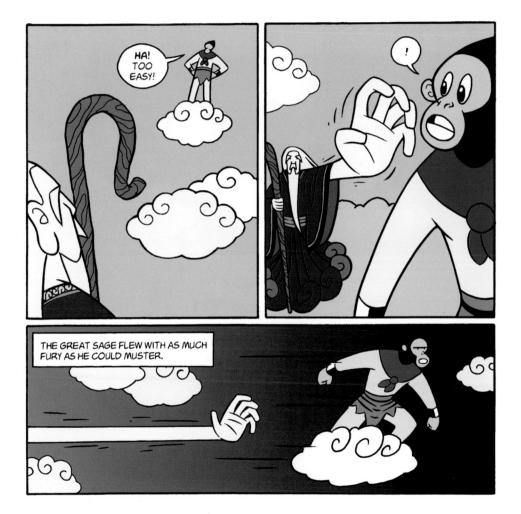

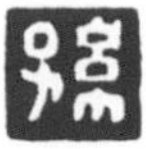

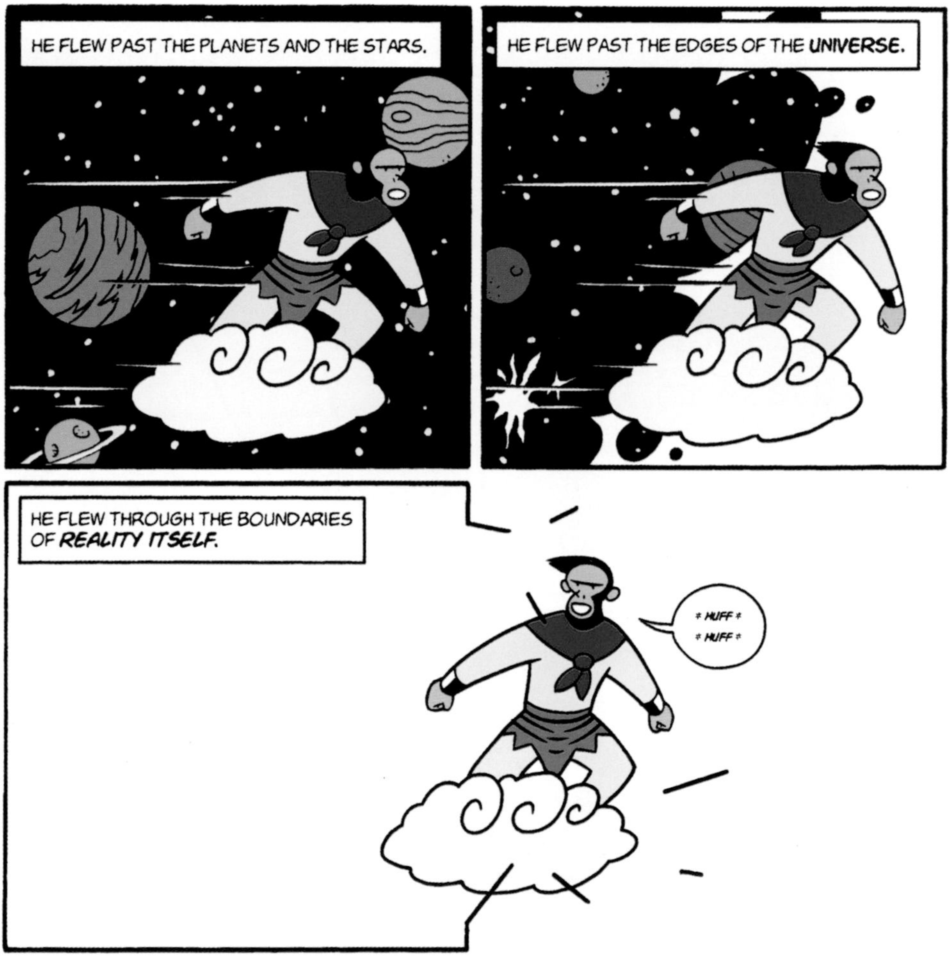
HE FLEW PAST THE PLANETS AND THE STARS.
HE FLEW PAST THE EDGES OF THE UNIVERSE.
HE FLEW THROUGH THE BOUNDARIES OF REALITY ITSELF.
* HUFF *
* HUFF *

THERE, AT THE END OF ALL THAT IS, THE GREAT SAGE CAME UPON **FIVE PILLARS OF GOLD.**

NEVER ONE TO MISS OUT ON A CHANCE FOR RECOGNITION, THE GREAT SAGE CARVED HIS NAME INTO ONE OF THE PILLARS.

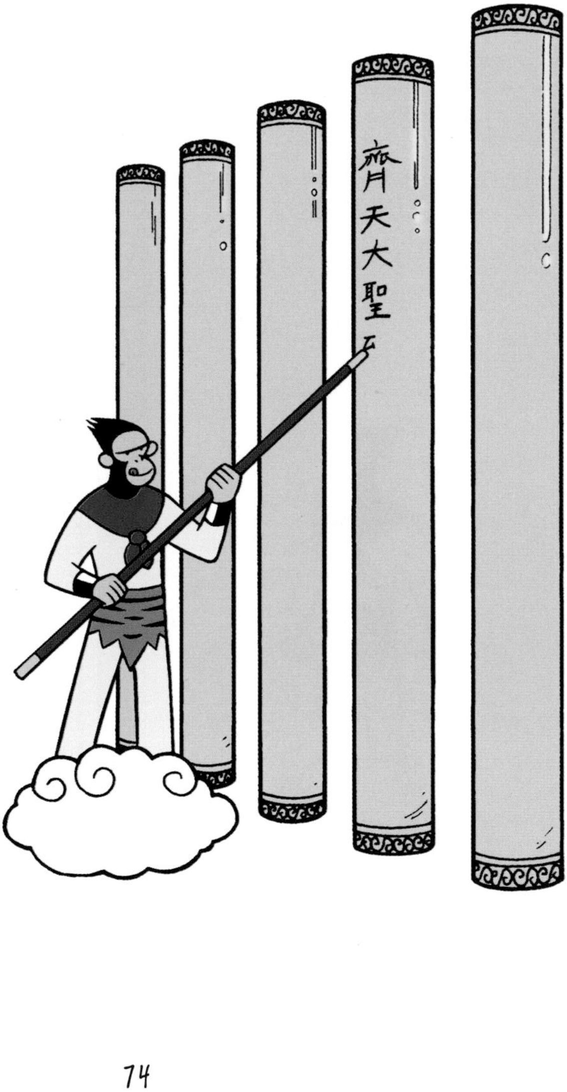
齊天大聖

THEN HE RELIEVED HIMSELF.
(IT HAD BEEN AN AWFULLY
LONG TRIP.)

齊天大聖到此一遊

齊天大聖到此一遊

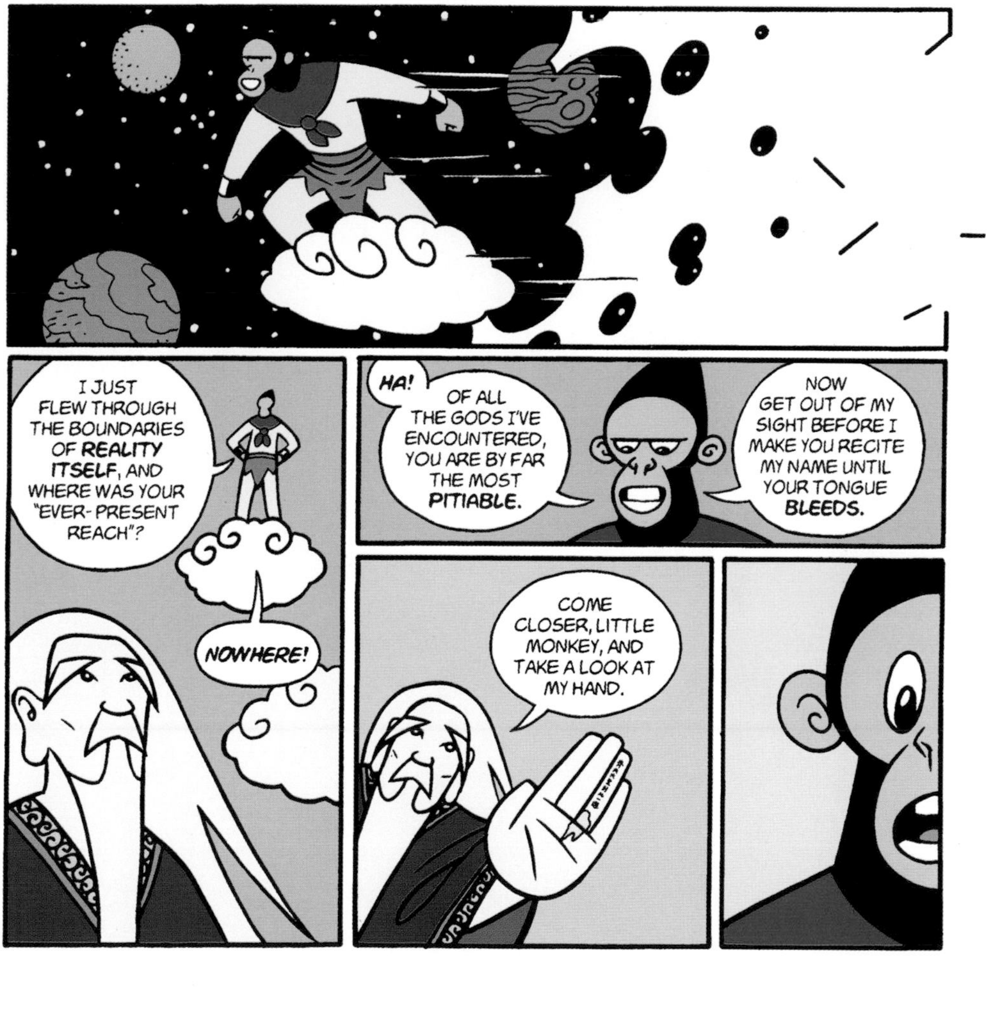
I JUST FLEW THROUGH THE BOUNDARIES OF REALITY ITSELF, AND WHERE WAS YOUR "EVER-PRESENT REACH"?
NOWHERE!
HA!
OF ALL THE GODS I'VE ENCOUNTERED, YOU ARE BY FAR THE MOST PITIABLE.
NOW GET OUT OF MY SIGHT BEFORE I MAKE YOU RECITE MY NAME UNTIL YOUR TONGUE BLEEDS.
COME CLOSER, LITTLE MONKEY, AND TAKE A LOOK AT MY HAND.

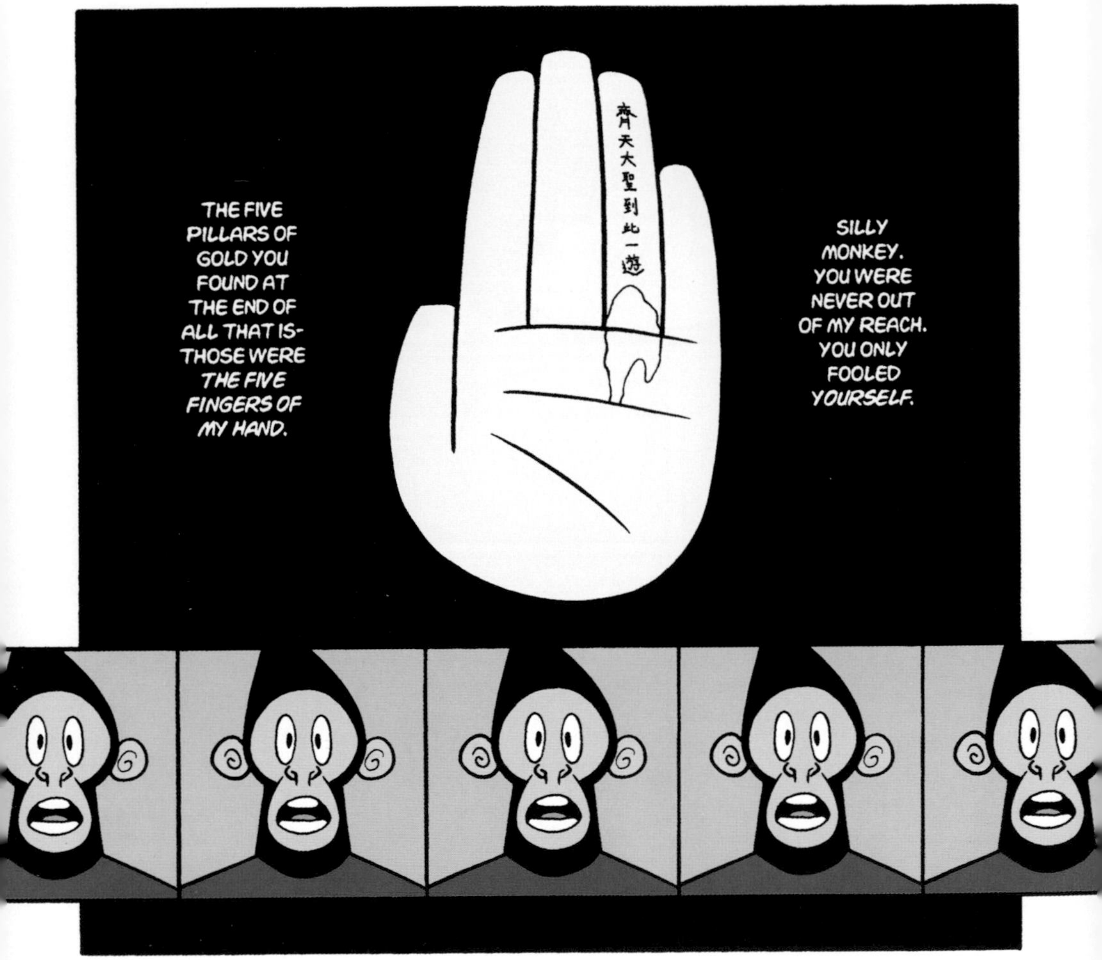
齊天大聖到此一遊
THE FIVE PILLARS OF GOLD YOU FOUND AT THE END OF ALL THAT IS- THOSE WERE *THE FIVE FINGERS OF MY HAND.*
SILLY MONKEY. YOU WERE NEVER OUT OF MY REACH. YOU ONLY FOOLED *YOURSELF.*

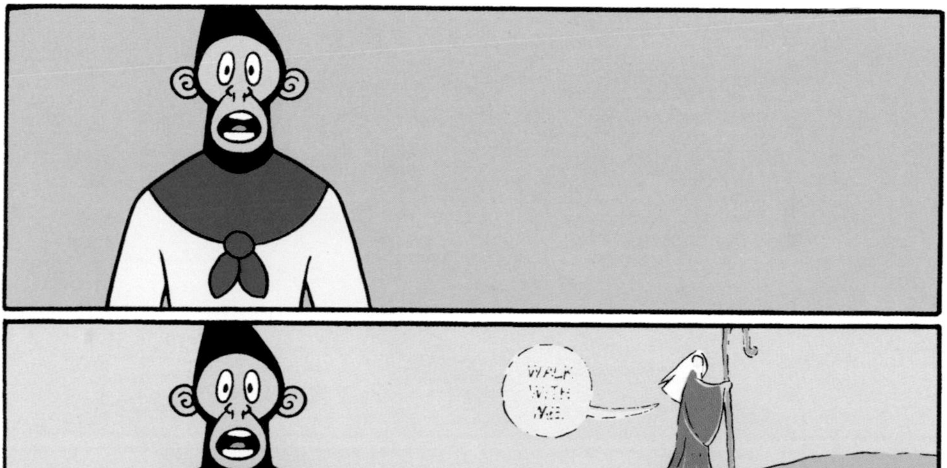
WALK WITH ME.
WALK WITH ME.

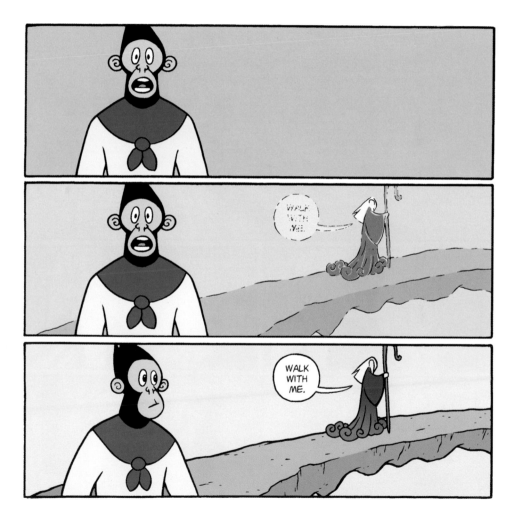

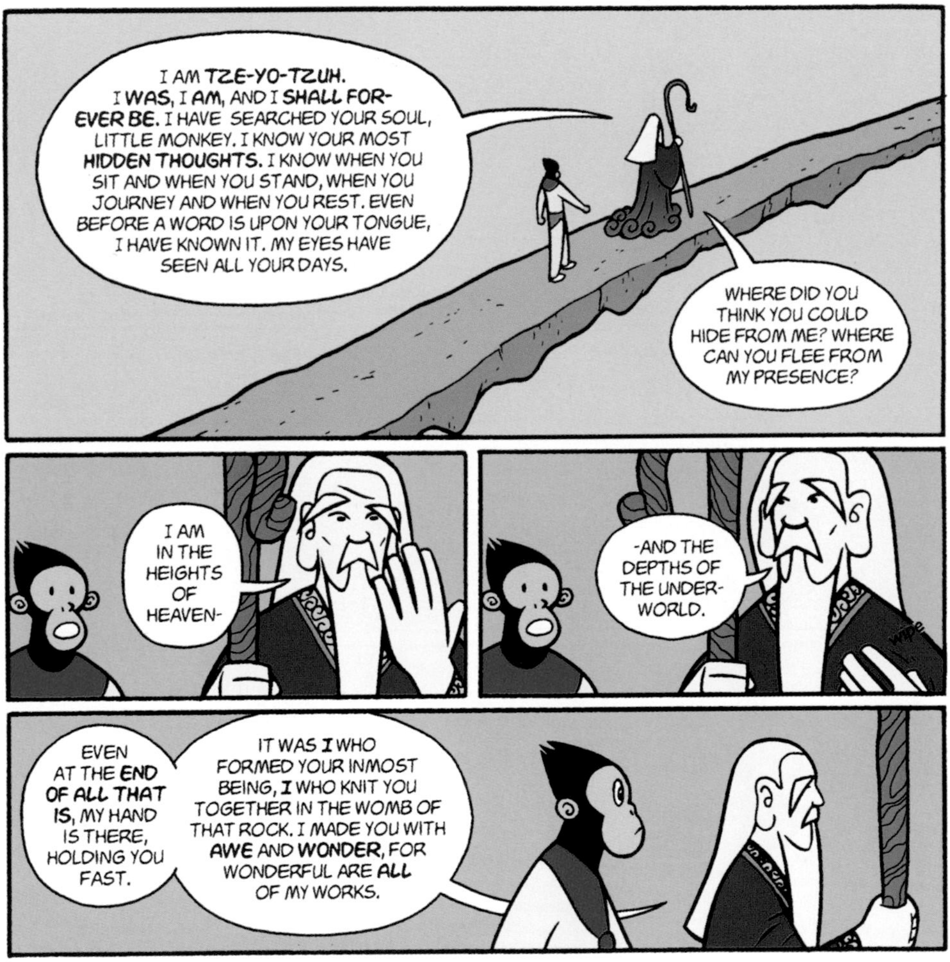

I AM TZE-YO-TZUH. I WAS, I AM, AND I SHALL FOR-EVER BE. I HAVE SEARCHED YOUR SOUL, LITTLE MONKEY. I KNOW YOUR MOST HIDDEN THOUGHTS. I KNOW WHEN YOU SIT AND WHEN YOU STAND, WHEN YOU JOURNEY AND WHEN YOU REST. EVEN BEFORE A WORD IS UPON YOUR TONGUE, I HAVE KNOWN IT. MY EYES HAVE SEEN ALL YOUR DAYS.
WHERE DID YOU THINK YOU COULD HIDE FROM ME? WHERE CAN YOU FLEE FROM MY PRESENCE?
I AM IN THE HEIGHTS OF HEAVEN-
-AND THE DEPTHS OF THE UNDER-WORLD.
wipe
EVEN AT THE END OF ALL THAT IS, MY HAND IS THERE, HOLDING YOU FAST.
IT WAS I WHO FORMED YOUR INMOST BEING, I WHO KNIT YOU TOGETHER IN THE WOMB OF THAT ROCK. I MADE YOU WITH AWE AND WONDER, FOR WONDERFUL ARE ALL OF MY WORKS.

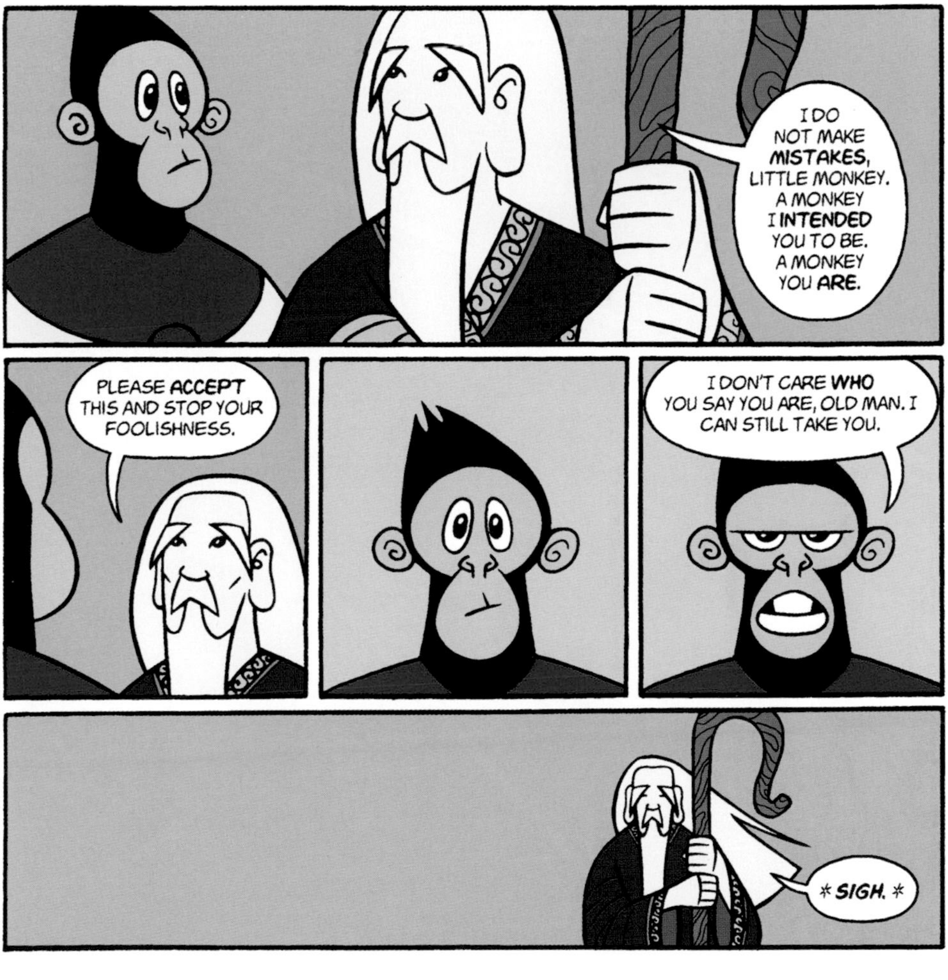

I DO NOT MAKE MISTAKES, LITTLE MONKEY. A MONKEY I INTENDED YOU TO BE. A MONKEY YOU ARE.
PLEASE ACCEPT THIS AND STOP YOUR FOOLISHNESS.
I DON'T CARE WHO YOU SAY YOU ARE, OLD MAN. I CAN STILL TAKE YOU.
SIGH.

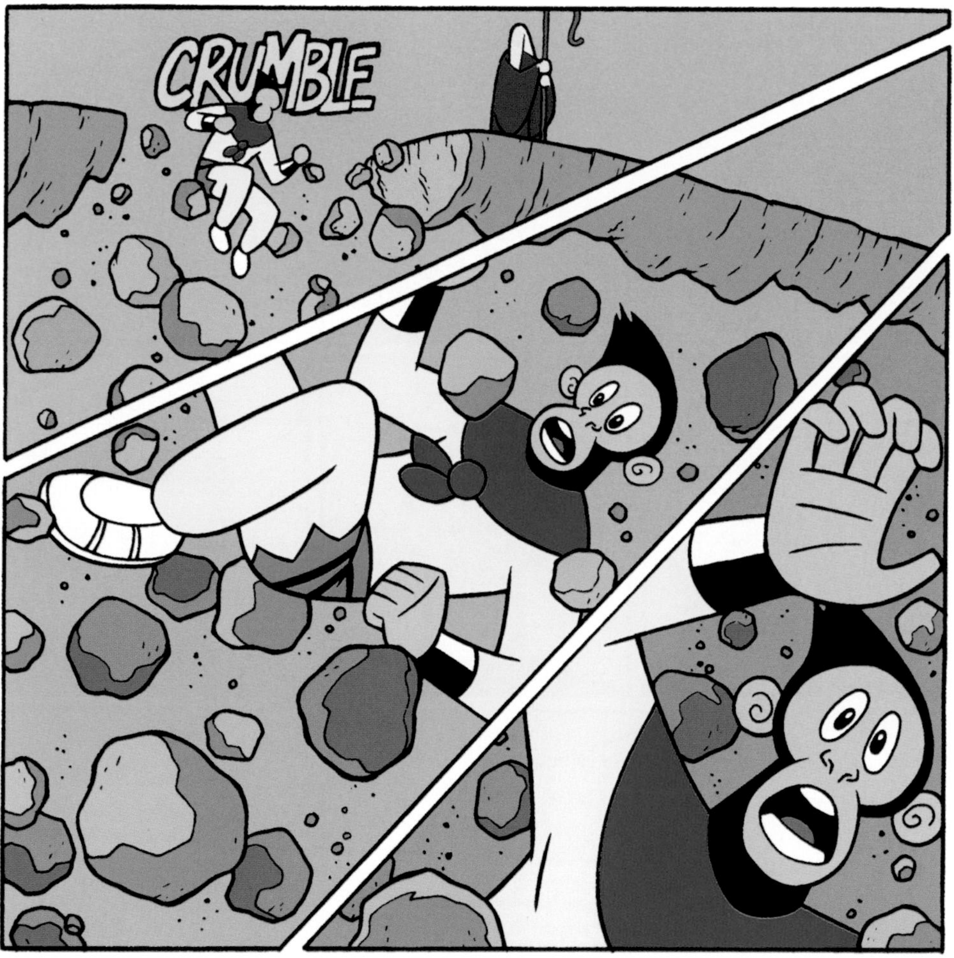
CRUMBLE

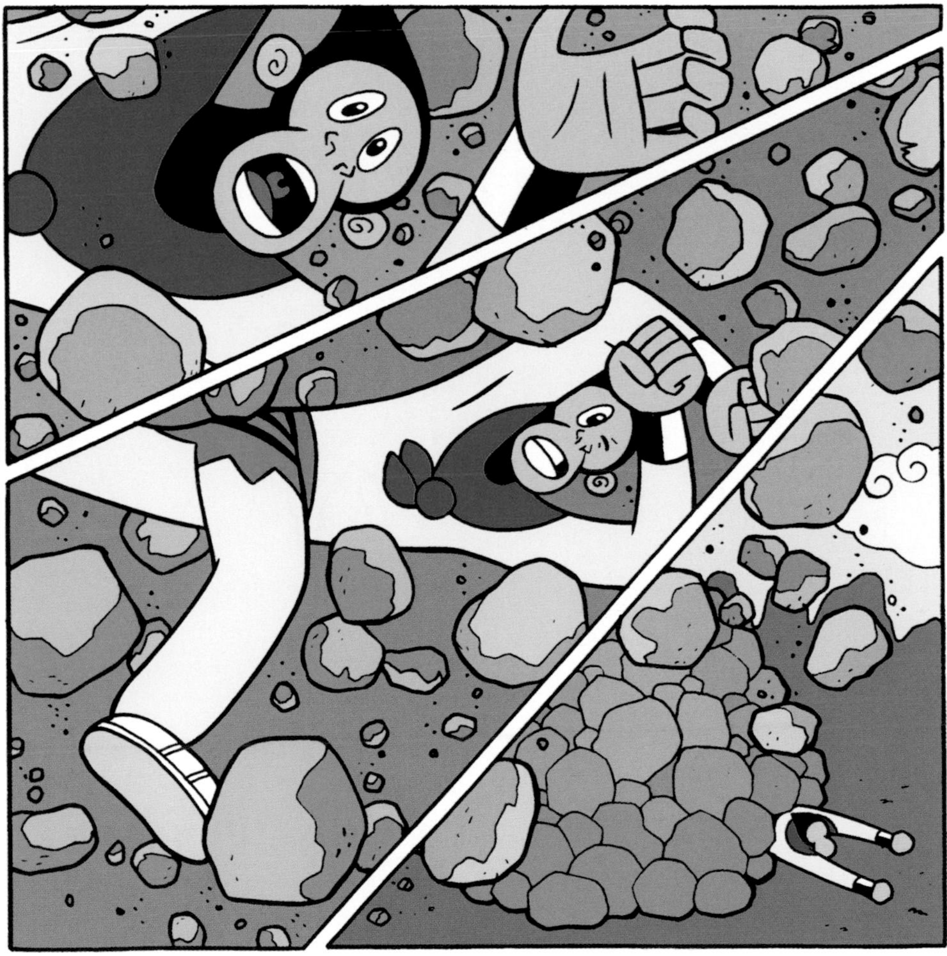

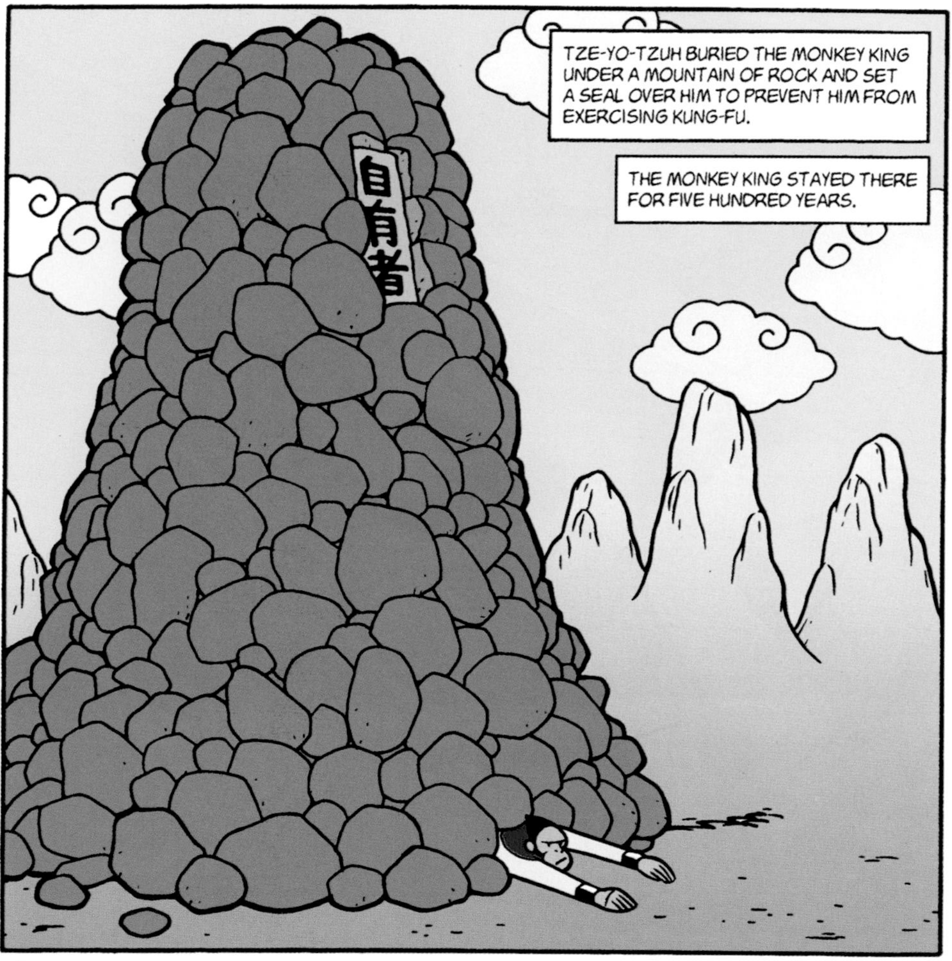
TZE-YO-TZUH BURIED THE MONKEY KING UNDER A MOUNTAIN OF ROCK AND SET A SEAL OVER HIM TO PREVENT HIM FROM EXERCISING KUNG-FU.
THE MONKEY KING STAYED THERE FOR FIVE HUNDRED YEARS.

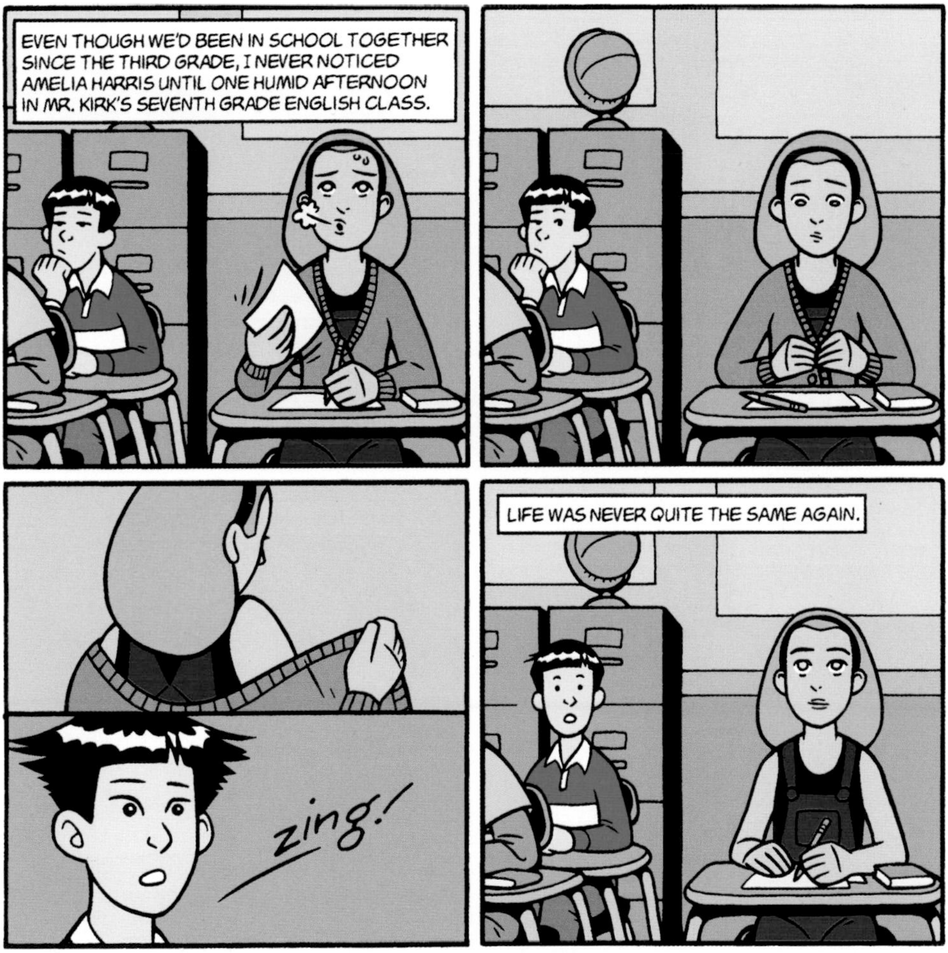
EVEN THOUGH WE'D BEEN IN SCHOOL TOGETHER SINCE THE THIRD GRADE, I NEVER NOTICED AMELIA HARRIS UNTIL ONE HUMID AFTERNOON IN MR. KIRK'S SEVENTH GRADE ENGLISH CLASS.
zing!
LIFE WAS NEVER QUITE THE SAME AGAIN.

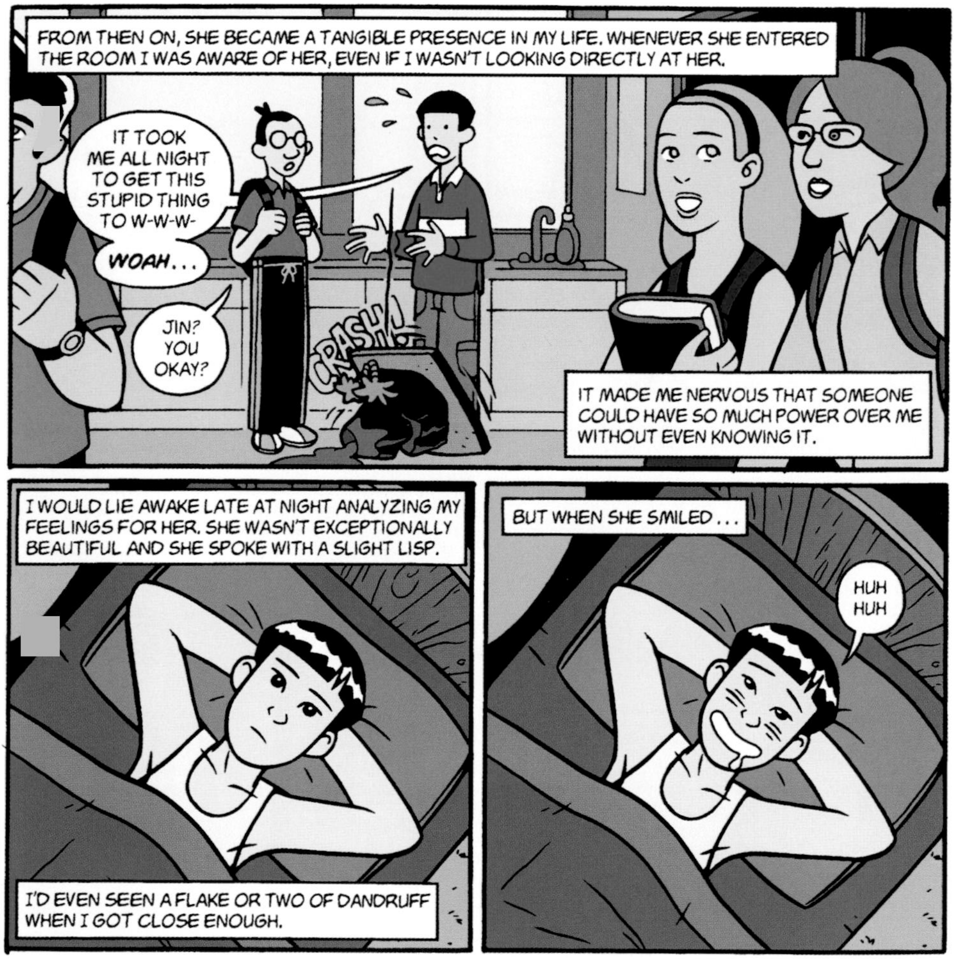
FROM THEN ON, SHE BECAME A TANGIBLE PRESENCE IN MY LIFE. WHENEVER SHE ENTERED THE ROOM I WAS AWARE OF HER, EVEN IF I WASN'T LOOKING DIRECTLY AT HER.
IT TOOK ME ALL NIGHT TO GET THIS STUPID THING TO W-W-W-
WOAH...
CRASH!
JIN? YOU OKAY?
IT MADE ME NERVOUS THAT SOMEONE COULD HAVE SO MUCH POWER OVER ME WITHOUT EVEN KNOWING IT.
I WOULD LIE AWAKE LATE AT NIGHT ANALYZING MY FEELINGS FOR HER. SHE WASN'T EXCEPTIONALLY BEAUTIFUL AND SHE SPOKE WITH A SLIGHT LISP.
I'D EVEN SEEN A FLAKE OR TWO OF DANDRUFF WHEN I GOT CLOSE ENOUGH.
BUT WHEN SHE SMILED...
HUH HUH

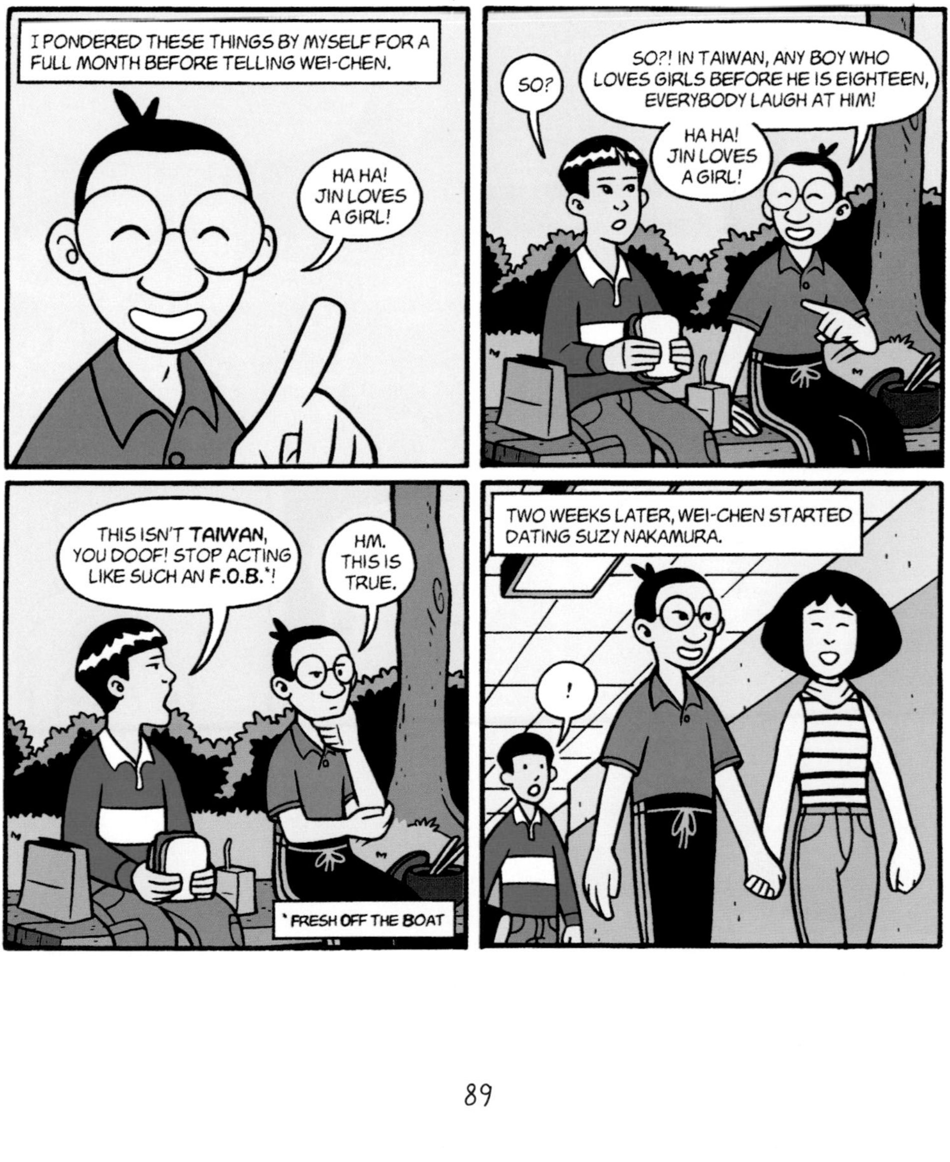
I PONDERED THESE THINGS BY MYSELF FOR A FULL MONTH BEFORE TELLING WEI-CHEN.
HA HA! JIN LOVES A GIRL!
SO?
SO?! IN TAIWAN, ANY BOY WHO LOVES GIRLS BEFORE HE IS EIGHTEEN, EVERYBODY LAUGH AT HIM!
HA HA! JIN LOVES A GIRL!
THIS ISN'T **TAIWAN**, YOU DOOF! STOP ACTING LIKE SUCH AN **F.O.B.***!
HM. THIS IS TRUE.
*FRESH OFF THE BOAT
TWO WEEKS LATER, WEI-CHEN STARTED DATING SUZY NAKAMURA.
!

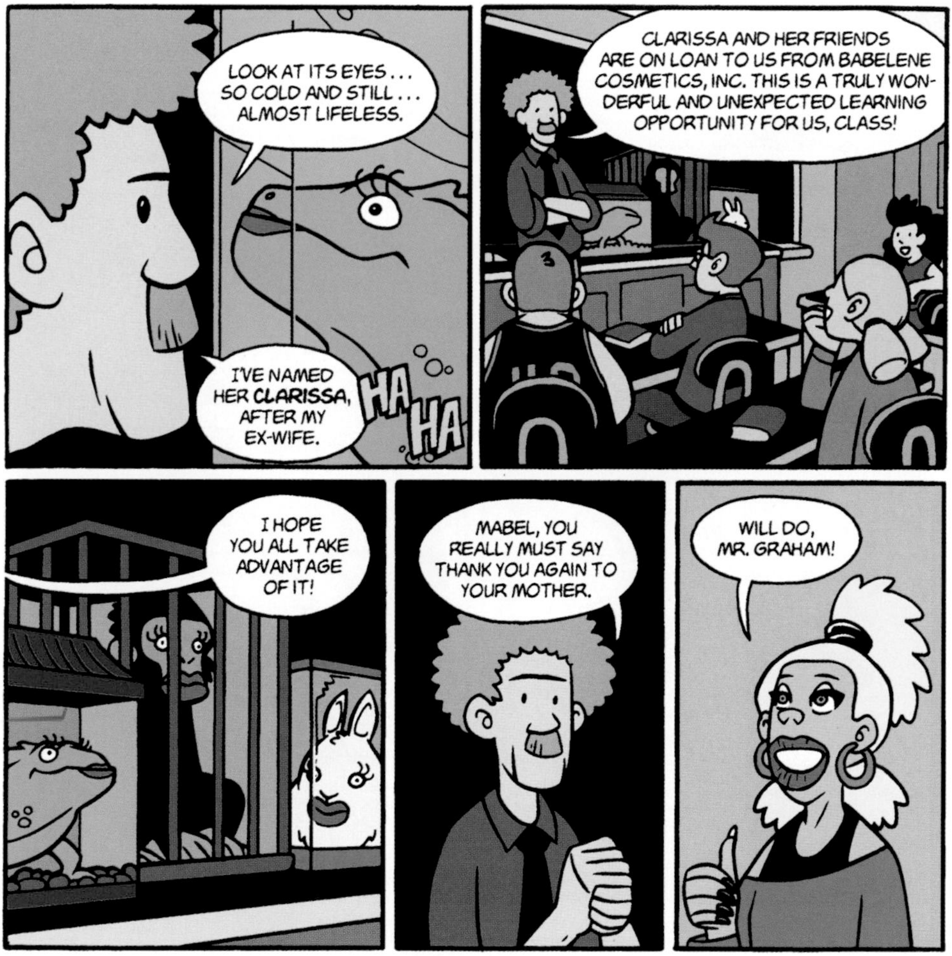
LOOK AT ITS EYES . . . SO COLD AND STILL . . . ALMOST LIFELESS.
I'VE NAMED HER CLARISSA, AFTER MY EX-WIFE.
HA HA
CLARISSA AND HER FRIENDS ARE ON LOAN TO US FROM BABELENE COSMETICS, INC. THIS IS A TRULY WONDERFUL AND UNEXPECTED LEARNING OPPORTUNITY FOR US, CLASS!
I HOPE YOU ALL TAKE ADVANTAGE OF IT!
MABEL, YOU REALLY MUST SAY THANK YOU AGAIN TO YOUR MOTHER.
WILL DO, MR. GRAHAM!

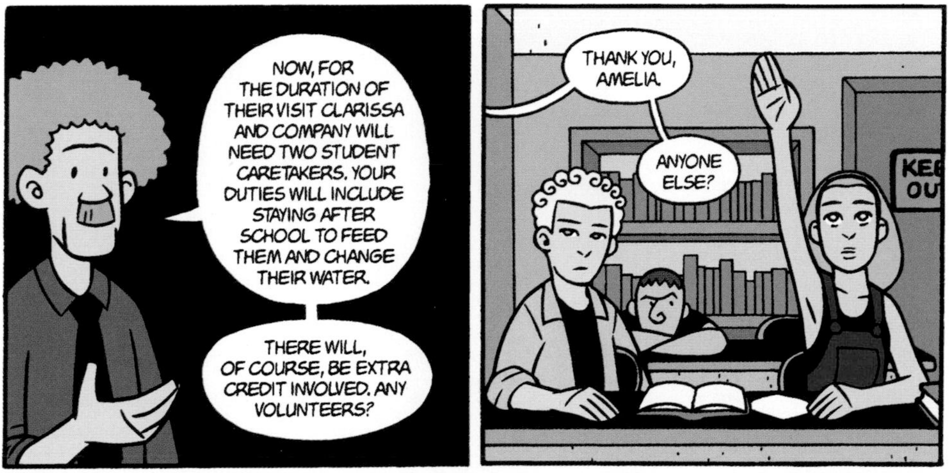
NOW, FOR THE DURATION OF THEIR VISIT CLARISSA AND COMPANY WILL NEED TWO STUDENT CARETAKERS. YOUR DUTIES WILL INCLUDE STAYING AFTER SCHOOL TO FEED THEM AND CHANGE THEIR WATER.
THERE WILL, OF COURSE, BE EXTRA CREDIT INVOLVED. ANY VOLUNTEERS?
THANK YOU, AMELIA.
ANYONE ELSE?
WHAT FOR, AMELIA? YOU CAN PET MY LIZARD ANY TIME YOU WANT.
TIMMY-!
I DON'T KNOW, TIMMY. YOU DO A PRETTY GOOD JOB OF THAT YOURSELF.
HA HA!

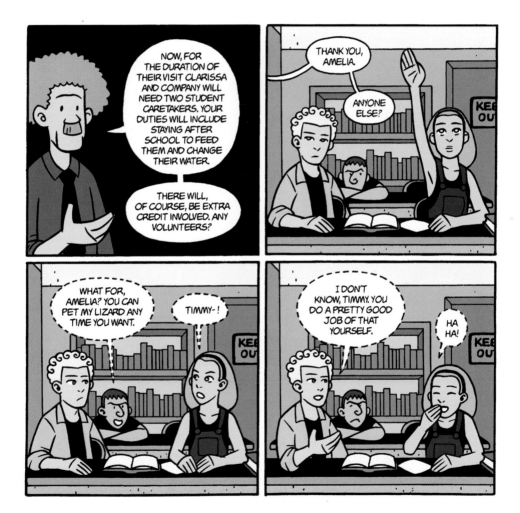

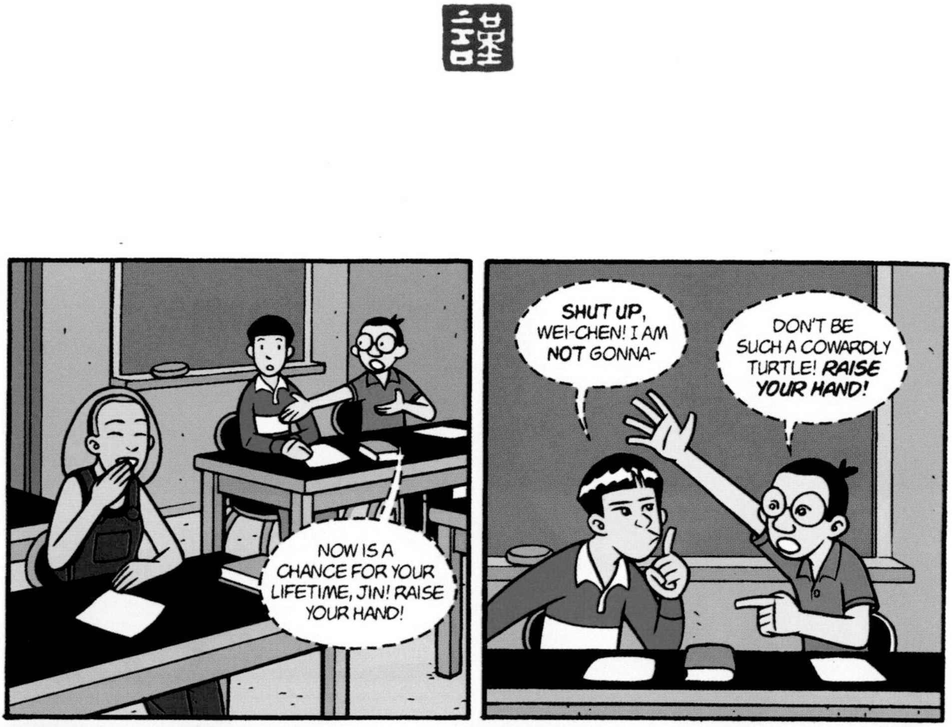
NOW IS A CHANCE FOR YOUR LIFETIME, JIN! RAISE YOUR HAND!
SHUT UP, WEI-CHEN! I AM NOT GONNA-
DON'T BE SUCH A COWARDLY TURTLE! RAISE YOUR HAND!
WEI-CHEN, ARE YOU VOLUNTEERING?
UH... IN ACTUALITY, MR. GRAHAM, JIN WOULD-
WEI-CHEN. IF YOU AREN'T VOLUNTEERING-
-THEN WHY ARE YOU MAKING SO MUCH NOISE BACK THERE?

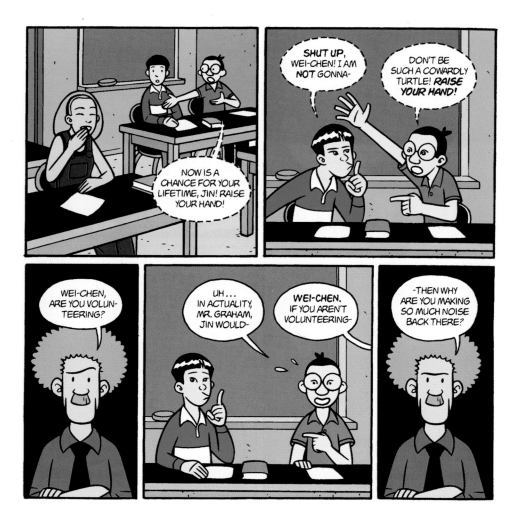

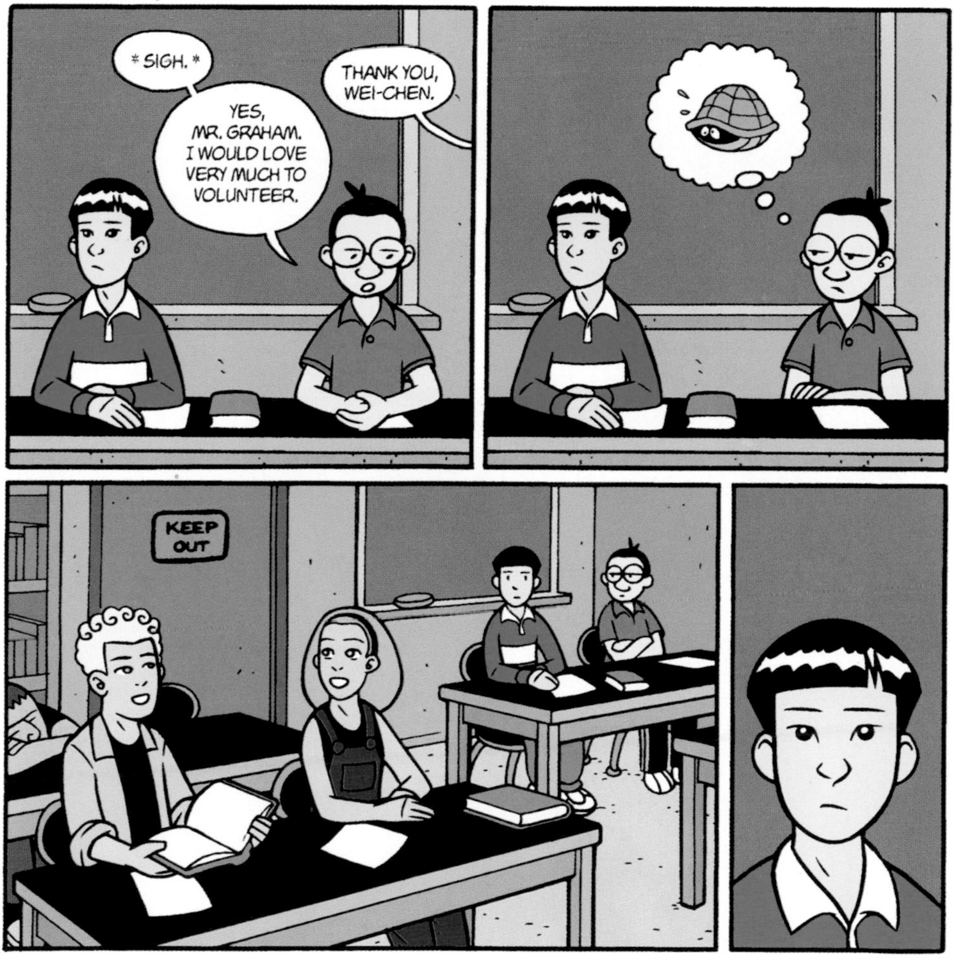
SIGH.
YES, MR. GRAHAM. I WOULD LOVE VERY MUCH TO VOLUNTEER.
THANK YOU, WEI-CHEN.
KEEP OUT

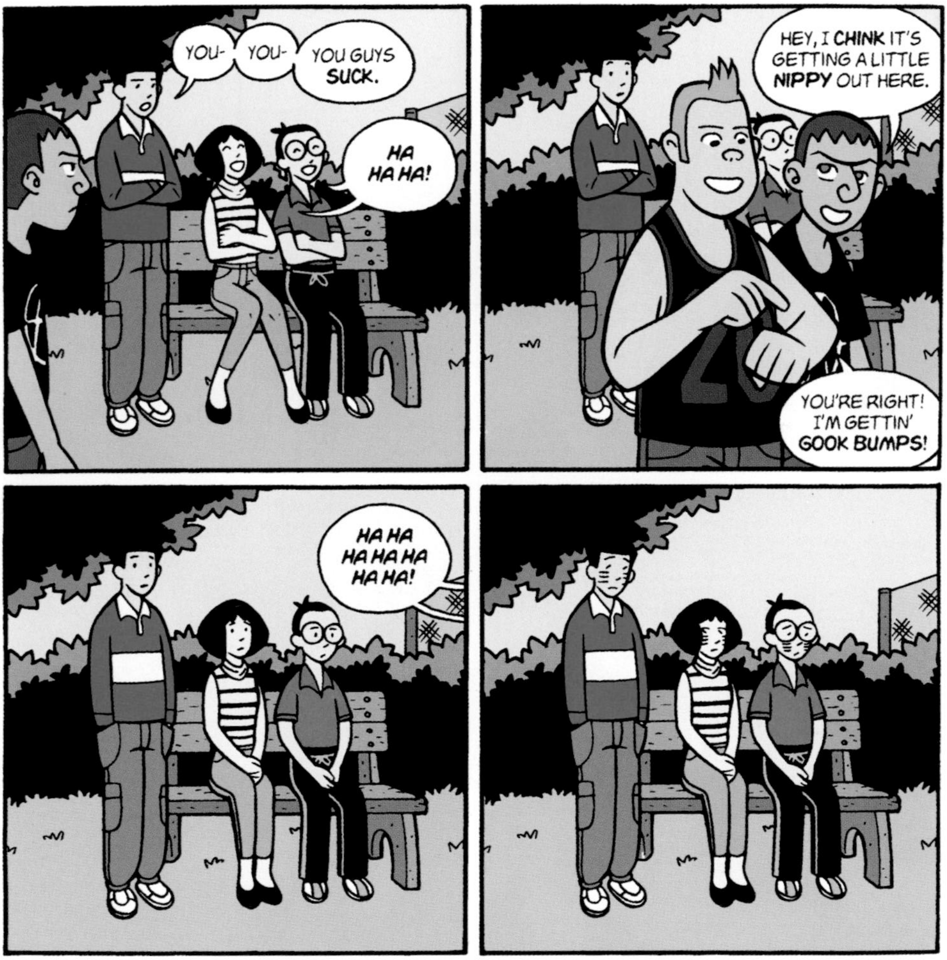
YOU-
YOU-
YOU GUYS SUCK.
HA HA HA!
HEY, I CHINK IT'S GETTING A LITTLE NIPPY OUT HERE.
YOU'RE RIGHT! I'M GETTIN' GOOK BUMPS!
HA HA HA HA HA HA HA!

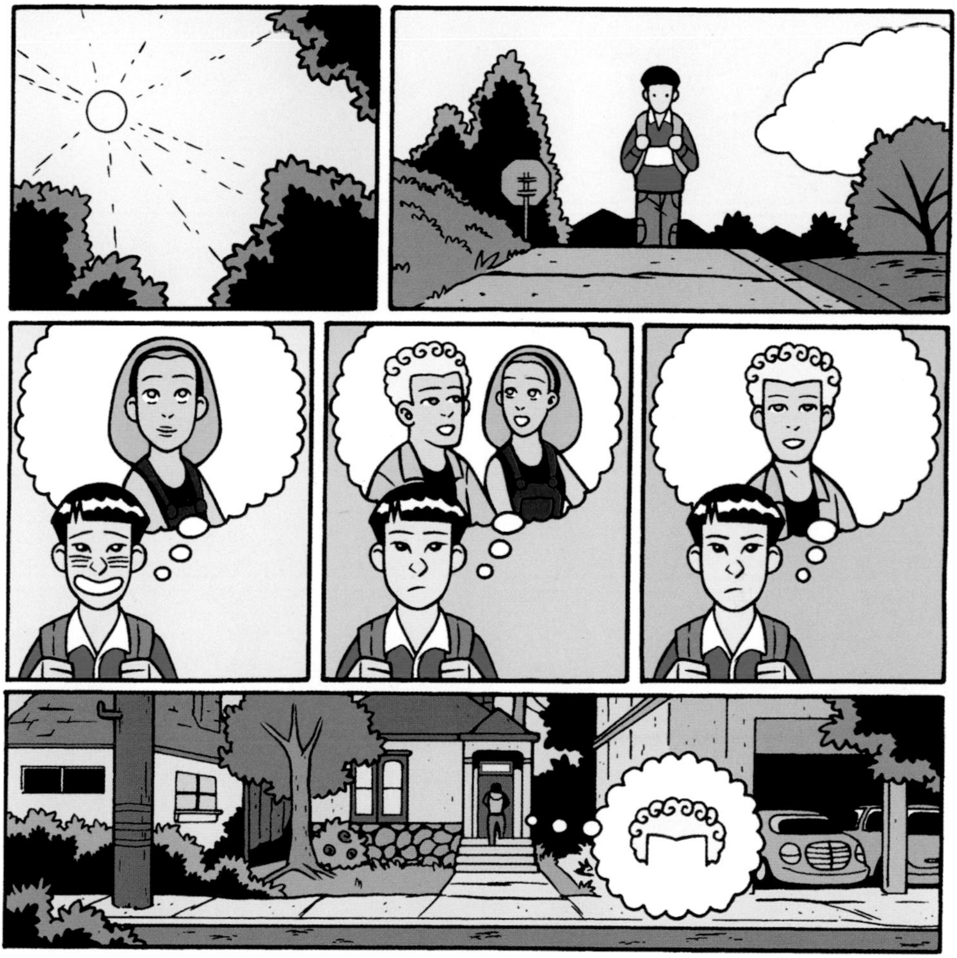

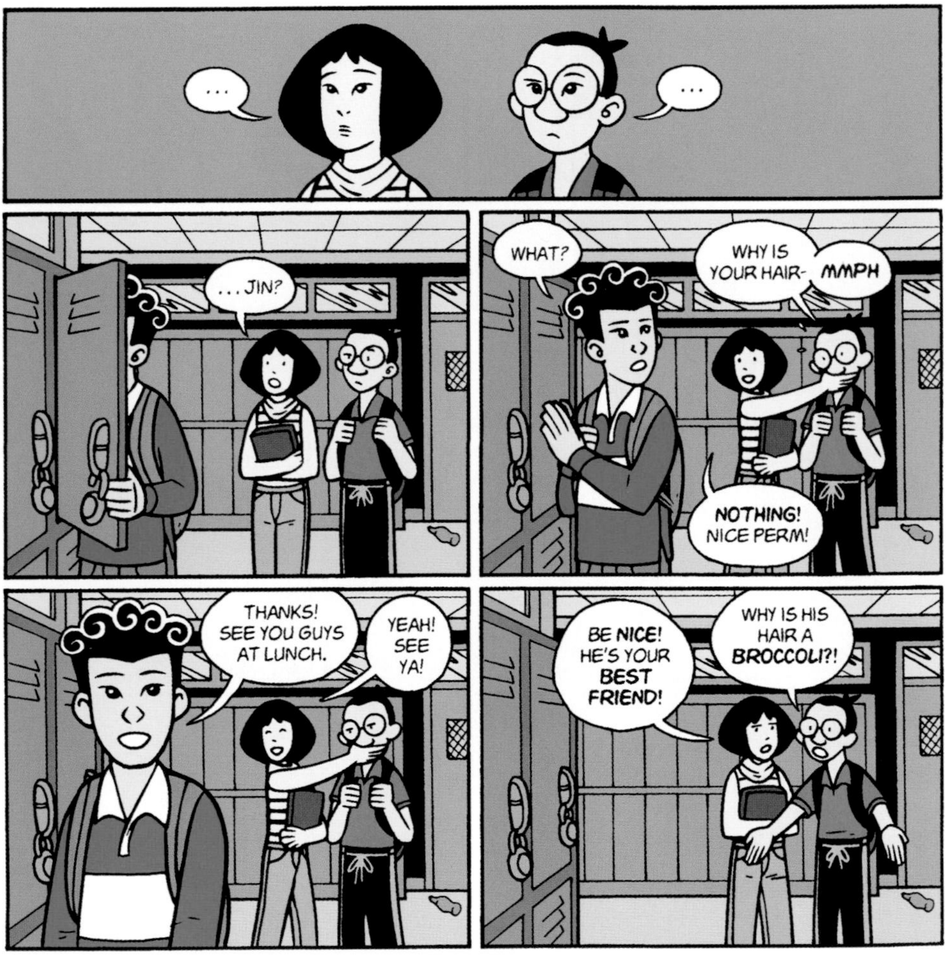
. . .
. . .
. . . JIN?
WHAT?
WHY IS YOUR HAIR-
MMPH
NOTHING! NICE PERM!
THANKS! SEE YOU GUYS AT LUNCH.
YEAH! SEE YA!
BE NICE! HE'S YOUR BEST FRIEND!
WHY IS HIS HAIR A BROCCOLI?!

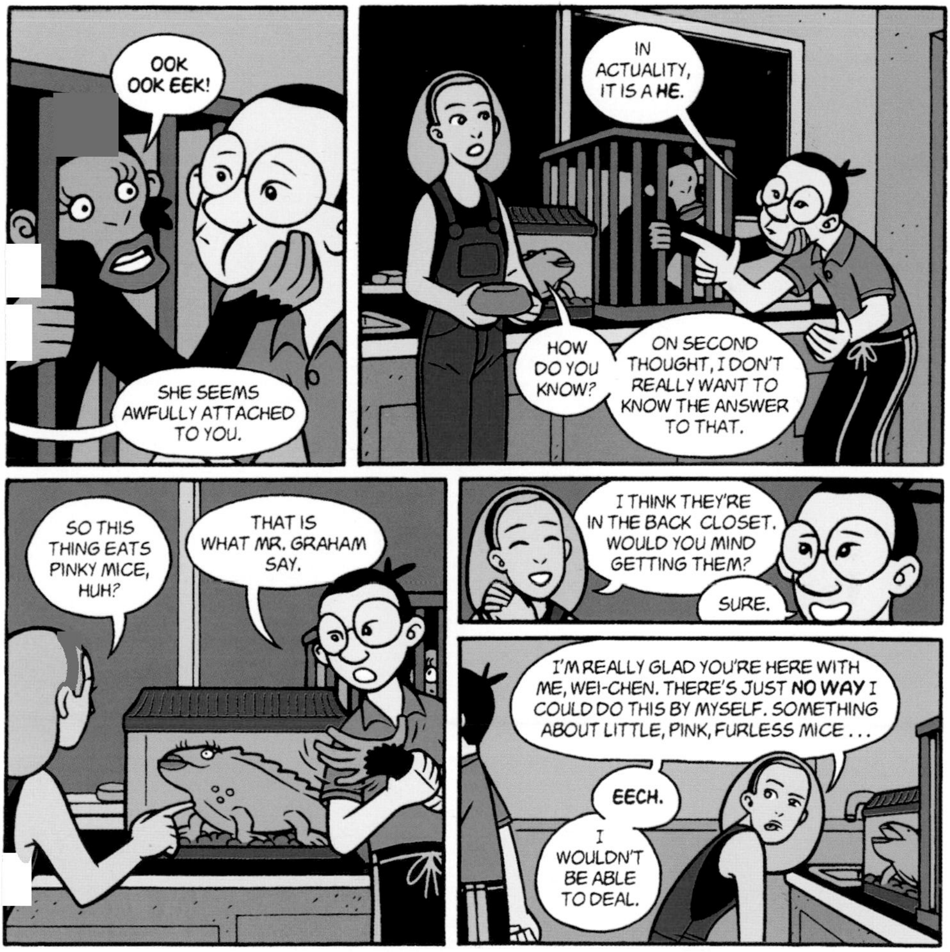

OOK OOK EEK!
SHE SEEMS AWFULLY ATTACHED TO YOU.
IN ACTUALITY, IT IS A **HE**.
HOW DO YOU KNOW?
ON SECOND THOUGHT, I DON'T REALLY WANT TO KNOW THE ANSWER TO THAT.
SO THIS THING EATS PINKY MICE, HUH?
THAT IS WHAT MR. GRAHAM SAY.
I THINK THEY'RE IN THE BACK CLOSET. WOULD YOU MIND GETTING THEM?
SURE.
I'M REALLY GLAD YOU'RE HERE WITH ME, WEI-CHEN. THERE'S JUST **NO WAY** I COULD DO THIS BY MYSELF. SOMETHING ABOUT LITTLE, PINK, FURLESS MICE . . .
EECH.
I WOULDN'T BE ABLE TO DEAL.

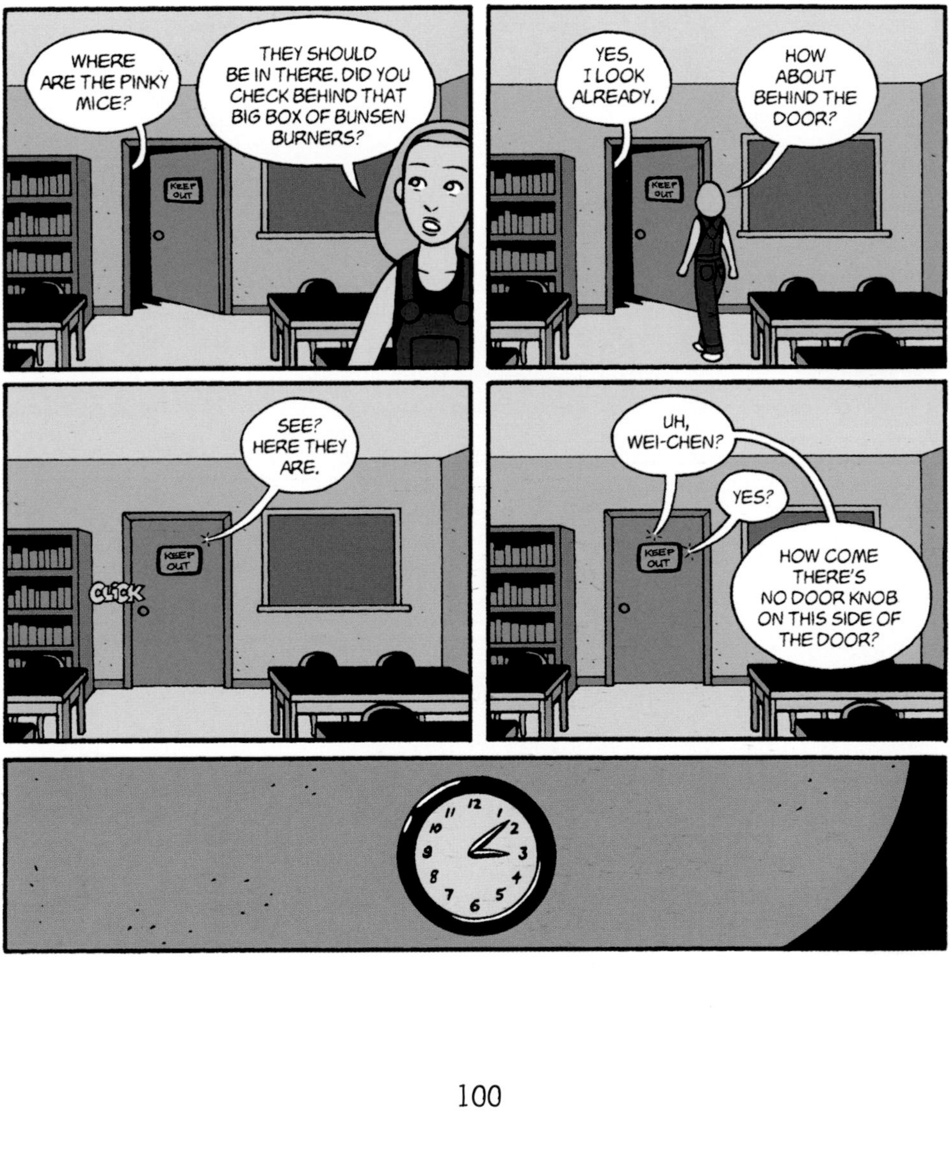
WHERE ARE THE PINKY MICE?
THEY SHOULD BE IN THERE. DID YOU CHECK BEHIND THAT BIG BOX OF BUNSEN BURNERS?
KEEP OUT
YES, I LOOK ALREADY.
HOW ABOUT BEHIND THE DOOR?
SEE? HERE THEY ARE.
CLICK
UH, WEI-CHEN?
YES?
HOW COME THERE'S NO DOOR KNOB ON THIS SIDE OF THE DOOR?

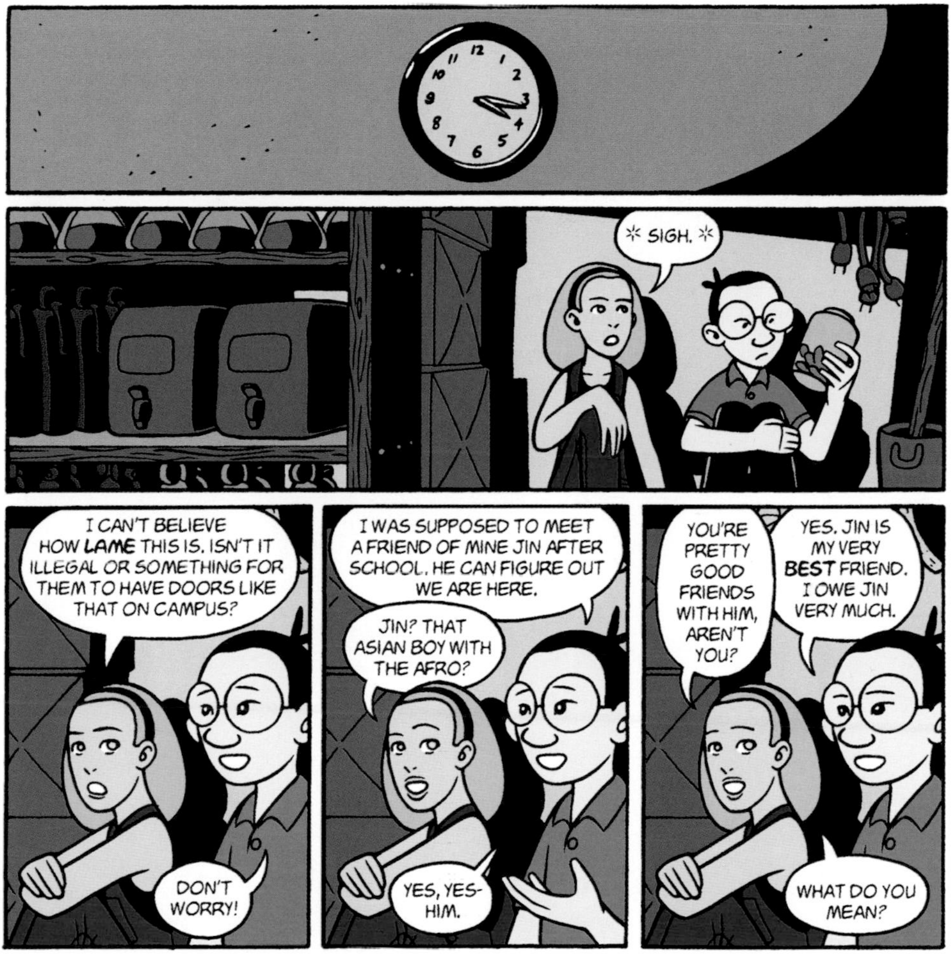

* SIGH. *
I CAN'T BELIEVE HOW **LAME** THIS IS. ISN'T IT ILLEGAL OR SOMETHING FOR THEM TO HAVE DOORS LIKE THAT ON CAMPUS?
DON'T WORRY!
I WAS SUPPOSED TO MEET A FRIEND OF MINE JIN AFTER SCHOOL. HE CAN FIGURE OUT WE ARE HERE.
JIN? THAT ASIAN BOY WITH THE AFRO?
YES, YES- HIM.
YOU'RE PRETTY GOOD FRIENDS WITH HIM, AREN'T YOU?
YES. JIN IS MY VERY **BEST** FRIEND. I OWE JIN VERY MUCH.
WHAT DO YOU MEAN?

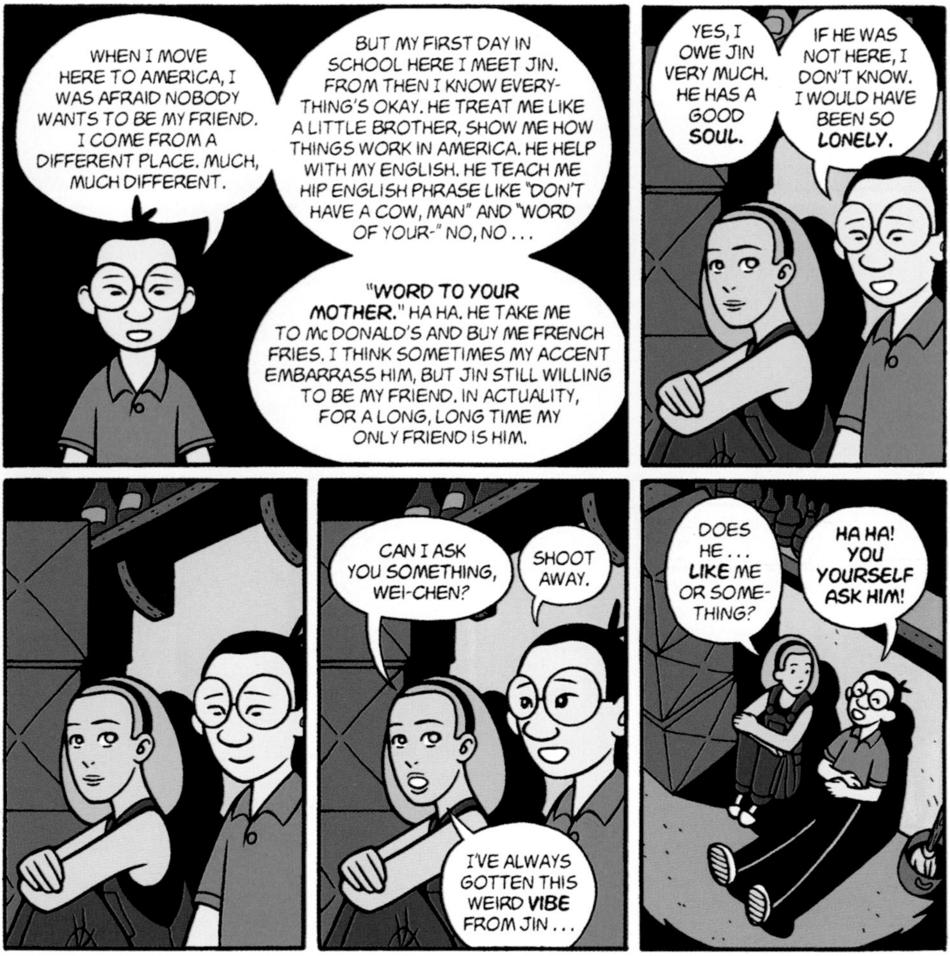
WHEN I MOVE HERE TO AMERICA, I WAS AFRAID NOBODY WANTS TO BE MY FRIEND. I COME FROM A DIFFERENT PLACE. MUCH, MUCH DIFFERENT.
BUT MY FIRST DAY IN SCHOOL HERE I MEET JIN. FROM THEN I KNOW EVERY-THING'S OKAY. HE TREAT ME LIKE A LITTLE BROTHER, SHOW ME HOW THINGS WORK IN AMERICA. HE HELP WITH MY ENGLISH. HE TEACH ME HIP ENGLISH PHRASE LIKE "DON'T HAVE A COW, MAN" AND "WORD OF YOUR-" NO, NO . . .
"**WORD TO YOUR MOTHER.**" HA HA. HE TAKE ME TO McDONALD'S AND BUY ME FRENCH FRIES. I THINK SOMETIMES MY ACCENT EMBARRASS HIM, BUT JIN STILL WILLING TO BE MY FRIEND. IN ACTUALITY, FOR A LONG, LONG TIME MY ONLY FRIEND IS HIM.
YES, I OWE JIN VERY MUCH. HE HAS A GOOD **SOUL.**
IF HE WAS NOT HERE, I DON'T KNOW. I WOULD HAVE BEEN SO **LONELY.**
CAN I ASK YOU SOMETHING, WEI-CHEN?
SHOOT AWAY.
I'VE ALWAYS GOTTEN THIS WEIRD **VIBE** FROM JIN . . .
DOES HE . . . **LIKE** ME OR SOME-THING?
HA HA! YOU YOURSELF ASK HIM!

謹

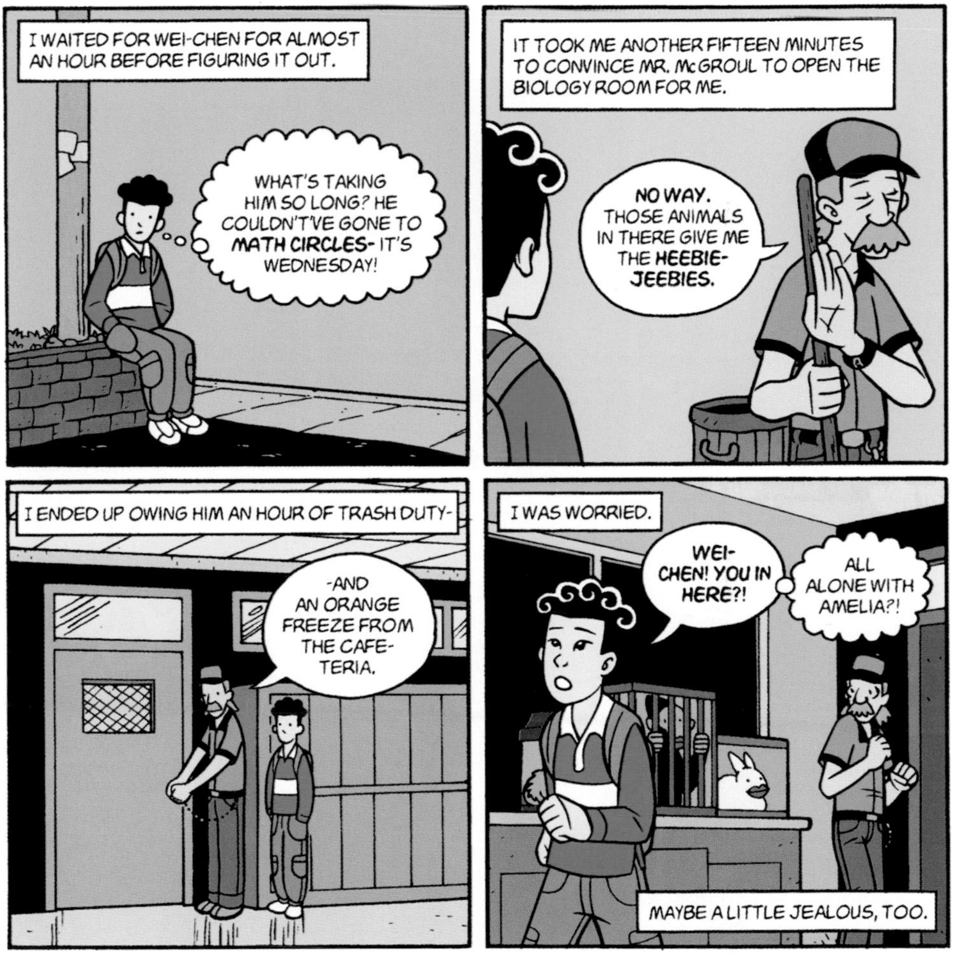
I WAITED FOR WEI-CHEN FOR ALMOST AN HOUR BEFORE FIGURING IT OUT.
WHAT'S TAKING HIM SO LONG? HE COULDN'T'VE GONE TO MATH CIRCLES- IT'S WEDNESDAY!
IT TOOK ME ANOTHER FIFTEEN MINUTES TO CONVINCE MR. McGROUL TO OPEN THE BIOLOGY ROOM FOR ME.
NO WAY. THOSE ANIMALS IN THERE GIVE ME THE HEEBIE-JEEBIES.
I ENDED UP OWING HIM AN HOUR OF TRASH DUTY-
-AND AN ORANGE FREEZE FROM THE CAFE-TERIA.
I WAS WORRIED.
WEI-CHEN! YOU IN HERE?!
ALL ALONE WITH AMELIA?!
MAYBE A LITTLE JEALOUS, TOO.

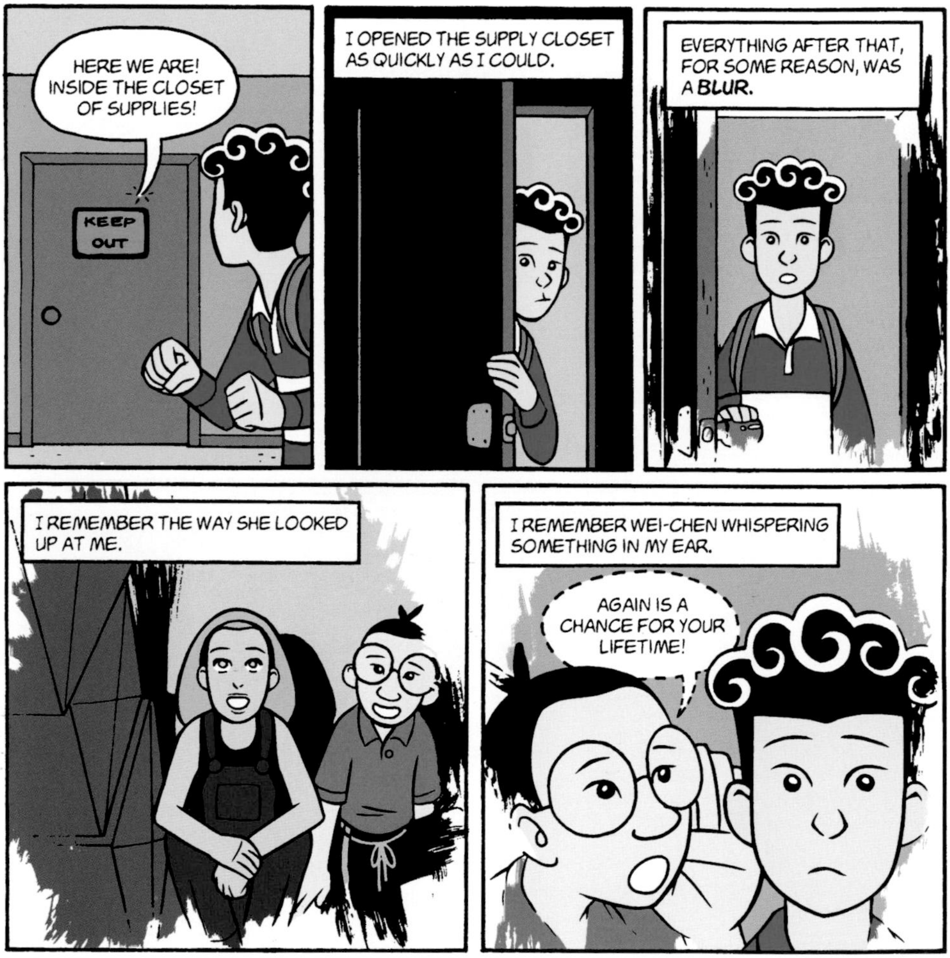
HERE WE ARE! INSIDE THE CLOSET OF SUPPLIES!
KEEP OUT
I OPENED THE SUPPLY CLOSET AS QUICKLY AS I COULD.
EVERYTHING AFTER THAT, FOR SOME REASON, WAS A **BLUR.**
I REMEMBER THE WAY SHE LOOKED UP AT ME.
I REMEMBER WEI-CHEN WHISPERING SOMETHING IN MY EAR.
AGAIN IS A CHANCE FOR YOUR LIFETIME!

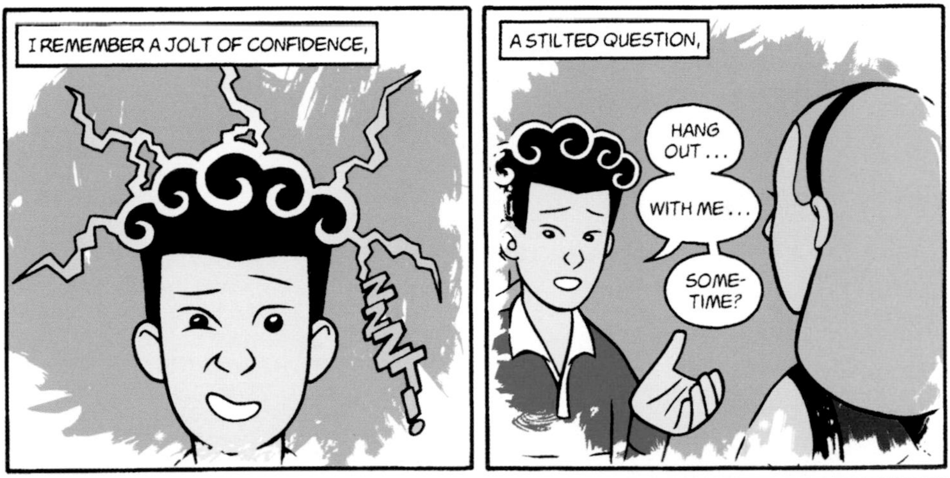
I REMEMBER A JOLT OF CONFIDENCE,
ZZZT!
A STILTED QUESTION,
HANG OUT . . .
WITH ME . . .
SOME-TIME?
AND A WORD FROM HER LIPS . . .
YES.
YES.
YES.

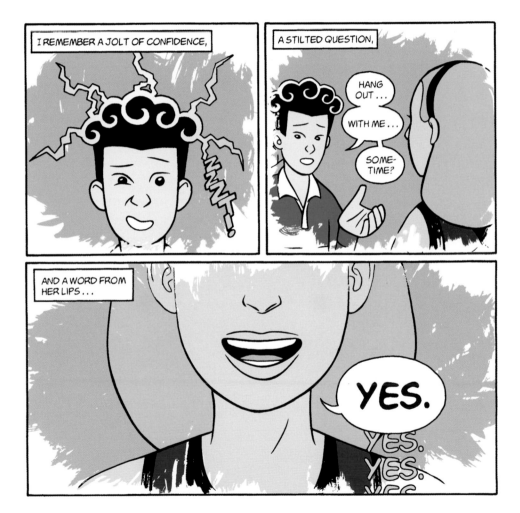

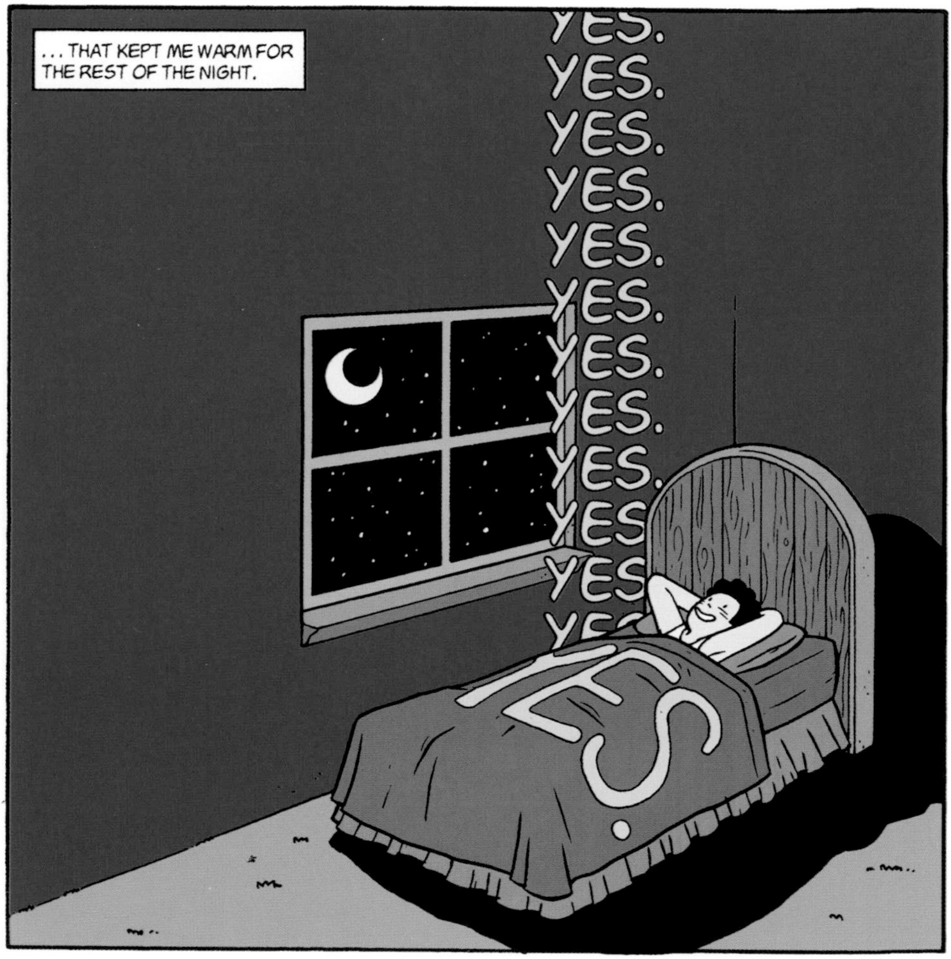

. . . THAT KEPT ME WARM FOR THE REST OF THE NIGHT.
YES.
YES.
YES.
YES.
YES.
YES.
YES.
YES.
YES.
YES.

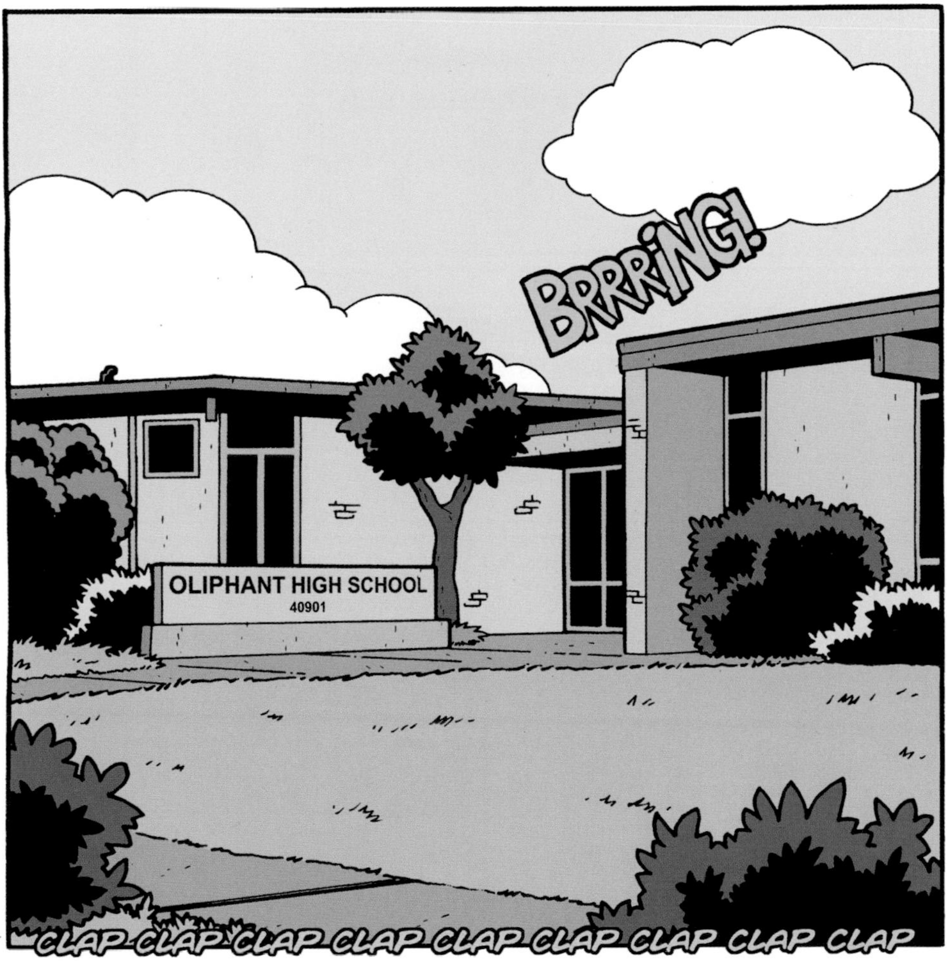
BRRRiNG!
OLIPHANT HIGH SCHOOL
40901
CLAP CLAP CLAP CLAP CLAP CLAP CLAP CLAP CLAP

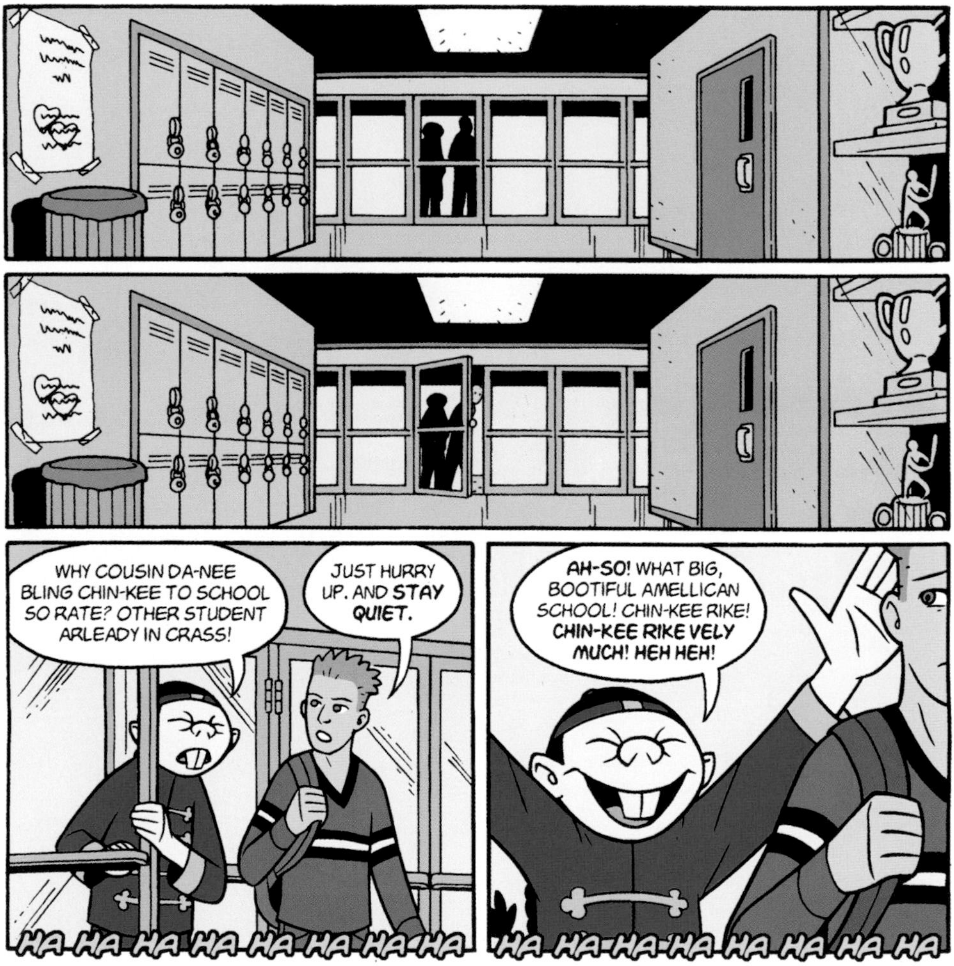
WHY COUSIN DA-NEE BLING CHIN-KEE TO SCHOOL SO RATE? OTHER STUDENT ARLEADY IN CRASS!
JUST HURRY UP. AND **STAY QUIET.**
HA HA HA HA HA HA HA-HA
AH-SO! WHAT BIG, BOOTIFUL AMELLICAN SCHOOL! CHIN-KEE RIKE! **CHIN-KEE RIKE VELY MUCH! HEH HEH!**
HA HA-HA-HA-HA HA HA HA HA

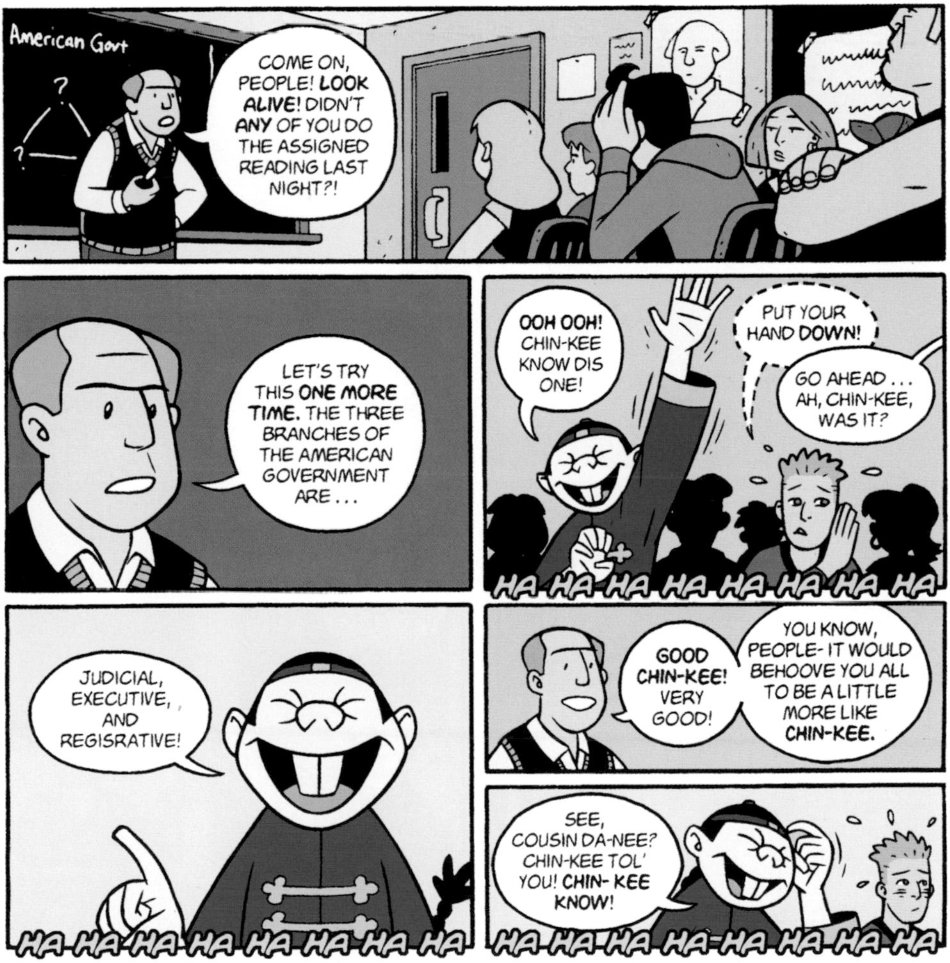
American Govt
COME ON, PEOPLE! LOOK ALIVE! DIDN'T ANY OF YOU DO THE ASSIGNED READING LAST NIGHT?!
LET'S TRY THIS ONE MORE TIME. THE THREE BRANCHES OF THE AMERICAN GOVERNMENT ARE . . .
OOH OOH! CHIN-KEE KNOW DIS ONE!
PUT YOUR HAND DOWN!
GO AHEAD . . . AH, CHIN-KEE, WAS IT?
HA HA HA HA HA HA HA HA
JUDICIAL, EXECUTIVE, AND REGISRATIVE!
HA HA HA HA HA HA HA HA
GOOD CHIN-KEE! VERY GOOD!
YOU KNOW, PEOPLE- IT WOULD BEHOOVE YOU ALL TO BE A LITTLE MORE LIKE CHIN-KEE.
SEE, COUSIN DA-NEE? CHIN-KEE TOL' YOU! CHIN- KEE KNOW!
HA HA HA HA HA HA HA HA

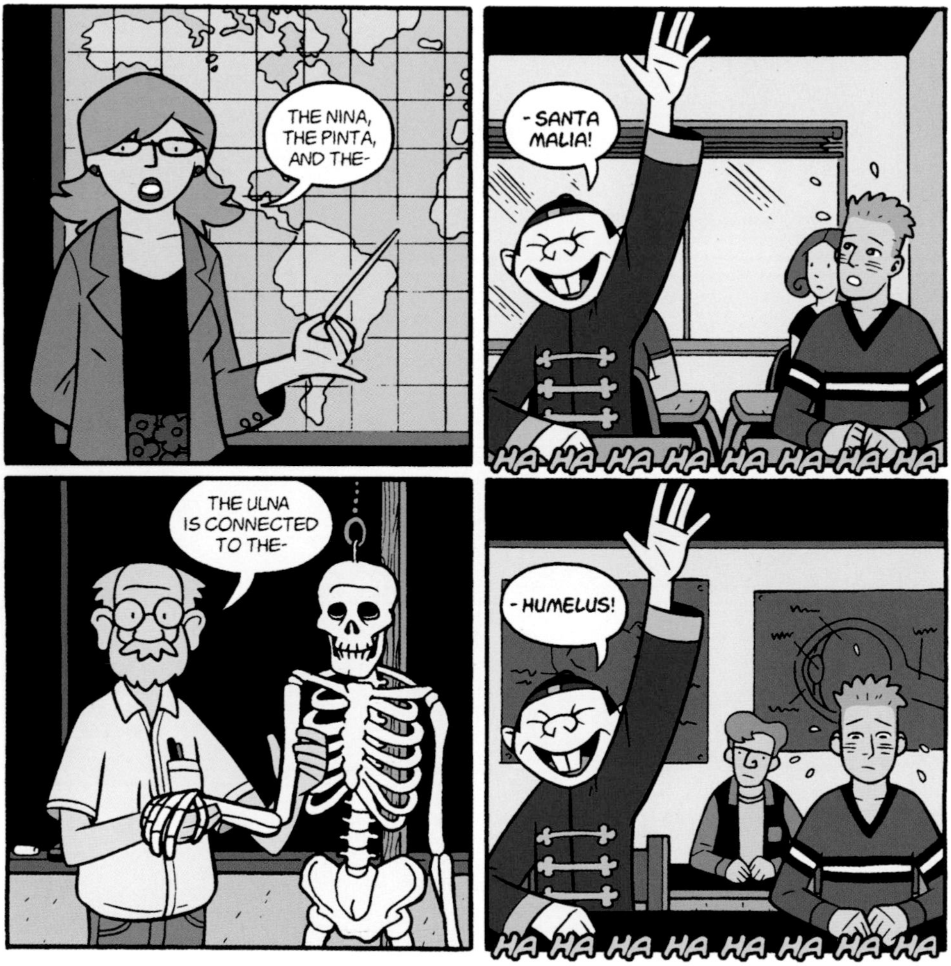
THE NINA, THE PINTA, AND THE-
- SANTA MALIA!
HA HA HA HA HA HA HA HA
THE ULNA IS CONNECTED TO THE-
- HUMELUS!
HA HA HA HA HA HA HA HA

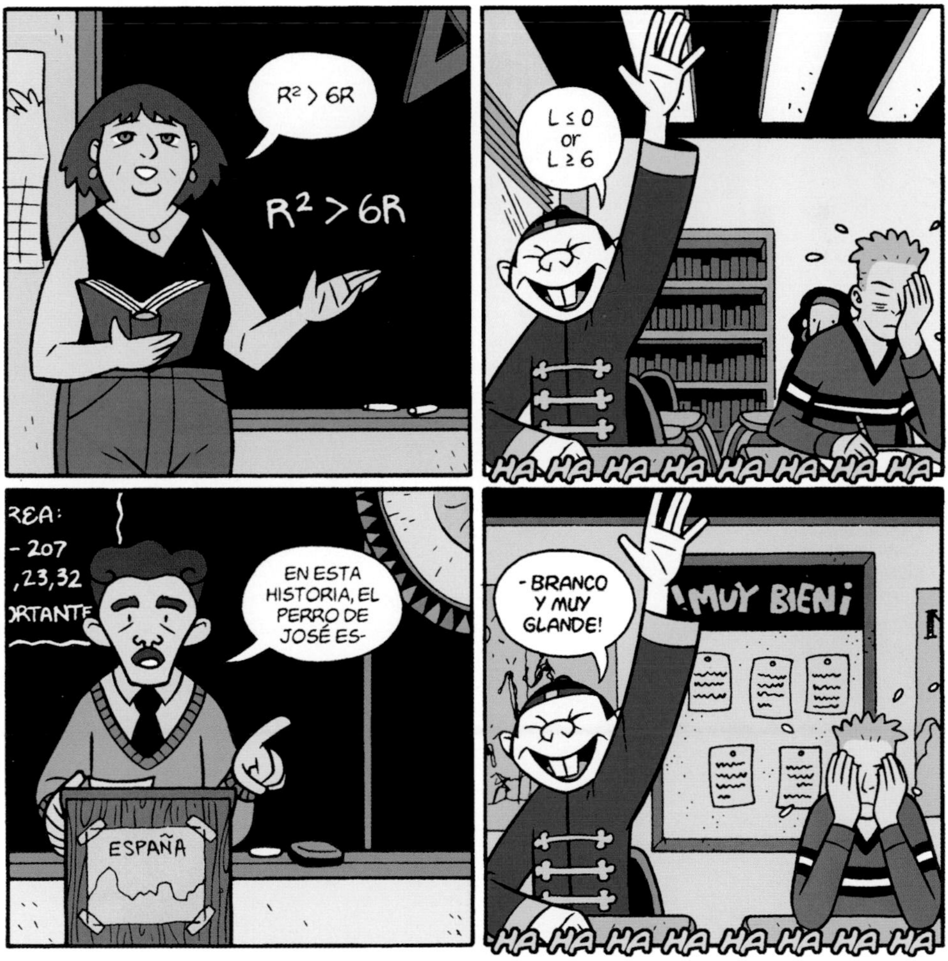
$R^2 > 6R$
$R^2 > 6R$
$L \leq 0$ or $L \geq 6$
HA HA HA HA HA HA HA HA
EN ESTA HISTORIA, EL PERRO DE JOSÉ ES-
ESPAÑA
- BRANCO Y MUY GLANDE!
¡MUY BIEN!
HA HA HA HA HA HA HA HA

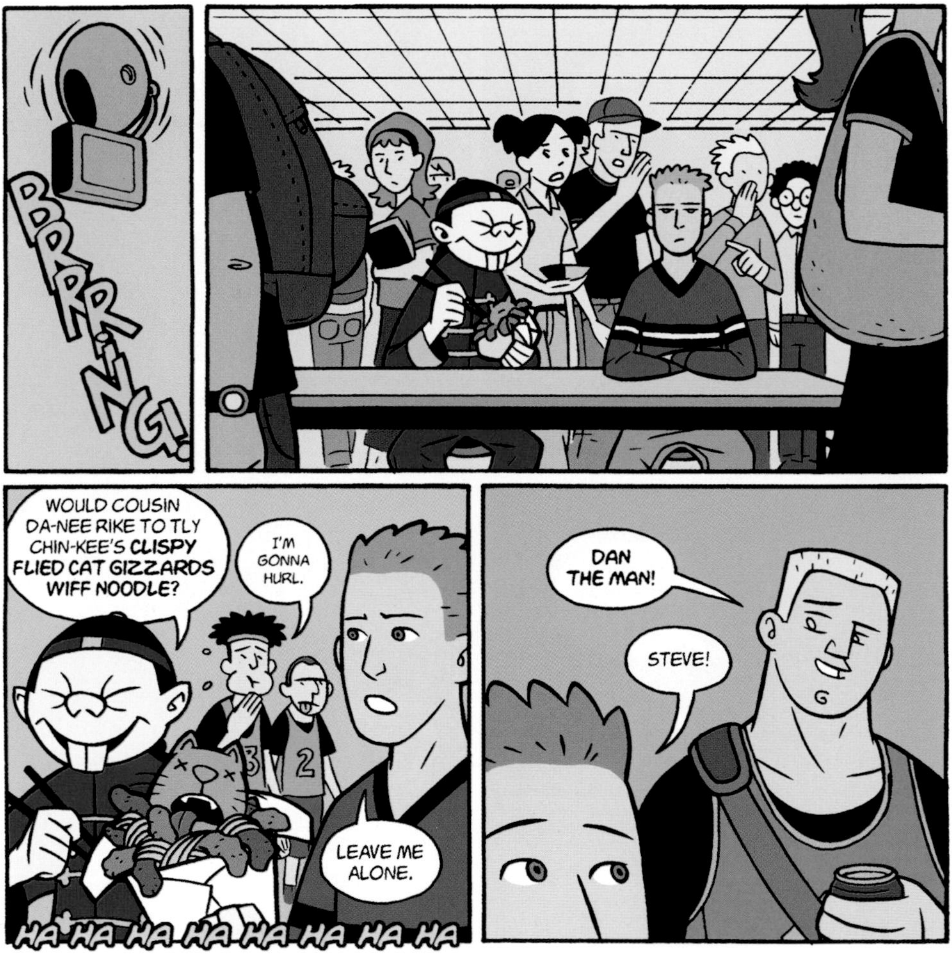
BRRRING!
WOULD COUSIN DA-NEE RIKE TO TLY CHIN-KEE'S **CLISPY FLIED CAT GIZZARDS WIFF NOODLE?**
I'M GONNA HURL.
LEAVE ME ALONE.
HA HA HA HA HA HA HA HA
DAN THE MAN!
STEVE!

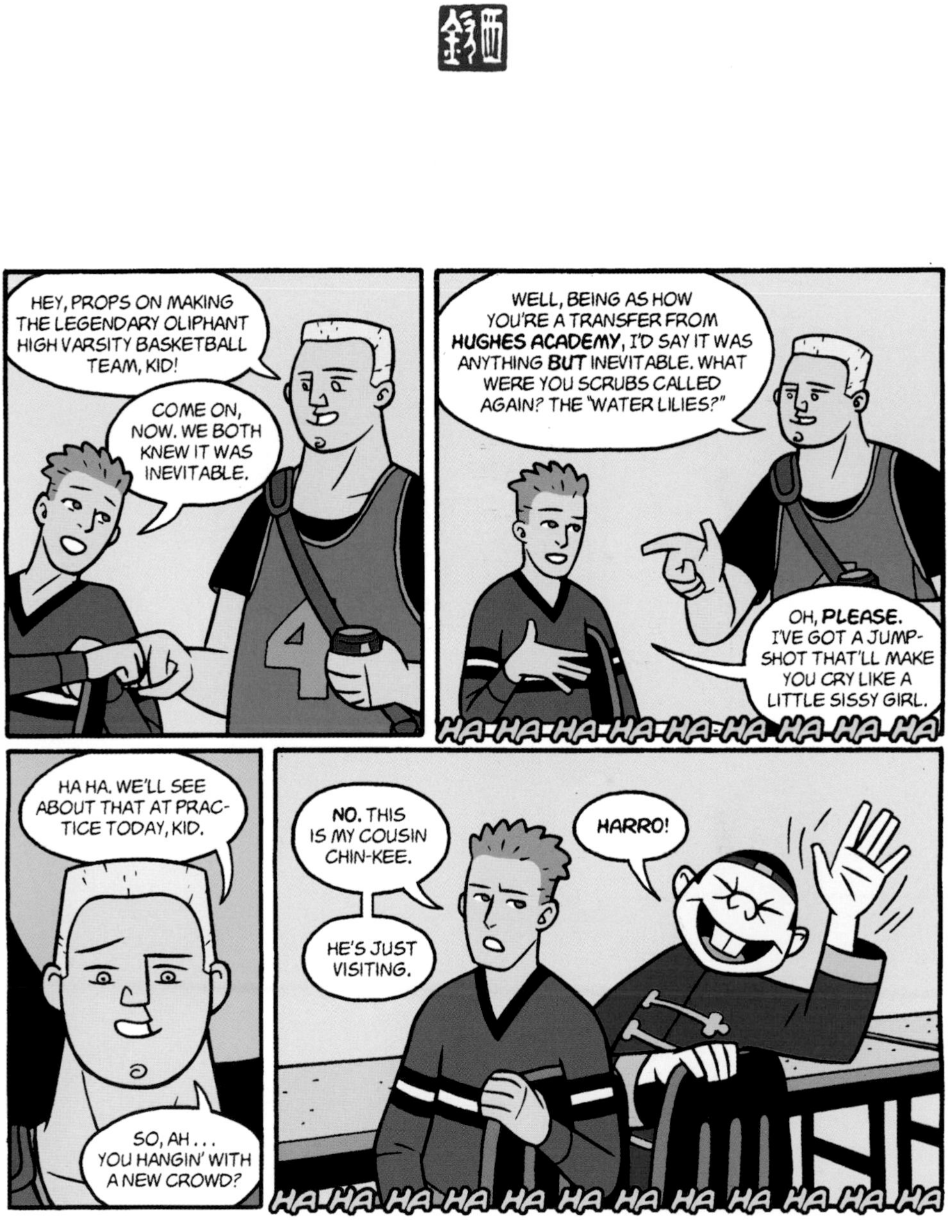
HEY, PROPS ON MAKING THE LEGENDARY OLIPHANT HIGH VARSITY BASKETBALL TEAM, KID!
COME ON, NOW. WE BOTH KNEW IT WAS INEVITABLE.
WELL, BEING AS HOW YOU'RE A TRANSFER FROM **HUGHES ACADEMY**, I'D SAY IT WAS ANYTHING **BUT** INEVITABLE. WHAT WERE YOU SCRUBS CALLED AGAIN? THE "WATER LILIES?"
OH, **PLEASE.** I'VE GOT A JUMP-SHOT THAT'LL MAKE YOU CRY LIKE A LITTLE SISSY GIRL.
HA HA HA HA HA HA HA HA HA
HA HA. WE'LL SEE ABOUT THAT AT PRACTICE TODAY, KID.
SO, AH . . . YOU HANGIN' WITH A NEW CROWD?
NO. THIS IS MY COUSIN CHIN-KEE.
HE'S JUST VISITING.
HARRO!
HA HA HA HA HA HA HA HA HA HA HA HA

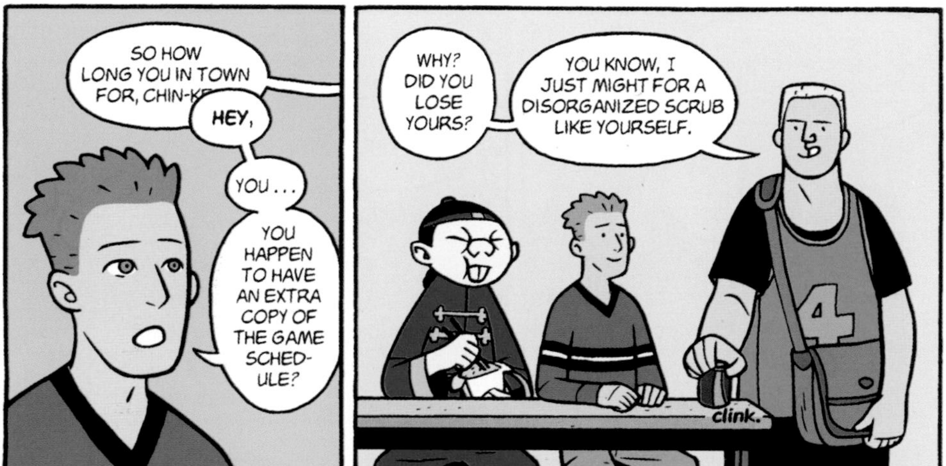
SO HOW LONG YOU IN TOWN FOR, CHIN-K
HEY,
YOU . . .
YOU HAPPEN TO HAVE AN EXTRA COPY OF THE GAME SCHED-ULE?
WHY? DID YOU LOSE YOURS?
YOU KNOW, I JUST MIGHT FOR A DISORGANIZED SCRUB LIKE YOURSELF.
clink.
Cola
GIMME A SEC . . .
HA HA HA HA HA HA HA HA
IT'S IN HERE SOME-WHERE . . .

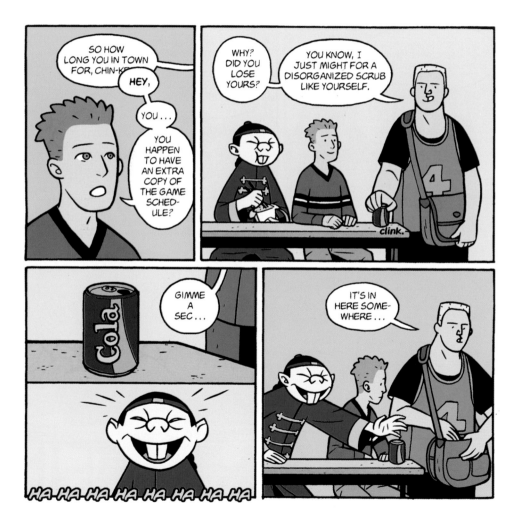

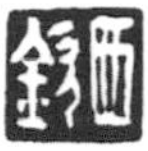

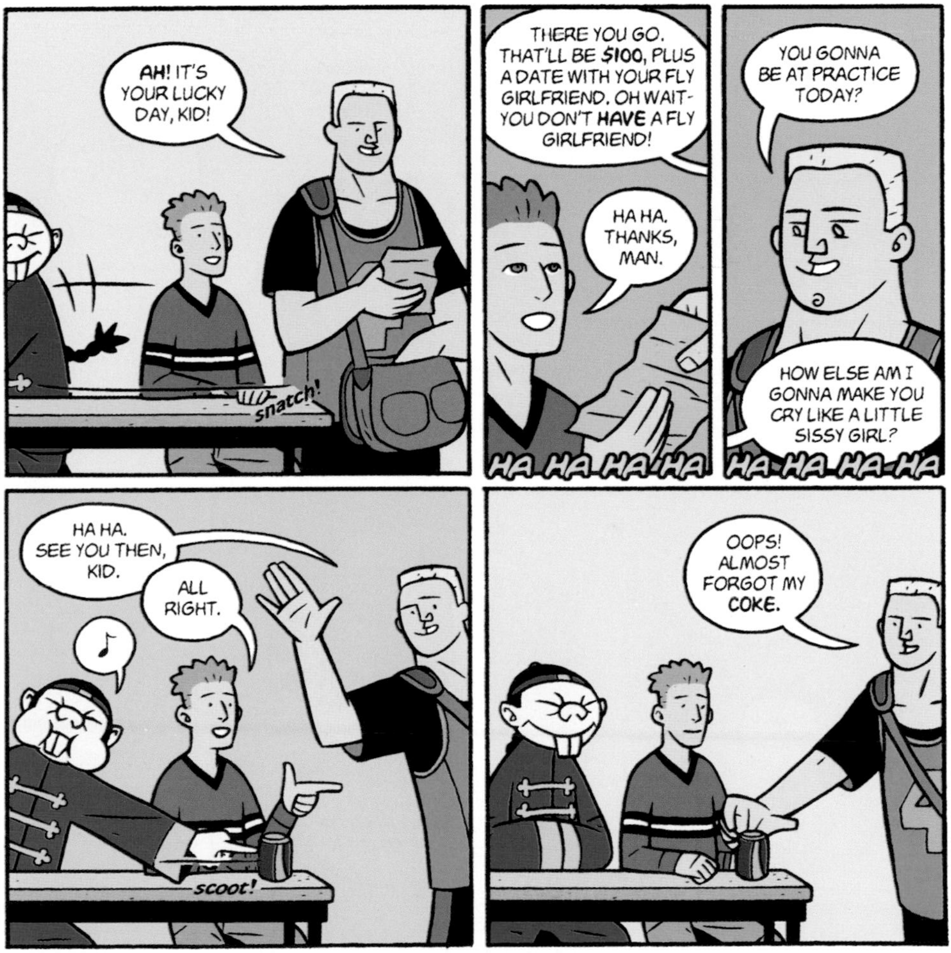
AH! IT'S YOUR LUCKY DAY, KID!
snatch!
THERE YOU GO. THAT'LL BE $100, PLUS A DATE WITH YOUR FLY GIRLFRIEND. OH WAIT- YOU DON'T HAVE A FLY GIRLFRIEND!
HA HA. THANKS, MAN.
HA HA HA HA
YOU GONNA BE AT PRACTICE TODAY?
HOW ELSE AM I GONNA MAKE YOU CRY LIKE A LITTLE SISSY GIRL?
HA HA HA HA
HA HA. SEE YOU THEN, KID.
ALL RIGHT.
♪
scoot!
OOPS! ALMOST FORGOT MY COKE.

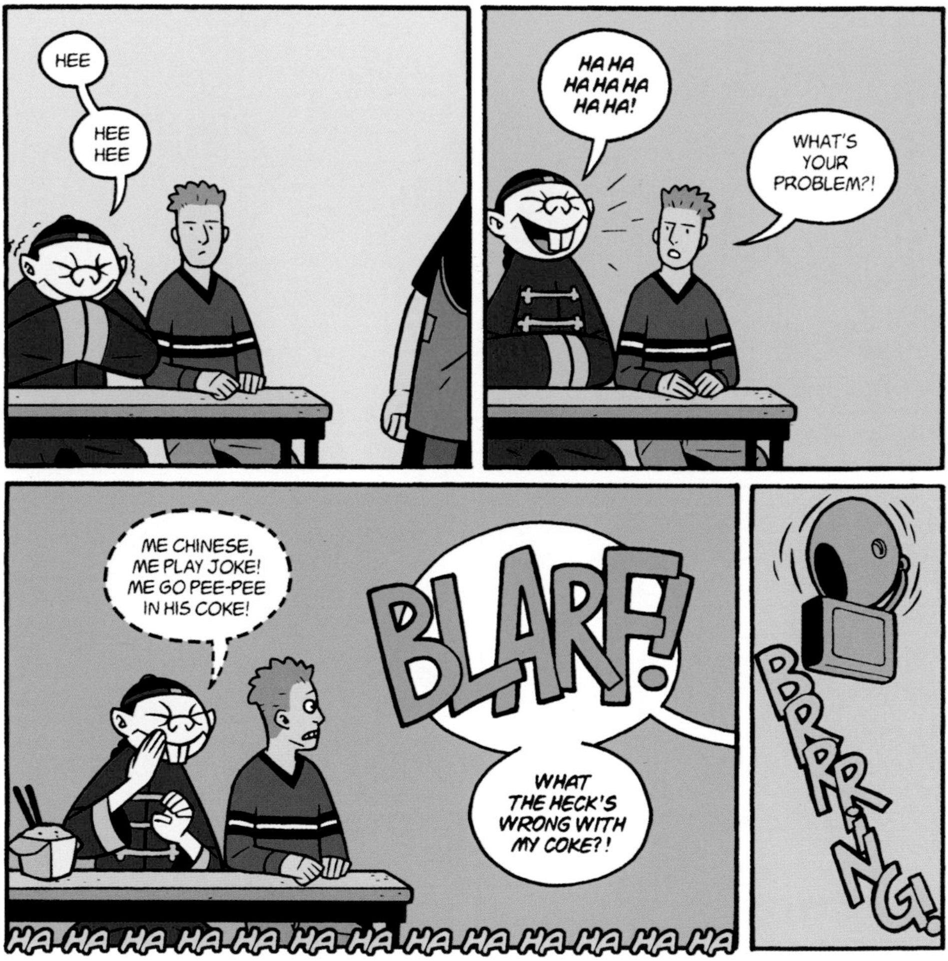
HEE
HEE HEE
HA HA HA HA HA HA HA!
WHAT'S YOUR PROBLEM?!
ME CHINESE, ME PLAY JOKE! ME GO PEE-PEE IN HIS COKE!
BLARF!
WHAT THE HECK'S WRONG WITH MY COKE?!
HA HA HA HA HA HA HA HA HA HA HA HA HA
BRRRING!

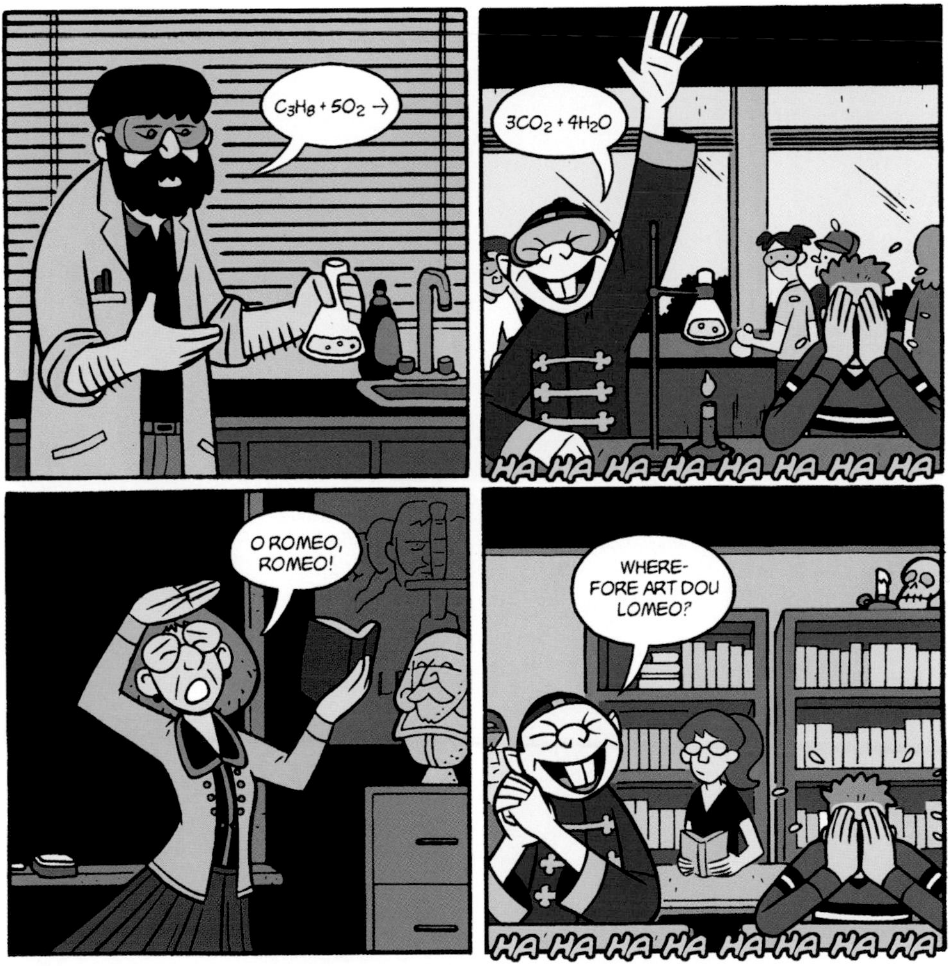
$C_3H_8 + 5O_2 \rightarrow$
$3CO_2 + 4H_2O$
HA HA HA HA HA HA HA HA
O ROMEO, ROMEO!
WHERE-FORE ART DOU LOMEO?
HA HA HA HA HA HA HA HA

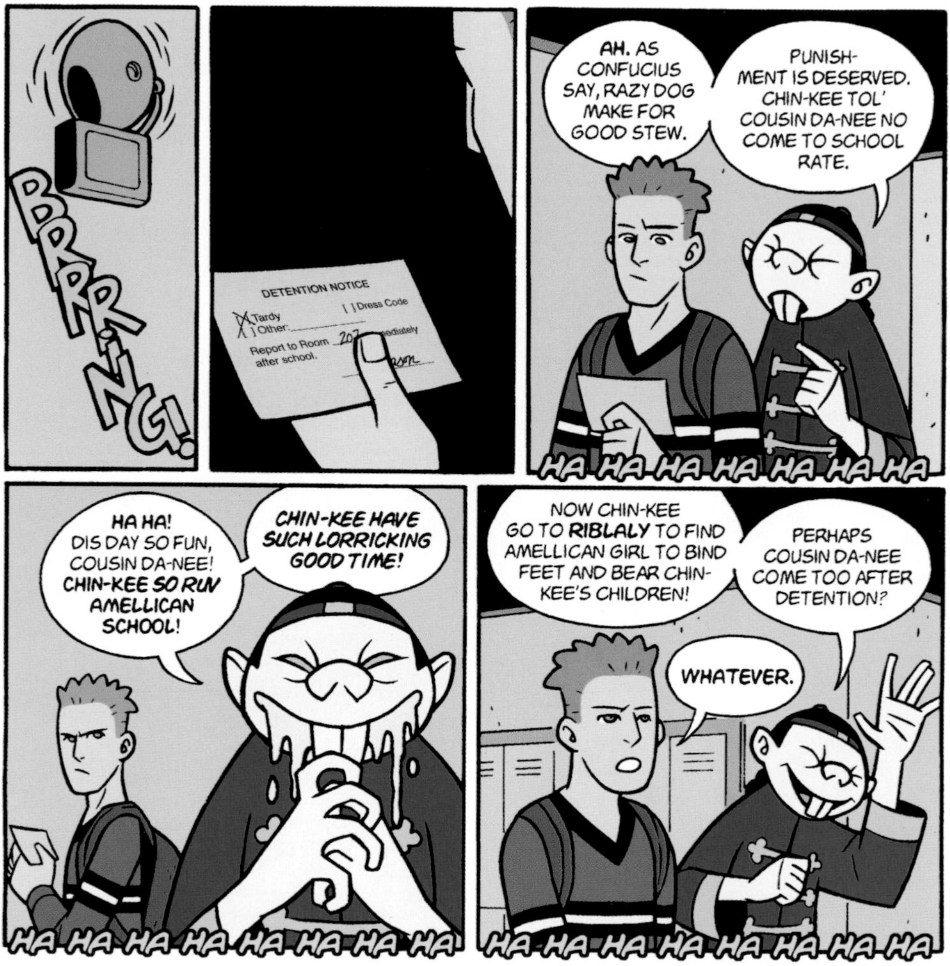
BRRRING!
DETENTION NOTICE
Tardy
[ ] Dress Code
[ ] Other:
Report to Room 207
after school.
AH. AS CONFUCIUS SAY, RAZY DOG MAKE FOR GOOD STEW.
PUNISHMENT IS DESERVED. CHIN-KEE TOL' COUSIN DA-NEE NO COME TO SCHOOL RATE.
HA HA HA HA HA HA HA
HA HA! DIS DAY SO FUN, COUSIN DA-NEE! CHIN-KEE SO RUV AMELLICAN SCHOOL!
CHIN-KEE HAVE SUCH LORRICKING GOOD TIME!
HA HA HA HA HA HA HA HA
NOW CHIN-KEE GO TO RIBLALY TO FIND AMELLICAN GIRL TO BIND FEET AND BEAR CHIN-KEE'S CHILDREN!
PERHAPS COUSIN DA-NEE COME TOO AFTER DETENTION?
WHATEVER.
HA HA HA HA HA HA HA HA

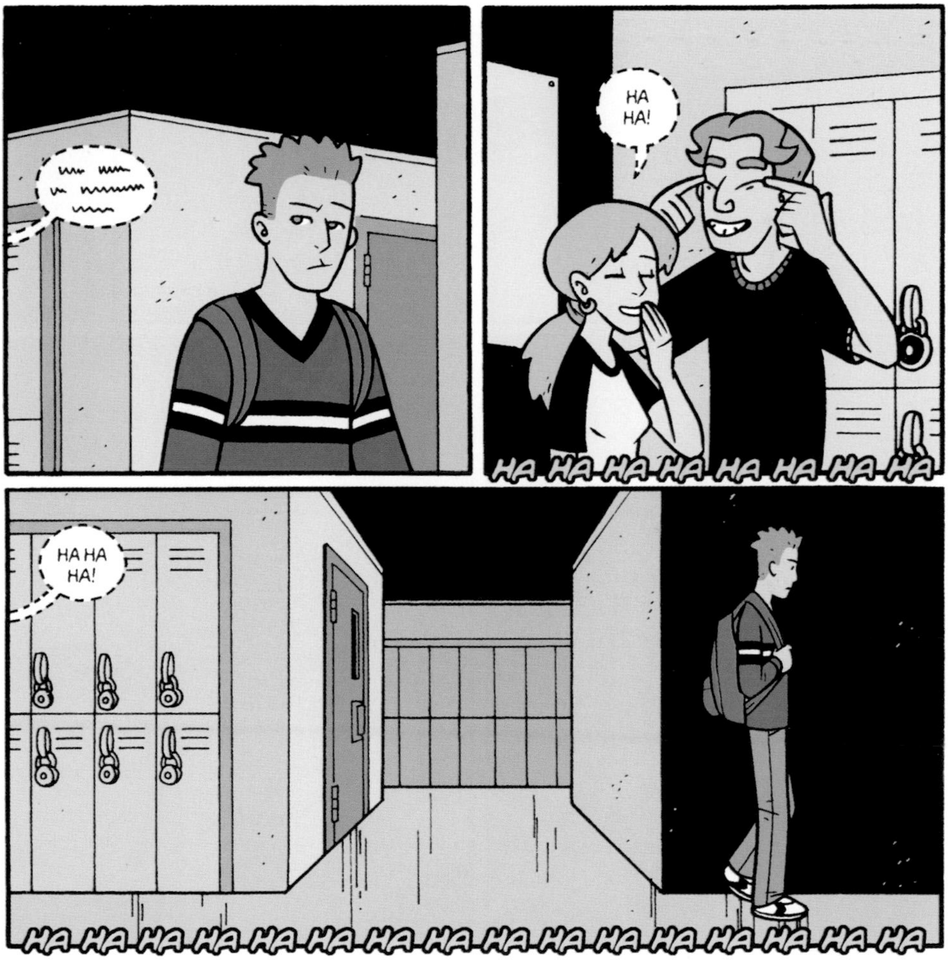
HA HA!
HA HA HA HA HA HA HA HA
HA HA HA!
HA HA HA HA HA HA HA HA HA HA HA HA HA HA HA HA

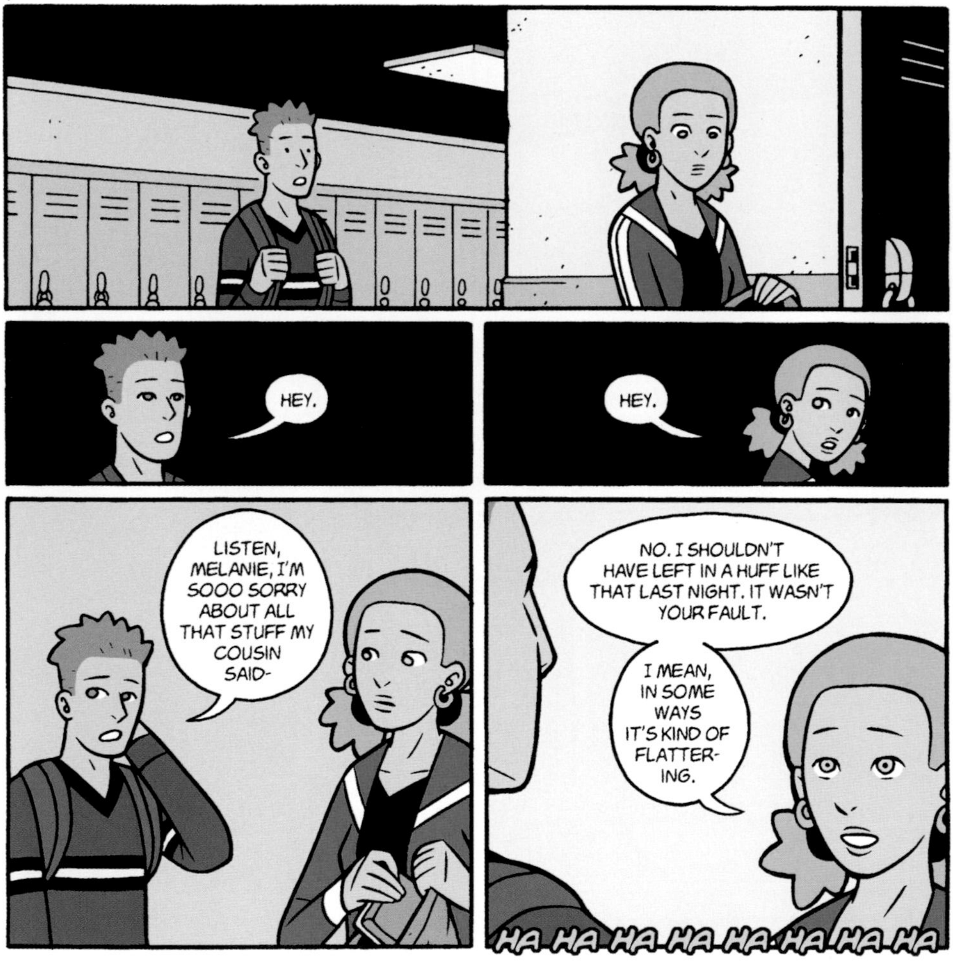

HEY.
HEY.
LISTEN, MELANIE, I'M SOOO SORRY ABOUT ALL THAT STUFF MY COUSIN SAID-
NO. I SHOULDN'T HAVE LEFT IN A HUFF LIKE THAT LAST NIGHT. IT WASN'T YOUR FAULT.
I MEAN, IN SOME WAYS IT'S KIND OF FLATTER-ING.
HA HA HA HA HA HA HA HA

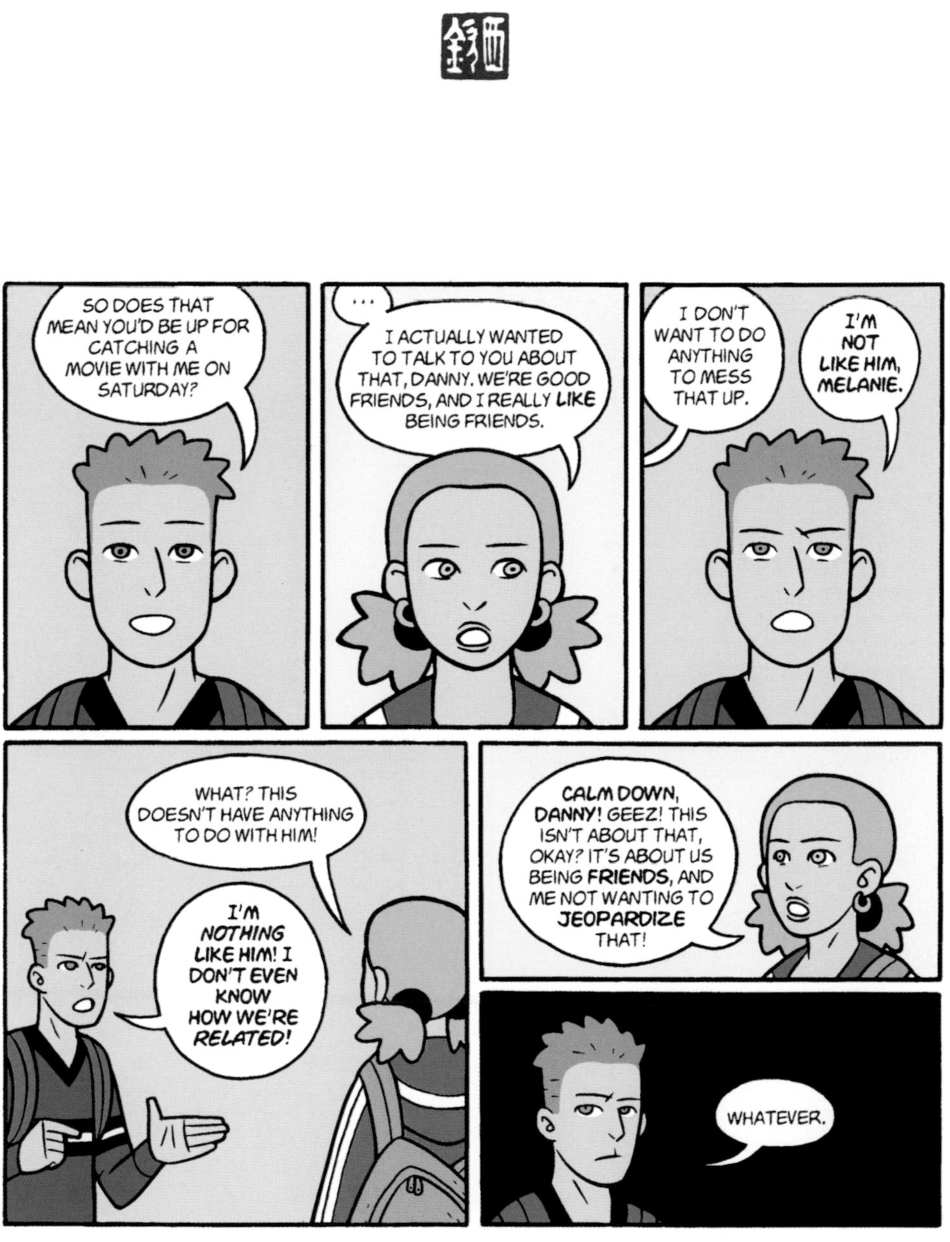
SO DOES THAT MEAN YOU'D BE UP FOR CATCHING A MOVIE WITH ME ON SATURDAY?
...
I ACTUALLY WANTED TO TALK TO YOU ABOUT THAT, DANNY. WE'RE GOOD FRIENDS, AND I REALLY LIKE BEING FRIENDS.
I DON'T WANT TO DO ANYTHING TO MESS THAT UP.
I'M NOT LIKE HIM, MELANIE.
WHAT? THIS DOESN'T HAVE ANYTHING TO DO WITH HIM!
I'M NOTHING LIKE HIM! I DON'T EVEN KNOW HOW WE'RE RELATED!
CALM DOWN, DANNY! GEEZ! THIS ISN'T ABOUT THAT, OKAY? IT'S ABOUT US BEING FRIENDS, AND ME NOT WANTING TO JEOPARDIZE THAT!
WHATEVER.

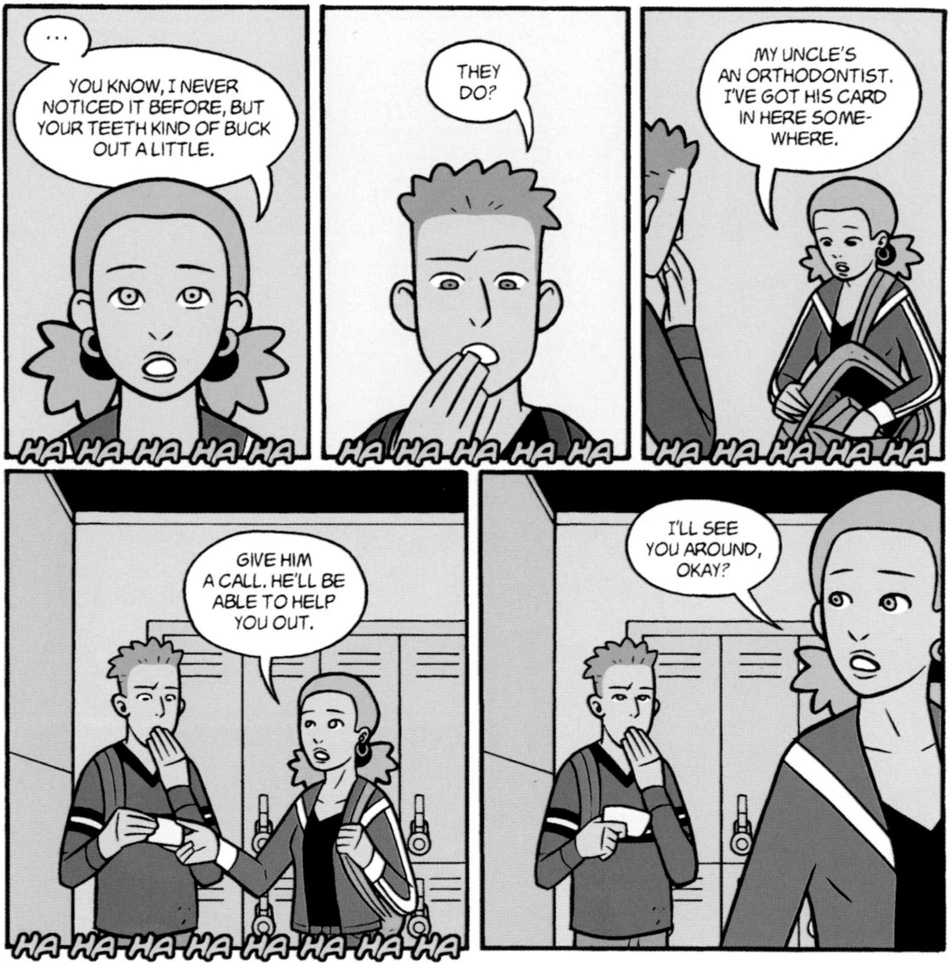
...
YOU KNOW, I NEVER NOTICED IT BEFORE, BUT YOUR TEETH KIND OF BUCK OUT A LITTLE.
HA HA HA HA HA
THEY DO?
HA HA HA HA HA
MY UNCLE'S AN ORTHODONTIST. I'VE GOT HIS CARD IN HERE SOME-WHERE.
HA HA HA HA HA
GIVE HIM A CALL. HE'LL BE ABLE TO HELP YOU OUT.
HA HA HA HA HA HA HA HA
I'LL SEE YOU AROUND, OKAY?

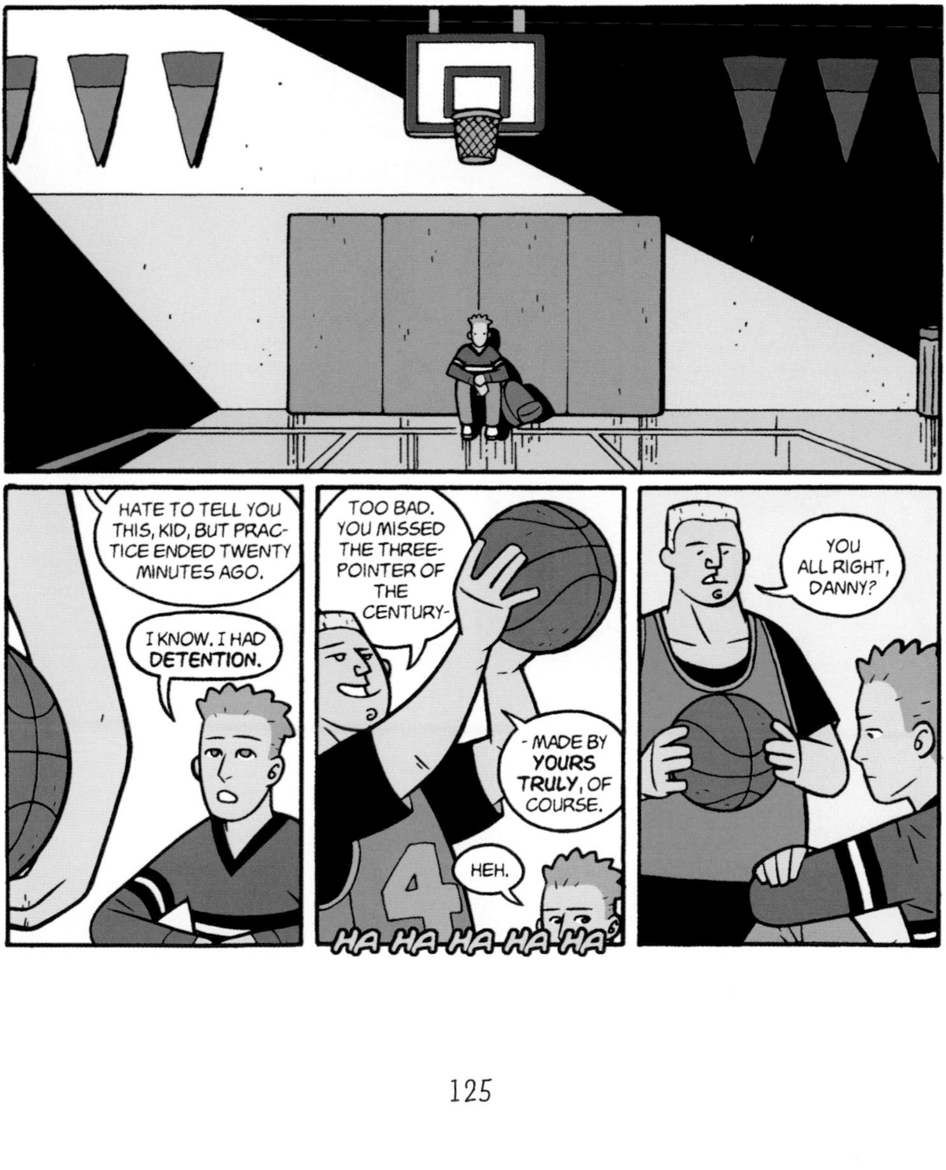
HATE TO TELL YOU THIS, KID, BUT PRACTICE ENDED TWENTY MINUTES AGO.
I KNOW. I HAD DETENTION.
TOO BAD. YOU MISSED THE THREE-POINTER OF THE CENTURY-
- MADE BY YOURS TRULY, OF COURSE.
HEH.
HA HA HA HA HA
YOU ALL RIGHT, DANNY?

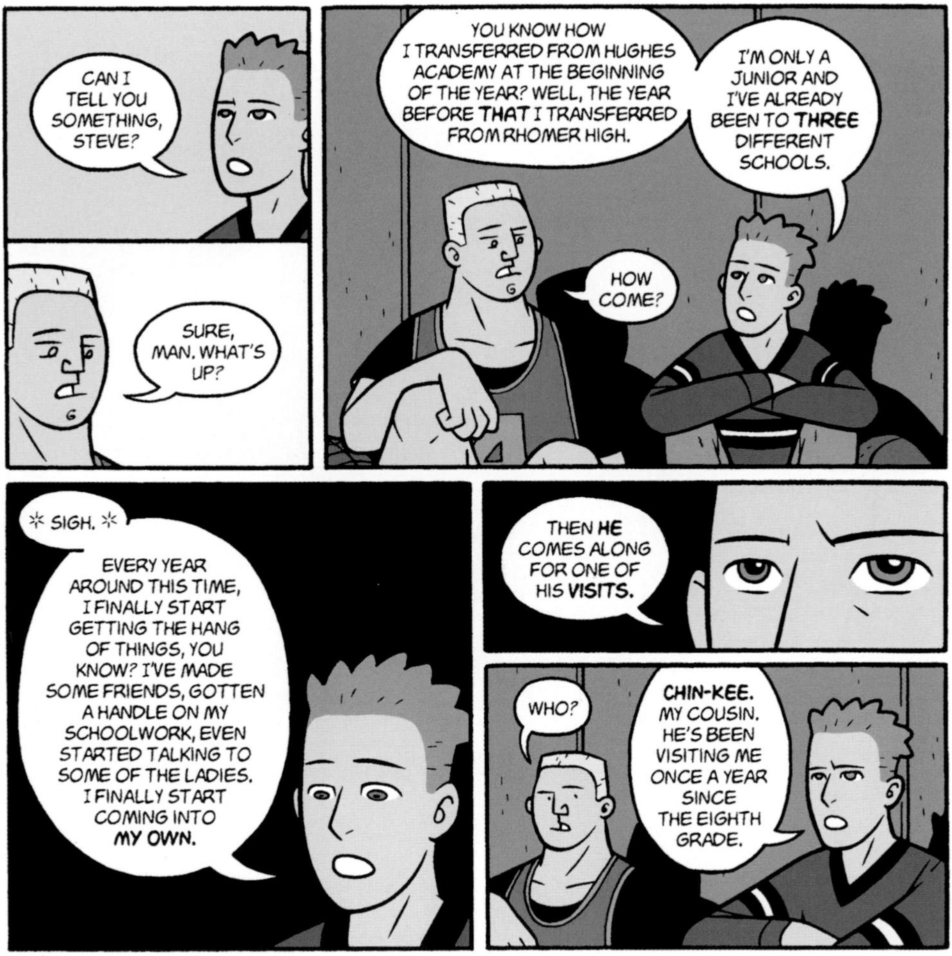
CAN I TELL YOU SOMETHING, STEVE?
SURE, MAN. WHAT'S UP?
YOU KNOW HOW I TRANSFERRED FROM HUGHES ACADEMY AT THE BEGINNING OF THE YEAR? WELL, THE YEAR BEFORE **THAT** I TRANSFERRED FROM RHOMER HIGH.
I'M ONLY A JUNIOR AND I'VE ALREADY BEEN TO **THREE** DIFFERENT SCHOOLS.
HOW COME?
* SIGH. *
EVERY YEAR AROUND THIS TIME, I FINALLY START GETTING THE HANG OF THINGS, YOU KNOW? I'VE MADE SOME FRIENDS, GOTTEN A HANDLE ON MY SCHOOLWORK, EVEN STARTED TALKING TO SOME OF THE LADIES. I FINALLY START COMING INTO **MY OWN.**
THEN **HE** COMES ALONG FOR ONE OF HIS **VISITS.**
WHO?
CHIN-KEE. MY COUSIN. HE'S BEEN VISITING ME ONCE A YEAR SINCE THE EIGHTH GRADE.

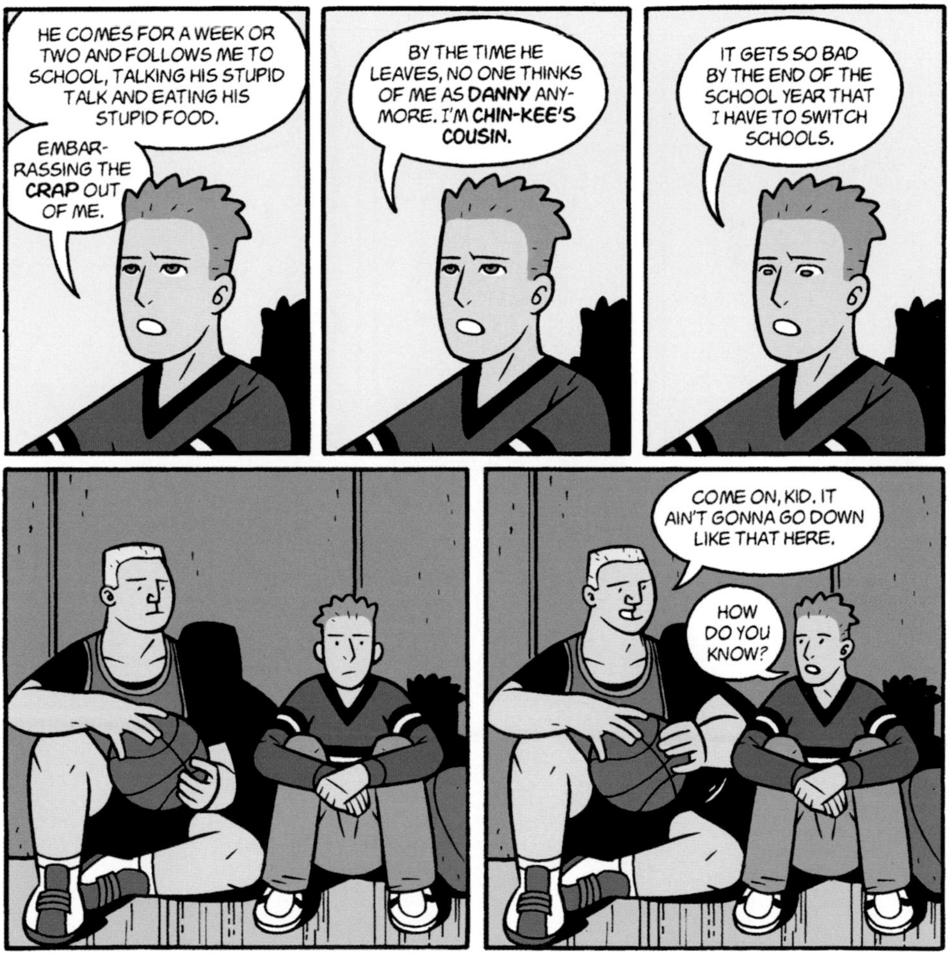
HE COMES FOR A WEEK OR TWO AND FOLLOWS ME TO SCHOOL, TALKING HIS STUPID TALK AND EATING HIS STUPID FOOD.
EMBAR-RASSING THE CRAP OUT OF ME.
BY THE TIME HE LEAVES, NO ONE THINKS OF ME AS DANNY ANY-MORE. I'M CHIN-KEE'S COUSIN.
IT GETS SO BAD BY THE END OF THE SCHOOL YEAR THAT I HAVE TO SWITCH SCHOOLS.
COME ON, KID. IT AIN'T GONNA GO DOWN LIKE THAT HERE.
HOW DO YOU KNOW?

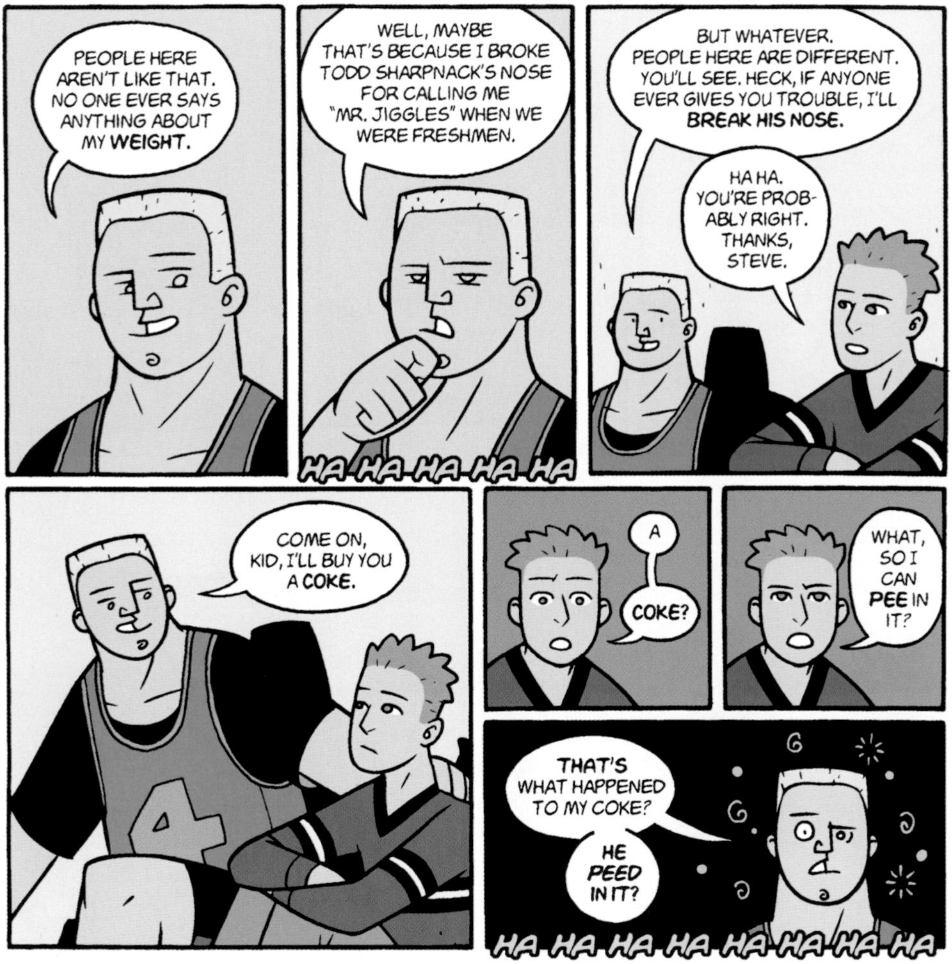
PEOPLE HERE AREN'T LIKE THAT. NO ONE EVER SAYS ANYTHING ABOUT MY WEIGHT.
WELL, MAYBE THAT'S BECAUSE I BROKE TODD SHARPNACK'S NOSE FOR CALLING ME "MR. JIGGLES" WHEN WE WERE FRESHMEN.
HA HA HA HA HA HA
BUT WHATEVER. PEOPLE HERE ARE DIFFERENT. YOU'LL SEE. HECK, IF ANYONE EVER GIVES YOU TROUBLE, I'LL BREAK HIS NOSE.
HA HA. YOU'RE PROBABLY RIGHT. THANKS, STEVE.
COME ON, KID, I'LL BUY YOU A COKE.
A
COKE?
WHAT, SO I CAN PEE IN IT?
THAT'S WHAT HAPPENED TO MY COKE?
HE PEED IN IT?
HA HA HA HA HA HA HA HA

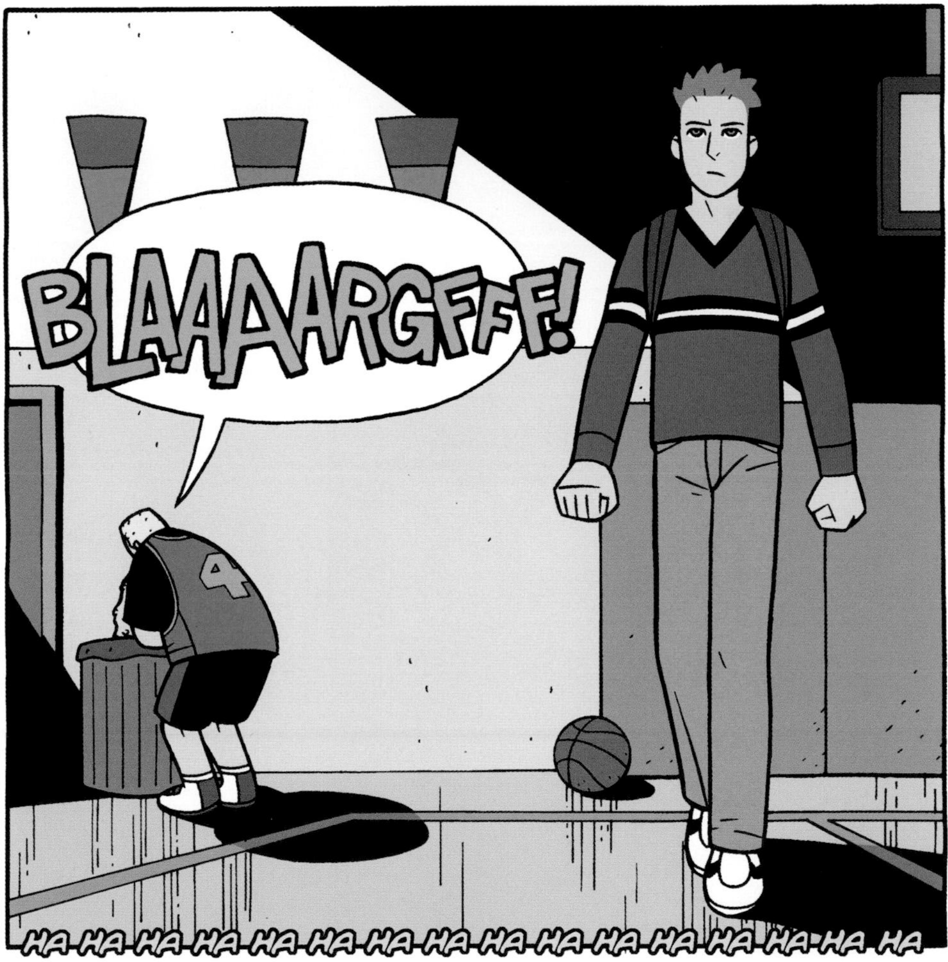
BLAAAARGFFF!
HA HA HA HA HA HA HA HA HA HA HA HA HA HA HA HA

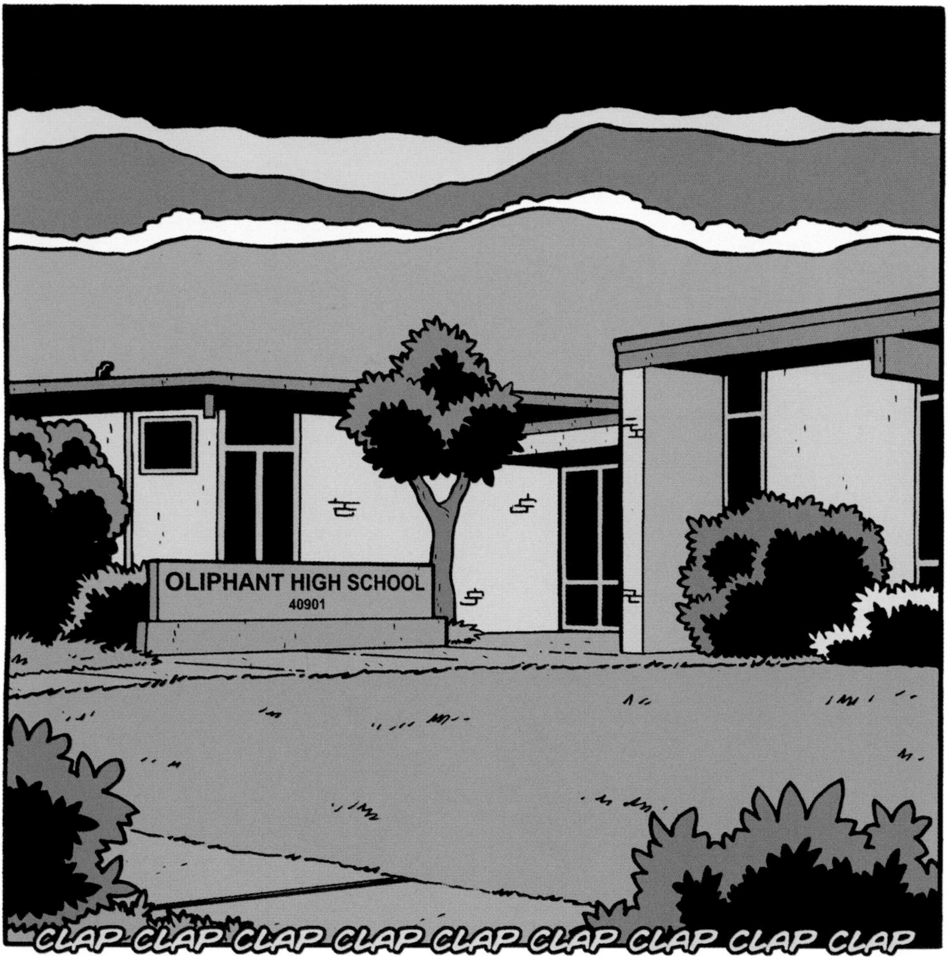
OLIPHANT HIGH SCHOOL
40901
CLAP CLAP CLAP CLAP CLAP CLAP CLAP CLAP CLAP

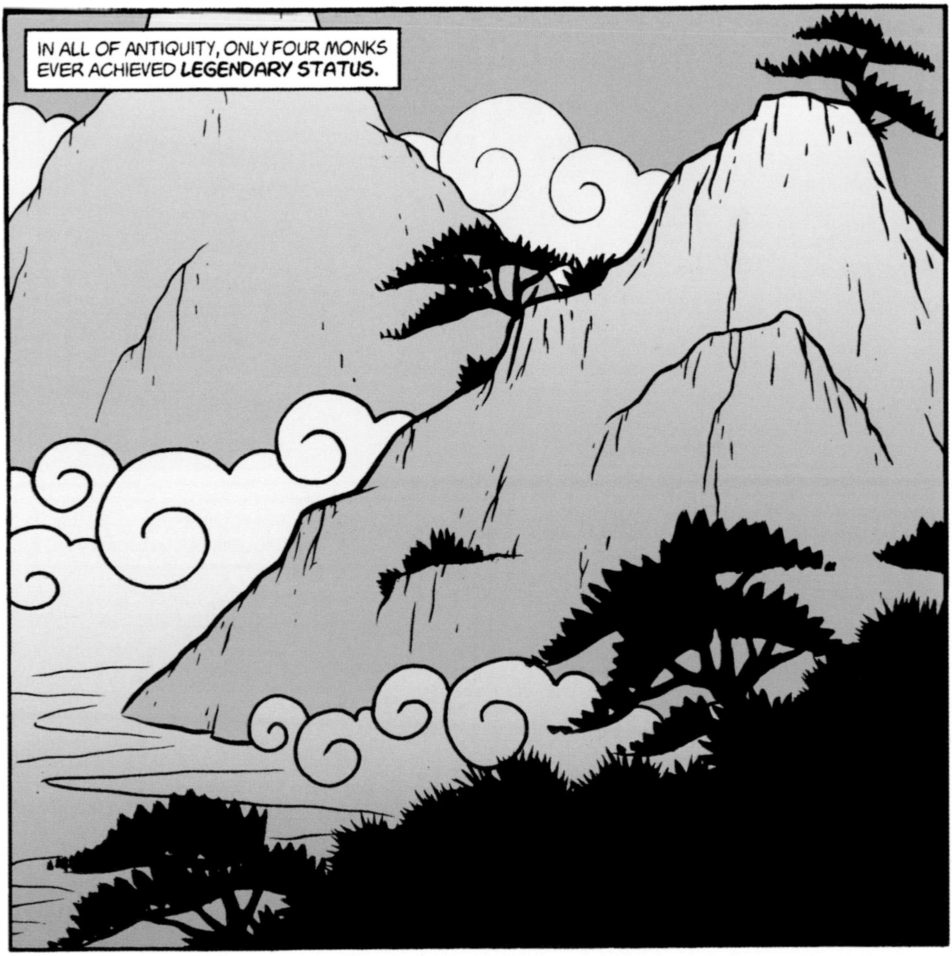
IN ALL OF ANTIQUITY, ONLY FOUR MONKS EVER ACHIEVED **LEGENDARY STATUS.**

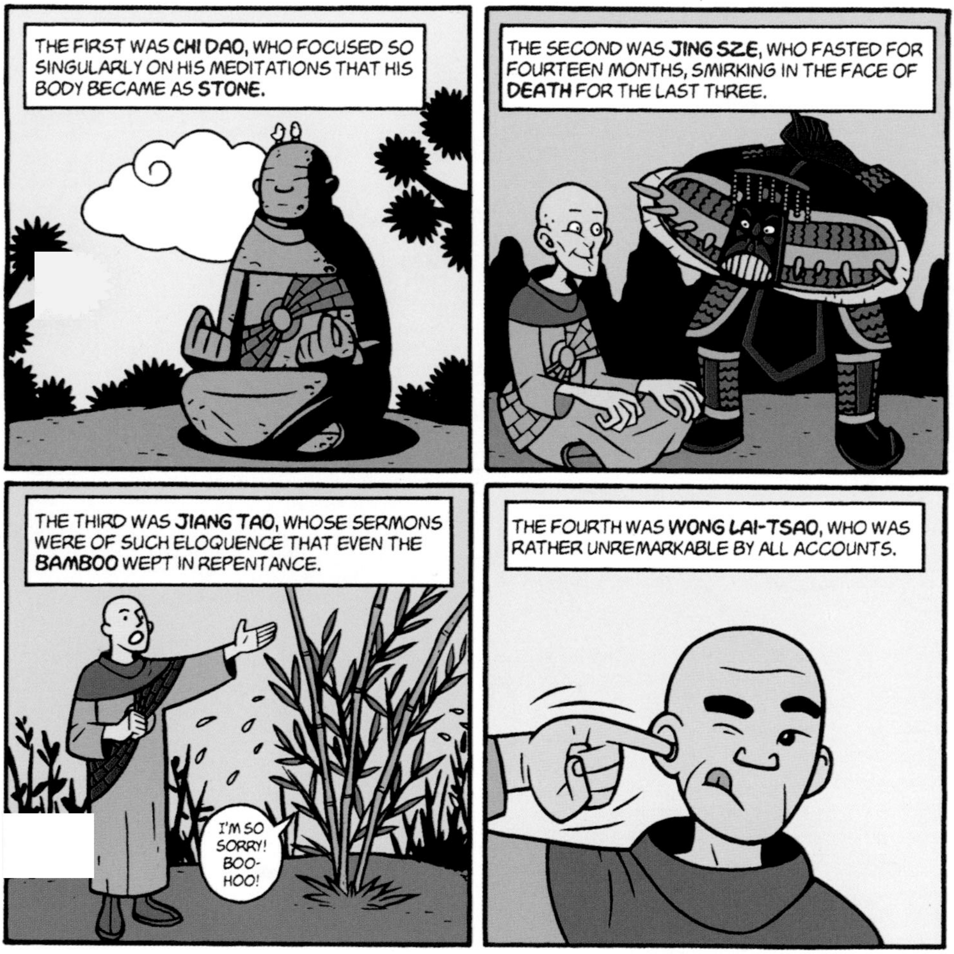
THE FIRST WAS CHI DAO, WHO FOCUSED SO SINGULARLY ON HIS MEDITATIONS THAT HIS BODY BECAME AS STONE.
THE SECOND WAS JING SZE, WHO FASTED FOR FOURTEEN MONTHS, SMIRKING IN THE FACE OF DEATH FOR THE LAST THREE.
THE THIRD WAS JIANG TAO, WHOSE SERMONS WERE OF SUCH ELOQUENCE THAT EVEN THE BAMBOO WEPT IN REPENTANCE.
I'M SO SORRY! BOO-HOO!
THE FOURTH WAS WONG LAI-TSAO, WHO WAS RATHER UNREMARKABLE BY ALL ACCOUNTS.

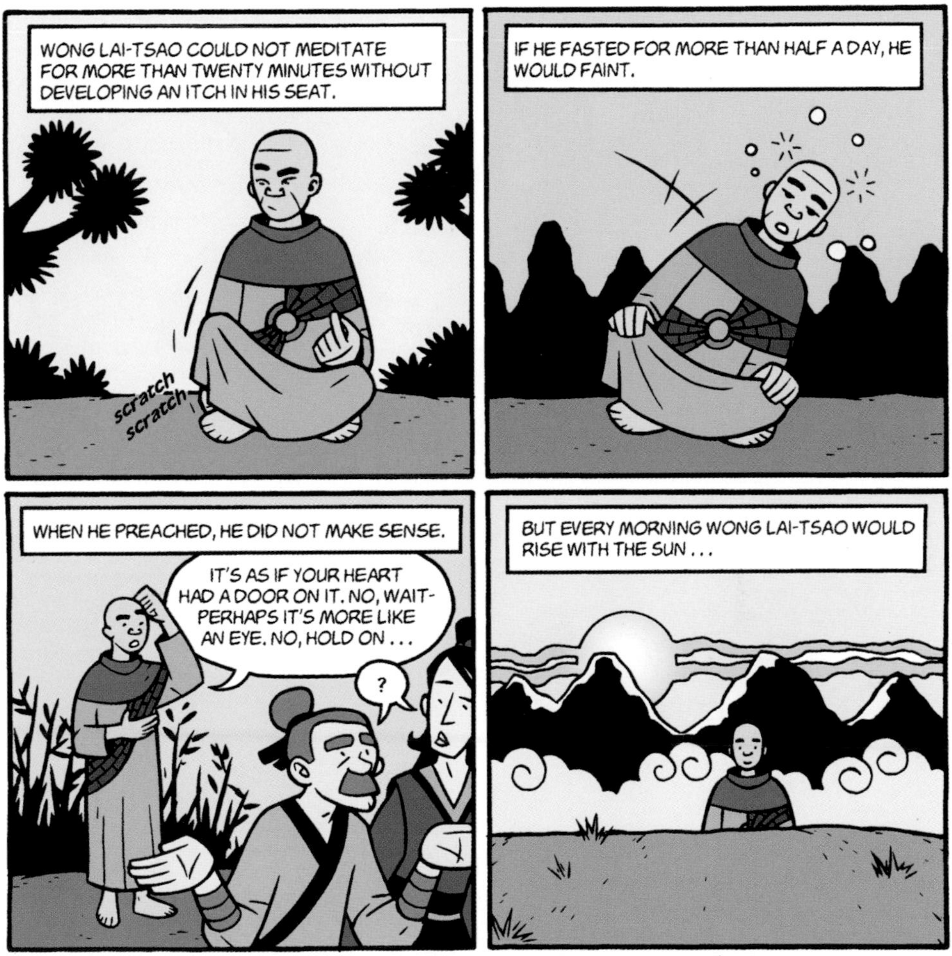
WONG LAI-TSAO COULD NOT MEDITATE FOR MORE THAN TWENTY MINUTES WITHOUT DEVELOPING AN ITCH IN HIS SEAT.
scratch scratch
IF HE FASTED FOR MORE THAN HALF A DAY, HE WOULD FAINT.
WHEN HE PREACHED, HE DID NOT MAKE SENSE.
IT'S AS IF YOUR HEART HAD A DOOR ON IT. NO, WAIT- PERHAPS IT'S MORE LIKE AN EYE. NO, HOLD ON . . .
?
BUT EVERY MORNING WONG LAI-TSAO WOULD RISE WITH THE SUN . . .

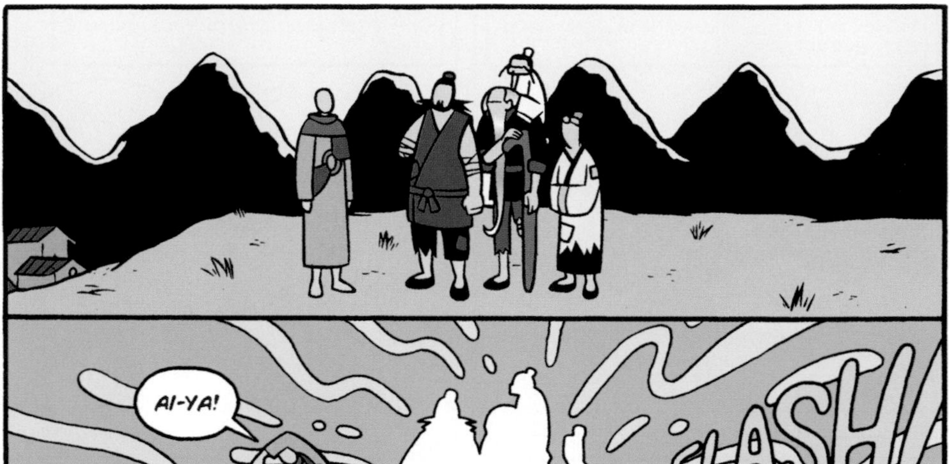
AI-YA!
FLASH!

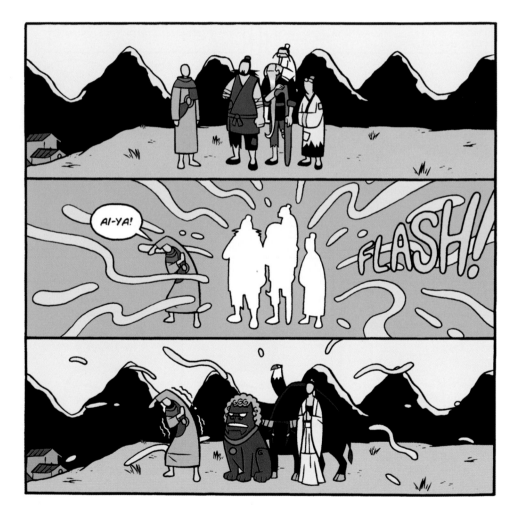

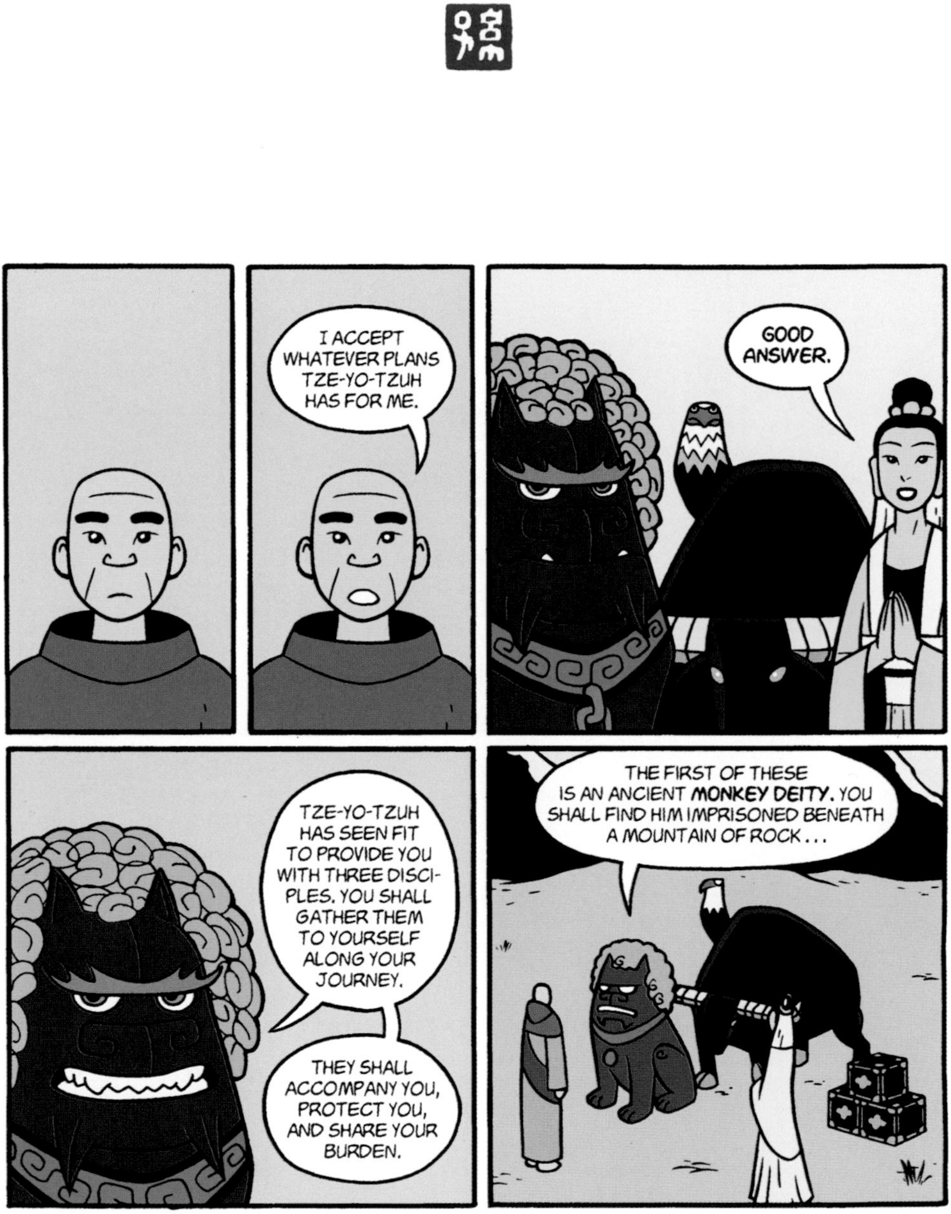

I ACCEPT WHATEVER PLANS TZE-YO-TZUH HAS FOR ME.
GOOD ANSWER.
TZE-YO-TZUH HAS SEEN FIT TO PROVIDE YOU WITH THREE DISCIPLES. YOU SHALL GATHER THEM TO YOURSELF ALONG YOUR JOURNEY.
THEY SHALL ACCOMPANY YOU, PROTECT YOU, AND SHARE YOUR BURDEN.
THE FIRST OF THESE IS AN ANCIENT **MONKEY DEITY.** YOU SHALL FIND HIM IMPRISONED BENEATH A MOUNTAIN OF ROCK . . .

THE NEXT MORNING, WONG LAI-TSAO ROSE WITH THE SUN AND SET OFF ON HIS MISSION.

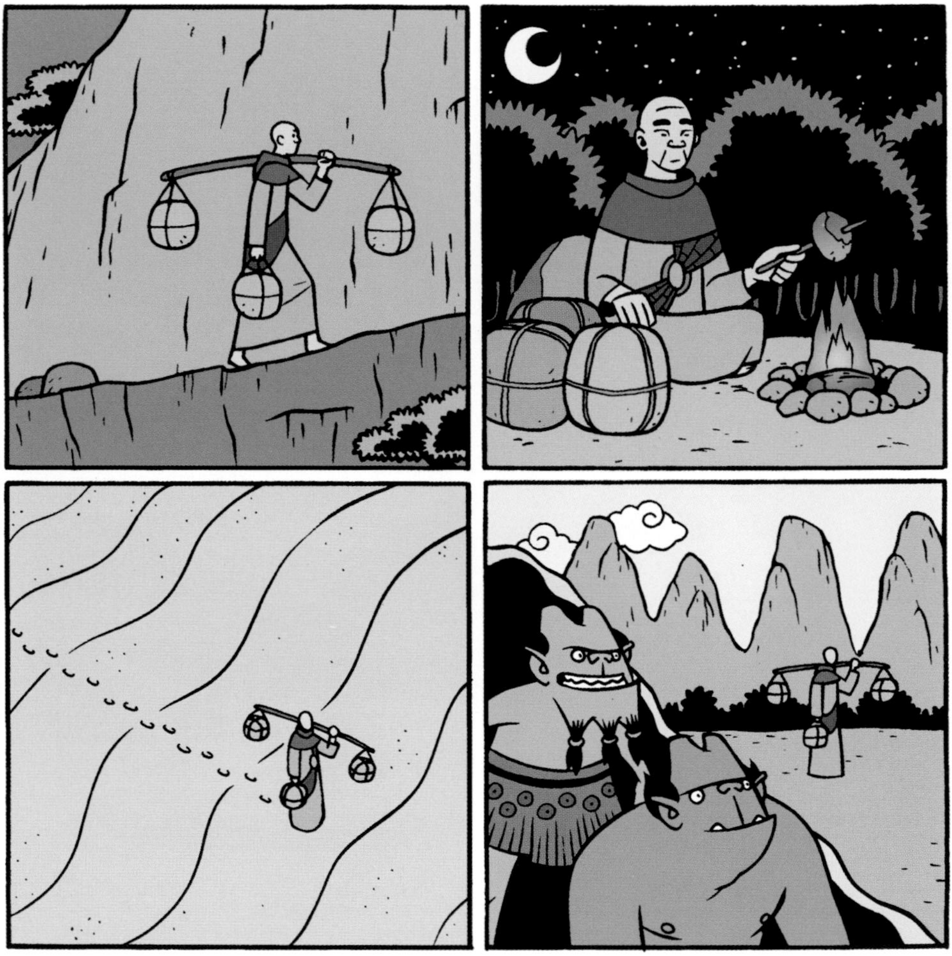

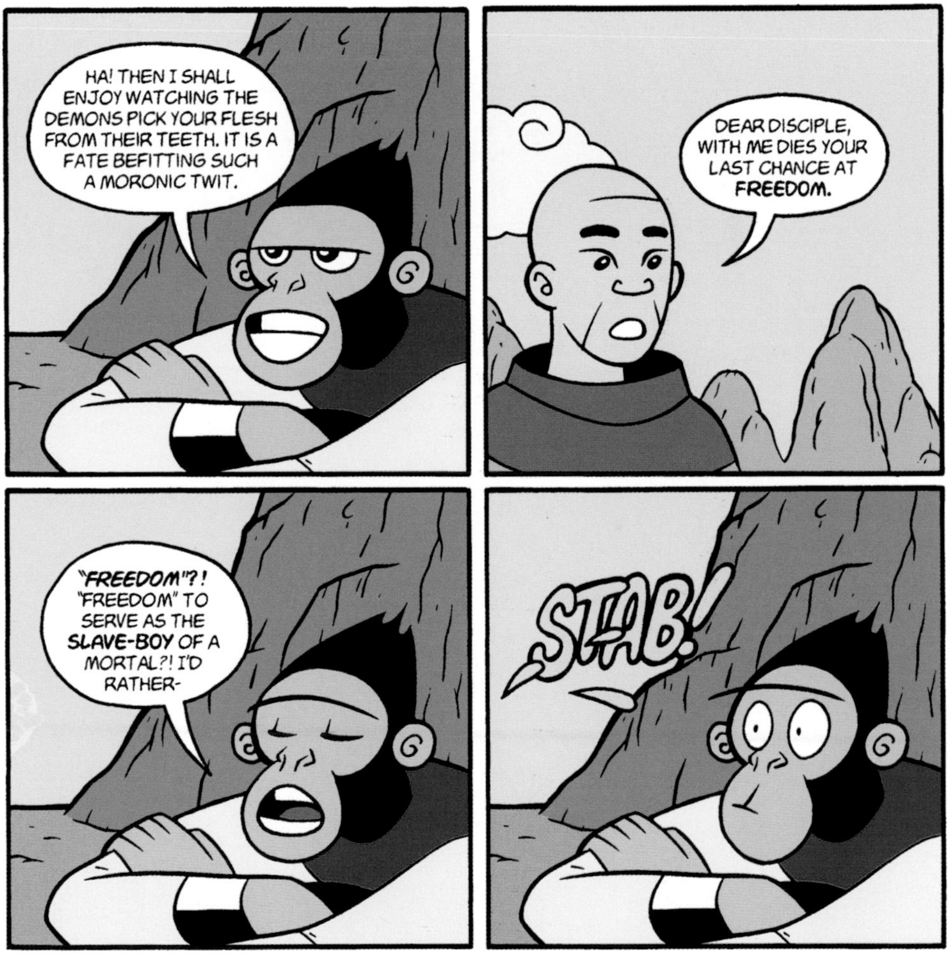
HA! THEN I SHALL ENJOY WATCHING THE DEMONS PICK YOUR FLESH FROM THEIR TEETH. IT IS A FATE BEFITTING SUCH A MORONIC TWIT.
DEAR DISCIPLE, WITH ME DIES YOUR LAST CHANCE AT FREEDOM.
"FREEDOM"?! "FREEDOM" TO SERVE AS THE SLAVE-BOY OF A MORTAL?! I'D RATHER-
STAB!

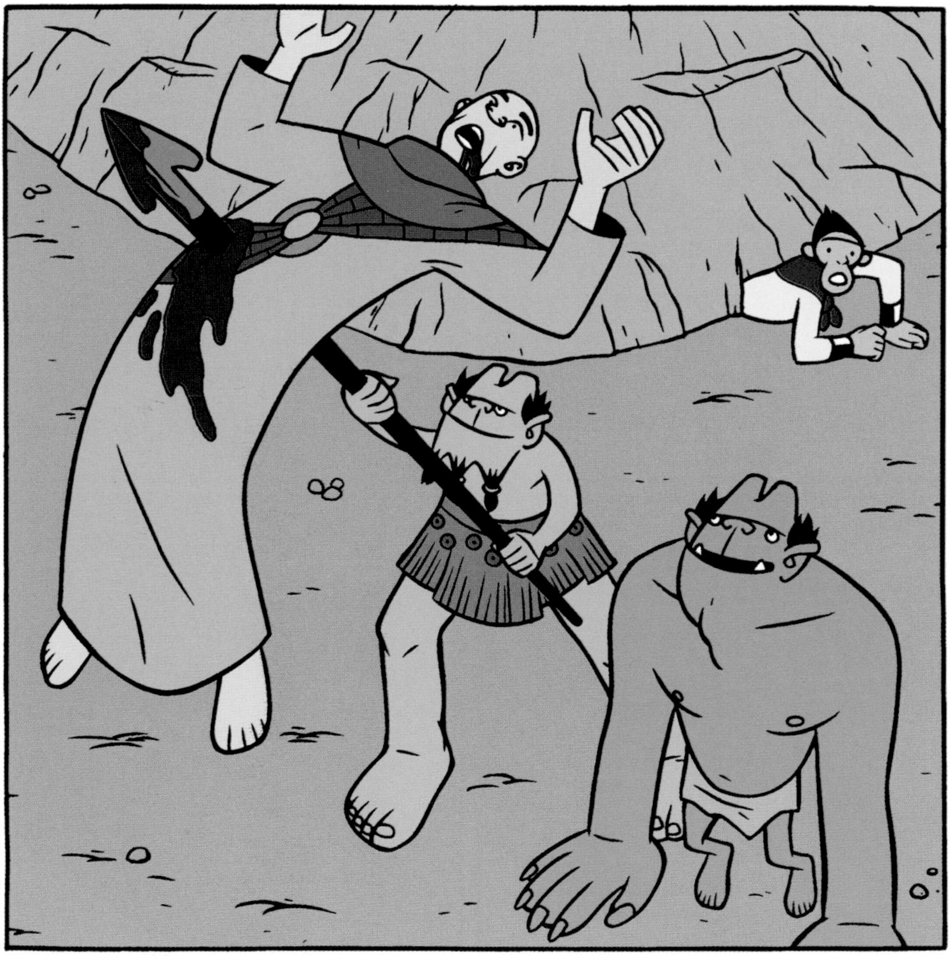

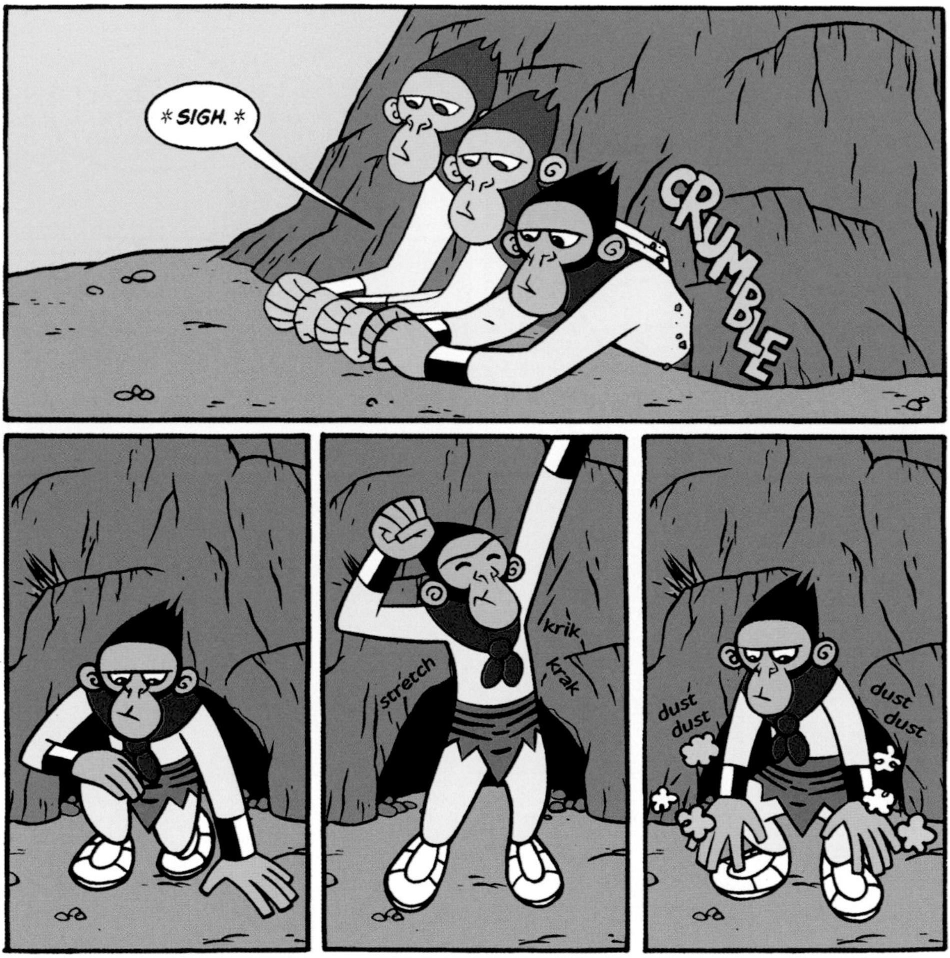
SIGH.
CRUMBLE
stretch
krik
krak
dust
dust
dust
dust

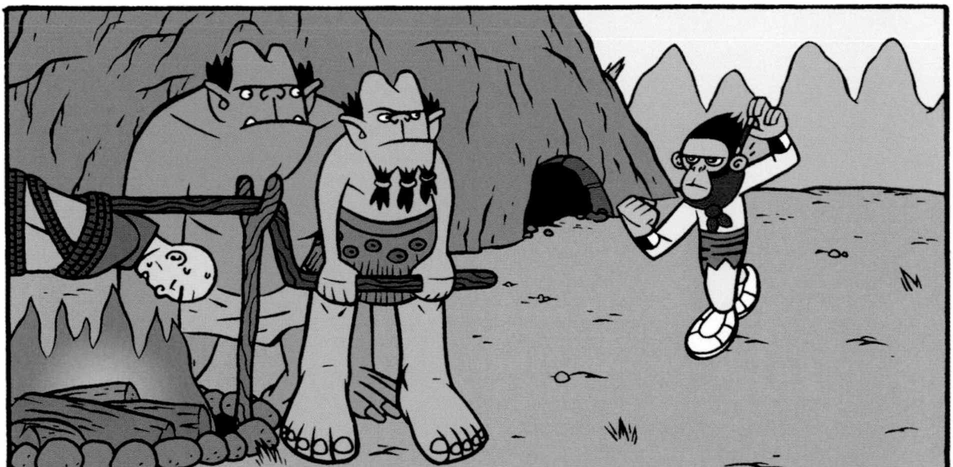
WACK!
WHUMP!

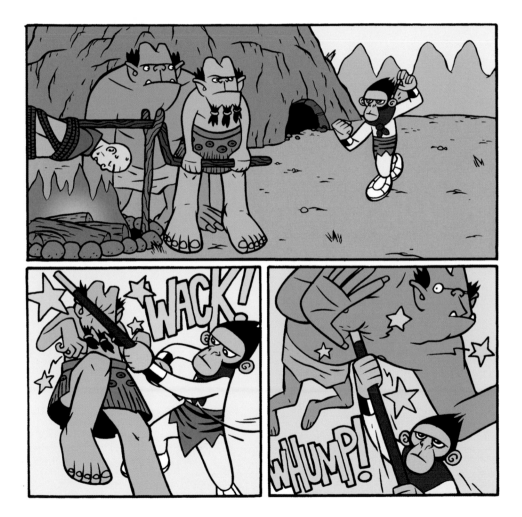

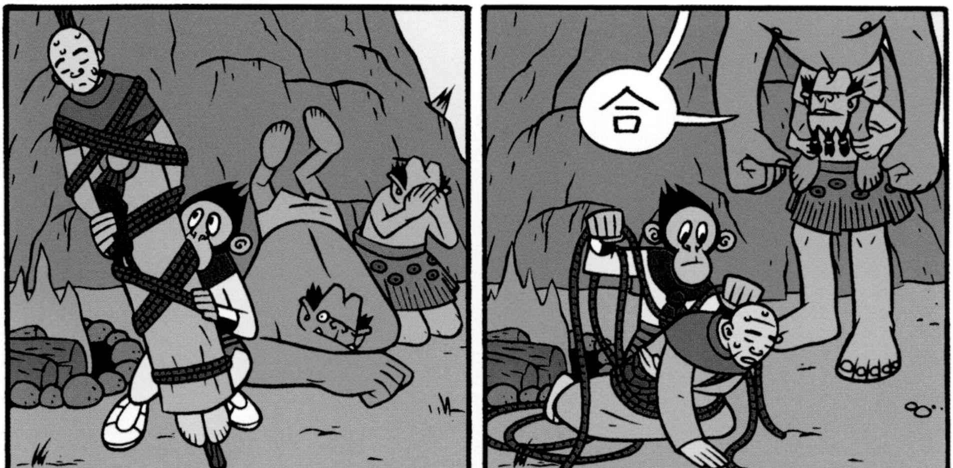
合
?!

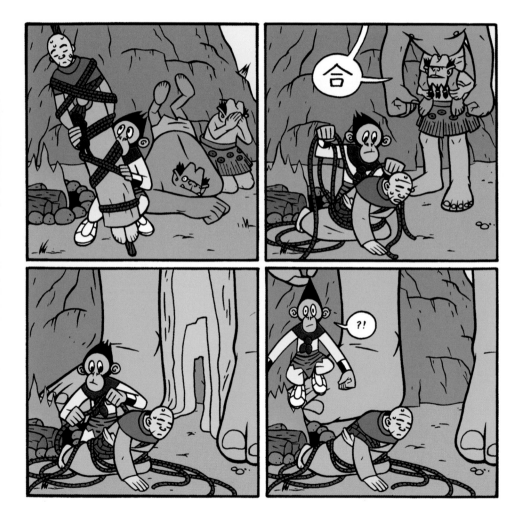

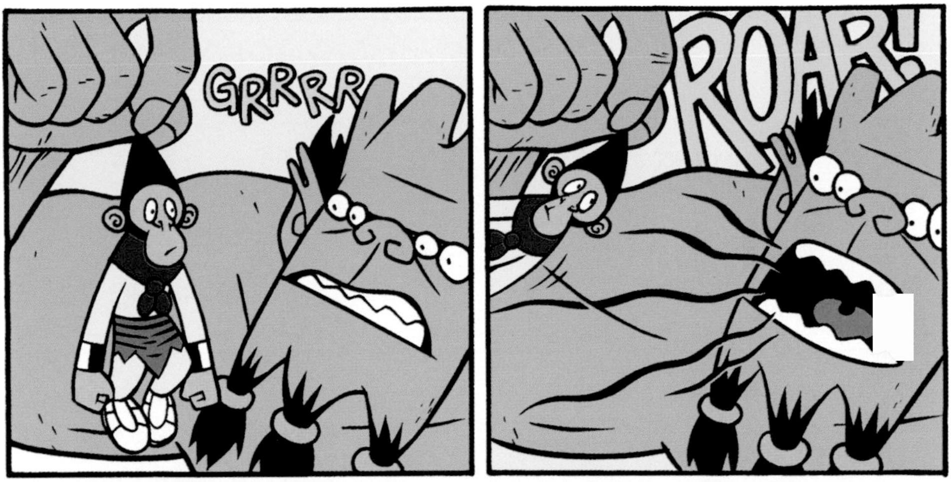
GRRRR
ROAR!
HUFF
HUFF
HUFF
swing
swing
!
ppft!

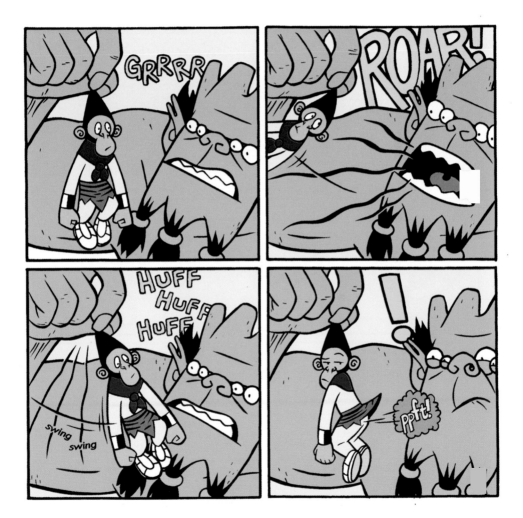

154

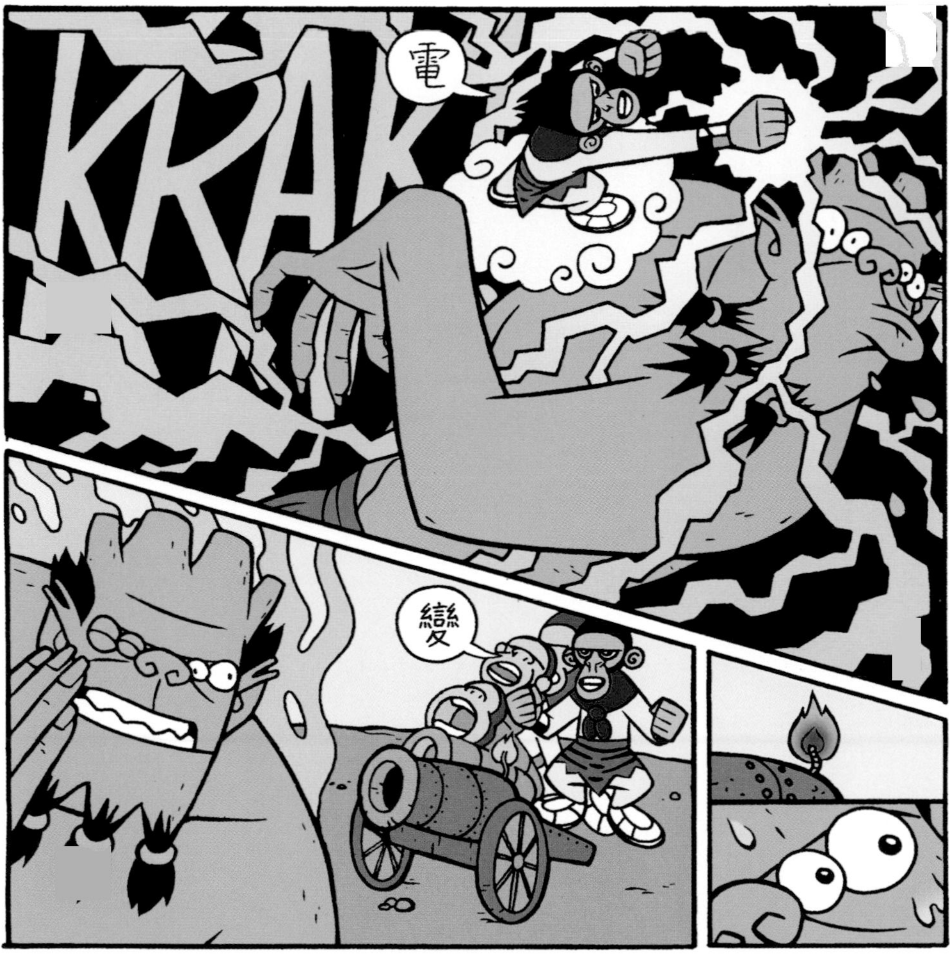
KRAK
電
變

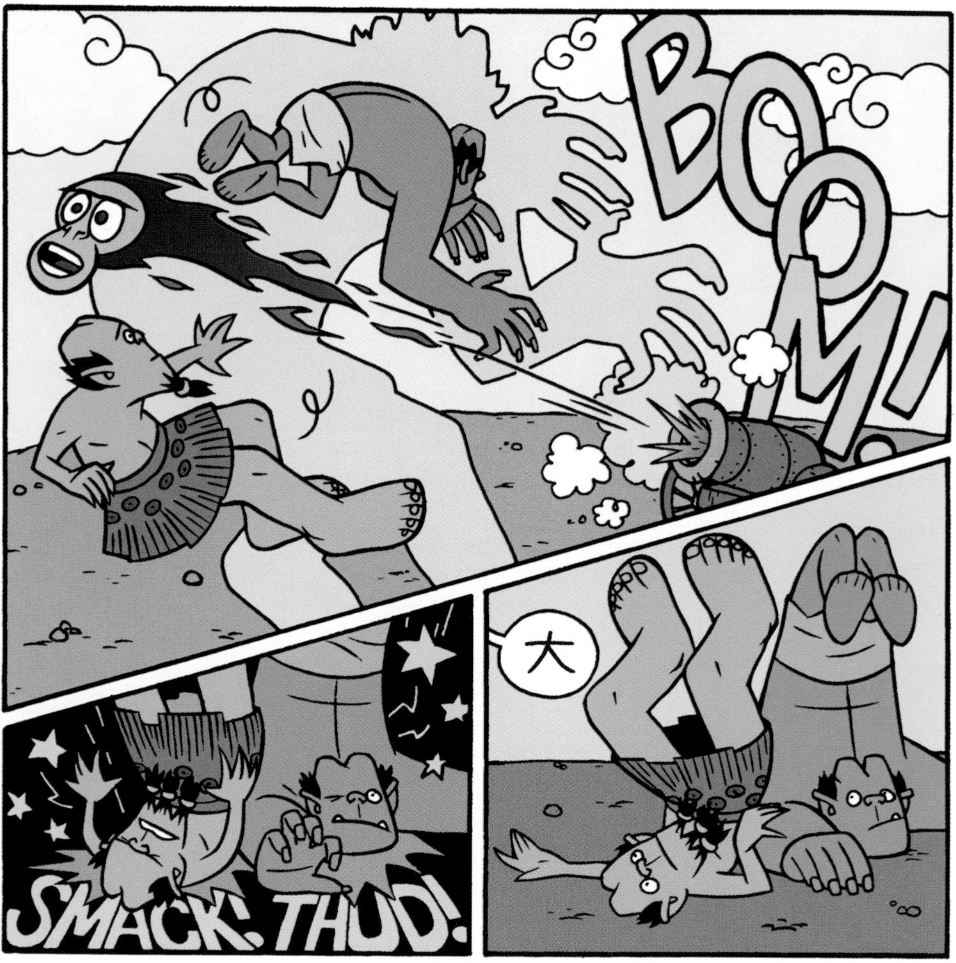
BOOM!
SMACK! THUD!
大

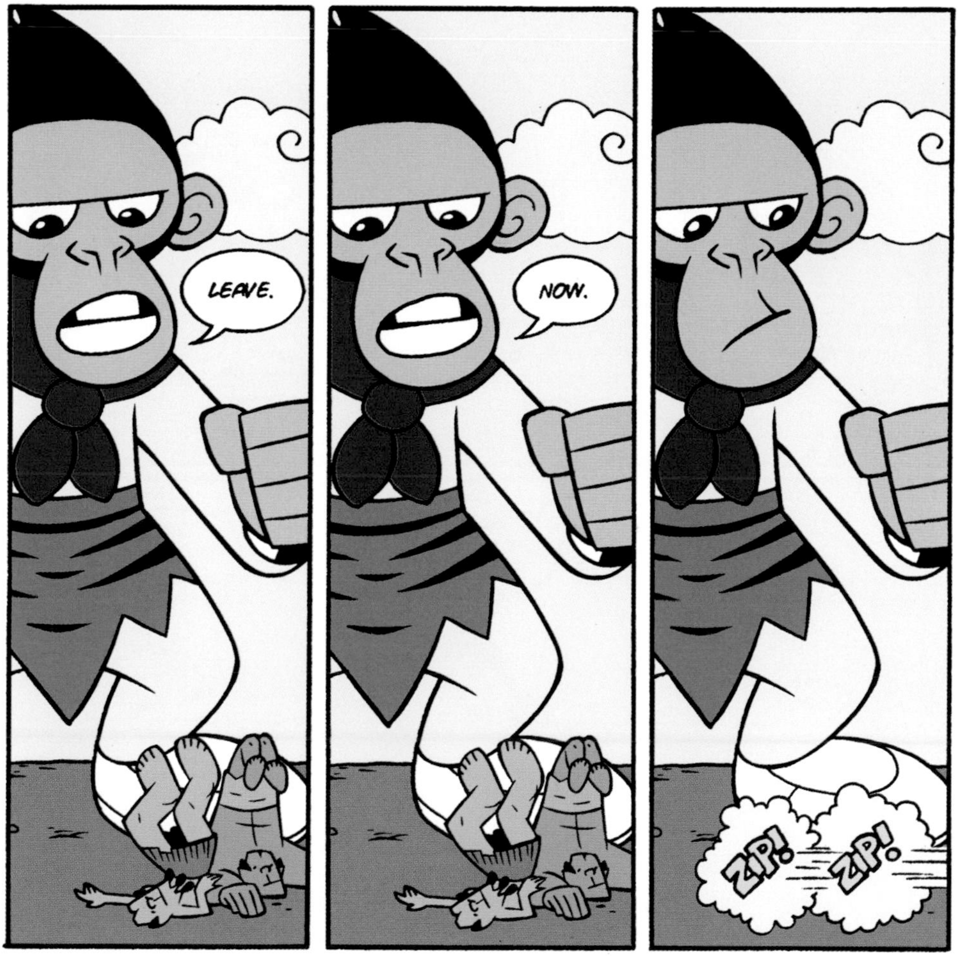
LEAVE.
NOW.
ZIP!
ZIP!

THE MONKEY KING ACCOMPANIED WONG LAI-TSAO ON HIS **JOURNEY TO THE WEST** AND SERVED HIM FAITHFULLY UNTIL THE VERY END.

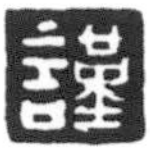

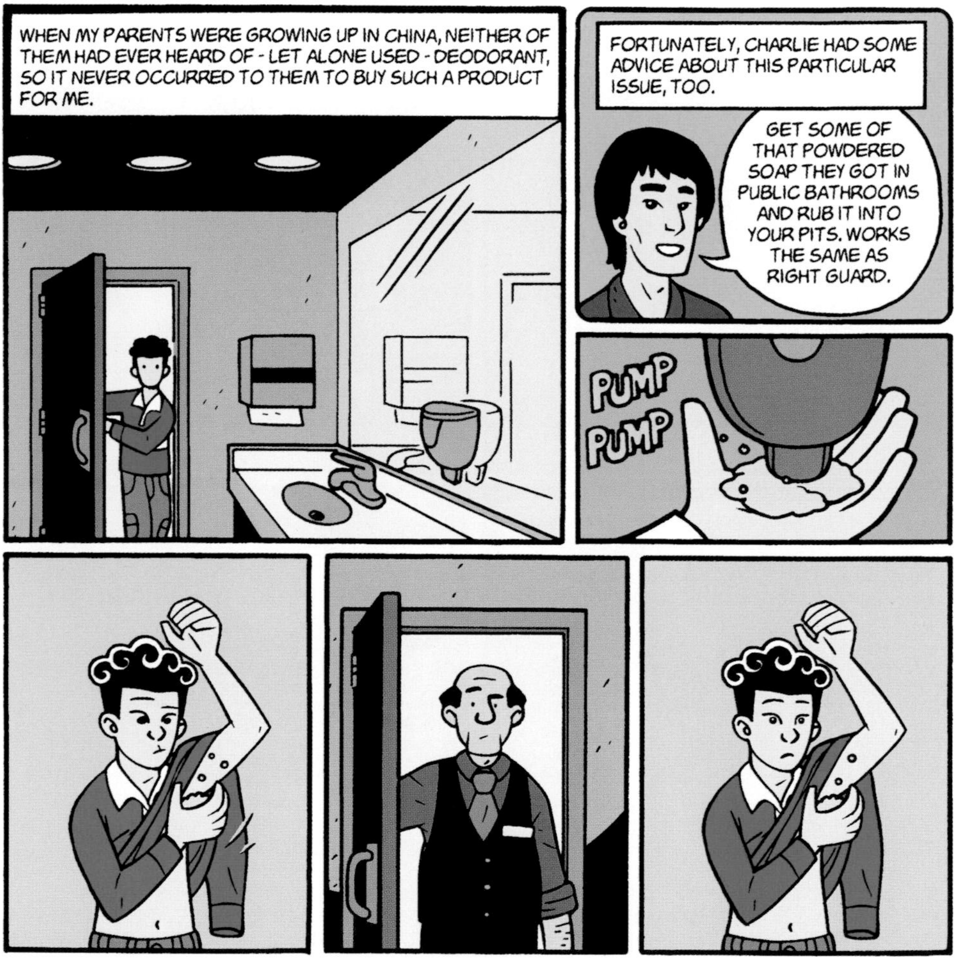
WHEN MY PARENTS WERE GROWING UP IN CHINA, NEITHER OF THEM HAD EVER HEARD OF - LET ALONE USED - DEODORANT, SO IT NEVER OCCURRED TO THEM TO BUY SUCH A PRODUCT FOR ME.
FORTUNATELY, CHARLIE HAD SOME ADVICE ABOUT THIS PARTICULAR ISSUE, TOO.
GET SOME OF THAT POWDERED SOAP THEY GOT IN PUBLIC BATHROOMS AND RUB IT INTO YOUR PITS. WORKS THE SAME AS RIGHT GUARD.
PUMP
PUMP

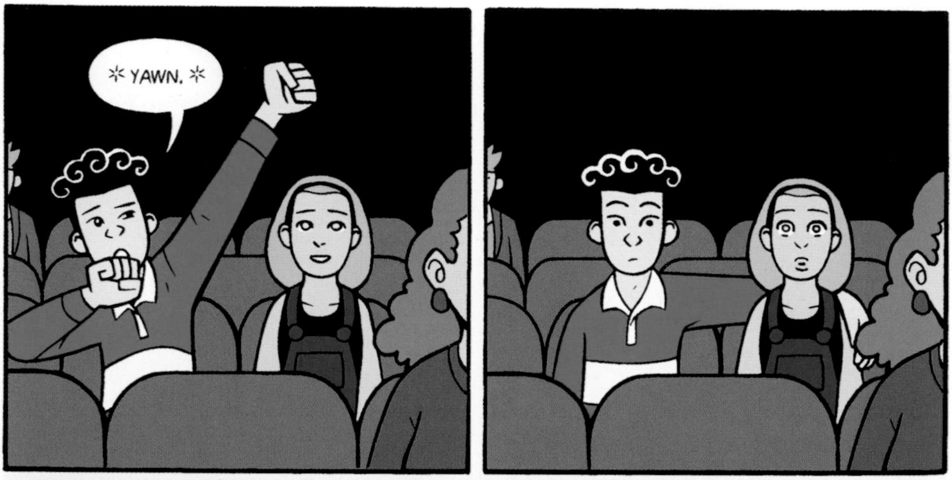
* YAWN. *

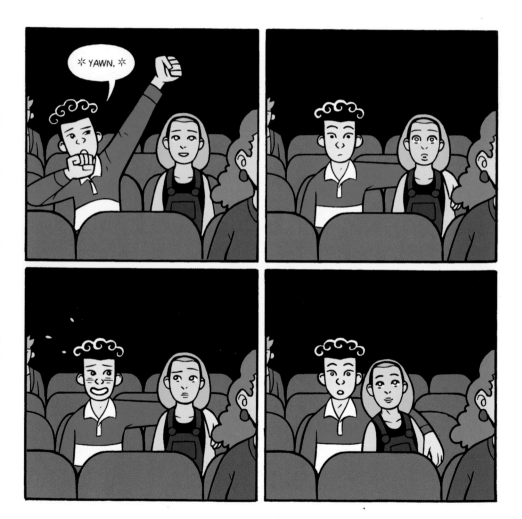

180

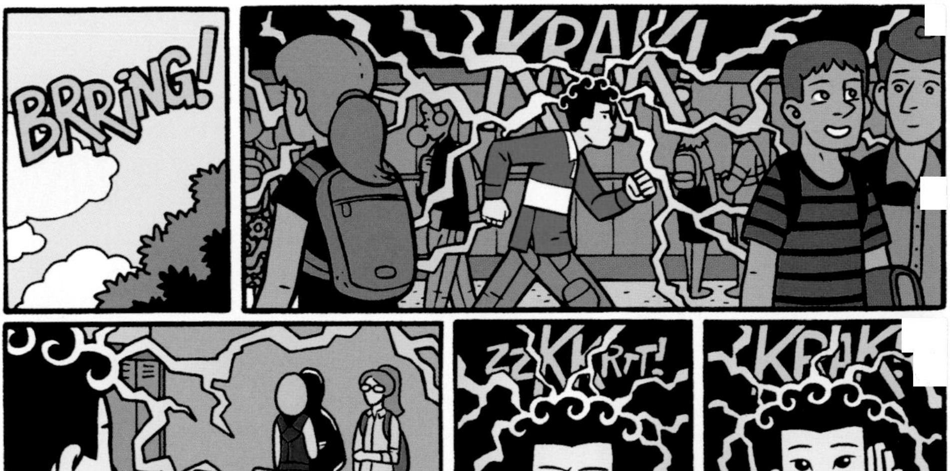
BRRING!
KRAK!
ZZKKRTT!
AMELIA!
HEY, JIN.
HOW'RE YOU DOING, JIN?

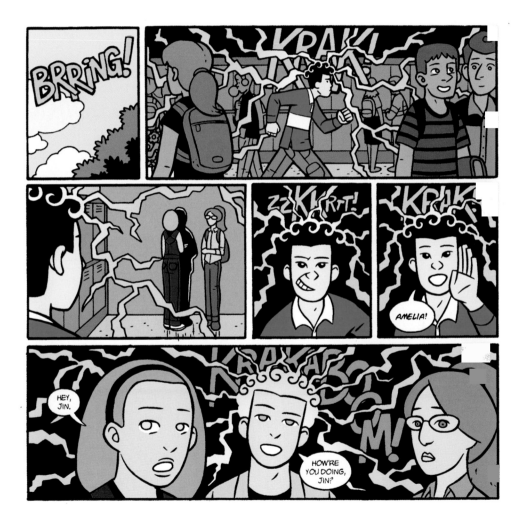

I HAD TROUBLE FALLING ASLEEP THAT NIGHT. I REPLAYED THE DAY'S EVENTS OVER AND OVER AGAIN IN MY MIND.

AND AT AROUND THREE IN THE MORNING, I FINALLY **BELIEVED** MYSELF.

EACH TIME I REACHED THE SAME CONCLUSION: WEI-CHEN NEEDED TO HEAR WHAT I HAD TO SAY. IT WAS, AFTER ALL, THE **TRUTH.**

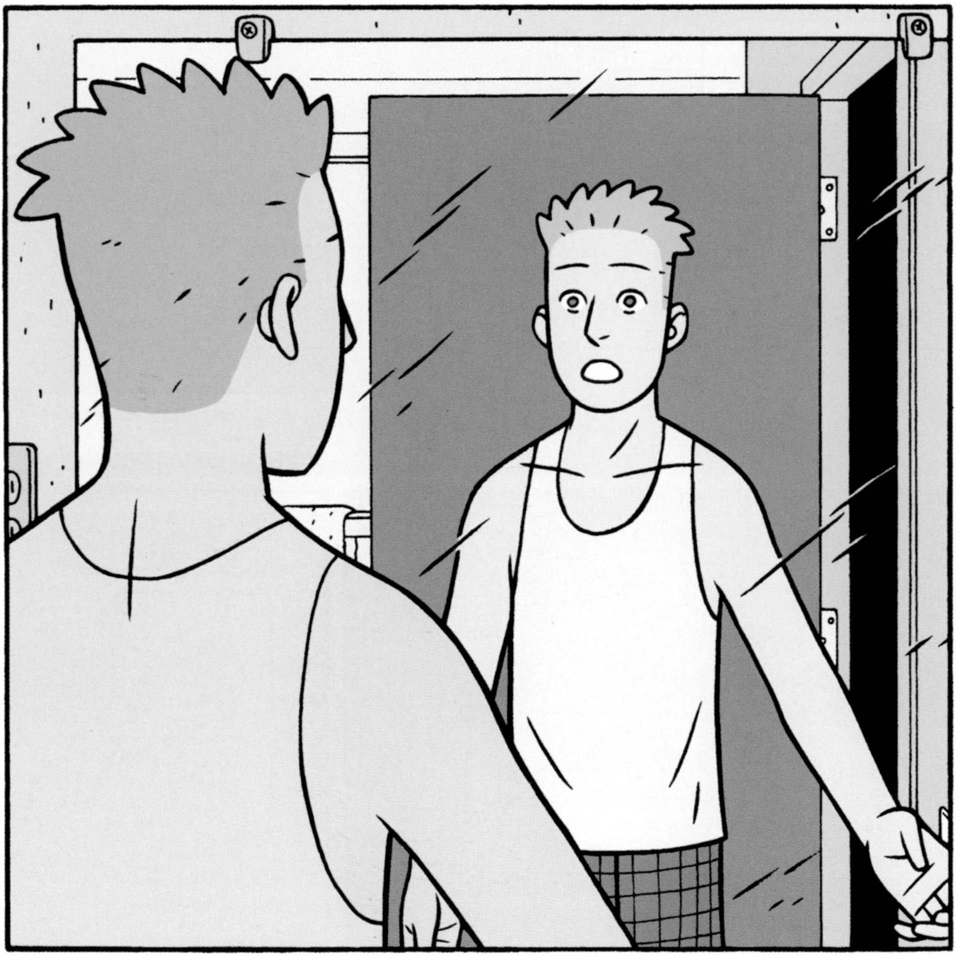

謹

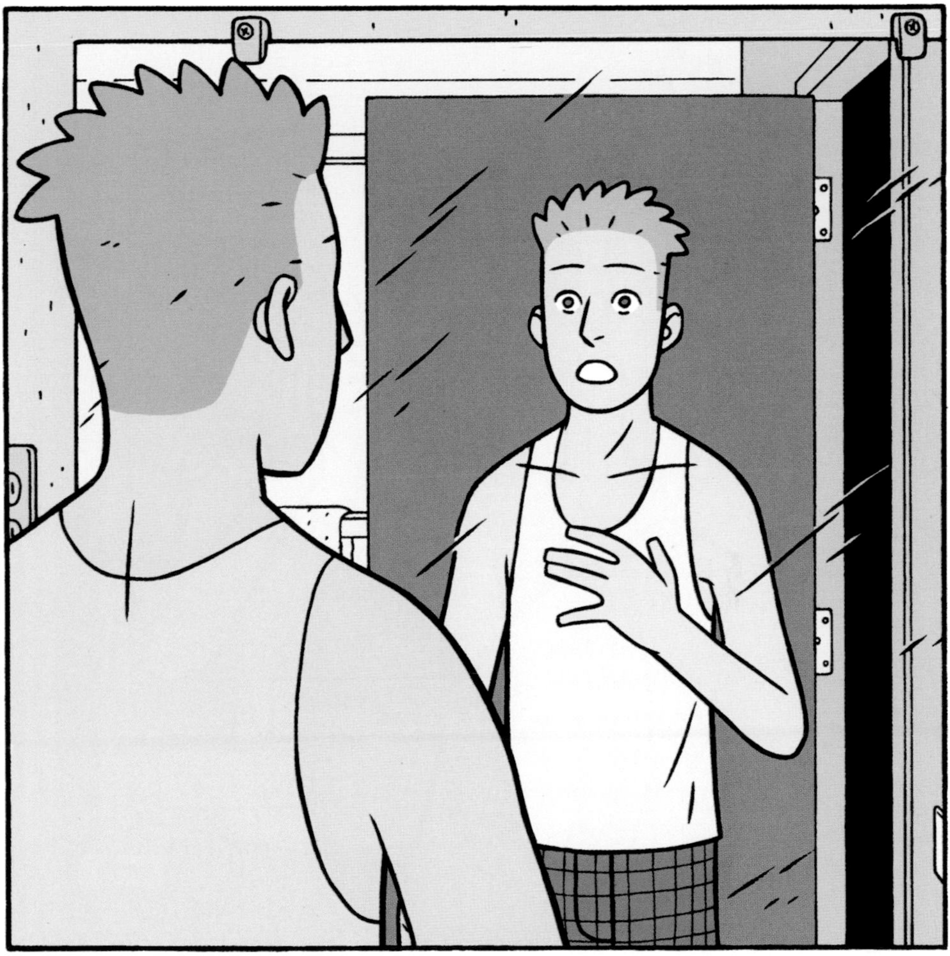

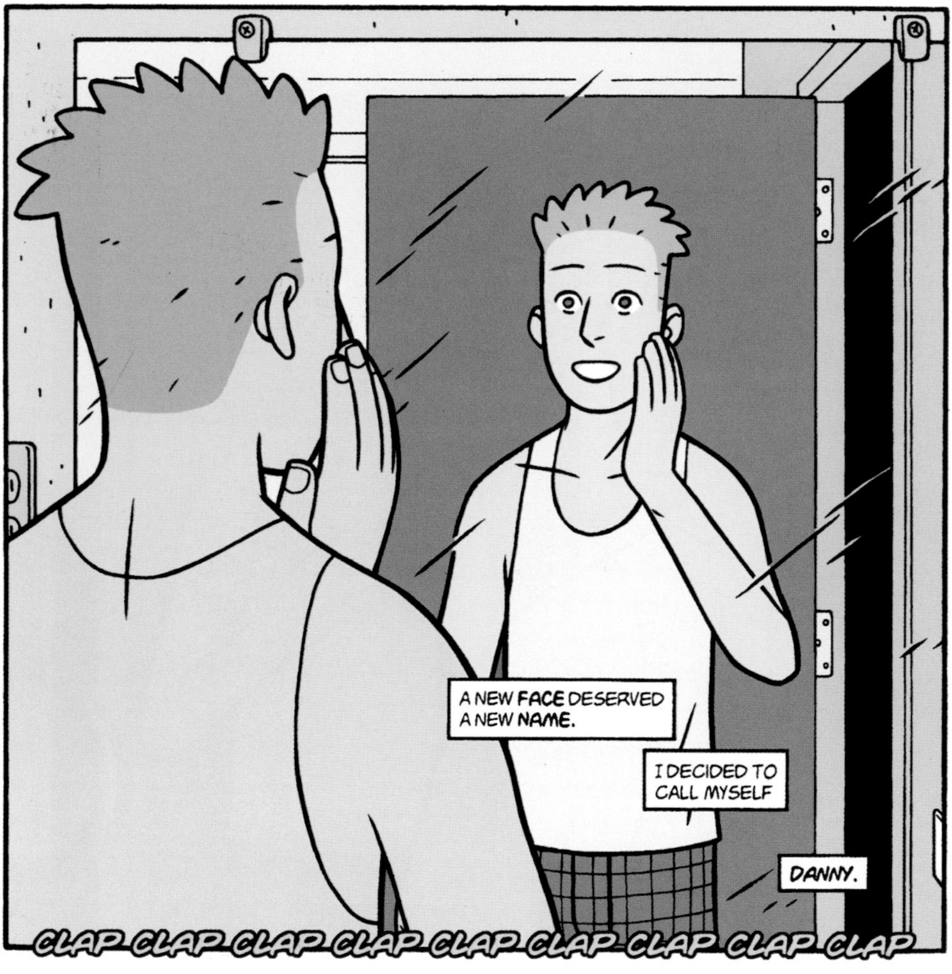
A NEW FACE DESERVED A NEW NAME.
I DECIDED TO CALL MYSELF
DANNY.
CLAP CLAP CLAP CLAP CLAP CLAP CLAP CLAP CLAP

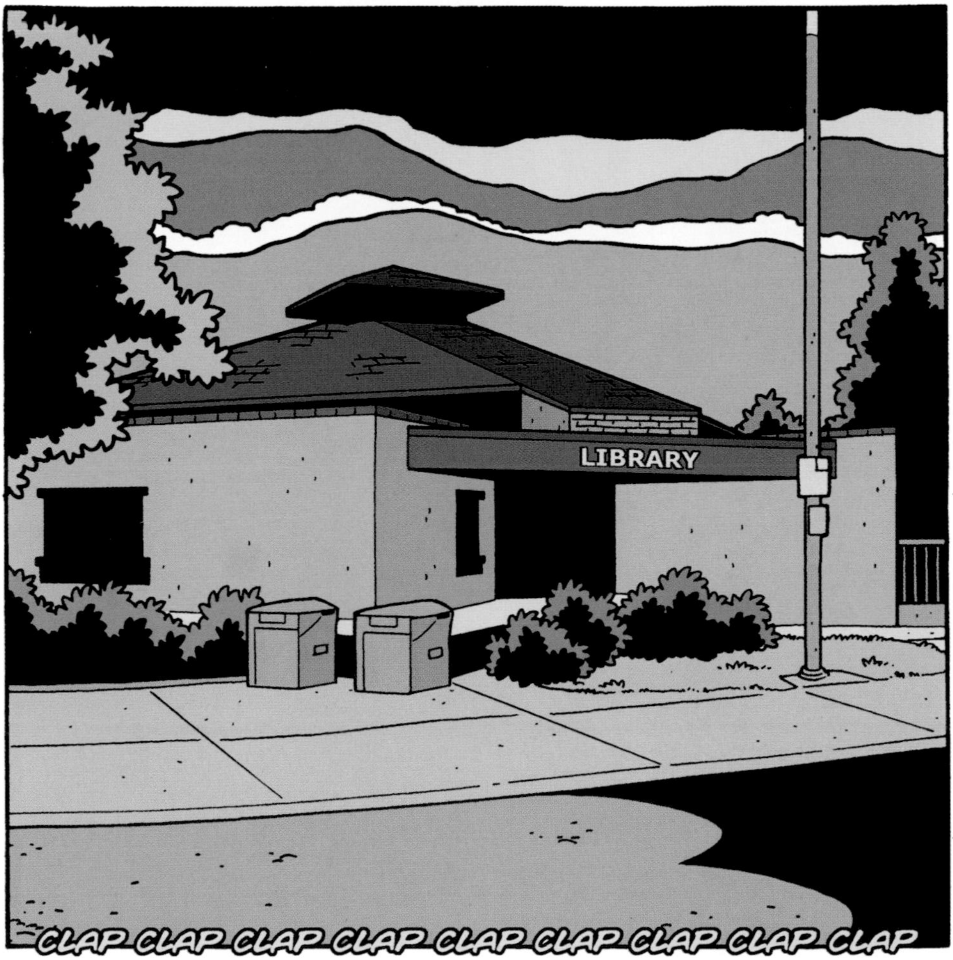
LIBRARY
CLAP CLAP CLAP CLAP CLAP CLAP CLAP CLAP CLAP

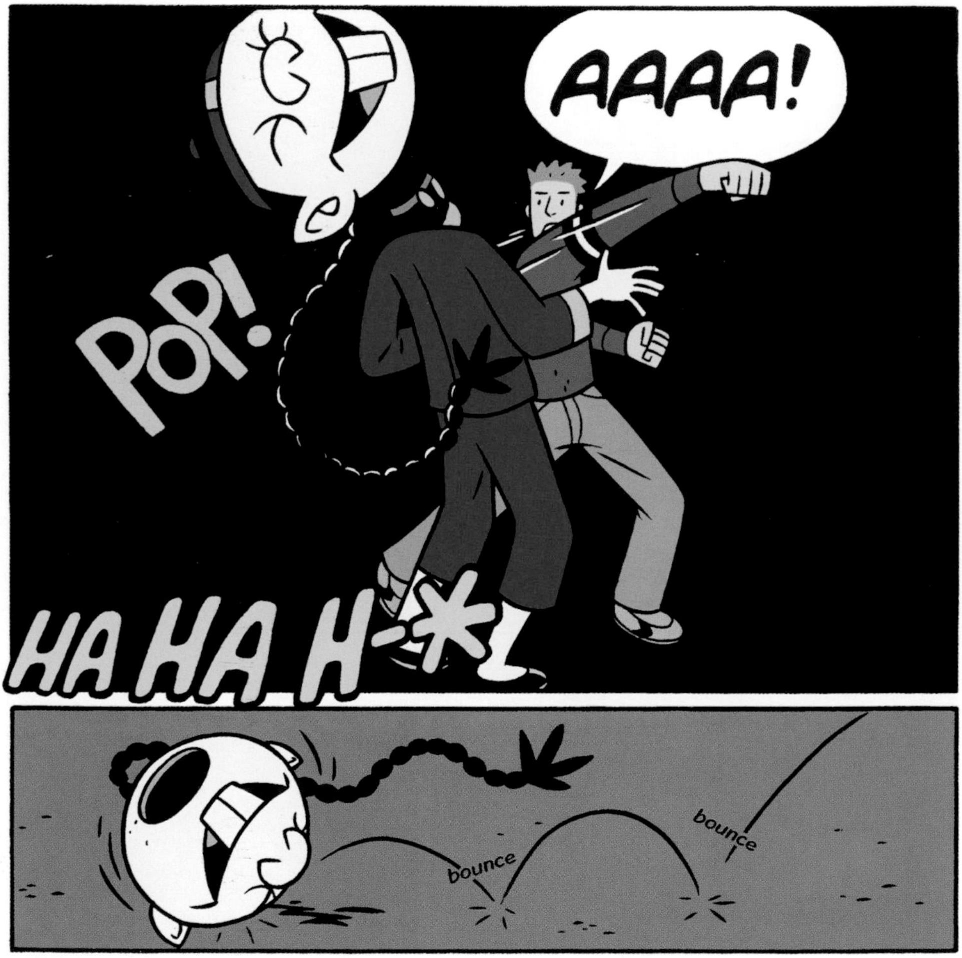
AAAA!
POP!
HA HA H-
bounce
bounce

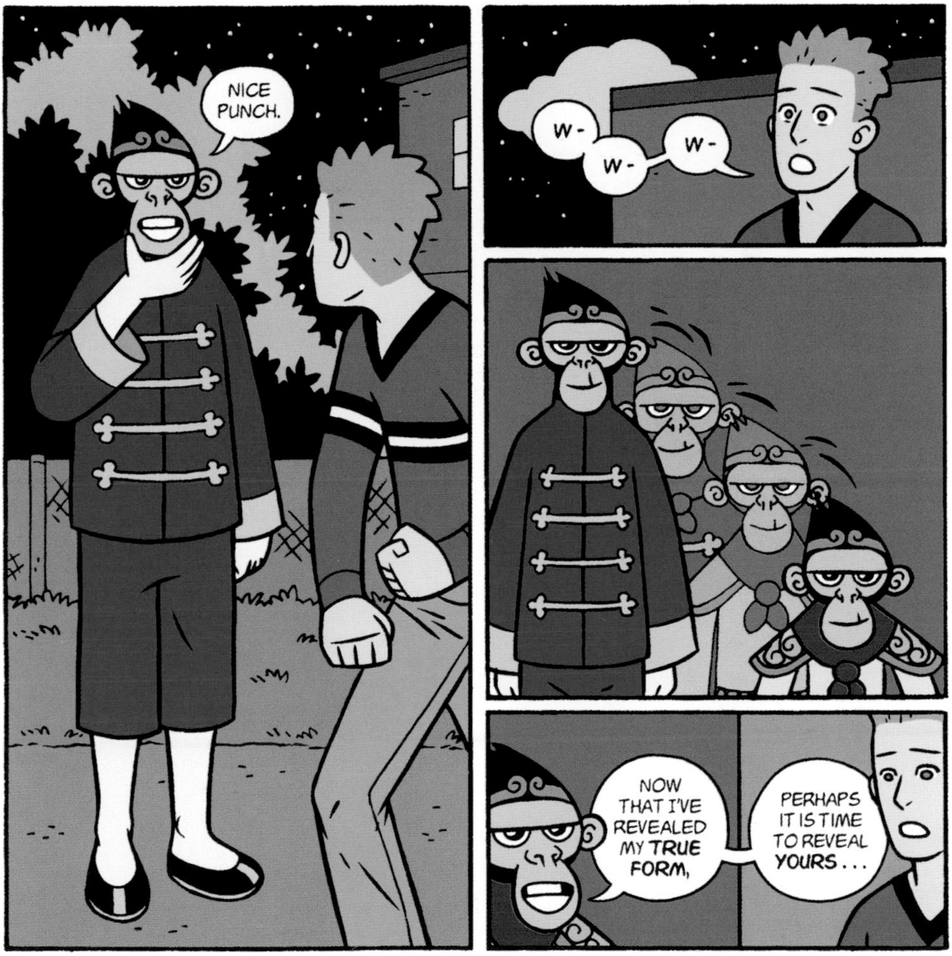
NICE PUNCH.
W-
W-
W-
NOW THAT I'VE REVEALED MY **TRUE FORM,**
PERHAPS IT IS TIME TO REVEAL **YOURS . . .**

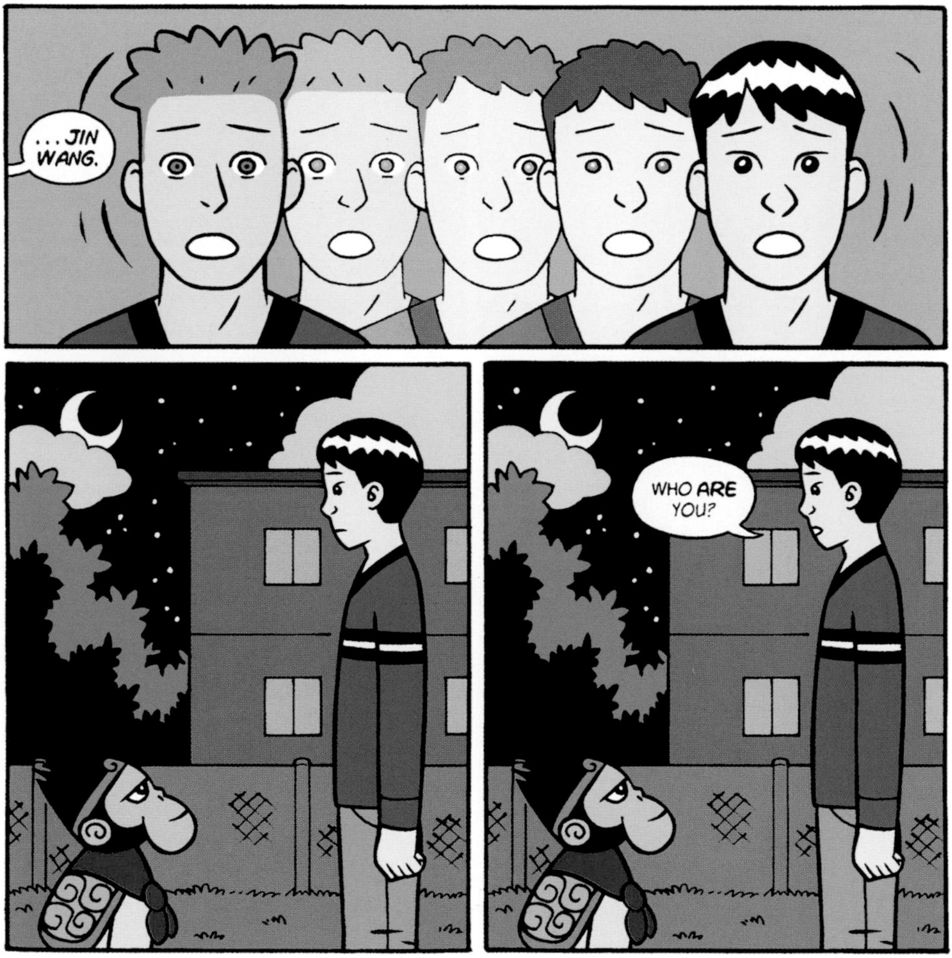
...JIN WANG.
WHO ARE YOU?

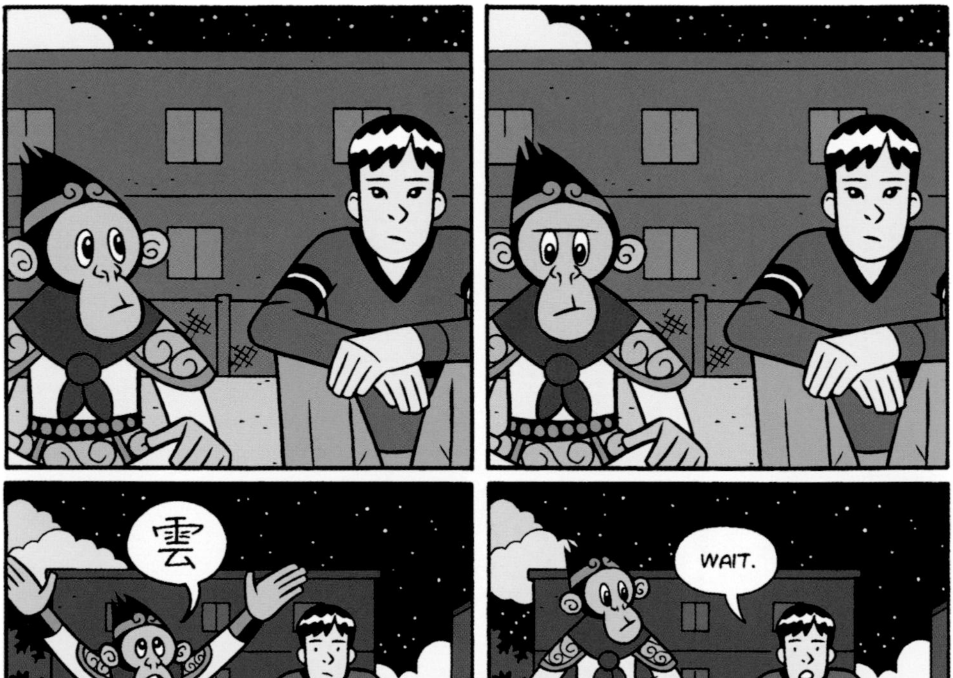
雲
WAIT.

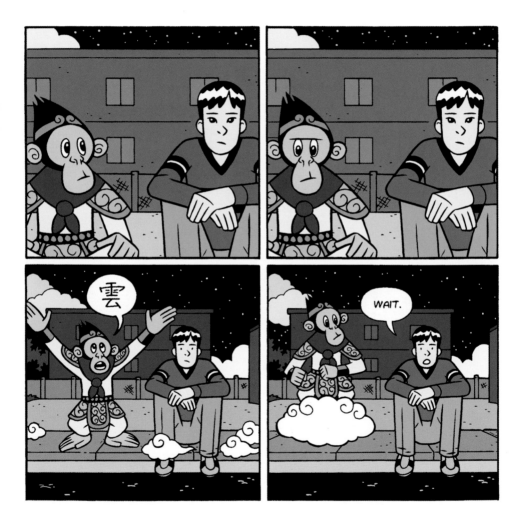

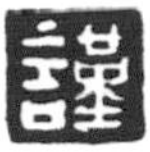

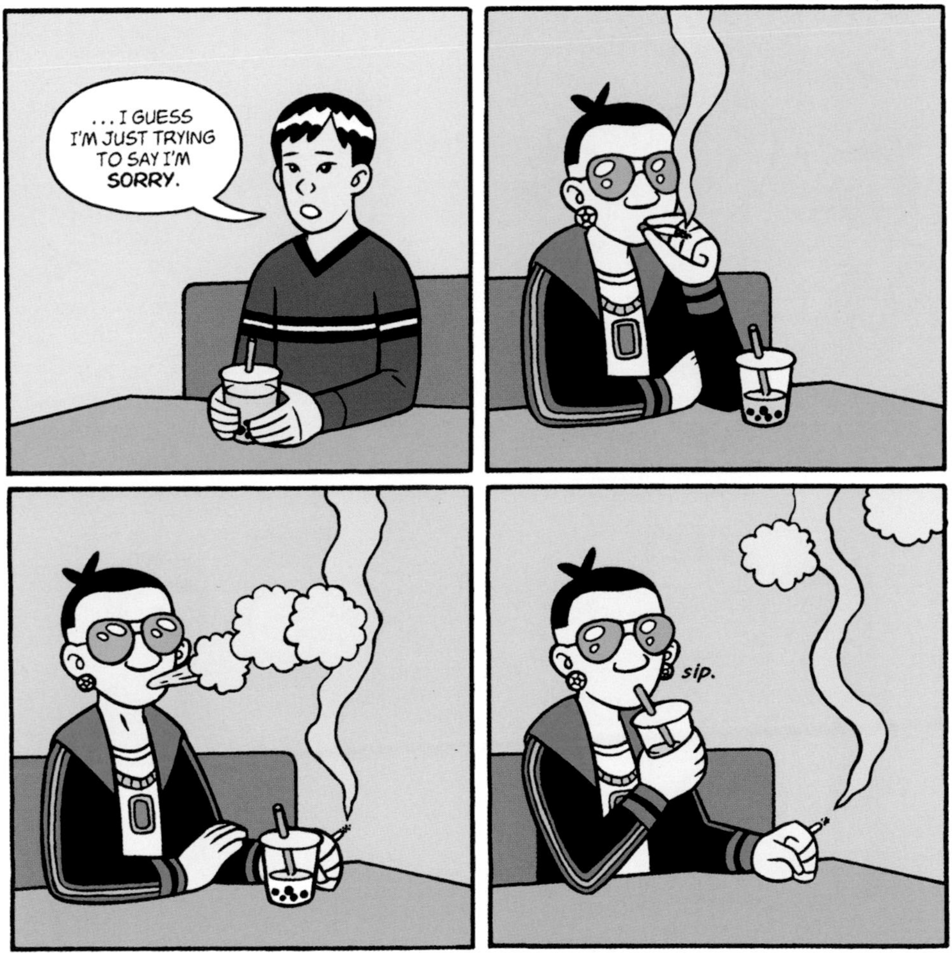
...I GUESS I'M JUST TRYING TO SAY I'M **SORRY**.
sip.

The End

Afterword

When I began working on *American Born Chinese* in the year 2000, I was a twenty-seven-year-old high school teacher making comics on the side. I'd been self-publishing comic books for about five years—most of them were photocopied and stapled by hand, and I'd sell them at local conventions for a couple dollars each. I lost money with every issue, but I didn't mind. It was glorious fun.

I believe that all the stories we tell—from the earliest fireside pantomimes performed by our ancestors to the most recent streaming service releases—collectively make up a millennia-long conversation about what it means to be human. Because my own cultural heritage is such an important part of how I've found my place in the world, I knew I had to do a story about it.

Even so, I was hesitant. To do it properly, I'd have to revisit my own painful memories. As a kid, I was bullied for being a Chinese American. My classmates made fun of the shape of my eyes, the food my family ate, and how my parents spoke English. I was constantly reminded that I was an outsider.

By the year 2000, I'd finally mustered enough courage to begin *American Born Chinese*.

The book took me five years to complete. When I was nearing the last chapter, a friend of mine named Derek Kirk Kim, one of the most talented cartoonists I know, introduced me to a young and ambitious editor named Mark Siegel. Mark was just about to launch his own graphic novel imprint called First Second. I was thrilled when Mark signed me. First Second published *American Born Chinese* in the fall of 2006 as a part of their second season.

The response was well beyond anything I could have imagined. Teachers, librarians, bookstore owners, and graphic novel fans supported my book with reviews, book talks, and enthusiastic word-of-mouth. They paved the way for me to become the full-time cartoonist that I am today. They changed my life.

Since then, I've been invited to communities all over the world to talk about the themes in *American Born Chinese*. Again and again, readers would approach me afterward to tell me their own experiences of being outsiders.

Many of them were the children of immigrants like me, though their parents might have come from India, Nigeria, Russia, or Mexico. Others found themselves on the outside for different reasons. Perhaps it was because of their sexual orientation or their faith tradition or the unconventional way their brain worked.

It didn't matter. The details might have been different, but the emotions were always the same.

What I've found is that the outsider's experience is nearly universal. Almost all of us have a story about not fitting in. It's so common that, ironically, it can be a way for us to understand and connect with one another. The outsider's experience can be our common ground.

Being on the outside can feel like pure agony, especially when we're young. It can strike at the very core of who we are. But if we're willing to work through our experiences and make sense of them, we'll find that we're not alone in our pain. Quite the opposite, actually.

That's what I've learned from taking part in this millennia-long conversation about what it means to be human. That's what I've learned from telling a story, and then having stories told to me in return.

So thank you for reading my story. And thank you for telling your own.

Gene Luen Yang
September 2020

Thank You

Theresa Kim Yang, The Yang Kids, Jon Yang, Derek Kirk Kim,
Lark Pien, Mark Siegel, Judy Hansen, Danica Novgorodoff,
Calista Brill, Gina Gagliano, Robyn Chapman, Molly Johanson,
Jon Yaged, Angus Killick, Allison Verost, Lucy Del Priore,
Simon Boughton, Lauren Wohl, Scottie Bowditch, Chloe Volkwein,
Julianne Lewis, Morgan Kane, Cynthia Lliguichuzhca,
Kate Kubert-Puls, Thien Pham, Jesse Hamm, Jason Shiga,
Jesse Reklaw, Andy Hartzell, Joey Manley, Alan Davis, Rory Root,
Albert Olson Hong, Shauna Olson Hong, Hank Lee, Pin Chou,
Jacon Chun, Jonathan Crawford, Jess Delegencia, Susi Jensen,
Margaret Bechard, Patricia McKissack, Linda Sue Park,
Benjamin Alire Sáenz, Jude Watson, Cindy Dobrez,
Eunice Anderson, Angelina Benedetti, Teresa Brantley, Vicki Emery,
Jana Fine, Michele Gorman, Jessica Mize, Sarajo Wentling,
Gillian Engberg, Robin Brenner, Whitney Matheson, Chris Reilly,
James Sime, Jeff Vander Mccr

First Second

Published by First Second
First Second is an imprint of Roaring Brook Press,
a division of Holtzbrinck Publishing Holdings Limited Partnership
120 Broadway, New York, NY 10271
firstsecondbooks.com

Library of Congress Cataloging-in-Publication Data
Yang, Gene.
American born Chinese / Gene Yang; coloring by Lark Pien
p. cm.
Summary: Alternates three interrelated stories about the problems of young Chinese Americans
trying to participate in the popular culture. Presented in comic book format.

Our books may be purchased in bulk for promotional, educational, or business use.
Please contact your local bookseller or the Macmillan Corporate and Premium Sales Department
at (800) 221-7945 ext. 5442 or by email at MacmillanSpecialMarkets@macmillan.com.

Edited by Mark Siegel
Cover and interior book design by Danica Novgorodoff
Color by Lark Pien
Chinese chops by Guo Ming Chen

Printed in China

ISBN 978-1-250-81189-9 (2021 paperback edition)
10 9 8 7 6 5 4

Don't miss your next favorite book from First Second! For the latest updates go to
firstsecondnewsletter.com and sign up for our enewsletter.

BY ART WE LIVE

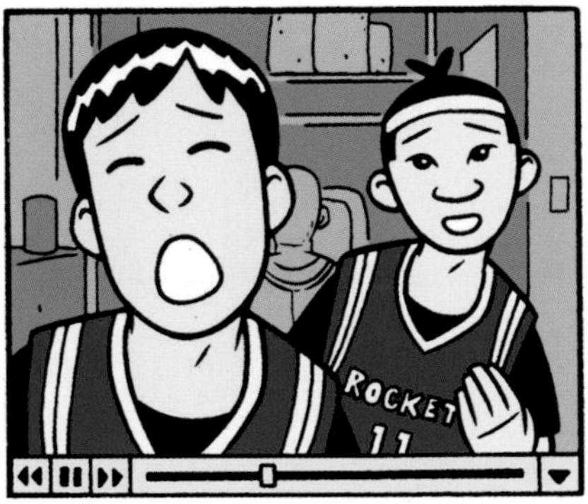
ROCKET
11